Frederick James Furnivall

Tell-Trothes New Yeares Gift and The Passionate Morrice...

Frederick James Furnivall

Tell-Trothes New Yeares Gift and The Passionate Morrice...

ISBN/EAN: 9783744715799

Printed in Europe, USA, Canada, Australia, Japan

Cover: Foto ©Andreas Hilbeck / pixelio.de

More available books at **www.hansebooks.com**

Tell-Trothes New-Yeares Gift

AND

The Passionate Morrice.

———◦———

JOHN LANE'S

Tom Tell-Troths Message, and his Pens Complaint.

———◦———

THOMAS POWELL'S

Tom of all Trades.

———◦———

The Glasse of Godly Loue.

(BY JOHN ROGERS?)

TELL-TROTHES NEW-YEARES GIFT

BEEING

ROBIN GOOD-FELLOWES NEWES OUT OF THOSE COUNTRIES WHERE
INHABITES NEITHER CHARITY NOR HONESTY,

WITH HIS OWNE INUECTIUE AGAINST IELOSY.

AND

THE PASSIONATE MORRICE.

1593.

JOHN LANE'S

Tom Tell-Troths Message, and his Pens Complaint.

1600.

THOMAS POWELL'S

TOM OF ALL TRADES.

OR

THE PLAINE PATH-WAY TO PREFERMENT.

BEING

A DISCOVERY OF A PASSAGE TO PROMOTION IN ALL PROFESSIONS, TRADES,
ARTS, AND MYSTERIES.

1631.

THE GLASSE OF GODLY LOUE.

(BY JOHN ROGERS?)

1569.

EDITED BY

FREDERICK J. FURNIVALL, M.A., CAMB.,

FOUNDER AND DIRECTOR OF *THE NEW SHAKSPERE SOCIETY*, &c.

PUBLISHT FOR

The New Shakspere Society

BY N. TRÜBNER & CO., 57, 59, LUDGATE HILL,

LONDON, E.C., 1876.

71989

Series VI. No. 2.

JOHN CHILDS AND SON, PRINTERS.

CONTENTS.

Contents.

Contents.

FOREWORDS.

§ 1. HERE are reprints of three rare tracts, of which the first two are on the England of Elizabeth's time (1593, 1600), and the third is written by a man of her time, tho' not publisht till the seventh year of Charles the First's reign (1631). The fourth scrap is before 1600.

The printing of the first tract was urg'd on me by my friend Mr W. C. Hazlitt, because there was only one copy of it known to him, and that at Peterborough Cathedral Library, quite out of the way of the ordinary student. As this tract dealt with the husband-and-wife question in Shakspere's young days, and mainly took-up the other side (the woman's) to that which Shakspere backt in *The Comedy of Errors* (Act II. sc. i. ; V. i. 68—86), I was glad to recommend it to the friend and fellow-member of our Society[1] who had offerd to give us a Shakspere's-England reprint of moderate size. Otherwise its inner worth would not have given it so early a place in our Sixth Series. But still, for the social condition of England in Shakspere's time, this *Tell-Trothes New-yeares Gift* of 1593 has great interest, so far as the family life of the middle classes is concernd. Oddly enough, too, it does illustrate aptly a bit of the last long speech of Suffolk in 1 *Henry VI*, V. v. 48—54 (tho' I suppose that is not Shakspere's), about the young king's choice of the dowerless Margaret :

[1] He has made it a condition that his name be not mentiond.

Suf. A dower, my lords ! disgrace not so your king,
That he should be so abject, base, and poor,
To choose for wealth, and not for perfect love
Henry is able to enrich his queen,
And not to seek a queen to make him rich :
So worthless peasants bargain for their wives, .
As market-men for oxen, sheep, or horse.

At p. 61-2, of Tell-Troth's Part II, *The Passionate Morrice*, we come on the following passage :—

" Fie, fie ! mariages, for the most part, are at this day so made, as looke how the butcher bies his cattel, so wil men sel their children. He that bids most, shal speed soonest ; & so he hath money, we care not a fart for his honestie. Well, it hath not been so, and I hope it wil not be long so ; & I wil assure you, loues commonwealth wil neuer florish vntil it be otherwise. Why, it is a common practize to aske the father what hee will giue with his childe ; and what is that differing from cheapening an Oxe ? And it is as common, that if she be fat, it is a bargaine, but if leane, she must stay another customer."

This cannot be calld an advance on the low part of the earlier *Paston-Letters* view of the marriage question.[1]

I do not want to puff our Victorian time against the Elizabethan. We have faults enough, God knows. There *may* be a few beings calld women now extant, who justify the sketches that reviews tell us sensation-novelists draw, and that prurient article-writers affect to denounce,[2] but surely no one can turn from the cuckoo cry which the *Love's-Labours-Lost* end song, and almost all Elizabethan books on social life, echo ; no one can contrast Shakspere's doctrine on the relation of husband and wife in *The Errors* (First-Period) and *Taming of the Shrew*, with Tennyson's in *The Princess*,[3] without

---

[1] There is also proof of plenty of true love in these Letters ; and Margaret Paston, the heroine of the volumes, is not far from being a model wife of the time.

[2] See my *Ballads from Manuscripts*, vol. i, p. 2.

[3] There's nothing, situate under hea-
ven's eye,
But hath his bound, in earth, in sea, in
sky :
The beasts, the fishes, and the winged
fowls,
Are their males' subject, and at their
controls :
Men, more divine, the masters of all
these,
Dear, but let us type them now
In our own lives, and this proud watch-
word rest
Of equal ; seeing either sex alone
Is half itself, and in true marriage lies
Nor equal, nor unequal : each fulfils
Defect in each, and always thought in
thought,
Purpose in purpose, will in will, they
grow,

feeling that enormous moral progress has been made since the Elizabethan time in the relations of the sexes, and of husband and wife.[1]

The comparison of *Love's Labours Lost* with *The Princess* is full of interest; and though the contrast of the converse excluders of the opposite sex in the two works strikes a student of both poets at first sight, I have never seen or heard it alluded-to in any criticism of the poem or play. The comparison of *In Memoriam* with the *Sonnets* has been indeed mentiond, but never workt out, full of interest as the subject is. Victorians need not fear to set Arthur Hallam by Shakspere's Will H., or the grounds of Tennyson's affectionate reverence for his friend, by those of Shakspere's love for his.

Assuming, then, that the full description by the unknown 1593 TELL-TROTHE[2] of the causes of Jealousy in English husbands, and

Lords of the wide world, and wild wat'ry seas,
Indued with intellectual sense and souls,
Of more pre-eminence than fish and fowls,
Are masters to their females, and their lords:
Then let your will attend on their accords.—Luciana, in *Errors*, II. i.
(Cp. Milton's view.)

The single pure and perfect animal,
The two-cell'd heart, beating, with one full stroke,
Life.
    The Princess, p. 157, 1st ed., 1847.

[1] The views of our narrow-minded (and often caddish) folk, as well as those of our broader-minded and more generous men, on the Woman-question, are annually stated in the House of Commons, in the debate on the Woman's-Suffrage Bill, or any attempt to admit women to the learned professions. Women still wait for justice and fair-play.

[2] *Indouinello*, a tell-truth, a tom-tell-troth.—1598; Florio. For the second name of the title, Robin Goodfellow (or Hobgoblin), see Shakspere's *Midsummer Night's Dream*, II. i. 34, 40, Cotgrave, and Florio:

Follet: or, *Esprit follet*. An Hobgoblin, **Robin-goodfellow**, Bugbeare.—1611; Cotgrave.

Luiton: m. A Goblin, Bug, **Robin-good-fellow**, merrie diuell, that vses to mocke, and deceiue, sillie people.—1611; Cotgrave.

Loup-garou: m. A mankind Wolfe ... also a **Hobgoblin**, Hob-thrush, **Robin-good-fellow**; also a night-walker, or flie-light; one thats neuer seene but by Owle-light.—1611; Cotgrave.

Lutin: m. A Goblin, **Robin-good-fellow**, Hob-thrush; a spirit which playes reakes in mens houses anights.—1611; Cotgrave.

Lutiner. To play the Goblin, or night-spirit; to keepe a foule rumbling, or terrible racket vp and down a house in the night.—1611; Cotgrave.

Fantasma, a ghost, a hag, a **robin goodfellow**, a hob-goblin, a sprite, a iade, the riding hagge, or mare.—1598; Florio.

the relation of father and daughter, husband and wife, justifies the appearance of our first tract, in this volume, I pass on to the second, John Lane's *Tom Tel-troths Message and his Pens Complaint*, of 1600, when Shakspere was writing, or had just written, his brilliant Second-Period *Much Ado* and *As You Like It*.

§ 2. John Lane is known to manuscript men by his still unprinted completion of Chaucer's *Squires Tale*,[1] and his re-telling of the Romance of *Guy of Warwick*, the prose Forewords to which are printed in the *Percy Folio Ballads and Romances*, ii. 521-5, from the Harleian MS. 5243 in the British Museum. He is not mentiond in Edmund Howes's list of English poets with "Willi. Shakespeare gentleman" (Continuation of Stowe's *Annales*, ed. 1615, p.

Mani ... hobgoblins, or elfes, or such misshapen images or imagined spirits that nurces fraie their babes withall, to make them leaue crying, as we say bug-beare, or els, rawe head and bloodie bones.—1598 ; Florio.

Lemuri, the ghosts or spirits of such as dye before their time, or hobgoblings, black bugs, or nightwalking spirits.—ib. And see *Manduco*.

[1] Thus describ'd in Black's Catalogue of the Ashmole MSS., 1845, col. 91-2 : No. 53. A small quarto volume, containing 81 leaves of paper, gilt at the edges, beside three on which are written the title and introductory pieces: it is very neatly written, as for a presentation copy ; and the royal Arms are stamped on the covers.

"Chaucer's Piller, beinge his Master-peece, called the Squires Tale, wᶜʰ hath binn given [up as] lost, for all most thense three hundred yeares : but now found out, and brought to light by John Lane. 1630."

On the back of the title is an acrostick (forming "Maria Anglie. C. M.") from "The Muse to the soveraigne bewtie of our adreadded sovereign lord King Charles :" which introduces an affected dedication, followed by 8 lines from "The Muse to the fowre winds," by "J. L.," and 6 lines to the author by Thomas Windham, of Keinsford, co. Somerset, Esq., one of the Justices. On the fourth page are 4 stanzas from the fourth book of the Faerie Queene by "The poet Spencer, uppon the loss of that peece of Chaucers." Then follow the Description of the Squier by Chaucer (in his prologue to the Canterbury Tales, v. 79—100), and "The Squires prolog, as it is in Chaucer," and "The Squiers tale as it is in Chaucer," the text of which on f. i.

The two first parts of this poem, and the two first lines of the third part, are copied from Chaucer ; at the end of the second (f. 10ᵇ) is this note—"Heare followeth my suppliment to bee inserted in place of that of Chaucer's which is missing. J. L." This long poem, which bears no just proportion to Chaucer's tales, consists of twelve parts or cantos, to each of which is prefixed a summary stanza of 4 lines. At the end are an Epilogus (f. 79ᵇ), "The Marchantes wordes to the Squier, and the Hostes wordes to the Marchant as they are in Chaucer" (f. 80), and "Comparatio," f. 80ᵇ.

On the back of f. 81, Ashmole has written an extract from Lydgate's "Temple of Glass," about Canace, the heroine of this story.

811, col. 2); but, as the friend of Milton's father, he is done more than justice to by Milton's nephew, Edward Phillips, who in his *Theatrum Poetarum*, 1675, thus describes Lane :—

"A fine old Queen Elizabeth gentleman, who was living within my remembrance, and whose several poems, had they not had the ill fate to remain unpublisht, when much better meriting than many that are in print, might possibly have gain'd him a name not much inferiour, if not equal, to *Drayton* and others of the next rank to *Spencer*; but they are all to be produc't in Manuscript: namely, his *Poetical Vision*[1]; his *Alarm to the Poets* [1648]; his *Twelve Months*[1]; his *Guy of Warwic*, a Heroic Poem (at least as much as many others that are so Entitled); and lastly his Supplement to *Chaucer's* Squires Tale."—1675, p. 111-12; edition 1824, p. xxiii. See also Winstanley's *Lives of the Poets*, p. 100 [which only repeats part of Phillips].—Hazlitt's *Handbook*, p. 326, col. 2.

Besides the above, John Lane[2] wrote

"An Elegie vpon the death of the high and renowned Princesse, our late Soueraigne Elizabeth. By I. L. Imprinted at London for John Deane, at Temple-barre. 1603 ; 4to, 7 leaves. *Bodleian* (Malone) *ib.*; and
"Tritons Trumpet, 1620." (Hazlitt.)

His *Tom Tel-Troths Message* is a poem of 120 six-line stanzas, in which he complains of his countrymen's naughtinesses. The closest handling of his subject is in pages 119—134, where he deals with the Seven Deadly Sins. This should be compared with the like part in *The Times Whistle*, by R. C., about 1616 A.D., edited for the Early English Text Society by Mr J. M. Cowper in 1871.

Lane first complains of the Pope, the Cardinals, priests, monks, friars, and all 'this popish ribble-rabble route,'[3] stanzas 14-19, p. 113-114. Then he laments vaguely the state of 'Englands two Vniuersities,' and the Seven Liberal Sciences, p. 115-118, of which, Grammar 'stands bondslaue-like, of Stationers to be sold,' l. 149, and Poetry brings no solace to country swains, who fancy more 'the winding of an horne,' l. 208, while ballad-makers pen 'new gigges for a countrie clowne,' l. 216, and 'bastard braines' with their base rymes work Poetry's infamy, l. 226.

[1] See *Percy Folio*, ii. 522, col. 1, at foot. The Poetical Visions was to have 'first and second partes.'
[2] Under A.D. 1572, Wood's *Fasti Oxonienses*, Pt. i, col. 189, notes,—when speaking of John Lane, of Christ Church, who died in 1578—"There was one John Lane, a poet, about this time."
[3] Compare *The Image of Ypocresye*, &c., in my *Ballads from MSS.*, i. 181-266.

Next come the Seven Deadly Sins. Under (1) *Pride*, Lane abuses the 'fine-ruft Ruffines,' st. 42, p. 119 ; the dandies 'full trick and trim tir'd in the lookinge glasse,' l. 255, casting sheeps-eyes[1], &c., walk-ing with fantastical gait, st. 45, wearing long hair or curld locks, st. 46, resembling every shape like Proteus,[2] and every colour like the chameleon, st. 47 ; drest in the snip-snap jagd clothes, st. 48, that in former fashions Chaucer in his *Parsons Tale*, and so many other complainers from time to time condemnd ; and with wingd sleeves, round hose, cloaks short and long, st. 51, p. 121.   Then the women are scolded for their dress : bold Beatrice with her wires—that movd Stubbes's wrath—tires, periwig, and caul (st. 52) ; with feathers (which men wear too), st. 53, 54 ; pumps, pantofles, corkt shoes (st. 55, p. 122), and fans (st. 56).   The picture alluded-to in stanzas 57-8, of the Englishman set alone, in other folks' feathers, I have not come across.[3]   Andrew Boorde's caricature, given at p. 167 of my *Harrison*, is the only one of the kind I know.

Under (2) *Envy*, the only special hits are at the Minstrels daily striving with blind fiddlers, l. 398, p. 124, the justling Jacks driving their betters to the wall, l. 400, and the scoffers 'with rimes and riddles rating at their foe,' l. 405.

Under (3) *Wrath*, we have the fights in Smithfield, the lines that make one think of the sad death of Marlowe in a quarrel for a drab, st. 76, p. 126.   Then Wrath's contraries are dwelt-on in st. 80-1, p. 127, Chaucer's other 'vertue that men clepe pacience or sufferaunce' (*Remedium contra Iram*), being treated as two.

(4) *Sloth* or Idleness has no local colour.

Avarice (5) repeats Harrison's complaints in his *Description*, II. 18, p. 296, &c., how ' She raiseth cheape things to the highest price,' st. 90, p. 129, and specially ' engrosseth all the corne,' l. 547 ; and leads to Usury (Harrison, p. 242), the two making the proudest cavaliers stoop, and penning ' them vp within the Poultries coope,' in gaol, st. 94.   Avarice too leads to landlords racking the rents of houses and lands, p. 130, of which Crowley, Harrison, my *Ballads from MSS.* i., the *Supplications* (E. E. Text Soc.), &c. &c., complain so bitterly.

Of *Gluttony* (6) Lane says, p. 131, that it is allied to Lechery and Drunkenness :—

---

[1] Compare Laneham with the Ladies, in his *Letter* of 1575, p. 60 of my ed.

[2] Compare Andrew Boorde, and Harrison's *Description*, II. vii, p. 167, &c. Also Stubbes.

[3] Perhaps it's in the *Recueil de la Diversité des Habits*, Paris, 1562 (A. Boorde, p. 323).

This trull makes youngsters spend their patrimonie   601
In sauced meates and sugred delicates,
And makes men stray from state of Matrimonie
To spend their substance vpon whorish mates.   604

Under *Lechery*, the seventh and last Deadly Sin, Lane's stanza
109, p. 132, evidently alludes to Shakspere's *Venus and Adonis*, and
Lucrece. He regrets the infection of the French disease, st. 110, p.
133, the wide-spread cuckoldry of his day, st. 113, and the 'light-
taylde huswiues' showing and vaunting themselves in (?) Shakspere's
Globe theatre, 'the Banke-sides round-house,' where in 1599—perhaps at its opening—he brought out his triumphant *Henry V.* Then
Lane stops, not for want of further matter, st. 120, p. 135, but because his pen is dry. And he affirms, l. 713-14,

    .... *Tom Teltroth* will not lie,
We heere haue blaz'd Englands iniquitie.

(I pay for the present reprint of Lane and thĕ extract from Pritchard or Rogers at the end of this volume.)

§ 3. Our third tract is by a reverencer of Bacon in his distress, a
rollicking attorney and Welshman, Thomas Powell, who seems to
have begun writing very bad serious poetry in 1598 and 1601, and
then turnd to chaffing prose,—still intersperst with scraps of bad
verse,—and divers professional handbooks, till he ended his career of
authorship in 1631[1] with his *Tom of all Trades*, here reprinted.[2] My
attention was first calld to the last-namd book during my inquiries
into 'Education in Early England,'[3] by Warton's extract from it in
his *History of English Poetry*, § 58, vol. iv, p. 304, note 3, ed. Hazlitt.[4]
There being no copy of the first edition in the British Museum,
and the second edition being conceald by its title, I waited till a
visit to the Bodleian enabl'd me to read the book there ; and I found
it interesting enough to justify its reproduction here. As Powell
was Shakspere's contemporary, his account of how fathers then pusht
their sons and daughters on in life, tho' not publisht till 1631,

[1] He may of course have seen through the press some of the later editions of
his *Attourneys Academy*, &c.
[2] There *may* have been two Thomas Powells. But as the one of 1603-1631
had both a serious and a humorous style in his prose, and in his verse in his prose-
books, I see no sufficient reason for supposing that he is not the serious-style
verse-writer of 1598-1601.
[3] See the Forewords to my *Babees Book*, E. E. Text Soc. 1868.
[4] I have also had copied for the Society, Edward Hake's *Touchstone for this
time present*, 1574, for its bit about girls' education and amusements, partly quoted
by Warton in the same note. But the rest of the book is preachy and dull.

covers Shakspere's time, and enables us to realize a bit of his fellow-countrymen's being. Our Member, Miss E. Phipson of Monk Sherborne, Basingstoke, kindly bears the cost of this Powell reprint.

Of Thomas Powell's first publication, *Loues Leprosie* (W. White, 1598), a quarto of ten leaves, only one copy is known, that of Mr Christie-Miller, at Britwell. It was reprinted by my friend Dr Rimbault for the Percy Society in his five "Ancient Poetical Tracts of the Sixteenth Century,[1] reprinted from unique copies formerly in the possession of the late Thomas Caldecott, Esq." 1842. The poem is on the death of Achilles, through his love for Priam's daughter Polyxena. Here are three extracts from it, on that love, on Achilles's fight with Troilus, and on Achilles's death from the arrow shot into his only vulnerable spot, his heel :—

"Achilles loues Polyxene : What is shee ?
The lyuing daughter of his enemie.
How shall he woe her, that hath wed another ?
How shall he winne her, that hath slaine her brother ?
His trophees and his triumphes she doth hate ;
In Hectors death his vallor liued too late ;
Liue blest in this, that thow art Orpheus brother :
Hee none of thine, nor Thetis is his mother."—p. 71.

" Well mounted and well met, they ioyne togeather
Like flowdes, whose rushing, cause tempestuous weather ;
And now their clattering shildes resemble thunder ;
The fire, a lightning when the cloudes do sunder :
Long did it thunder ere the heavens were bright ;
So long, that when it cleered, the day was night ;
A night perpetuall vnto Priams sonne ;
His horse was slaine, the day was lost and won ;
And heere each one might heare windes whispering sound,
When earst the drums their senses did confound ;
Troilus dethes chiefe conquest from the fielde ;
Wrapt in their colours, couered with their shielde,
They carry him to make the number more,
Whose bleeding sydes Achilles speare did gore."—p. 78.

" Foorthwith a marriage twixt them was concluded ;
Alas, that true loue should be so deluded !
The sunne is rose, sees Thetis sonne to fall
Vnder this false pretended nuptiall.
The Delphick oracle is now fulfilde,
' Eare Troy be wonne, Achilles must be kilde.'

[1] 1. The Doctrinall of good Servauntes. 2. The Boke of Mayd Emlyn. 3. The New Nutbrowne Mayd. 4. The Complaynt of a dolorous Louer. 5. Loues Leprosie.

This is the day wherein they surfet all,
With blood of his who made the Troians thrall;
And this the day wherein he did appease
Vnquiet soules, which earst could find no ease.
This day was nyght to him, and day to those
By whom vntimely death did heere repose.
His liues familliar starre doth shoote and gall,
The fairest starre the heauens weare gracte withall,
Euen when his steppes salute the temple porch
With hymmes, and Hymæn[e]us burning torch,
A shaft from Paris hand did soone disclose
Where Styx had kist him, and how high it rose.
Where the Stygian flood did neuer reach,
Deathes winged messenger did make a breach,
Whence from each veine the sacred breath descending,
Polyxens ioyes began, and his had ending.
                                    Finis."   p. 79.

Powell's second book, I have not seen.   Mr Hazlitt believes
that the unique copy from Heber's sale is at Britwell, and gives it as

"The Passionate Poet.   With a Description of the Thracian
Iemarus.   By T. P.   London, printed by Valentine Simmes, dwell-
ing on Adling hill, at the signe of the white Swanne. 1601. 4to.
26 leaves."

Of the third book, which is a very rare[1] black-letter quarto
of 16 leaves, Mr Henry Huth has, with his unvarying kindness, lent
me his copy.   It is a tract written just before and just after Queen
Elizabeth's death: 1. justifying the reasonableness of her dealing
with Papists on the one hand, and Dissenters on the other (see the
first two extracts on p. xviii, xix); 2. chaffily describing the effect
produc't by the news of Elizabeth's death, the disturbances likely
to arise from it, and the quieting of them by the happy proclamation
of James I; 3. arguing that the Scotch and English are of like
nature, and fit to form one nation; in this, the opposite of the
author of *The Complaynt of Scotland*,[2] and too of Andrew Boorde
with his "Trust yow no Skott, for they wyll yowse flatteryng wordes;
& all is falsholde:" see the amusing bits in my edition of Boorde (E.
E. T. Soc.), p. 59, note 3, p. 135-8.   The title of this third book is

[1] It was suppresst.   Valentine Simmes was fined 13*s.* 4*d.* on Dec. 5, 1603,
for printing it and a ballad.   See p. 192, below.
[2] "there is nocht tua nations vndir the firmament that ar mair contrar and
different fra vthirs, nor is inglis men and scottis men:" for, in short, the Englishmen are devils, and the Scotchmen are angels.   But note Andrew Boorde's
"Also it is naturally geuen, or els it is of a deuyllyshe dysposicion of a Scotysh
man, not to loue nor fauour an Englyshe man." p. 137.

A / WELCH BAYTE / to spare Prouender. / Or, / *A looking backe vpon the* / Times past. / Written Dialogue wise. / *This booke is diuided into three parts,* / The first, a briefe discourse of *Englands Securitie,* while her / late Maiestie was liuing, with the maner of her proceeding in / Gouernment, especially towards the Papists and Puritanes of / *England,* whereof a Letter written late before her death, speci-/fies, as followeth in this first part. / The second, A description of the Distractions during her / Maiesties sickenesse, with the composing of them. / The third, Of the Aptnesse of the English and the Scotte to / incorporate and become one entire Monarchie : with the / meanes of preseruing their vnion euerlastingly, added there-/vnto.   [*Scroll.*]   Printed at London by Valentine Simmes. / 1603.

The extracts above referrd to, p. xvii, on Elizabeth's treatment of Romanists and Dissenters follow :—

" But when about the twentieth yeare of hir raigne shee had discouered in the King of *Spaine* an intention to inuade hir dominions, and that a principall point of the plotte was to prepare a partie with in the realme that might adhere to the forreiner, and that the Seminaries began to blossome, and to send forth dayly, priests and professed men, who should, by vow taken at shrift, reconcile her subiects from their obedience, yea and binde many of them to attempt against her Maiesties sacred person, and that by the poyson which they spred, the humors of most *Papists* were altered, and that they were no more *Papists* in conscience and of Softenes, but *Papists* in faction ; then were there newe lawes made for the punishment of such as should submitte them selues to such reconcilements . or renuntiations of obedience ; And because it was a treason carried in the clowdes and in wonderfull secrecie, and came seldome to light, and that there was no presumption thereof so great as the recusancie to come to diuine seruice : Because it was sette downe by their decrees, That, *To come to Church before reconcilement, was to liue in schisme ;* But, *To come to Church after reconcilement, was absolutely hereticall and damnable,*

Therefore there were added Lawes containing punishment *pecuniarie* against such Recusants, not to enforce consciences, but to enfeeble and impouerish the meanes of those of whom it rested indifferent and ambiguous, whether they were reconciled, or no.

And when, notwithstanding all this prouision, this poyson was dispersed so secretly, as that there was no meanes to stay it but by restraining the Merchants that brought it in,

Then lastly, was there added a Lawe whereby such seditious priests of the new erection were exiled ; and those that were at that time within the land shipped ouer, and so commanded to keepe hence, vpon paine of treason.

[sign. B 4. bk]   This hath beene the proceeding, though intermingled, not only with sundrie examples of hir Maiesties grace towards such as in her wisdome she knewe to be *Papists* in Conscience, and not in Faction and Singularitie ; but also with an ordinarie mitigation towards the offenders in the highest degree conuicted by lawe : If they would but protest, that if in case this realme should be inuaded with a forreine armie by the Popes authoritie, for the Catholique cause, (as they terne it) they would take part with hir Maiestie, and not adhere to hir enemies.

For the other part which haue bin offensiue to the State, though in other degree, which name themselues *Reformers*, and we commonly call *Puritanes;* this hath bin the proceeding towards them.

A great while when they inueighed against such abuses in the Church, as *Pluralities, Nonresidence* & the like; their zeale was not condemned, only their violence was sometimes censured.

When they refused the vse of some ceremonies and rites, as superstitions, they were tollerated with much conniuence, and gentlenes : Yea, when they called in question the Superioritie of Bishops, and pretended to bring a *Democracie* into the church ; Yet, their Propositions were heard, considered, and by contrarie writing, debated, and discussed. Yet all this while, it was perceiued that their course was dangerous, and very popular ; as, because *Papistrie* was odious, therefore it was euer in their mouthes, that they sought to purge the Church from the reliques of *Papistrie;* a thing acceptable to the people, who loue euer to run from one extreame, to another.

Because multitude of Rogues, and Pouertie were añ eye-soare, and dislike to euerie man, therefore they put it into the peoples head : That, if Discipline were planted, there should be no vagabonds, nor beggers (a thing very plausible,) and in like manner, they promised the people many other impossible wonders of their Discipline.

Besides, they opened the people a way to gouernment by their *Consistorie*, and *Præsbyterie*, a thing though in consequence no lesse præiudiciall to the liberties of priuate men, then to the soueraignty of Princes, yet in first shew very popular. Neuerthelesse all this (exept it were in some few that entered into extreame contempts) was borne, because they pretended but in dutifull maner to make propositions, and to leaue it to the prouidence of God, and the authoritie of the Magistrate.

But now of late yeares, when there issued from them, as it were a Colonie of those that affirmed the consent of the Magistrate was not to be attended ; when vnder pretence of a confession, to auoide slaunders and imputations, they combined themselues by classes and subscriptions ; when they descended into that vile & base meanes of defacing the gouernment of the Church by rediculous *Pasquils* [1]*;* When they beganne to make many subiects in doubt to

[1] The Martin Marprelate controversy began in 1589.

take an oath, which is one of the fundamentall parts of Iustice in
this Land and in all places; When they beganne both to vaunt of
the strength and number of their partizans, and followers, and to
vse communications that their cause would preuaile, though with
vproare and violence ; Then it appeared to be no more zeale, no
more conscience, but meere faction and deuision : And therefore
though the State was compelled to hold somewhat a harder hand to
restraine them then before, yet it was with as great moderation as
the peace of the Church & State could permitte.

And therefore, Sir, (to conclude,) consider vprightly of these
matters, and you shall see her Maiestie is no temporizer in religion ;
she builds not religion vpon policie, but policie vpon religion ; It is
not the successe abroade, nor the change of seruants here at home
can alter her ; onely as the things themselues alter, so she applieth
hir religious wisdome to correspond vnto them, still retaining the
two rules before mentioned, in dealing tenderly with consciences, &
yet in discouering Faction from Conscience, & Softnes from Singularitie.   Farewell.

Your louing friend

T. P."

The *Welch Bayte* is dedicated by Powell to Shakspere's patron,
Lord Southampton, but oddly makes no allusion to that Lord's
being set free from the Tower on James I.'s accession.   He was
committed there for his share in Essex's rebellion in Feb. 1600-1.
Perhaps lines 2 and 4 below mean that his committal was unjust.

[sign. A, back]   A Prelude vppon the name of
Henry VVriothesly *Earle of*
South-hampton.

Euer.

W Hoso beholds this Leafe, therein shall reede,
     A faithfull subiects name, he shall indeede ;
The grey-eyde morne in noontide clowdes may steepe,
But traytor and his name shall neuer meete.

Neuer.

[sign. A 2]   To the right Honorable *Henry Wri-*
othesly *Earle of* South-hampton
Baron of Tichfield : and of the Noble Order of the Garter.

L Et golden artists practize quaint imposture,
   And study to a semblance of perfection,
   Let Leopers sweate to shew the world their moisture,
   We study not to Patrones for direction :

Vnlesse the Honor that my lines shall owe,
Can both protect vs, and approoue them too.

And such is thine, whose beames of Patronage
Doe heate alike in Iudgement, and in blood,
Both, with pure fires deriu'd from parentage,
Preserued in the Arke of Fortunes flood,
When Neptune, *and the sea gods did abette,*
With Cynthia *in her fullest veines aspect.*

Thou wholesome Honour, Chaste Nobilitie,
Be in protection mine, as Generous,
Without distent though all thy auncestrie:
It was thy wont, Thou canst not erre in vs:
And for the Test sufficeth me to know;
Thy Iudgement best deserues my lines to owe. ,

Your Lordshippes
In all the nerues of my ability,
Tho: Powell.

At the end of the *Welch Bayte* are 8 lines of verse 'To the vnparaleld blesst disposition, *The Lady* Elizabeth Bridges'; two 6-line stanzas 'To the noble Gentleman, Sir Thomas Kneuet'; and one stanza of 6 'To the Right Worshipfull Sir Edward Dyer.' The book's signatures are A 1. 2 ; B, C, D, in fours, E 1, 2:

Though Powell's notions of girls' education are not ours,

"Instead of songes and musicke, let them learne cookerie and laundrie : And instead of reading in Philip Sidney's *Arcadia,* let them reade the *Groundes of good Huswifery.* I like not a female poetesse at any hand":

yet no doubt Mrs Wm Shakspere shar'd them. Powell was a practical, sharp, business man, with a gift of racy speech. He was evidently a searcher of Records—see his book on them, and his advice to a father, p. 143 below, and specially his proposal to search the Wills Office for grants to charitable uses. I hope his readers will take to him somewhat.

The fourth book of Powell's was a professional one of 78 pages, whose title is overleaf:—

DIRECTION FOR SEARCH OF

RECORDS

Remaining
in the

{CHANCERIE,
TOWER,
EXCHEQUER, with the *Limnes*
thereof : *viz.*

The {
Kings *Remembrancer.*
Lord Treasurers *Re-membrancer.*
Clarke of the *Ex-treats.*
Pipe.
Auditors.
}

The {
First Fruits.
Augmentation of the *Reuenue.*
Kings *Bench.*
Common *Pleas.*
Records of Courts *Christian.*
}

For the clearing of all such *Titles,* and *Questions,*
as the same may concerne.

With the accustomed Fees of Search : And
diuerse necessarie Obseruations.

Cui Author
THOMAS POWELL, *Londino-Cambrenfis.*

——— —— *Cum tonat ocyus Ilex*
Sulphure discutitur sacro, quam tuque, domusque.

LONDON,
Printed by B. A. for *Paul Man,* and are to be sold
at his Shop in *Chancerie* Lane, at the Signe of the
Bowle; or in *Distaffe* Lane, at the Signe
of the *Dolphin.* 1622.

Powell's fifth book is a merry one of 34 leaves :

Wheresoeuer you see mee, / Trust vnto your selfe. / Or, / THE MYSTERIE / OF LENDING / AND / *BORROWING.* / *Seria Jocis* : / Or, / The Tickling Torture. /—*Dum rideo, veh mihi risu.* / *By* THOMAS POVVEL, / London-Cambrian. / [4 *bits of old ornament.*] LONDON, / Printed for *Beniamin Fisher*, and are / to be sold at his shop in *Pater-noster-row,* / at the signe of the *Talbot.* / 1623

It is a chaffy rollicking description of the different kinds of Borrowers—Courtier, Inns-of-Court man, Country Gentleman, and Citizen—and Lenders, Debtors' places of refuge, and debtors' shifts to avoid payment. (For the 2nd edition, see below, p. xxvi.)

Here is the beginning of how the Courtier handles the Citizen he wants to borrow money of, p. 3 :—

" The Courtiers method followes.

First he invites his Creditor, to a dish of Court-Ling, with Masculine mustard plenty.

Then shewes him the priuie lodgings and the new banquetting house.

Perhaps the Robes next.

Then the great Magolls tent in the Wardrobe : And so much serues for the first meeting, and to procure an appetite to the second.

To the second Meeting our Creditor is summoned, and brings behinde him his wife, like to a broken wicker glasse bottle hanging at his taile, and enters into the Masking roome.

Whereat the Courtiers skill in deliuering of the Maskers names, vnder their seuerall disguises, did purchase an euerlasting and indissoluble citie-consanguinitie with his female charge, ouer whom, the more sleepy hir spouse, the more vigilant was my cousen courtier.

And now he hath made his partie strong enough to visit my citizen, and to borrow and take vp of him at his own home, in the most familiar phrase that can bee deuised for such like vse and purpose.

Then for the quickning, continuing, and inlarging of his credit, our Courtier pretends how he has receiued newes that his feign'd kinred is very sicke ; and thereupon a takes occasion (in stead of venison) to send her a bottle of that famous and farre fetcht *fronti-neack :* He bids himselfe to dinner the same day, and there in a cursorie way of commending the art of man, in matter of Manufacture, he falls by chance vpon the remembrance of an extraordinarie stuffe, which hee saw a great personage weare lately in Court, not doubting but that his cousens [the Creditor or citizen's] shop did afford the like : His purpose was to haue a suit of the same very shortly, if they would but lay it by for him till his moneyes came in : Yet with a very little intreaty so cleanly expuompted, he was persuaded to take it along with him, but onely for feare lest the whole peece might be sold by the foolish foreman vnawares before his returne.

> Giue vs old Ale, and booke it,
> O giue vs old Ale, and booke it :
> And when you would haue your money for all,
> My cousen may chance to looke it."

This larky book of Powell's was followd by his sober sixth :—

The / Attourneys Academy : / *or*, / The Manner and / forme of proceeding practically, vpon / any Suite, Plaint, or Action whatsoeuer, in any / Court of Record whatsoeuer, within / this Kingdome : / especially, / in the Great Courts at / *Westminster*, to whose motion all other Courts of / Law or Equitie ; as well those of the two Pro-/uinciall Counsailes, Those of Guild-Hall / *London ;* as Those of like Cities / and Townes Corporate, And / all other of Record are diur-/nally moued : / *With the Moderne and most vsuall Fees of the* / Officers and Ministers of such Courts. / Published by his Maiesties speciall priuiledge, / and / Intended for the publique benefit of all / His Subiects. / *Summum hominis bonum, bonus ex hac vita exitus.* / Tho : ˙Powell / *Londino-Cambrensis.* / London, / Printed for *Beniamin Fisher :* and are to be sold at his / Shop in *Pater-noster* Row, at the signe of the / *Talbot :* 1623.

This is a regular Attorney's Handbook, dedicated to the " Lord Bishop of Lincolne, and Lord Keeper of the great Seale of England," and with a second dedication which does credit to Powell :—

" To / trve Nobilitie / and tryde Learning, / beholden / To no Mountaine for Eminence / nor Supportment for his Height, / Francis, Lord *Verulam*, and / Viscount S^t. *Albanes.*

O Giue me leaue to pull the Curtaine by,
      That clouds thy Worth in such obscuritie,
Good *Seneca*, stay but a while thy bleeding,
T'accept what I receiued at thy reading :
Heere I present it in a solemne straine,
And thus I pluckt the Curtaine backe again.
                                        The same
                                 THOMAS POWELL."

There were later editions in 1630, 1647, &c. Then came in 1627, Powell's seventh book, a professional one in 72 leaves :

The / Attornies / Almanacke, / Provided / & / desired / For the generall ease and daily vse of all / such as shall haue occasion to remoue any / Person, Cause or record, from an / inferiour Court to any the / higher Courts at / *Westminster.* / By THOMAS POWELL. / *Summum hominis bonum, bonus ex hac vita* / *exitus.*

London. / Printed by B. A. and T. F. for *Ben: Fisher,* and are to / be sold at his Shop at the signe of the *Talbot* without / *Aldersgate.* 1627.

Next appeard, in 1631, his eighth book, to which he did not put his name, as not half of it was his own work. The title is given by Mr Hazlitt in his *Collections and Notes,* 1876,[1] as

"The Repertorie of Records: remaining in the 4. Treasuries on the Receipt side at Westminster [and] the two Remembrancers of the Exchequer. With a briefe introductiue Index of the Records of the Chancery and Tower: whereby to giue the better Direction to the Records abouesaid. As also a most exact Calendar of all those Records of the Tower: in which are contayned and comprised whatsoeuer may giue satisfaction to the Searcher for Tenure or Tytle of any thing. London, Printed by B. Alsop and F. Fawcet for B. Fisher, &c. 1631.

4to, A—Ee in fours, first leaf blank."

"Dedicated in verse 'To the Vnknowne Patron,' which is followed by a leaf with a somewhat enigmatical heading 'To the same Patron the great Master of this Mysterie Our Author payeth this in part of a more Summe due.' There is also a prose address to the Reader, in which Powell gives some account of the circumstances attending the publication."

Powell says he first thought of dedicating his book to Mercurie, who'd inspir'd him to write a bit of verse again, but as he can't find a Patron, he dedicates it to an unknown one, whom Mercury is to find out. The address to the Reader follows :—

To the Reader.

IT may be obiected vnto me, that the collation of these things, is not all made vp and digested into this fabrique of mine owne materials and structure, and I doe ingenuously confesse it: Seeing the Foure Treasuries [p. 17—120] were collected by Mr. *Agard,* his priuate notes, a man very industrious and painfull in that kind[2]; and one who had continual recourse vnto the most, & custody of many of the rest of the same: And the latter Callender of the Records of the Tower [? p. 211—217], came to my hands from an Author vnknowne, euen as the Printer was drawing the last sheet of the precedent worke from the Presse. I was content to giue it wharfage, and to let it be layd on shore with the rest, but very vnwillingly; because I had no conuenient roome left where to dispose it, without blaming of my Methode, in that it was not layd

---

[1] Mr Hazlitt also notes that "Verses signed *T. P.* are attached to Ford's *Fames Memoriall,* 1606."

[2] See his collections in the Public Record Office.—F.

in his proper place, with the rest, that is, vnder the Title of the Tower, in the first Station : whereof I hope an equall censure, ever resting

Sub rostro Cycaniè.

The book is a 4to of 217 pages, besides Title and four pages of dedication, and describes where the Records are, what bundles of them, &c. are in the several rooms, and what Countries and places some of them refer to.   Here's a short extract :—

"*And now to the foure Treasuries.*

The first is, the Treasurie of the Court of Receipt.   In which are Two of the ancientest Bookes of Records in this Kingdome : made in William the Conquerours time, called *Doomes-day.*

The one Booke in Quarto, containing the Description or Suruey of Essex, Norfolke, and Suffolke.

The other in Folio, being the like, for all the Shires in England, from Cornwall, to the Riuer of Tyne.

Here is a Booke called the blacke Booke, made in Henry the seconds time, *De necessarijs Sca[ca]rij observandis :* And in the same, are the Oathes and Admittances of Officers inrolled, and other Notes of some consequence." [and so on].

This was followd by his 9th work, the last I find under his name, his *Tom of all Trades* printed below, p. 137—175.   In 1635 came out a second edition of both his *Tom of all Trades* and earlier *Mysteries of Lending and Borrowing,* in one little volume with the following title, no doubt written by himself :—

The Art of Thriving. / Or, / The plaine pathway to / Pre-ferment. / Together with / The Mysterie and Misery / of *Lending* and *Borrowing.*   Consider it seriously. / Examine it judiciously. / Remember it punctually. / And thrive accordingly. / [by Thos. Powell, Gent. *in MS.*] Published for the common / good of all sorts &c / London, / Printed by *T. H.* for *Benjamin* / *Fisher,* and are to be solde at his shop / at the signe of the Talbot in Alders-/gate street. 1635.   [120 pages : at p. 121 a fresh title,]

The / Mistery / and / Misery / of / Lending / and / Borrowing / By / Tho : Powel, *Gent.* / London : / Printed by *Thomas Harper* for / *Benjamin Fisher,* and are to be / sold at his shop in Alders-gate / streete at the signe of the / Talbot. 1636.   [p. 121—254.]

Of the Sir Edward Hales whom Powell praises so warmly in his Dedication to his *Tom of all Trades,* the Rev. W. S. Scott Robertson of Sittingbourne sends me the following account :

"Sir Edward Hales was the first of his name at Tunstall.[1]   He

[1] "I come now to speak of the Hales, present lords of Tunstall, a family of

was originally of Tenterden, but marrying the Harlackenden heiress, of Woodchurch, he removed to her seat. He was created a baronet in 1611. After the death of his first wife he married the widow (*née* Martha Carew) of Sir James Cromer of Tunstall, and removed thither. Sir James Cromer died in 1613, and left no son. One of his three daughters, Christian, the youngest, who inherited Tunstall, married Sir Edward Hales's eldest son John, and thus the Hales family became fixed at Tunstall. John Hales died in his father's lifetime, but his son Edward,[1] who was born about 1626, ultimately succeeded his grandfather Sir Edward.

" The first baronet, with whom your author Thomas Powell was so pleased, died in 1654, and was buried in Tunstall Church. The present representative of the family is Miss Hales of Hales Place, Canterbury, whose name figured in the statements of the claimant to the Tichborne estates. She has very recently sold her Tunstall property."

great antiquity ; but as their interest here is not of so long standing, I shall go no higher than the last century, beginning with

" *Sir Edward Hales*, Knight, who was advanced to the dignity of a baronet 1611 ; he served in several parliaments, and took part with those that raised the rebellion against king Charles I. He died October 6th, 1634, aged 78.* This is he for whom the noble monument in Tunstall church was erected with his effigies in full proportion cut in marble. His wives were Deborah, da. and heir of Martin Lackenden of Woodchurch, Esq., and Martha the relict of Sir James Crowmer.

" *John*, the eldest son of Sir Edward, by Deborah his first lady, married Christian, the youngest of the daughters and co-heirs of Sir James Crowmer aforesaid ; and by this marriage was Tunstall brought into the family of Hales. This John died in the life-time of his father, and left issue *Sir Edward Hales*, baronet, a zealous royalist, who in his younger years risqued his person and fortune in the cause, insomuch that he was forced to abscond and live beyond the seas on account of the great debts he had contracted for the king's service. He died in France some years after the Restoration." From the ' History and Antiquities of Tunstall in Kent.' By Ed. Rowe Mores, printed in Nichols's Bibliotheca Topographica Britannica, vol. i. pp. 33, 34. (Mores died in 1778, this History was publisht in 1780.)

" This Sir Edward Hales was a commissioner for the survey of Aldington in 1608, Sheriff of Kent in a year between 1611 and 1620, and M.P. for Kent in a Parliament preceding the Long Parliament."—Furley's *History of the Weald of Kent*, Ashford, 1874, vol. ii. Pt. II. pp. 522, 602.

¹ Sir Edward Hales, the third of that name, but the first baronet, of Tenterden, Kent, was knighted, and on June 29, 1611, was created a Baronet. He was twice married, first to Deborah, only daughter and heir of Martin Herlackenden of Woodchurch, Esq., by whom he had issue four sons, viz. John his eldest son,

* See the cp. ded. to Powell's *Tom of all Trades*. Lond. 1631, 4to.

§ 4. The last piece in the present volume, " *The Glassé of Godly Loue,* Wherein all married couples may learne their duties, each toward others, according to the holy Scriptures,"—I was tempted to add because it made a kind of Appendix to the *Tell-troth* tract of 1593, and because it was part of a thin treatise belonging to me, that Mr Hazlitt believes to be unique, but which is unluckily imperfect. It is undated, but is printed by Richard Jones, who took up his freedom of the Stationers' Company on the 7th of August 1564 (Arber's *Transcript,* I. 278), had one press in May 1583 (ib. 248), and printed till 1600. Whether the *Glasse* is by Thomas Pritchard,[1] the writer of the first part of the volume, or I[ohn] R[ogers] who seems to have written the second part, I cannot tell. It follows the I. R. Discourse. The title-page of Pritchard's tract is on p. xxix, opposite.

§ 5. I have now but to thank the Librarian of Peterborough Cathedral for trusting his unique 1593 *Tell-troth* to me ; Mr Henry Huth for his loan of Powell's *Welch Bayte ;* Mr W. G. Stone of Walditch for so kindly making the Contents, Notes, and Index to this volume ; Miss E. Phipson for paying for *Tom of all Trades,* and our friend who hides his name, for his gift of the first *Tell-troth* reprint.

F. J. FURNIVALL.

3, *St. George's Square, London, N.W.*
    July 11, 1876.

---

who married Christian one of the daughters and co-heirs of Sir Jas. Cromer, knt., and in her right became possessed of the manor of Tunstall and other large estates, and died in his [father's] life-time ; his other children were Edward, Samuel, Thomas, and a da. Christian. His second wife was Martha, da. of Sir Mathew Carew, and relict of Sir Jas. Cromer. He died Oct. 6, 1654, in his 78th year, is buried in Tunstall Church. His grandson Edward (son of his eldest son John) succeeded him ; this Edward was about 13 years of age at his father's death in 1639. "He succeeded his grandfather in title and estate in 1654 ; but being most zealously attached to the royal cause, he risqued his fortune as well as his person, in the support of it ; by which means he ruined the former, and was obliged on that account to abandon his native country, to which he never afterwards returned, but died in France soon after the restoration of K. Charles II." He was one of the three who escaped with James II. in 1688. Abstract taken from Hasted's History of Kent, vol. ii. p. 576.

[1] On ' 1628, July 9, Thom. Prichard of Jesus College,' Oxford, was admitted to the degree of Doctor of Divinity. Wood's *Fasti Oxon.,* pt. 1 (*Athenæ,* vol. ii.), col. 443, ed. Bliss. But I do not suppose that this is our T. Pritchard.

THE SCHOOLE

of honest and vertuous lyfe :

Profitable and necessary for

all eſtates and degrees, to be trayned in :
but (cheefely) for the pettie Schollers, the
yonger ſorte, of both kindes, bee they men or
Women.　by T. P.

Also, a laudable and learned
Diſcourſe, of the worthyneſſe of honorable Wedlocke, written in the be=
halfe of all (aſwell) Maydes as Wydowes,
(generally) for their singuler instructi=
on, to chooſe them vertuous and honeſt

Husbandes :

But (moſt ſpecially) ſent writtē as a Iewell
vnto a worthy Gentlewoman, in the
time of her widowhood, to direct & guide
her in the new election of her seconde
Huſband.　By her approoued freend and
kinſemen.　I. R.

Imprinted at London by

Richard Johnes, and are to
be ſolde at his ſhop ouer againſt S. Sepulchers Church without Newgate.

Tell-Trothes New-yeares Gift

Beeing

*Robin Good-fellowes newes out of thofe Countries, where inha-
bites neither Charity nor honefty.*

With his owne Inuectiue againft Ielofy.

LONDON
Imprinted by Robert Bourne.
1593.

Tell-Trothes New-yeares Gift.

 Marry, fir, now you looke as if you expeƈed newes: me thinks I fee your cares open to heare what Robin good fellow will tel you; & becaufe your defire fhal not be altogether fruftrate, you fhal, if you will, be fomewhat the wifer before you goe. I am affured it is not ftale; and were you as long in reading of it, as the Senators haue bene in agreeing vppon it, I know you would craue many baetes before you had paffed the mainger. But behold, they had the paine, and you may haue the pleafure; and I am glad that it was my fortune to meete with it; and doubtleffe it was a great haffard, that a worfer carrier had not hapned on it. For thus it fel out: walking towards Iflington in a frofty morning, I by chaunce lighted into the company of a boone companion, that feemed no leffe pleafing in fhew, then he prooued in fubftaunce. A merry mate hee was, and matched with one of his owne minde, a fimple fellow, that marchinge vnder the habbite of true meaninge, tels all that he fees, and euery thing he thinkes to be true: *Tell-troth* is my name, and you may truft me if you will, for I affure you, that he that crediteth me moft, fhall not fpeede worft. We two matches mated by good fortune, *Robin good-fellow* the one, who neuer did worfe harme then correƈ manners, and made diligent maides: and I, *Tell troth*, the other, who euer haue beene a fworne enemy to lafye lurdens, and a profeffed foe to *Iack No-body:* no fooner fettinge our eyes, the one on the other, but knew each others conditions, falling forthwith into familiarity. And it being my hap to enquire firft from whence hee came, hee made it not fcrupulous to certifie his comming from hell, a place (fayde hee) that is odious, and yet to none but to them that feare it: Mary (qd. hee) *Robin good-fellow*, that could go inuifible from [1]his infancy, had it by nature giuen him, that he fhould bee fubiect to no inferiour power whatfoeuer, either ruling or inhabiting vnder the higheft elemente, with a generall priuiledge to fearch euery corner, and enter any caftell to a good purpofe. By libertye of which pattente, I croffed the riuer *Stix* in *Carons* boat without his leaue, giuinge him a patt on his drowfie pate for my paffage. And from him vnknowne, I came to *Cerberus* (that Lubberly Porter), who was makinge fafte of the brand gates, which were faine to bee opened, that the greate *Magog* with his companye that were fummoned to the Parliamente, might enter without interruption. He heard my trampling, and therefore asked who was there? but when I would not aunfweare, he thought it was *Lelaps* his curre, bidding him to lie downe, and fo likewife I eafely entred the dungion. To tell what I there faw, were no newes: becaufe it hath beene tolde by fo many, whereof foome of them haue not reported amiffe. But going on to the mercileffe pallace, the gates ftoode wide open, fo that any might enter ther without controlement. With in the great Hall whereof, were affembled the whole fociety of bad company, a generall conuocation beeing called about the deciding of many matters which were not altogether perfected. There was a greate thronge, and no little fturre, the feuerall billes of complainte which were there exhibited of many matters, beeing fo many, as they would require an age to rehearfe them, efpecially feeing this one matter wherof my newes confifteth, was a hearing and deciding feauen yeares.

But to come to the matter, all the worft diuels being placed in their orders according to their cuftome (which is needleffe to fet downe, for that I hope there is none heere that euer meane to be partakers of any of their Offices) the Speaker vttered an Oration that would haue made a maftie to haue broke his collor with girning thereat, declaringe what a continuall profite Ielofie, aboue all other vices, brought to that place, praifinge fo highly the commodity thereof as, in his diuelifh iudgement, hell would be paffinge beggerly without that helpe. Manifeftinge how eafely mens and womens mindes were drawn to all cor¹ruption thereby, with fuch a dilatinge narration as neuer an Orator in hell could haue fpoken more. After the finifhinge of whofe fuftie framed fpeech, there was a queft of enquiry called, whofe forman deliuered a whole bundell of fcroles and papers,

[¹ sig. A 3]

wherein were fett downe the caufes that helped Ielofie, with the
meanes that hindered the fame, as alfo the kindes thereof, with
feuerall complaintes made both by men and women that were vexed
with the like. The which I will, quoth Robin, deliuer vnto thee if
thou fo wilt : whereof, I beeing wonderfull defirous, for *Mens hominis
nouitatis auida*, hee went on with it as followeth.

The firft caufe (quoth he) is a conftrained loue, when as parentes ~Parents~
do by compulfion coople two bodies, neither refpeftinge the ioyning ~f[or]ced loue~ ~a cause of~
of their hartes, nor hauinge any care of the continaunce of their ~Ielofy.~
wellfare, but more regardinge the linkinge of wealth and money
together, then of loue with honefty : will force affeftion without
liking, and caufe loue with Ielofie. For either they marry their
children in their infancy, when they are not able to know what loue
is, or elfe matche them with inequallity, ioyning burning fommer
with kea-cold winter, their daughters of twentye yeares olde or vnder,
to rich cormorants of threefcore or vpwards. Whereby, either the
diflike that likely growes with yeares of difcretion engendereth difloyalty in the one, or the knowledge of the others difability leades
him to Ielofie.

What is the caufe of fo many houfholde breaches, deuorcements, ~Rob. Goo[d-]~
and continuall difcontentmentes, but vnnaturall difagreementes by ~fellowes~ ~digres-~
vnmutuall contraftes ? Will the Turtel change while her mate is ~sion. The~ ~natu[re] of~
true, or the Swanne be cruell as long as his female is loyall ? If ~the Sw[anne]~ ~is, that at~
there be difloyalty betweene mates linked by their owne eleftion (as ~such time[as]~ ~he sees an~
doubtleffe there is), how can vnconftancy be condemned in thofe that ~vnconstan[t]~ ~tricke to b[e]~
neuer had that liberty ? were the hart as fubieft to the law as ~perfourme[d]~ ~by his~
the body is, I would thinke fuch marriages lawfull, but fince ~fem[ale.]~ ~he neuer~
the one hath liberty, when the other is in captiuity, I know, *Tell troth*, ~[t sig. A 3,]~ ~back]~
(quoth *Robin*) it will not ceafe to feeke reuenge for his bodies ~a the~ ~Swan~
flauery, vuleffe grace [1] correfteth, by fhewing what the law of God ~commit~ ~the fault~
forbiddeth. Pretious iewels are chofen, and deere thinges loued ; but ~her vn-~ ~e hath~
at what price are thofe rated at which are eafely obtained ? Doubt- ~d him &~ ~he bee-~
leffe at fo low a reckoninge as pipple ftones are, in comparifon of ~Liine, he~ ~es the~
pearles ; the one had without coft or trauell, and the other not to be ~with~ ~his own~
obtained without both. A leffon learned with ftroakes, ftaies with ~a.~
the fcholler, when a fentence read without regarde, is not fo foone in
at one eare, as out at the other : And loue gained with fighes &

flightes encreafeth, when obtained otherwife, it foone decayeth. *Durum pati meminiſſe dulce*, & an ounce of pleafure ftolne with feare of a pound of vnreft, makes vs ftill to thinke on the fweeteneſſe of loue, and all wayes to be ftriuing to continue it, when the contrary will procure lighte regarde thereof. How farre more delightfome is ftolne venifon to him that hath inough, then his owne? And how pleafant is that meat in tafte which is dainty? Thinges farre fetchte and deere boughte, are good for Ladies: and trifles will often better content then treafure. The Diuels crye for miflike, but who beares the brunt of it? The feete that flie from it, not the head that bredd the baite; the man can prouide for himfelfe, when the poore woman is voide of all fuccour, and he will haue a cloake to hide his mifery when ſhe ſhall want a cap to couer her [1] extremitye. She muft beare the lumpes and lowres; if happily ſhe efcapes the blowes, the biting [2] woordes, if not worfe, euen cruell hart-breakinges and back-beatinges. Thus ſhall the Fathers couetuoufnes be caufe of the childes vndooing, and his harts-eafe beginning of her woe, and ende of her happineſſe: his likinge meeting with her loathing, which ſhall vndoe her by Ielowfy. Hath God by an inftinct of nature ingrafted loue fo farre forth in vnreafonable creatures, as they doo not ~onelye choofe their mates (as all creatures doe), but liue faithfullye to them, and con-ftantly with them, fo longe as life endureth; and ſhall that priuiledge be taken from man-kinde, whome onely he hath endowed with reafon and difcretion? The birdes bringe vpp the yong, vntill they can ſhift for themfelues, and then giues them leaue to vfe their liberty: the beaftes of the fielde haue the felfe [3] fame freedome, and the fifhes in the Sea, no other reftrainte; onely man is iniurious vnto himfelfe, by vnnaturall vfage of his deereft bloud. They care for their children vntill they be paft care: and euen then themfelues freed from that charge, they bring their young ones to a greater croffe: geuing them forrow for their pleafure, and vnreft in fteede of hartes eafe. They doe not matche them with the mates their childrens eies haue chofen, but with the men their owne greedy defire haue found out: little fore-thinking of their childrens after-greeuinge, and their owne repenting. They regard not now a dayes the old fayinge of the wife man, *I had rather haue a man then mony*, but teftify by their doinges that they efteeme more of wealth then of

[1] *orig.* his]
[2] *orig.* bting]
[3] leaf A 4]
Men [make] themfel[ues] vnnatur[al] to their[chil-] dren by t[heir] matches

humanity. They forget what themfelues haue beene, and will not
remember what themfelues haue done. Their coueteoufneffe choak-
eth their charity, and their worldly care keepeth em¹ for knowinge [¹ *orig.*
diuinity. They abhorre and grow mad to heare their children entreat keepe them.
for ⸗ from.]
for the maides that pleafe them, or for the men their foules loue, but
tirant like they fay, *fic volo fic iubeo, ftet pro ratione voluntas :* I like
him, and thou fhalt haue him; loue this man or I will loath thee.
This effecte hath coueteoufneffe in the father; and beholde what dif-
contentmente it worketh in the childe.

He or fhee by duety is bound to their Parentes commaundement,
and for feare of their difpleafure are linked to continuall mifery.
What faith the hufband to the wife, but, this was thy fathers worke,
to winne me by his mony; and fince hee hath his will with the want
of my weale, I wil not liue alone in forrow, but² will make thee tafte [² *orig.* bnt]
of the fame fauce. Thy Father hath his, and why fhould I not haue
mine ? So faith he, and fo fareth fhee : hee inuentes meanes to
make her mourne, and leaues no practife vntried, which is like to
procure her mifery. They liue in one houfe, as two ennemies lie in
the field : their habitation being feuered, like twoo campes that bee
ready for battell. Hauocke is made lauifhly, of that their fathers
gathered corruptly, that either being fpente lafciuioufly in the company of ftran³gers, or licentioufly in controuerfies at law. So great [³ an- *orig.*
au-]
⁴mifchiefe arifeth of coueteoufneffe in matches of matrimonye. [⁴ leaf A 4,
back]
Touching the faluing of which fore, it is moft requifite that the
children fhould haue their free liberty in likinge, as the fathers haue
had theirs in choofing. For as thofe matches are beft, wher there is
a mutuall agreement betweene parentes and their children, fo do
thofe for the moft part loue beft, that haue the priuiledge of
choofinge for themfelues. My cheefeft reafon may bee drawne from
contentment in loue, which is fatisfied with any thinge, according to
the faying, *Loue hath no lacke ;* and my old leffon, *Selfe do, felfe haue,*
makes the patient often not to complaine of a great fore, when an
other will cry out for no harme. Experience hath beft difplayed it
to fome : and common reafon cannot but make it knowne to all.
For who that hath done him felfe an iniury will complaine thereof,
for feare of beeing ⁵accompted a foole ? Or what woman that hath [⁵ aco- *orig.*
arc-]
burnte her finger will blame others for the deede done by her felfe ?

You might haue tooke better heede, and *It was your owne fault,* are two fhrode plafters for a greene wound: and the minds of men are beft pleafed with their owne thoughts, & women with nothing more contented then to haue their willes. When a woman diftruftes of any helpe to come from any part-taker, fhee will bee glad to pleafe hir hufband, & they two falling foorth, fhe (hauing none to maine-taine her in her pride) will bee contented to reconcile her felfe vnto him by kinde fubmiffion. And where a louing kiffe will faue a great deale of coft, if there it bee not vfed, mony cannot be better beftowed then in buying wit to faue the next charges. But how now, *Robin !* thou haft beene ouer longe in thy digreffion. I haue indeede, and therfore, frend *Tell-troth,* I returne to my matter.

Indiscreete gouernment the second cause of Ielosy. A fecond caufe of Ielocy fpringeth from indifcretion in gouern-ment, which is either in one or both of them *that* are linked together in mariage, neither of them hauing reafon to knowe what belonges to either, or neither of them difcretion rightly to correct what is amiffe in either. Loue will bce too wanton vnleffe he be whipped with rufhes, and ouer dull if his winges be clipped ; giue him his [¹ sig. B] liberty, and he will runne at raudum ; ¹ fhut him vp in prifon, and he will be ftarke mad ; fo that gentle correction muft barre his liberty, and mild chafticement preuent his madneffe ; a wanton toung be-wraies a lafciuious hart, and by the vttraunce of the toung, wicked thoughts are manyfefted ; therfore, either to gaze lafciuioufly, or to fpeake wantonly, may moue Iellofy. Modefty in a young woman is as a garland of wheat in a ioyfull harueft ; and difcretion in a man like an oliue braunch after long difcention : fhe honoureth her huf-band with a figne ot happineffe, and he contentes his wife with a pledge of loue ; by his wifdome hee teacheth her knowledge, and by her obedience fhe makes him glad ; his correction is as a warme cup of drinke to a cold ftomake, and her reformation as a fonne-fhine daye after much raine. Peace flourifheth where wifdome ruleth, and ioy raigneth where modefty directeth. To pleafe the harte of a huf-bande, is to ioyne vnity with the whole world ; and to be in the loue and fauour of a wife is a freedome from much care ; wifdome there-fore in men to gouerne their common wealths, and modeftie in women, are of no fmall meanes to continue vnity, and deftroy Iellofy.

Another caufe is caufeleffe difcontentment, when the man will ^{Causles} lowre without occafion, and the woman fret, not knowing any reafon, and efpecially when either of them wil oppofe them felues againft other, and both of them maintaine their hartes pride : when a man will finde fault without caufe, or a woman complaine of two much eafe, it fhowes a troubled minde and breeds fufpeĉt. He that cannot be merry at home, goes about to perfwade hee will be mad abroad; and fhee that lowers on her hufband when he comes home, fhowes fhe had as liue haue his roome as his company : where loue is, there is no thought of battell; and there, what abfence hath hurt, prefence will heale. A kind and louing wife forgetteth all vnkindneffe by the fight of her beft beloued, as a child doth the correĉtion of his mother by the receipt of an apple from her; and a difcreete hufband is no longer difpleafed then a fault is a doing. Contentment is an excellent fauce to eury difh, and pleafantneffe a finguler portion to preuent mifchiefe: the head is neuer[1] euill; but either it is [2]pleafantly difpofed or knauifhly occupied. A merry countenance is a figne of content- ment, but froward wordes are meffenger of melancholly. In what the hart delighteth, with that it is beft pleafed; and harde it is to hault before a creppell. A frowne lodeth, and a fmile lightneth; to frowne therefore kindly, is a barre to Iellocy : but loading crabbedly, men vndoe themfelues fpeedily.

Many men delighting in much company, cannot be contented to follow their defire abroad by vfing new familiarity, but wil bring daily grief vnto their houfes, as little regarding their difpofitions with whome they ioyne frendfhip, as the occafions that may be offered of diflike by after repentings; fo that following their pleafure in fatisfieng that humor, they fall afterwards into a worfe vaine, being fufpitious of ouer much familiarity to haue crept with their acquaintance, and doubtful leaft their copefmates are matched with them in their darlinges bofomes. When they will begin fo to watch their wiues eies, and dogge their frendes lookes, as the mife fhall not pepe with- out daunger of the cats, nor the filly women fpeake without fufpition of falfhood, Others will bring ftrang women vnto their wiues to welcome : fpeaking lauifhly of their beauties, and vn- decently in their praifes, they will make comparifon without difcretion, and giue iudgement without wifdome. They regard prefent pleaf-

Caufles d[is]con-tentme[nt] the third.

[1 orig. nener] [2 fig. B, back]

[M]ens follye [the] fourth.

ure, but care not for future profit, not fo much as thinking on the
chilling winter in the heate of fummer, nor of warre in time of
peace. They confider not how loue wil brooke no equalitie, nor
marriage allowe of the leaft vnconftancy; and both thefe, though
themfelues haue beene the procurers of their own difcontentment,
yet will they lay all the burthen on their wiues backes, either plaging
them in beeing fufpitious, or punifhing them by making them
ielious. The old fayng is, that he which will no pennance doe, muft
fhonne the caufe that belongs thereto : had I wift, is a flender
remedy to remoue repentaunce, but a manifeft badge of folly,
efpecially when a man will leaue the bridg, to trie to leap ouer the
ditch and fall into it. Thought is free; but when the toung blabs, it

is figne the hart ¹ aboundes. What an euident token of folifh blind-
neffe is it, for a man to feeke many daies to pleafe his mind, when
afterwards, hauing found and inioying it, he will miflike thereof in a
moment, by fight of a new obiecte? O! that is a weake harte that
hath fuch a wandring eie! and hee is no fmall foole that fo little
efteemes of experience, as hee delighteth in the practife of vnknowne
conclufions. Might it pleafe them to vfe leffe wordes and more wit,
fewer companions or kinder familiarity, they fhould not fo lightly
enter the hazard of Iellofy.

Ill counfell is the next caufe of Iellofy; wher by the wicked
(whofe immaginations are only to foe difcentions by bruting euil
fuppofes, bred of a fufpitious braine, & vttered with colored hipocrifie)
labour to fette debate betweene true hartes, and to fhuffle in fufpition
amongft thofe that are free from thought thereof. They will ftriue
to perfwade by liklyhoods, & confirme afcertions with falfe oathes.
They will place betweene man and wife a tree of difcorde, and plant
in peacable houfes, rootes of variance; their toungs fhall be wagging
to wifh them to taft of the fruit thereof, their heads ftudying how to
bring them to like of the practife of their premeditated mifchiefe.
They will alleadg, lo thus it hath proued by others, and fo hath it
fell out vnto them for want of fufpition. Think on the worft (fay
they) for the beft is not hurtfull; but thinke of them as of the worft,
fay I, for they are moft hurtfull.

And thefe make-bates will not let to brute reportes, though
meerely falfe, to confirme their fayings, cloking their mifchiefe with

the habit of good meaning, and hiding their knauery with a fhow of
puritie. They will tatle tales as if fraught with truth : and vtter
flanders, with proteftations. They will inuent to perfwade, and
fweare to confirme : fticking burres on their backes, that were free
from motes; and filling their heads with wonders, that before were in
quiet. They ioy to fet difcention in a louing plat, and reioyce to fee
debate betweene faithfull frendes; they hunt after controuerfie, and
honour Iellofy. And becaufe themfelues are old, they will hate all
that are younger then themfelues, and fufpeδ all, for that themfelues
haue loued [1] the game : experience of knauery is a peftilent helpe to [1 sig. B 2,
Iellofy; and if the mother hath loued to playe falfe, fhee will bee fure ^{back]}
to miftruft the daughter. Beware, for I haue tried: tis a vile whip to
fcourge a fearefull hart with; and perfwafions from a diffembling
hart are wondrous hurtfull to an vnconftant louer. It is a fmall bit
that will not make a hungry dogge gape; and an vnfauery morfell
that will not content a longing appetite. A will, with a diuelifh wit,
will praδife any thing; and what is it that they cannot effeδe?
Marry, the beft helpe to preuent their mifchiefe, is mifbeliefe; and the
readieft mean to trie truth, is, to fearch into their own liues. And for
that you fhall, Tell-Troth, quoth hee, the better vnderftand the
diuelifhneffe of fuch creatures as are thefe makebates, I will tell thee
a merry tale, I haue hard there tould, of one who was croft in her
wicked fufpition.

There was an olde trott, that in her youth hauing beene a true [A m]erry
traueller, and now through her loofe life was worne to the bones and ^{tale [of a]} ^{make [bate.}
paft all goodneffe, dwelled neere vnto a proper young woman matched
with a very honeft man. This olde beldame, being good for nothing
but to keepe the cat out of the afhes, and to prattell ouer a pot of
nut-browne ale, would fpend the reft of her time which was not imployed ouer the fagget, in fitting at the dore to watch what company
reforted to the young mans houfe afore faid. . Whether, for that he
was of a trade, did come diuers, fome to bargaine, other about other
bufineffe, and amongft the reft, this man had a frend, being a young
man, which did often repaire thether. The olde cat hauing feene him
there twife or thrife, beeing at a certaine time amongft many of her
other goffopes, (like vnto her felfe in condition and of her own
ftampe by antiquity,) called this honeft mans wiues name into queftion,

ſo ſetting her worne chappes a wagging, as ſhe burthened her conſcience with the confirmation of her miſtruſtfullneſſe concerning her
luing. The reſorte thether was her reaſon, and the ſight of the
former younge man her concluſion for the truth thereof. Some of
her companions (ſomewhat better diſpoſed then her ſelfe) gaue their
[¹ ſig. B 3] iudgement with ſome tol·leration concerning the ſuſpected diſhoneſty,
of which ſhe miſliking, reproued their light of beliefe with a ſhameleſſe interrogation, howe ſhee could bee honeſt, ſeeing ſuch a one
doth reſorte daily vnto her, who is like to bee a wild youth, and
therefore cunning, and ſhe a young woman ſoone to be inticed : we
know (ſaid ſhe) by experience the dealings of ſuch mates, hauing our
ſelues beene fully tried by their ſlightes : verily they cannot be well
thought on; nor may ſhe be liked, nor her huſband praiſed, for giuing

A fires-bir[d,] ſuch entertainment.   Vpon which report, her withered goſſipes gaue
for that she
ſat continu- vppe their verdict, that then indeede ſhe could not be honeſt; and ſo
ally by the
fire ſide.   for that time the court broke vppe.   They gon, this wether-beaten
ſieres-bird could not be ſatisfied with thus much, but the chuffe her
huſband comming in, ſhee could not chuſe but tell him of the company that had beene with her, and of the talke that had paſſed betweene
them, with a recitall of her newly broched miſchiefe, affirming it
was great pittie, ſeeing ſhe was a very proper young woman, and hee
an honeſt man, a young beginner that was like to doe well, were he
not ouer-reached by ſuch companions.   Doubtleſſe (quoth ſhee) it
were good, and a thing well pleaſing vnto god to impart thus much
vnto her huſband, peraduenture he, ſilly man, miſtruſt no ſuch matter,
or is loth to offend his wife by telling her of it ; but if hee ſeekes not
preſent remedy, howe is it poſſible hee ſhould eſcape vndoing ?   To
which ſuppoſed impoſſibility hee agreed ; I thinke, lead thereunto
rather for feare then otherwiſe, as you ſhall hereafter gather.   Well,
ſhortly they agreed to ſend for the yong man, and at his comming
ſent for a pinte of wine, giuing him therewith to gnaw, ſuch cruſtes
of ſmall comfort, as tended both to his owne diſcredite & his wiues
diſhoneſty : both their opinions concerning ſuch men which reſort to
his houſe, as they feared, rather to her then to him : as alſo the
reportes of other their neighbours that greatly pittied them, miſtruſt-
ing no leſſe then they had ſaide, confirmed their ſlaunders, endinge
their tittell tattell with perſwaſions to forewarne their wiues of ſuch

company. With which vnlooked-for banquet, the younge man, being
ſtroken amaſed (and maruell not, ſince it was meat ¹ of ſo hard a diſ-
geſture), ſtoode ſtill for a ſeaſon ; but after callinge his wittes together
(of which he had no ſmall neede being mated with two ſuch rookes)
aſſured them of his wiues conſtancye toward him, that loued him moſt
intierly, and obeyed him moſt duetyfully. And touching the reſorte,
his trade required cuſtomers, and not of the worſt ſort (for he was a
ſhoomaker) ; and ſo lightly thanking them for their proteſted good
will (giuing as ſmall credit to their prittell prattell as he had ſtomacke
to their cheere) he departed home, nothing leſſe louing, or thinking
worſe of his wife then hee did before. But they, ſeeing their purpoſe
tooke ſo little effecte, grewe mad, eſpecially the ſhe beetell, that in a
great rage ſhe poſted to the tauerne, where ſhe found ſome of the
queſt of inquiry aforeſaid, to whome ſhe blaſed the rancour of her
hart, ſhowing them howe ſhamefully their young neighbour was
wronged, and diſhoneſtly abuſed, through his kind ſimplicity. Wherevppon this honeſt man was dubbed amongſt them a wittall ; but while
mother trot and her fellowes were deſcanting on others honeſty, there
came in a new goſſip, and not without newes, aſſuring this breede-bate
that her huſband (the olde fornicator that had beene with his wife a
bate-maker) was at the flower de luce, a houſe of as good reſort of
honeſt women as any be in brid-well, and had ſent for thether wine
and other good cheere; which brought ſo bad cheere to her hart, as in
all haſte ſhee did runne thether : where not finding him, but vnderſtanding, I know not by what meanes, that hee was newe gon, ſhee
fals ſo hot to ſcoulding with the whipperginne her oſtice, as from
wordes they fell to blowes, ſo as in the ende our good neighbour
came home to her huſband with a painted face, as if ſhee had beene
at her nuntions with cats. Well, beeing come, Ioane Stoomp-foot
and Tom Totty, fell to 'thou knaue' and 'thou queane,' with other ſuch
ſhameleſſe tearmes, as her huſband, not able to ouermaiſter her that
way, began to beelabour her faire and handſomely with a faggotſtick,
a preſent remedy to charme ſuch diueliſh tounges. With which
noiſe (for doubtleſſe it was great, eſpecially the longe toungd beare
getting the worſe), the neighbours beeing troubled, were ²forced of
pitty to come in, who, ſeeing the fray bloody, ſeuered the knaue and
the queane, and ſo parted the combate. But the ſcoulding champion

[¹ ſig. B 3, back]

They are
[ro]okes for
[th]eir trou-
[bl]ing tongs.

The nature
[of] a Hee
bee[te]ll is,
with [th]eir
whole
[fo]rce to flie
[a]gainst
ei[th]er man
or [b]east,
toſting
[th]em.

Which was
the Shee
make-bate.

[² leaf B 4]

(hauing good occafion to fet her chappes a-wagging, that were faine
to flaunder before, for want of other matter) curfed the time that euer
fhee met with fuch a whore mafter knaue, telling the whole circum-
ftaunces of the matter, with tearmes fit for women of her owne
ftampe. And her hufband, on the contrary part, forced to heare her
tale, requites it with a iadifh tricke, that fhe was taken with before
time by him in his celler with a collier vpon two fackes of coales.
And thus both of them that accufed others fo lately of difhonefty,
were now by all condemned for a Ielious knaue and a miftruftfull
baude, worthy titles for fuch makebates.

  I therefore warne (quoth Robin) both all fuch Ielious goffipes
as loue to haue owers in euery mans bote, and could wifh that all
mens daggars belonged to their fheathes, and alfo thofe driggell drag-
gells (whofe wicked and lafciuious liues haue wafted their bodies to
the bones, and yet not worne the tippes of their tounges) to leaue to
be fo rafh in their iudgementes, or to let their fhameleffe inftrumentes
to blabb fuch vnconfcionable vntrothes to fo abhominable an ende.
And I alfo councell both men and women, lightly to regard their
backebitings and flaunders, that by vncharitable intermedling with
their doings, feeke to moue ftrife and procure diflike, betweene thofe
that loue faithfully and liue quietly together, neuer giuing occafion
of fufpition the one to the other, feeing that flaunders are onely likely hoodes, and no likelyhood certaine.

The hard
vsage ether
of a man to-
wardes his
wife, or of
[a] woman
towards her
husbande,
i[s] the
seauent[h]
cause of
Ielosy.
  A feauenth caufe proceedeth of hard vfage, when as a man will
brutifhly vfe his wife by ftrokes, and currifhly barre her of matrimoniall kindneffe. The man that will lifte vp his hand againft his
wife, is like the horfe that doth fling out his heeles to ftrike his
keeper; the one hauing a knauifhe, and the other a iadifh tricke.
Will a man of loue launce his owne flefhe, thoughe fome of deuotion
fcourge their owne backes? Doth not the dog feare the ftaffe that
hath ftroken him? and can a woman like of the hand that hath hurt
[' leaf B 4,
back]
her? He that calleth his brother foole in ¹anger, is in daunger of hell
fire: and thinkes the other man that hatefully beates his wife, or the
woman that reuiles her hufband, which are neerer the one to the
other, to efcape that furnace? It is an eafie matter to find a ftaffe to
beate a dogge, but vnpoffible to meete with a dogge that will loue to
be beaten with a ftaffe, and as hard to finde a kinde hufband that

will hold vppe his hand in anger againft his wife, which is as his
owne hart vnto him; but it is very eafie, for that they are ouer-com
mon, to light vppon breakers of wedlocke, that will hold vp their
armes, bend their fifts, and beat their filly wiues, at their comming
home from bad women, loathinge thofe that loue them, and louing
thofe that lothes them but for aduauntage. There was alfo information made of many, that hauinge vfed their wiues wondrous ill all
their life time, dealing with them as rigoroufly as many iades do with
the Oftlers knauifhly, that notwithftanding their cruelty hath beene
manifeft to the whole world : yet lying vpon their deathes bed, as
late as poffible they could, and yet better late then neuer, haue, ftroken
with penitencie, confeffed their faultes with forrow, and affirmed
with proteftations that they know there were, nor euer haue beene,
more faithfull, carefull, obediente, nor louinge wiues then theirs : I
pray you what would fuch haue prooued, if they had beene matched
with like kind-harted men. Well, I leaue that to your iudgement,
and will come to the laft caufe of Ielofy.

Which being not the leaft, is a leaud behauiour in company, when
by loofe trickes it may bee adiudged that nothing but oportunity is
wantinge to their inciuillity. But where fhame tames not, there
blame maines not. A feftred fore muft haue a fearching falue; and a
fhameleffe fmile an open frowne. They that carelefly offende the
law of modeftye, muft not tafte of the fweete of courtefy; and they
which refpect not humanity, fhalbe troubled with Ielofy. Blame
not the childe that feares the rod, hauing felt the fmart therof, nor
miflike thofe that fhonne foure thinges, hauing tafted of fuger. A
hound that knowes the game, delightes in hunting; and geue the
keeper leaue to beftirre him1felfe when a curre chafeth his deare. Hee [ɪ sig. C]
that fteales by night, efcapes often when the day-theeues is apprehended; but an impudent and defperate robber muft haue a fhort
dome, for that a plaine matter needes a fmall triall. He that feares
not the halter will hardly become true; and they that care not for
fufpect, are feldome honeft. A ftill dogge bites fore, but the barking
cur feares more. The hart is the director of the other partes. I pray
you then what thinkes he that fhames not who fee ? Fy of hipocricie,
but the diuell take impudencie.

Thefe caufes thus fet downe were reduced into thefe eight kindes.

Knauifh and foolifh doters and fornicators, backebiters and liers.
Bankrotes and hipocrites: the two firft kindes haue effectes from the
third, fourth, and eight caufes, the two fecond from the firft and fift;
the fix and feauen kindes, of the fourth and fift caufes; and the two
laft proceede, of the fecond, third, and feauenth caufes, of euery one
of which there was a feuerall bil of complaint deliuered, which for
that they were very tedious, I haue but onely brought awaye the
endorcementes of them.

The firft was, that whereas Iafper Impudencie lately entertained
into the familiarity of one Ioone, good wench, that had vfed him
very kindly in fecrete, had to her great difcredite, for that fhe barred
him of that Priuiledge in an open affembly, called her name and
fame in queftion, by accufing her of plaing faft and loofe (about a kind
glaunce that fhee had geuen vnto an other, that had better deferued
her fauour), in confideration of whofe foolifh knauery and knauifh
folly, fhee defired redreffe againft him.

The fecond was, againft the folly of a yong nouice, that was fo
paffionate for the loue of a maide, that he could not fee any to fpeake
vnto her, but ftraighte would fall into a founde through Ielofy. An
other complained of an old dotor of fourfcore yeares of age, that had
gotten, through the compulfion of her parentes, her felfe in marriage,
being but two and twenty. Who through his watching, and the
dodging of an old beldam his fifter, being in houfe with him, was fo
tormented, that if fhee were neuer fo little out of both their fightes:
he prefently thought his head belgan to bud, though it were in the
deade of winter, and woulde moft fhamefully raile vpon her. And
fhee, hauing learned fome fubtelty by the old foxes craft, on a time
ftole foorth to her fathers to fupper, not making any priuy to her
parting, and there ftayed vntill nine of the clock. When comming
home, fhee found her hufband a bed, that had almoft fretted his hart
out for his wiues long tarrying: who no fooner faw her, but fell a
threatning of her, and ftricktly examining her where fhee had beene:
But fhee, beeing well acquainted with that cuftome, fained, that by
chaunce, comming from her fathers, fhee met with a younge gentleman, an old frend of hers, that would not be faid nay, but fhe muft
of force go fup with him. And affirming that to be true, fhee fell

[¹ sig. C,
back]

downe vppon her knees and craued his pardon. At the hearing of
which, yea, and before fhee had quite done (now thinking that to be
certeine, which before he onely miftrufted, being verily perfuaded
that the deftinies hadd crowned him with a paire of hornes for his
New-yeares gift), he fpitted at her, laying Bridewell in her difh, and
the cart for her trencher : not only refufing her company for his bedfellow, but driuing her out of his chamber with a bedftaffe. Neither
contented with this, but in all haft in the morning hee trotted vnto
her fathers : infourming him of many falfe tales, and amongft the
reft, her laft nights tricke was brought in for a confirmation of his
hard fortune in beeinge matched with fuche a one. But her father,
knowing that to be falfe, and the other as likely, perfuaded him from
his Ielofy, which would not be, notwithftanding.

The fourth kind defired iudgement againft their hufbands, that,
hauing beene married to them the fpace of threefcore yeers, and
growing wery of them, brought home to their houfes yoong men,
vnder the titles of their kinfmen, to haunt their companies, with com-
mandment that they fhould vfe them as well as them felues. Who
(through their ciuill behauior deferuing no leffe) being on a certaine
time in their chamber with them, were taken by their hufbandes with
other of their copefmates, that through bribes proued falfe wittneffes,
by which the old fornicators procured deuorcementes, and married
younge wenches.

[1] As for make-bates, there was framed againft them a bill, to the [1 fig. C 2]
effecte of the tale aforetould of them. And touching their commo-
rades the liers, they were complained of, for that in open affemblies
they would fpeake againft Ielofy, curfing him and his followers. But
beeing matched accordinge to their hartes defire, with women that
are moft faithfull and honeft, enioying through them the happineffe
of a bleffed eftate, they, ouercloyed with the fweete it yeeldeth, and
wearied with the gainefull fruite which arifeth therof, will (for that
ther are no occafions of Ielofy offered) themfelues nourifh caufers by
moft vnciuill companions. Talke of Ielofy in their company, they
wil vtterly condempne fuch fickell headed Buffardes, that vppon euery
light occafion are miftruftful of their wiues, fwearing and protefting
that they are not, nor would bee of fuch a fufpitious fociety for the

world : when their priuy checkes for their wiues modeft familiarity
fhall be fo openly executed, as their actions fhow their tounges haue
lyed.

But thefe of the fixt kinde are knaues in graine, that hauing
lauifht their ftockes leaudly by badd meanes, and feeing their eftates
to grow weake, will feeke out wiues, not of the common forte for
propernelle, but fuche matchlelle paragons as are for neatnelle not to
be mated in a countrey.   Thefe muft bee fett in their fhoppes to tole
in cuftomers; vnto whome, if they fhow not themfelues good-fellowes
by gentle fpeeches, their houfes will proue to hoat for them.   They
muft not fticke to promife fairely and to kiffe, fo they do it clofely;
onely this prouifo muft be had, that they keepe them out of their
mony boxes and clofecubberds.   Which practife proouinge profitable,
and thereby their eftates being amended, ftraight falfe meafure
is fufpected, and thervpon, this their owne inuention mifliked
off.   Then they will fay that they do more then their commiffion
alloweth, though leffe a great deale then in the beginning was commaunded.   Yea, thence after they muft fit no more in the fhoppes for
feare of thunderclappes; and if perchaunce once in a moneth they
are there, in which time it may happen fome of their olde cuftomers
to come to renue their acquaintance, priuy frownes fhalbe geuen
them [1]of the wittals their hufbandes, their chapmen beeing in company; and in their abfence, bitter woordes, if not bitinge blowes.
Then fhall they not bee fuffered to looke on a man without controlement, nor dare to fpeake to any for feare of buffets.   If any aske for
them, buying there, prefently they are thoughte to be their wiues
cuftomers, and therefore fhall haue bad entertainement, and be ferued
with the woorft ftuffe, if any be worfe then other.

[¹ sig. C 2,
back. Catch
word by]

The laft were cried out vppon, for that, whereas they are married
with honeft mens children, beeing beloued of them far better then
they deferue, they will fhowe them fo much kindneffe in their
wooing time, and on their marriage day, as they leaue neuer a whit
for the time following.   For, hauing reaped the firft dayes roit, and
beeing inriched with the profit thereof, they growe careleffe of that
which might infue, thinking there is no heauen but the time prefent,
nor any commodity like to arife of the remnant.   Before company,
their kindneffe fhall bee fo freely vfed, as when their wiues and they

are alone, noughte but bitter wordes and worfe fhall followe. Abroad,
their behauior towardes them fhall bee paffing louing, mingled with
kinde mirth; but at home they will fo lumpe and lowre, as it were
better to be in hel, then to liue in houfe with fuch hipocriticall
Ielious hufbandes. At feaftes and at affemblies they will vfe themfelues like faintes, affirming they are matched with pearleffe wenches
for good and honefte behauior; but in their chambers they are
diuels, fufpecting falfhood and clofe dealings betweene their deareft
frends and faithfull wiues. And to make an end of the meffe, I
will tell you of an euidence giuen there againft a moft notable affe.

There was one that, to fhonne his predeftinated fortune, and to
preuent his hard hap fore-told him by fome diuell incarnate, did
fearch to fee if hee mighte finde fuche an ill-fauoured peece of ftuffe
as all men els would miflike of, not efteeming how deformed fhee
were, fo fhee brought money with her. And at laft, Nature had
fhapen a morcell for his tooth, fuch a matche as it was impoffible to
mate her, vnleffe her forenamed mother had bene [1] hired therevnto. [1 fig. C 3]
Shee was beetell-browed, goggell-eyed, blobber-lipt, wry-necked,
crooke-backt, and fplay-footed : hauinge the huckle bone of her
breech burft, whereby fhee wente wriggling with her taile like a
broken legged dogge; with fo fweete a breath, as a man had beene as
good to haue gone faftinge into the common gardens about London,
as into her chamber when fhe was in it. With this vnmatchable
creature did this ftripling marrie, fuppofing it vnpoffible that fhe that [2 orig. thã]
had neuer a good part in her body, fhoulde haue fo bad a tricke as to
lende his muftard pot to others vfes. Wherevppon, ioying that hee
alone liued with an honeft woman (as hee thought), hee would laugh
at his neighbours folly for choofing wiues to ferue other mens
turnes, beeing, by feeding of their owne fancies, cuckold by fuch
as himfelfe was, who had notwithftandinge at home for his owne
diet fuch an one as would not bee of others regarded, nor himfelfe
coulde fnuffe it off. But his tender crippell, knowing that there were
Vulcans that woulde fometimes looke into ftraunge Smithes fhoppes,
and perfuading her felfe that *Pecunia omnia poteft*, did hire a plow-
man fhee had, to fupplye fome wants in her fweete hartes abfence.
Who, agreed on the matter, did fo clofely perfourme their knauery, as
to their thinkinge the Diuell himfelfe perceiued not their villauy.

Well, foone after there came certaine chapmen to this clothiers houfe,
(for he was of that trade) to make merry with him al the Chrift
maffe holly dayes, in which time they vfed this kinde crippell for his
fake fo familiarly, as they would ieft with her before his face. Who,
watchinge for a difhe from off Ielofies table, feared his owne fhadow
would beguile himfelfe, and therefore would neuer leaue, vntill by a
fhift he had got them forth of his doores. So played hee with euery
one that came after vnto his houfe, warning his wife from vfing fuch
companions familiarly : neuer mifdoubtinge Lobb, his man, that did
daunce trenchemore once euery day in his priuy kitchin. But the
deftinies that had fworne his horned dubbing, to let him fee the
fruite of his choice, and the certainety of his fortune, (for to be a
cuckold, and know it not, is no more (fayes fome) then to drincke

with a flye in his ¹cuppe, and fee it not,) brought him on a time into
his barne ; when thinking to finde his man a threfhing, he found him
a kiffing of his crippell, with fo plaine further euidence of his hard
fortune, as he killed both man and wife ; and himfelfe was hanged for
it afterwardes.

    Of thefe fortes were the billes of enditementes, beeing practifes
fo well liked and allowed off by this confocation, as the perfourmers
of them were rewarded with the beft entertainement Hell affoordes.
And laying plats to effect further mifchief, they concluded that,
by cutting one an others throat, their kingdome might fooneft be
enlarged. To which end they inuented thefe meanes, which I will
rehearfe vnto thee.

    Firft, that knauifh Ielofy fhould be requited with clubbing iniury :
namely, that they that fhal abufe their loues with lauifh fpeeches, fhall be
lubberly beaten by champions, which fhall be prouided for that purpofe : fo that, through knauifh miftruftfulneffe and murthering reuenge,
they may all purchafe Hell. Then that thofe fooles, which (being
lodgde in the bed of conftant amity, taking their reft in Pleafures
armes : and rocked a fleepe louingly, like infantes in the cradle of
Difporte, by their nurfes Carefullneffe & Security) toffe their loues
conftancy fo lightly with ftroakes of biting and iniurious wordes, and
baule fo vnquietly, fhowing moft ielious trickes of childifhe miftruftfullneffe, as they force thereby their nurfes to bee careleffe of their
vndifcreete quietneffe, and to turne their bliffe into bane, That

thefe (I faye) for requitall of fuche foolifhneffe, fhoulde bee caft off, neuer againe to tafte of the fweeteneffe of their looues wonted curtefy, by which meanes they may become defperate and hang themfelues.

And touching doating or dolting Ielofy, that their wiues, to pay them for their fufpition, fhoulde not wander much abroade, nor giue entertainement to any gallants at home, but to growe familiar with their feruauntes, and ioyne fuch a helper to their hufbandes im-perfe&tion as Iacke the fcullian is, which fhall neuer bee miftrufted. And the better to effe&te their knauery, it was agreed that they fhould bee councelled that euer after Ie¹lious complaintes made by [¹ leaf C 4] their hufbandes to their frendes, they fhoulde fitte withe them at dinner and fupper for company, to preuente mifdoubte, but fhoulde not eate a bit, nor drinke a droppe, without their kindnes, for their hufbandes vnkindnes did yeeld fufficient teares to quench their thirft with. Marry, in a corner with iacke their partners, to fare as well as money and mirth could make them, Whereby it was thought that they would recant of their Ielofy, and giue them liberty to vfe it at their pleafure, fo far as themfelues might be affured how much they were vnhappy. And that fornicators (after they had obtained their defires according to the courfe of lawe) fhould, ftroking vppe their crooked fhankes, and belabouring their rufty beardes with their wetherbeaten fingers, feeking other wenches, meet with whipper ginnies that fhould knowe how to vfe fuch old leachers fo hand-fomely, (beeing contented to indure difcontentment, with the thought of the coine that lines their olde bagges,) as they fhall be reputed by them for as honeft women as liue, vntill the wedding day bee paft, when in the euening (fore-thinkinge of the fmall pleafure is like to enfue by their paftime) they fhal faine themfelues fo ficke, as of force they will lye alone, or at leaft without thofe old wretches. So fhall they ferue them by the fpace of a moneth, by which time (and it is no marueil) the churles will beginne to mifdoubt fomewhat. But what fhall they care, feeinge they are miftriffes of all they haue, and can keepe the chuffes from their owne? When they tell them of their vnkindneffe, thefe wil be ready to fpit in their faces, bidding them to goe trott vnto their trulles. As for them felues, they cannot abide fuch olde fooles; their breath ftinckes, they flauer with their

kiffinge, with fuche other opprobrious fcoffes, as by their harde
fpeeches and woorfe vfage, they fhall make the olde fooles to betake
themfelues to their beades, confeffing with fhame their fhameleffe behauiour towardes their late faithfull wiues, and, curfing
the caufe of this hapleffe fortune, cry *Peccaui*, and die quite difcontented.

It was further agreed vppon, that backebiters, that will not ceafe
[¹ leaf C 4, back] to blaze ielious vntrothes, fhall bee plagued with hauinge ¹their
tounges pulled foorth, or elfe woorfe punifhed by loofinge the
regardes of fuppofed honefty. And all the commodity fuche malicious Impes fhall reape for their knauery, is, a faire purchafed
place called Bridewell; and for their falfe reportes they fhall bee
fure of a proper cage to finge in; where their good names dyinge
with their honeftye, they fhall bee carried from thence in cartes of
reproach, and be buried in continual infamy, ronge to hell with
lafhes of whip-corde. And the liers: they, becaufe they would not
be iellious, but cannot leaue it, fhal weare hornes, whether they will
or no.

But the grand wittalls, that will alure cuftomers by the fine
wenches, and with hauing inriched themfelues thereby, will turne
their knauery into villanie. They by their crabbedneffe fhall come
to extreame pouerty, and then endeauoring to put in triall their olde
cuftome, their wiues fhall either growe ftuborne and reape no profit,
[² orig. librrall] or elfe too too liberall,² fpending the remnant which is left, leauing
their hufbandes as monyleffe as witleffe. As for the laft fort, not
leaft, whofe miftruftfullneffe cut their owne throates, caufing their
[³ orig. lewdensse] wiues to fall vnto lewdneffe³ by ouer rulinge them with hippocr[i]ticall
iurifdiction. Onely this fhall be added vnto the forwardneffe of their
diftruction, that their halting diff[fi]mulation fhould breede vpftartes to
faue their fore forheades; and they, regarding to maintaine their owne
good names with hipocricie, fhall thereby plante newe trickes of
hufwiuerie in their wiues confciences.

Thus, *Tell troth* (quoth *Robin*), thou haft hard fome thinge that
thou neuer hardft of before, which, when it fhall come vnto the
diuells eares, I knowe hee will bee monftrous collericke; but it mat-
tereth not: it is better he fhould fret, then humanity fade. For vnleffe
thefe his inuentions fhould be knowne, how fhould they be preuented?

I tell thee (frend), howfoeuer fome thinke of me, *Robin*, as he is a good fellowe by name, fo is hee no leſſe in minde; and I ſweare vnto thee I had rather fee the diuells dance the morice alone in that fiery hellhoufe, then a chriſtian to foole it there, through want of know-ledge of their [¹] inuentions. O, tell troth, is it not great pittie to fee fo [¹ ſig. D] manye thoufandes, through folly to inthrall themſelues to tormentes euerlaſting? thou wouldeſt thinke it vnpoſſible that the hundred part of them which are there onely for Ielofy, ſhould bee bred in a world. Why, man, I haue onely tould thee of the Ielofy betweene man and wife, and the louer and his ſweet hart; I haue not touched the Ielofy betweene frend and frend, the father and his ſonne, the mother and her daughter, yea, and betweene whome not, that are ioyned together, either by confanguinity, neighbourhood, by office, or duety. I let thefe paſſe, becaufe I meane not to meddle with them; onely, becaufe thou wanteſt fome way to thy iornyes end, I will tell thee a pretty ieſt, which though it bee mifplaced for want of memory, yet here it may come in very good tim[e]. And it is of an olde dotor that was very well ferued.

This dotor, who, though he were a man of fowerfcore yeares of age (knowing himfelfe vnable to fatisfy the expectation of a widow of his owne ſtanding), yet would he needes marry with a girle of foureteene; Who, being conſtrained thereunto by her freendes com-pulfion, not knowinge what belonged to the rites of matrimony, was contented to loue him entierly, and to liue truely vnto him without thought of diſhoneſty. Yet fo ill conceited was this foolifh dotor, and fo weary of his happy eſtate, as although he knew aſſuredly the cubbard was clofe ſhutt and without any crannes, yet could he neuertheleſſe fufpect the filly moufe, and would fet trappes, hopinge to catche her, counfelled therevnto by his mifdeeming thoughtes. If ſhee had beene neuer fo little out of his fight, he thought it was the ſpring time, being but Chriſtmas; to ſtay the forwardnes whereof, his froſt-biting wordes ſhould nippe her. The younge cubbe at laſt (learning fubtilty by the olde Fox), fufpectinge there was fome further ſweete in a marryed womans life, then as yet ſhee had taſted off, onely perfuaded thereunto by her huſbandes Ielofye, tooke harte at graſſe, and woulde needes trie a newe concluſion. The nexte day beeing foorth at dinner with him, where were likewife many women

[¹ sig. D,
back. *Catch*
word foorth] of all degrees, fhee amongft the reft chofe ¹ forth an old matron to
paffe away the time with, which in communication, finding her to be
of fuch a courteous difpofition, as vnto her fhee made complaint of
the feruile bondage her frends had brought her too. Which fhee
pittying (for what hart fo hard as would not pitty her, that wanted
alltogether contentmente?), gaue her fuch good councell as fhee her
felfe had tried, hauinge beene peftered with the like inconuenience,
though not with fo many hart-breakinges : whereof this younge
woman liked fo well, on the morrow fhe meant to put fome of her
conclufions in practife. And a brother of hers comming home vnto
her the next day, fhe likewife fhowed vnto him howe the Ielofy of
her hufband increafed, defiring him to help her to effect a practife
fhe determined to try ; to which he foone agreeing, they ftole both
into one of her chambers, there fpending the day in fecret communication, How it might bee beft performed ; which beeing earneft,
paffed away the time fo foddenly as night was come vpon them ere
they thought on it, fo that thereby he, forced to departe, was let
foorth at the dore by her felfe, whome a maied fhee had (which the
olde dotor made more of then of her felfe) did efpy, not knowing who
it was. But fhee had newes inough that it was a manne, and fo good
to her liking, as in all haft her maifter muft be made acquainted
there with ; he, vpon the hearing thereof, growing fo hot, as he did not
onely beate his wife, but in a great rage turned her forth of the dores,
reuiling her moft fhamefully. The filly woman had no other
fuccour but to goe to her brothers that was married, in the fame
towne (for fhe durft not complaine to her father on a foddaine, he
was fo cruell), who receiued her kindly, and lodge[d] her for that night,
becaufe it was fo late. And in the morning betimes hee went with
her to her fathers, making him acquainted with the whole matter.
Who, after the true fearch of the certainty thereof, condemned his
owne folly for the match, fending for the olde mifer, that was met
at the dore pofting thetherwards to complaine. But at his comming
his expectation was quite fruftrated, for wher, according to a former
courfe had in the like practife, he looked to haue his wife rebuked &

[¹ sig. D 2.
Catch word
he] himfelfe moned, ¹ hee was nowe, not onely fharpely threatened for his
mifufage towardes her, but alfo deferuedly fcoffed at, and driuen force
perforce (becaufe hee was matched with his fuperiours), to bee there-

with contented. And vppon the triall of the truth he found himſelfe ſo
plainely conuicted, as hee confeſſed his faulte, and aſked her forgiue-
nes, ſewing for a reconſciliation to bee made between them. Which
done, they departed home, & his wife, not forgetting the ſhame ſhee
had indured by his meanes, ſtuddied to requite his villanye, and
effected it after this manner. Her huſband kept a proper man whome
he did put in ſo great truſt, as he hiered him for a ſtale to deceiue
himſelfe by wiſhing him to trie his wiues conſtancy, Who dallied ſo
long with the flame, as at laſt he was burnte with the fire of deſire,
his affection ſo iumply meeting with her conceipt, as within a ſhorte
time, what by faire promiſes, larg[e] giftes, and her beauty (three
notable baites to catch a kind foole with), ſhe had ſo won him to
her will, as he would not onely reueale vnto her what ſo euer his
wife maiſter would ſay, but alſo would euer by falſe oathes ſobbe him
vppe with a thouſand vntruthes concerning her approued honeſty.
Well, his good reportes encreaſed but further miſlike in his maiſter,
with a more earneſt deſire to finde her falſe; and there vppon he
would teach his man how he ſhould further trie her, ſetting downe
ſuch plaine plots as by the[1] practiſe of them hee was ſhortly after [1 orig. thy]
ready at any time to doe his miſtreſſe any good turne in his maiſters
abſence. He had ſubtill wit inough, and therefore they both ſped
the better, he prouing ſo good a plaiſter to her ſore, as if ſhe and her
huſband fel out in the night, ſhe with her man would ſport in the
day time; and becauſe the olde foole was ſo couetous as he would
drinke onely ſmall beere to ſaue charges, they two would courroſe
whole gallons of wine at their going abroad, which was often without ſuſpition to the olde fooles hornes. Allwayes at dinner and
ſupper he ſhould haue her with him to ſhaddowe miſtruſt, but ſhee
would not eate a bit with him, becauſe his fare was ſo baſe, collour-
ing her nicenes with want of ſtomacke, and with ſorrow for his
churliſhnes towardes her. With which [2]diſſembling (for what cannot [2 ſig. D 2,
women doe by teares?) her huſband, what betweene his mans flattery   back]
and his wiues hipocricy, was quite chaunged, being verely perſwaded
now that ſhe is a ſaint, repenting he euer miſtruſted her, & recanting
of his folly in falſly accuſing her. For a mends whereof, hee confeſſed the ſecond time to her parents and frendes that he had moſt
vndeſeruedly ouerawed his faithful wife, greeued with nothing more

then his hard vfage towardes her, in reftraining her, beeing young, of
honeft liberty.   In requitall whereof, it was lawfull for her with his
young ftripling to goe forth and returne at her pleafure, to be in what
company fhe beft liked of, and nothing fufpected, for at this time he
would not let to fweare he had the onely honeft woman in the
worlde.   And if anye of his frends had reproued him of fuch folly,
aleadging that youth was foone inticed to lewdneffe, his aunfwere was,
hee cared not, and his thankes were fharpe wordes.   But if his
neighbours tould him fhee kept bad companye, affociating other
women that were good fellowes, hee, forth with, would raile vpon
the reporters for flaundering his wiues honefty, and would ftraight
haue the lawe of them for calling her good name in queftion.
And thus liued this dotor as long as the diftinies woulde permit
him, at his death leauing onely his hornes for his fucceffors portion.

How like you this, Tell-troth? you fmild at this mans folly, but
you had more neede to pittie the weaknes of fuch as, onely led with
extreames, ether hate deadly, or effecte too too childifhly.   But nowe,
becaufe thou art in a manner at thy iourneys ende, I muft leaue thee,
yet, before I goe, knowe this farther newes.   That at my comming from
hell, the affemblie aforefaid had thought to haue broke vppe, and gon
euery gouerner to his prouince to take their pleafures, beeing ouer-
toyled with their tedious confultations.   But as they were a rifing,
there came one in fweating, with a fupplication from Pierce-Penni-
leffe, inforfing them thereby to a newe labour.   Which I perceiuing,
and immagining it woulde bee long before it were ended, beeing
[¹ leaf D 3]   allready weary of their company, lefte that ¹ newes for the knight of
the pofte, and fo you are wellcome to your iourneyes ende.   Robin
good fellow, looking for no other thankes for his company, but that
(frend Tell troth) thou doft me the fauour to publifh this my inuectiue againft Ielofy.

[² orig.
deliuering]   Wherevpon he deliuerd ² vnto me a fcroule of paper with the
contents hereafter followinge, and fo hee vanifhed awaye, I know not
howe.

[*Large Coat of Arms in the original.*]

Robin Good-fellowe his Inuectiue [¹ leaf D 3, back]

againſt Ielofy.

He Poetes altogether aymed not amiſſe in their fiction, whereas, ſetting downe the torments of hell, they affirme ther is no torture that inflictes the furies with more extreame cruelty then the fond conceites of a ielious harte; and why? for that the reuenge of a diſdainefull woman is deadly, and her rewardes for miſtruſtfullneſſe, guiftes of vnceaſinge griefe, which in the ende woorke vtter deſtruction. The cauſe nouriſhed in men maketh the effect poſſible and the practiſe intollerable.

There is no ſweete ſo ſtronge, but the delighte thereof may bee croſſed by the contrarye; nor anye hart ſo firme, but continuall vnkindnes maye remooue it. The tall oake, that waueth not with euerye puffe of the winde, is eaſelye throwne to the ground by an extraordinary tempeſt. The hardeſt flint is pierſt with often droppes; and it is not impoſſible, thoughe vnlikelye, that the ſkie ſhould fall. Are they not woorthy to be nipte with the piercing ſtormes of a biting winter, that, hauing a ſhelter to defend themſelues from ſuch outragious wether, and knowing a tempeſt will come which may ouerthrow it, neglecteth neuertheleſſe to preuent that daunger by vnderpropping the ſame? or deſerue they to haue their eſtate pittied that wilfully ſeeke their owne vndooing? As it is a part of wiſedom to foreſee a daunger, ſo, not to withſtand and to endeuour to fruſtrate the ſame with reaſon and forecaſt, is a badge of extremeſt folly. *[a]ſpice, vt [imme]ritus mis[er]andæ [ſorti]s aſel-lus [a]ſſiduo [d]omitus ver[b]ere tardus [e]rit.*

And *Peccaui* deſeruedlye falles on their backes, that wittinglye and willinglye incurre the baſſard thereof. If men had no vnderſtanding of the plagues of hell they would be too too vitious, and their pleaſure could not but bee their deſtruction, vnleſſe euery one had a hale-backe for his companion. If Ieloſy be a torment more *Principiis obſta . ſero medicina paratur, Cum mala per longas conualuere moras.*

mercileſſe then diueliſh Pluto, and his common ¹wealth more greeuous
then the ſorrowes of hell, I ſorrow to thincke that men ſhould be ſo
witleſſe as to honour the Diuell, and ſo careleſſe as to delight in ſuch
a weale-publike. But be it as it is, or let it be woorſe, as it is vnpoſſible it ſhoulde, their conceites are grown to be ſo baſe, and their
enterpriſes ſo beaſt-like, as for the moſt part they follow Ieloſy ſo
eagerly, as they conſtraine their deereſt freendes to cut their throates
with the knife they moſt feare, when both the euell it ſelfe and the
cauſe therof might be remooued, ſo euery one would ground their
loue vpon diſcretion.

If the practiſes and proceedings of loue be ſo forcible as they
bring death with them to the hopeleſſe harte, hee is vnwiſe that will
ſtriue to encreaſe thoſe affections which are allready more then extraordinary. Waxe, by a temperate heat is mollified and formed, being
ſofte to any ſhape, but through a furious flame it either waſteth and
conſumeth, or els will not be touched without defiling of our fingers.
The hartes of women are like vnto waxe, that, tempered by the
paſſions of loue, are ready to take the impreſſion thereof; but if it
coole againe before the printe of kindneſſe be ſurely ſet on, or if the
flame of fury breake foorth about it, being ſett on fire by the coales
of miſgouernemente, to what bad ende will the good beginning be
turned? and how many hartbreakinges by quarrels and diſagree-
mentes will ariſe in the ſmoother of ſuch ſmoaky miſrule! Doubtleſſe the experience thereof hath taughte too too many to their griefe,
and will teach more to their vndooing, vnleſſe the ſwelling of that
ſore be aſſwaged with ſom wholſome medicin. But they that only
haue entertained the ſuperficies of loue, neuer harboring him in their
hartes, affirme that he and Ieloſy are brothers, and that the one cannot bee without the other. If they that holde the ſame for a
maxime, meane in the defence of their freendes honours, and to be
Ielious of their wiues good name and reputation, I graunt that that is
moſt kinde affection.

        But when Ieloſy ariſeth of a fooliſh fondnes, grounded with out
reaſon, to bee remooued with euerye lighte occaſion; or of miſtruſtfullneſſe of the partye loued, without triall of anye vn²conſtancy; or,
laſtly, of childiſh affection, lead away with an vnruely appetite, and
nouriſhed with diſpayringe conceites, conceiuing what is not, and

iudginge onely by fhadowes which remoue all hope, caufing continuall difcontentment,—that maketh the ielious mans cafe defperate, and the thinge foolifh.

There is no concorde betweene water and fire, nor any medium
betweene loue and hatred; for either the hart fighes vnder the
burthen of entiere affection, or groanes throughe the waight of
greeuous diffimulation. Loue couereth a multitude of finneful
offences, and loyalty recouereth a world of ouerflipt infirmities; but
diflike findeth rottenneffe in found timber, fpots in the pure white,
and vnkindneffe in the conftant harte; it engendereth Ielofy, and
procureth enmities; it hatcheth breakepeace, and glories in quarrels;
all it delighte is in findinge of faultes, and all it ioy to encreafe
miflike. If it hath it beginning of loues contrary, yea, in nature,
how can there bee anye brotherly equality betweene them? vnleffe,
vnhappilye, wee will make the eye father to both, that feeinge
afwell good as euell, entifeth the hart, through corrupt affections, to be
mifled by wicked elufions, bringing foorth baftardes in fteede of true
begotten children: For if Ielofy be loues brother, it is by corruption
of nature brought foorth vnlawfully, which may thus be manifefted.
After the eye hath chofen an obiect which brings fo fweet contentment to the hart, as it highly delighteth in the fame, that prouing fo
kinde loue and fuch feruent affection in both, as lawfull requitall
makes a pleafing fatisfaction, the eye receiuinge kinde glaunces for
amorous glotinges, and louinge harte-breakinges for affectionate hart
fighings. The eie beeing pleafed with an eye, and the hart contented
with a hart, they frolique both in glory as long as they reft in conftancie; but wandring from forth that fanctuary, the eie either fpies
another eie that better pleafeth it, and the harte likes of another
harte that better contentes it, or elfe the eie lookes curifhly into his
owne hart, and fpies fome fault in himfelfe, which, difpleafing, beget-
teth Ielofy: whereby the eie may be faid to be originall and father of
both.

¹ How is it poffible that falfhood fhould be in frendfhip? or`can [¹ fig. E]
the hand beguile the hart that ruleth it? no more will a louing wife
playe falfe with him to whome fhee is ioyned both by the lawe of
god and man, or a frend croffe her louing exceedinges, in whome his
hart delighteth. That which is bred in the bone will neuer out of

the flefhe; and what *Nature* hath made, *Arte* cannot marre. If
Enuie hath a tricke with her heele, all the diuells in hell cannot alter

it. And I maruell menne are fo foolifhe as to matche themfelues
with fuche women whome they haue caufe to fufpeсt. Doubtleffe,
either their own life hath beene lafciuious, by which they iudge others,
or their meaning bad in chufing fuch companions; when nowe, ouerlate repentinge of their bargaine, they light on a worfer mifchiefe.
Allthough the fox be fo crafty as he deceiues many, yet fometimes
he meeteth with a champion more fubtill then himfelfe. The pitcher
goeth long to the water, but at lafte getteth a knocke through the

bearers fault, and is brought home broken. The Ielious man feareth
his owne fhadow, and looketh narrowly vnto it, yet (likely) at laft
commeth a fubftaunce, who (when he thinketh leaft on it) entereth,
doinge him iuftice, though hee neuer the wifer. It is ftraunge that
menne are fo foolifh as to feeke their owne vndoing, for affuredly
looke, by what meafure they fell by, the fame fhall they receiue their
owne, without aduauntage. The quarreling mate fhall not complaine
for want of knockes, or the ielious man longe defire hell, when
the one fhall finde like fwafhbucklers vnto himfelfe, and the others
wife will not fticke to cut his throat with the knife hee hath fo long
feared.

If mens loue be fimplie good, women cannot but affeсtionate them
with like fimplicity; but if they playe falfe (Ielofye beeing their
cloake), they will be fure to keepe knaues to croffe their cardes with.
In thefe dayes euery cobler doth feare the carter, and fetes vppe his
whippe at his dore to keepe Iohn Cobbilero from his lattice. And I
pray you vppon what reafons fhall thefe ielious trickes be difcarded?
Somme haue it by nature, and fay, 'kit muft after kind, bee it but in

fcraping of a ¹ frying panne.' Beware of naturall foolles as long as
you liue; for a bad tricke ingrafted in them, neuer leaueth them
vntill he hath brought feauenty worfe into his roome. And, as for
the inuention of their prediceffors, they muft needes goe to the diuell
with them for companie. Others builde their knauery on other
mens misfortune, that are matched with Ioone, *communis omnibus*,
that could play at bucklers fo foone as fhe was paft her cradell. Oh,
fhee is a tall peece of flefh, and will ftand to her tackling fo ftoutly,
as the diuell himfelfe fhall not get the waifters from her. I counfell

him that thinketh hee hath met with her companion, to ceafe to
greeue at it, and ftriue not to remoue that he cannot ftirre, leaft
happily fhee falls quit from him, & neuer ferueth him after. Manye
honour him of cuftome, becaufe they hold their landes of him by
homage, their prediceffors allwayes hauing beene his fworne fubiectes.
A pittifull cuftome, that tendeth to the tenauntes vndoing, and a
title that might very well bee refigned ouer and denied; feeing it
only toucheth free taile, or feruices vnreafonable to be performed.
And a great part obtaine his entertainment by vfe and practife: thofe
are greene headed that long for reformations, & would haue new
lawes inftituted euery quarter, defiring to try new conclufions,
whether it were poffible for a man to liue vnto himfelfe. Which are
fo delighted with common cafes, as they make honefty a neceffity,
thrufting him out of the dores at their pleafure, by vfing them moft
fhamefully whome they ought· to loue entirly. But moft playe
ielious parts of knauery and bad entention, meaning to make a
practife of paltry peuifhneffe and knauifh conceiptes. They will be
ielious to try their wiues or frendes conftancy, being neuer afhamed
of their owne villany.

What fhall I faye ? I greeue to thinke on mens hard happe, and
womens vnkindneffe; the one nourifhing mifchiefe, and the other
perfewing, with deadly execution, the tormentes they fufpecte and
greeue at. I haue hard (euen of kinde gentlewomen reported, whoe
haue beene ouer vexed with the fufpitious conceiptes of ielious
hufbandes) that their flaunderous thoughtes [1] concerning the fufpected
crimes, did not fo much aggrauate their owne griefe (though it were
intollerable), as the fight therof did encreafe their wiues ioy and
delight, onely pleafed with this fweet melody : That they knewe
themfelues to bee moft conftant and faithfull, though fufpected of the
contrarye, and their hufbandes, defiring no more then conftancy,
cannot content themfelues with their defired felicity, but greeue their
own foules with triphells, and eate vppe their owne harts through
fufpition of difloyalty. I would but demaund· what recompence a
ielious man receiueth by all his trauell, or what little ioy he reapes by
his miftruftfullneffe and continuall penfiueneffe ? The loweft ebbe
is counteruailed with as high a floode, and boyftrous ftormes with
calme wether; the glomeft daye maye darken the funne, but not

Quidquid
[fe]ruatur,
cu[pi]mus
ma[gi]s:
ipsaque
[fu]rem cura
[v]ocat :
pauci [q]uod
fin[it]
al[t]er,
amant.
[1 sig. E 2]

abate his pride; and as there are extreame droughtes, fo fometimes
falls the contrary by extraordinary tempefts. There is no fowre but
may bee qualified with fweet potions, nor any doubtfull malady that

[¹ orig.
unuliicke] may not be allied with delightfull muficke¹; onely ielious thoughts
with loue are vncurable, and that a corafiue moft dangerous to mens
hartes. It is vaine to ftriue againft the ftreame, and as foolifh to build
caftels in the aire. He that thinketh to catch the aire in a bottle,
deferueth to be laft at; & he that would ty vp his wiues or frends
honefty in a ftring, to bee pitied : both follies fit for inno[c]ents &
practizes without end. I thinke *Vulcans* Ielofy preuailed him
nothing, & his catching of *Marce* & *Venus* in a purcenet as little,
except a confirmation of his great grief, & an affured knowledg of
his horned head, prouing a continuall badge of his infamy. The
like followed many others fufpition, and the like will enfewe of fuch
folly. *Vulcan* knewe that *Mars* was a copartner with him in *Venus*
bofome. And he himfelfe could not but blufh when hee had
wooed his owne fpoufe (the goddeffe of loue), in fteede of *Briceris*,
his beloued paramore. I knowe that euery one hath his faulte, and
all deferue equall punifhmente ; onely *Robin good fellow* wifhes, that
mens & womens prefumtions may be certaine, and that their fufpecte
may bee built on a fure ground.

[² sig. E ₂,
back] ² If men would imitate the fame rule, to auoide Ielofy, which
Cicero hath fet downe in his Offices, as moft requifite to maintaine a
happy weale publike (alleaginge, *it was the parte of mad men, to wifhe
for a gloomy day when the fonne fhined moft glorioufly ; or to defire
warre and turmoyling troubles, when the common-wealth flourifheth
moft happily through peace and tranquillity ; But, to alay hurly
burlies with councel, and to make warres ceafe by aduice, was greate
wifedome,)*—They would not encreafe their owne greefe and forrow :

[³ orig.
heigth]
reus est,
niumque
fauet ille
ori, cui
itur victa
ma cru-
a, rea. or rather, beeing at quiet, and obtaining the height ³ of pleafure by
mutuall loue and affection, they woulde not (I fay) long after vnreft,
or purfue troubles, and continuall difquietnes, with might and maine,
without meafure ; feeing the obtaining of their owne defire is a
proofe of their misfortune, and the iudgemente after the verdict of
fuch a title, continual fhame and infamy. The man is happy that
is accounted happy, and none are richer then thofe that be fo

adiudged of. If, then, fame be fo fauourable as to reckon a beggar equall with a kinge, is not hee a foole which will himfelfe reprooue her of an vntrueth? The prouerbe adiudges that 'an il bird which will defile his owne neft;' and is not he a bad cuckold, that will regifter himfelf one when the clarke hath left him out of fauour? By how much it is better to be one, beeing accounted none, then to be none, and reputed one,—by fo much the more are they beholdinge to themfelues for the horne that blowes their Ielofy vntill it flames. An extraordinary fmoake breedes fufpect of a hurtefull fire, and many fparkes make men to wonder; yet the harme of both of them is preuented by care and diligence.

I would but know the manne (*femper excipio*, the wittall) that would not be loath to be pointed at with a paire of hornes, & yet I know very many, and haue hard of an innumerable company, that haue made the whole parrifhe, yea, the country, priuy to their misfortune by defarte of them. Well, then, hereafter if there be any that hath a tooting head, and would not haue it fene, let him keepe it fecretely to himfelfe, and make the beft of it. He goes farre that neuer turnes, and fhee is a diuell that will neuer [1] mende; and fince the diuell is good to fome body, let the ielious man make much of her, that the fhee diuell may bee good to him. [1 leaf E 3]

Sorrow craues pitty, and fubmiffion deferues pardon. Hee is ouer hard harted that will not be entreated, and diuelifh that cannot forgiue. If, then, vpon penitent fubmiffion, a man fhalbe forced to receiue her into fauour that hath offended, will it not be fo much to his better contentmente, by how much a few are acquainted with the mifchiefe? That grief is beft difgefted that bringes not open fhame, but a fpightefull blow prooues a noted fcarre. But fuppofe the worft that can happe, imagine fhee will neuer be good, building vpon the old fayinge : *Shee that knowes where Chriftes croffe ftandes, will neuer forget where great A dwels*,—yet a man were better to bee troubled with a queane alone, then to bee forced to keepe both a queane and a knaue : for as the law grantes a deuorcement, fo is it requifite it fhoulde allow the woman maintenance; and what fhall her knaue lacke that fhe hath? Whofoeuer, therefore, that is bound to a bad bargaine, whereof comes two mifchiefes, either to keepe a queane or

[margin: Flectitur lus voce p gante de]

[margin: Quo sem[el] est imbuta recens seruabit odo[rem] Testa diu.]

F. duob[us] to parte with money, if he will follow Robin good fellowes councel,
malis, mi- let him rather choofe to diet her in his owne houfe, then to pay for
n[i]mum est
el[i]gendum. the boord of her and her louer in a ftrange place.

But becaufe it is the beft labour to woorke the confufion of fuch
an ennimy as Ielofy is, whofe company encreafeth multitudes of in-
conueniences, My meaninge is to fet downe fome neceffary helpes
how fuch a mifchiefe may bee beft preuented. And firft, I councel
euery one that is enfefted with fuch a plage to feeke to foreftall the
Obfequium daunger thereof, by kinde and gentle plaifters. I meane, that fhee
tigrefq[ue]
domat. who hath a ielous hufband, fubiect to the like infirmities before
timido[s]que
leones. mencioned, fhoulde reclaime him by gentle vfage, and ouercome his
vaine fufpition with modeft behauiour, not vfinge any vnciuill tricke
in difdainefull manner before his face, he hating the fame; or vfing
other fufpitious practifes, onely to croffe him with them; and fo to
carry themfelues in all places, and at all times, as they may neither
giue caufe of offence vnto them or of miftruft vnto others. The like
meane ought to be executed by men, that they ouerlay not their
[1 leaf E 3, [feare]'full wiues, brauing them with difdainefull likelyhoodes of dif-
back.
Cafchword honeft behauiour, but that they diffuade them from fufpition by the
fearefull]
[Fle]ctitur contraries, remoouing their ielious conceites by kindneffe and louely
ob[feq]uio
cur[ua]tus dalliance. It is eafy to cure a greene wound, but the daunger of a
ab ar[bo]re
ramus: feftred fore is mortall. The young tree will ftoup, when the old
[fra]nges, si
[vir]es fhrewd cannot bend; and new conceites are eafly remoued, but
experi[ar]e
tuas. engrauen thoughtes will not be rubbed forth; and loue is of fo great
force, as he fooner ouercomes with a faire word, then his enimye fhall
conquere by all his forces. Howe happie is that common wealth
where peace raigneth, and that family which concord gouerneth, the
one nourifhing true amity amongft her fubiectes, the other eftablifh-
ing vanity betweene man and wife.

What greater griefe then life with difcontent,
When difcontent of want of loue arifeth?
Loue hath no lacke, but allwayes liues content,
And any thing to pleafe his mind fufficeth;
Rich is true loue, abounding ftill with ftore,
The lacke whereof makes want a grieuous fore.

The sweete of loue doth yeeld so sweete a tast,
As mixt with gall, he turnes the sower to sweete :
By him is strength and blessed weale imbrast ;
By him is harts-ease gaind, and ioy most greet.
Strong is true loue, whose strength is kindly set :
To heape with sweete, that sower his ioy ne let.

The sport of loue is full of ioyfull smiles,
He cures all sores with one most kindest salue ;
A pleasing kisse his frowning rage beguiles,
And one faire word his anger doth dissolue ;
Pleasant is loue, he ioyes in weale and woe ;
His rage with smiles, his wroth with kisses goe.

[1] Thus liueth loue, and no otherwise fare they that be his followers ; [¹ leaf E 4]
they are neuer hart sicke, becauses they neuer suspecte ; nor euer dis-
pleased, becauses for that by themselues they are not grieued. Who
is more tormented then he that teares his owne flesh ? or who
deserues more griefe, then they that will not vse the remedy ? To
lock vp ones wife, for fear of sparrow-blasting, dub himselfe a cuckould
within an iron cage, and to seeke to [2] rule her by correction, when [² orig.
he cannot gouerne himself with discretion, is to gather a rod to beate ↓seeke is to to]
his owne breeche. For whiles she is lockte in her studie, her mind Non men-[tem]
hath the more liberty to inuent a fit reuenge againft her going seruare po tes, licet
abroad. What is it they cannot effecte, if they haue a will therevnto ? o[m]nia claudas omnibus
And what woman is there that liues without a meanes to repaye a e[x]clusis, int[us]
good turne, or to requite a bad ? Vse them, therefore, well, is the adulter eri Si sapis in-
wiseft way to liue quietly ; to loue them entirely, the onely meanes to dulge dom[i]n[æ]:
bee long happy. vultus[que] seueros exue.
If she meanes to deceiue thee, her inuention is hard to be pre- Centum
uented, for, watch her neuer so narrowly, she will finde a time to fron[·]te occulos,
performe her knauery. The silieft creatures are sildome catcht in centum cer[-] uice gere-
ordinary trappes : and can women want wit to fruftrate a common bat Argus, & hos vnu[s]
ftale ? If it wer possible to know their thoughts, it were likely their sæpe fesellit
practises might be hindered ; but as long as *secreta mihi* raignes, the amor.
rains of their liberty are at their own pleasures. And I thinke men
are beft at ease when they are so pleased,—at leaft, wise men are, or

fhould be, feeing their contentment hanges in their wills. For what
houfe is in quiet where the goodwife is out of patience ? If the maifter
bee angry, the fault onely lies on the miftriffe her necke; but be fhe
moued, about goes the maides, away runne the menne, and I make
a doubt whether her hufband dares to out ftand her. I am affured
fhee will out chide him. Flatery is a fweet baite, and kindneffe a

Qnod licet
ingratum
est : quod
non licet
acrius vrit.
wholefome potion ; & nothing more then vnlawfullnes, enticeth vs
vnto lewdneffe. The delighte of fweete is taken away by furfiting
of fuggar; but who by nature is not defirous of nouelties ? There
would not fo many purcafe Tiborne, vnleffe there were a Bull to

[¹ leaf E 4,
back]
[Flec]timur
in [v]it[i]um
semi[per]
cupinus-
[qu]e negata
[cu]i pec-
care [lic]et,
peccat
[mi]nus[.]
ipsa
[po]testas
se[m]ina
nequi[ti]æ
langui[di]ora
facit.
hange them ; nor fo many yeeld vppe ¹ the poffeffion of their garmentes
to the hangmen, were ther not a lawe to condemne them. And I
warrant you, there would be fewer horned heads, if ielious hartes
were fcanter, wherby the practife of watching might decay. Who
knowes liberty better then they that haue beene in bondage? And
whoe, for the moft parte, vfeth it worfe then they that knowe it
beft ? A mind ouerladed with ioy, committeth manye errours in his
iolity ; & a harte preffed downe with forrowe, thinkes of manye mifchiefes. Extreames are neuer good : and howe can one fooner fall
into them, then being made acquainted with one of them ? Hauing
beene in the dungion of difcontent, and being fet free to range at
our pleafure, we thinke we are neuer at the territ of delight, before,
with *Ouids* builders, wee touch the heauens, fo imperfect is our
nature.

O vtinam
[a]rguerem
[si]c, vt non
[v]incere
pos[s]em :
Me mi[s]e-
rum quare
[t]am bona
causa mea
est ?
Perfwafions are of great force to moue women, whofe harts,
though moft tender, withftand nothing more then crabbed vfage.
Vowe loue vnto them, and they will fweare conftancy vnto you; and
if perchance they make fome ouerflip by their deferuing Ielofy, yet
grow not ftraight collericke, but fay your paternofter before you
reprehend them for it ; in which time which is as fmall as may be,

Per vene-
rem iuro,
pueriq[ue]
volatilis ar-
cus : me non
admissi cri-
minis esse
reum.
you fhall, by tempering your wit with wifdome, finde fo tractable a
medicine to drawe her from a fecond fault, as her penitencie will take
away all fufpition of hipocricie. Say but you are forrowfull to heare
it, or afhamed to fee it, and, of my word, her next fhall be an oth
neuer to commit the like folly. What a cheape *fubpena* is this to
drawe an anfwere from the confcience ! When, paraduenture, to
deale otherwife, would come to neede a writ of rebellion. There is

no affurance better then that which is made with a fafe confcience ;
and no man ftands on a better ground, then he that buildes on his
wiues word. If fhe fpeaks it, why fhould we not rather belieue her,
then an other that fhould report no more vnto vs ? Oh, I knowe
what you will fay, becaufe fhe fpeakes in her owne defence ; and maye
not the other flaunder vppon a malicious will ? What will not the
diuell doe for aduauntage, and what can hee doe without his inftrumentes ? To bee too too cruell [1] breedes repentaunce, as well as care- [¹ sig. F]
leffenes forerunnes forrow. When tender droppes will pearce the
flint, the hard ftele is vnneceffarye ; and where good counfell will cor-
recte, a rod were better awaye then prefent. They fay that ouer-
awing makes fooles, and what will they let to doe ? It is as hard to
get any good out of them that are witleffe, as to force water out of
a flint ; and yet I fay not but that good may be gotten of them ; but
with it, I affirme it muft be by kind meanes. *Fy, fy, fweete hart,*   Hæc tib̨[i]
what lofe trickes are thefe ! or what immodifty will this be accounted !   sunt
Will ftrike fo deeply into a reformatiue confcience, as there fhall   mecu[m],
not neede out vpon thee, with fome beaftly tearme of a brutifh   communia
tecum : in
toung for a whit of correction.   And they will driue an obe-   bona cur
quisquam
dient wife to fuch contrition, as there fhall be no thought of an   tertius ista
venit ?
vnkind extrution, either of her out of dores, or of her good name and
fame from it wonted reputaation. Why is the hufband called his
wiues good-manne, but becaufe hee ought to be a meane to withdraw her from fuch imperfections as nature hath left in her ? He, in
my iudgement, can be but a bad common wealthes man which is an
ill hufband, for, looke what ill fafhions raigne vncorrected at home,
the like inormities fhould reft in his forrain charge. For who knowes
not that we haue the greateft care (if we haue any at al) of thofe
things which are neareft vnto our felues ? and why may not I affirme
that fuch a one will refpecte little a common profitte, when hee
regards fo lightly his owne priuate wellfare ? Oh, I woulde Robin
might be tedious, not troublefome, hee would then endeauor a
further probability of the ielious mans folly, but fearing he hath
offended too too much already, hee will euen but fhut vppe his
remnant breefely.

   The fweeteft flower whofe ftaulk fharpe prickles gard,
   Yeeldes pleafant fent, through care, without annoy :

The Goosbery, with hurtfull bushes ward,
Surrenders vp it selfe, through care to ivy.

[¹ sig. F,
back]

¹ *The rammish hauke is tamd by carefull heed,*
And will be brought to stoope vnto the lewre ;
The fercest Lyon will requite a deed
Of curtesie, with kindnesse to endure.

What fish so proud as doth disdaine a baite ?
Nor fish, beast, foule, nor fruit, but takes the mate.
Then since that care speedes best with curtesie,
Vse care and kindnesse to mate Ielofy.

Nec blan-
[   ]atis, nec
[eri]t tibi
cn[mi]s
amica,
[pe]rfer
& ol[du]ra :
post[m]odo
mitis [eri]t.
[² orig.
noysommes]

This is Robins counsell, a foueraigne oyle of experience to drawe away the droppinges of Ielofyes nofe, that fo much anoyes the patients harte. Which muft be wrought moft gently, laboured with the perfwafions of reafon, the effecte wherof, I warrant you, wil proue fo profitable, as either he will be freed from noyfomnes,² or haue his nofe put out of ioynt. Conetuoutnes is a peftelent help to Ielofy ; for how can he that hath fet al his loue on his money, be drawn to beftow part thereof on his wife ? No, of my credit, he that hath crept into that vaine, bath fo far crawled from honefty, as hee cares not what iniury hee doth. He knowes that loue will afke coft ; and why doth he loue the diuell, but to faue charges ? For could he be contented to doe good, as he is forward to worke mifchiefe, he would deale with loue better then to locke him vp in his coffers. Oh, it is a fweete thing to him to diue vppe to the elbowe in a bagge, while the kind man beftowes his time in kiffes. But let the other be affured, that whileft this inioyes paradice, he fhall be ftriuing to paffe through the eie of an nedle, which fhall proue vnpoffible. It is a gay thing to come to dignity, but it is a more benificiall thinge to vfe honefty ; but whye doe I talke of honefty to them that neuer meant to enter eternity ? Surely for no other caufe, but for that Robin, knowinge the flauerye that is prepared for you, is moued to pitty, and could wifh you had care to preuente the punifhment of the cormor-antes dungion. But I care not howe little honefty you haue, fo you fhunne Ielofy, for I onely harpe on that ftring at this prefent, which

I fay cannot bee a[1]voided without the entertainment of loue, who will [1 sig. F 2]
foone thruft him headlong befides his poffeffion.

Omnia vincit Amor, et nos cedamus amori.　The paffions of loue
are fo paffing kinde, as they fubdewe wherefoeuer they become, yea,
affuredly they will either conquere or kill; and becaufe life is moft
fweete, we will rather yeeld to affe&tion then die for Ielofy.　Loue is
a pleafing gout, which will fuffer vs no more to be mifled by vnreft,
then the tormenting gout wil giue his patientes leaue to reft while
the paine is vnceafing.　And fuch a hartie dropfie is he, as he fwels
his criples affe&tions with fo great kindneffe, as they fing no fong, but
Ah, I loue.　He is a nettle that ftinges the hart with continuall pleafure; and that babie which lodges in womens and mens eies, on
whome none fhall fix the fancy kindly, that fhall not be ftroken with
a darte of conftauncy; hee is the greeuing woe that breedes continuall
ioy, the fond conceipt that faftens faithful thoughts in his place, and
that euill that reapes eternall good.　To rehearfe her qualities, were
a new worke for Robin-good-fellow, and to followe his properties,
not a labour without profit.　But his chiefeft qualitie [2] is to be kind
and his next to be conftant; he euer forgiues, and ftill forgetes faultes.
He delightes not in breed-bates, nor doth he glory in the quarrells of
deereft frendes, but all his actions are faithfull, and all his thoughts
frutfull.　Dandill him, and he will fporte thee; fet him in thy lappe, [2 *orig.* qua
and hee will comfort thy hart; Speake him faire, and hee will kiffe
thee kindly; like him onely, & he will loue thee euer.　He neuer is
hafty, but hee repentes thereof prefently, paying for euery vnkinde
worde a forrowfull hei ho.　As he will be foone angry, fo is hee
ftraight pleafed, & therfore was he fained to be little in being neuer
long troubled with extreames.　But there is a certaine madneffe
which men call loue, the fame prouing fo great fondneffe, as euery
frowne of a miftriffe makes fome melancholy a quarter after, and to
match that, is foolifh dotage fet, both fo hot paffions for a while, as
they proue in the end to be loues greateft enimy, euen peftelent
Ielofy.　The one will die if hee hath not his longing; as for the other
(for that hee is more craftie), hee hath [3] many fubtill meanes to [3 sig. F 2,
obtaine his defire; yet both of them are fo far from reafon, as they
hurt themfelues willingly.　Nowe, to iudge howe kind they will be

[marginal notes:] Define (c[re]de mihi [vi]tia irritar[e] vetando: [nb]fequio v[in]ces aptius ipfe tuo. En ego co[n]fiteor tua fum noua praeda, C[u]pido. Porrigim[us] victas ad t[ua] vincla manus. Blanditiae comites t[ibi] erunt tetr[i]que furo[res] affidua pa[r]tes turba [fe]cuta tuas. His tu mi-[li]tibus fuperas homin[es] deosq[ue] que Nil opus e[ft] bello: ve[ni]am pacem[que] rogamus. litle] back. Catch word man]

to others, that be fo crabbed to themfelues, Robin leaues that to common reafon. Yet becaufe thefe two extreames, namely, mad fondneſſe and dottage, are the onely meanes to helpe Ielofy, I will bee bould a little to touch them.

The extraordinary conceipt of obtained curtify, moues ſuch a liking in the ouer paſſionate louer, as all his fences are onely tied to one obiect, & his whol hart dedicated to that faint, the fole miftriſſe of his hart. As the extremity which tormentes him, is eafed with nought except what comes from her kindneſſe, ſo his mad fittes, once croſſed with difcourtefie, breed that vncurable melancholy, which deadly grife and vntimely death do followe. But both of them being perchance ftroken with the felfe fame arrowe, ſhot from the vm-pertiall blind boy his bowe, are rauiſhed with the delighte they conceiue the one from the other, their thoughtes beeing heauenly, becaufe true to each other, and their true loue vowed to eternity, manifefted by no fmall fauours. Which happily euery day more and more encreafing frendſhip, remaines to both with wifhed contentment, vntill vnhappily, Ielofy (the profeſſed enimye to louers profperity) picketh a quarrell with one or both, by falfe vnconftancy. Then beginnes our hot loue to turne to burning coles, prouing ſuch fondneſſe, as wee fufpecte our owne fhadowes. Wee gorge our felues fo vnreafonably with the delight of our faintes beautie, as wee caft vppe the hope of their faithfullneſſe. We wil make them faintes, and thinke them diuells, louing them ſo entirely, as our ouer much makes them vnhappy. Wee doe fet them vp in vndecent brauery, and fet them out with foolifh praifes; yet, fhould any ftrangers (though of the familiars forte) feeme to fue to them,—nay, I may truely fay, fpeake to them, it may bee the better for the men, but bee aſſured it fhall bee the worfe for the women. And now comes in diſſimulation, by which we moft practife to vfe them kindly, whome wee hate deadly; to fpeake them faire to their faces, whome wee curfe behind their backs, ¹ and to feede them with dainties, whom wee could wifh poifoned. After the felfe fame manner fare our wiues: they haue a kinde dinner and a crabbed fupper, fweete meate with fower fawce, and a pleafaunt drinke with a poifoned potion; fo fonde extreames falling one on the others backe, as in a moment wee will vfe them like Goddiſſes (if we doe not confeſſe vnto them, they are no leſſe

[I] meane
the [de]ath
of hyr[spir]it
or of hir
[lo]ue.

[P]inguis
a[m]or
nimium[u]ue
patens, [in]
lædia
no[b]is
vertitur, [et]
stomacho
[d]ulcis vt
ef[c]a,
nocet.

[¹ sig. F 3]

vnto vs), and no otherwife then diuels, fwering now we hate them O facies &
moft deadly, whome euen now wee protefted to loue moft diuinely; oculos ma[ta]
fuche monftrous vnconftancy dooth this fondneffe nourifh. Neither tenere me[os]
fhall thefe trickes be extraordinary once in feauen yeares, but I would
Robin could not avow that he hath feene them performed on[c]e euery
day in many places. Well, I will leaue them to their amendes, and
touche as briefly the dotor.

Who, after a little pampering (hauing perchance had his liberty
in good pafture for halfe a yeare, without exercife), doth grow fo
frollicke, as he thinkes himfelf as youthfull as the yongeft nagge,
though he hath as many difeafes as a iade can haue. In this brauery
hee muft bee furnifhed with a gay faddell, and none vnder a ladye
maye ferue his tourne; I meane, while his prouender prickes, he wilbe
fo lufty, as hee thinkes no woman too yong for him. In which
vaine, beeing thus couragious, hee fpendes franckly, and fettes himfelfe foorth in the braueft manner, fo that by his hope, *quid non
aurum?* he will hap vppon fo vnequall a match (by practife prooued),
as after one nights iourney, he begins to be iadifhly tired, euery day
after growing miftruftfull. So that as his monftrous defire hath bene
the meane to ioyne himfelfe with fuche inequallity, fo fhall his
knowne cold courage and her youthfull yeares be a line to leade
him to Ielofy, Whofe perfuafions as yet haue taken fuch defired effect,
as at this time, where loue feekes to builde his kingdome, this his
ennimy (I meane Ielofy) neuer furceafeth from armes vn till he hath
loue out by the eares, being ftill accompanied with like bats, &
alwaies followed by vnhappy difcontentment. His profperity, generally allowed off in mens conceits, is greedely followed by their vnconftant hartes, which loue nothinge that [1] is eternall, nor like of any [1 sig. F 3,
loue but what wil alter dayly. And becaufe I haue entred fo farre back]
into the gouernement of Ielofy, I will prefume to wade a little
further into his kingdome.

In the countrey of Euery-place he raigneth, a ruler as pernitious
as mightye, and more mightye then either vertuous or peaceable. As
his kingdome is large, fo his fubiectes are many, his land beeing
inhabited by people no leffe vnruely then himfelfe, and his right
mainetained by make-bates that neuer are fatiffied, vntill their owne
bloud hath raunfomed the delight of their defired death. Manye are

his aduerfaries, and more his freendes, euery difpofition drawne to
follow his humours, and defirous of his entertainement, by reafon his
actions feeme pleafing, and his caufe righte and profitable. His
regimente is well ftrengthned by force of men, hauing ftronge
holdes, feeming no leffe delightfull in fhow, though by experience it
prooues moft fruitleffe and barren. His chiefeft citty and feat of
pleafure (accompted of his fubiectes the feconde Parradife) ftandes on
the top of a high hill, called Miftruftfullneffe, at foote whereof run-
neth the fwift riuer Vnconftancy, hauing this effecte in operation,
that whofoeuer inbathe themfelues therein, finde continuall altera-
tions in their harts before fetled, and now tormented with variable
thoughtes. In this ftreame are manye fandy fhallowes, and as many
daungerous holes, both continually vfed and frequented vnto, as well
by the inhabitantes of that citie, as alfo by all fuch who chaunce to
trauell that way. This citty hath his name 'Light of loue' maine-
teined by elders, whoe are elected, not for their wealth and wit, as in
other countries, but for their envy and foolifhneffe. Their common
trafficke is Exchaunge of Loue; and their profites, Difquietneffe and
Hate. The fruite that delighte[t]h their appetites, is Faith-leffe
Fancies; and the meates they feede on, Care & Vnreft. The fportes
they ioy in, are continuall brawles, and the walkes they take pleafure
in watching, and hope of finding. All their triumphes are Controuerfies in law, and all their turnies, for broken pates, with faggot
ftickes; their feaft day is repentaunce, and Death their Saboath.

[¹ leaf F 4] ¹This citie bearing the chiefe fwaie for vnrulineffe, hath fo difperfed
her inhabitaunce into the other partes of the cuntrey, as, for the moft
part, there is neuer a cottage in Ielofyes common wealth, but harbours
iourney men as bad as their maifters in condition. His houldes and
caftels are both ftronge and many, being fortified with deepe caft-
rauelinges, and furnifhed with all kindes of ingions fit for warre.
Theire artillery for defence, fo wel placed on the battlements of their
towers, as they wonderfully and daungerouflye annoye their ennemy.
Curfes and Banninges are the leaft fhot they carry, and a thoufande
bitter wordes will do no more then charge one of them. The natures
of thefe people are variable, and they, beinge for the moft parte falfe
harted, are likewife defirous ftill of new freends. The enterteine-
ment they will giue ftrangers is verye good, but the vfage of their

frendes and familiars, efpecially of their wiues (as you haue hard
already), is generally too too bad. They, alltogether reiecting reafon,
performe rafhly what fo euer they thinke, and effecte diuelifhly what
fo euer they practife. Their wills are their lawe, and fufpecte their
iudge, their iudgments being as lawleffe as their lawe is wanting
reafon and difcretion. They bandy honefty as a tennis-ball, and play
with good report, as a childe doth with an apple,—the one not being
in quiet vntill it bee eaten, & the other neuer fatisfyed vntill their
good hope be quite extinguifhed. The bufy Ape comes not to fo
many fhrowde turnes by his vnhappye trickes, as they come vnto
mifchiefe by their troublefome difpofitions; nor doth he deferue fo
much the whip to keepe him in awe, as they merrit the halter for
bringing fo many vnto mifery. For if the law rewards him with a
halfe penny corde, that doth rob a ftranger of thirteene pence halfe
penny, I knowe no reafon howe they can bee accompted leffe then
theeues, that either robbe their neighbours, or fpoile themfelues of
their good names. He that killes himfelf, fhalbe buried by the law
in the commons; and why fhoulde not he be intoombed vnder the
gallowes, that not onelye cuttes his owne throate, hafting thereby
to the diuell, but cuts his wiues alfo, toling her thither for company ?

[1] *Ah, foueraigne loue, whofe fweetneffe falues the fowre,* [1 leaf F 4, back]
And cures the woundes of euery dying hart :
Thou kilft by kindneffe, if thou kilft ; No lowre
Ads greater griefe to them that feele thy fmarte.

Thou countes it paine enough, by proofe to finde,
How two kind hartes may faft remaine in one.
Thy captiue bounds make but a conftant mind,
And all thy warre is for long Peace alone.

Thou ties the mind, and lets their handes goe free :
Thou woundes the hart, and neuer hurtes the fkinne :
Thy victory is, loue for loue to fee :
Thy greateft conqueft, where there is leaft finne.

Ah, fweeteft loue, thou wounds to cure for aye,
Whofe fharpe fhort-night[2] *procures a fweete long-day.* [2 orig. shor-nitght]

Such is loues enuy, and himfelfe no worfe an ennemy ; hee fightes
ftrongly, but to free euerlaftingly ; he tormentes happily, and cheereth

Non mihi
[m]ille
placent.
[n]on sum
de[sul]tor
amo[r]s:
Tu mi[h]i
'si qua
fi[d]es' cura
pe[r]ennis
eris. Tecum,
quos
dederint
annos mihi
fila
[S]ororum,
vi[v]ere
contingat
teq[ue]
dolente,
mori.[1]

frowardly; and both his fmiles & frownes are fo equally tempered, as his pleafing mixture makes a perfect medley, which yeelds moft melodious conftancy. One loue and one life fhall knit fo perfect a knott of amity, as one death fhall ende both their ioyes and miferies. Her loue fhalbe his life, and his life her loue, fhee fhall endure no torment without his torture, nor fhall he fuffer any extreamity without her agony. His fickeneffe fhalbe her forrow, and her griefe woorfe then his deathes wound. Their care fhalbe to encreafe each-others hartes-eafe; and their ftrifes, which of them fhall exceede the one the other in courtefy. Their dalliaunce fhall bee rewarded with darlinges, whofe fweete fauoured faces fhal be continuall pledges of their faithfull kindneffe. The daughters fhalbee like to their fathers, and the fonnes haue the countenances of their mothers. Their encreafe fhalbe multiplied, their fubftance doubled and trebled, till it

[2 sig. G]

come to aboundance, liuing fo longe as three folde gene[2]rations fhall make ioyfull great grand-mothers, and degrees of honour make happy pofterities. They fhall adde fo great a bleffing to their ftore, as time fhall not take away the memory of them, nor fame fuffer their antiquitye euer to die. A woor[l]d fhall ende with their honour, neither fhall that world decay vntill their dignity be regiftred in the true cronicles of eternity.

Thus fhall loues followers be thrife happy, and thus Robin goodfellowes well-willers, in imitating his care, bee manifolde bleffed. They fhall haue their hartes defire, and I
my wifhe, which I pray may happen to
both our contentmentes; and
fo, farewell.

[1] A good deal of the Latin fide-notes comes from Ovid's *Amores*, book 3, elegy 4.—W. C.

[1 sig. G back]

¹ *To the Gentlewomen and others of England.*

Ourtious and louely Dames, fome, to winne your fauour, prouid fuche coftly giftes as may befeeme your acceptance; and others, fo rare deuifes as a yeares trauell hath purchafed; but Tell troth, though as feruiceable as they which are moft paffionate, and as amorous as who exceedes in affection, hath only bought for you a dramme of wit, amounting to fower pennye charges to paffe for a new-yeares gift. The dedication whereof, I haue rather fubiected to your curtefie, then to mens patrocinie; for that your felues, being of the pureft mettall, and hauing your hartes framed of the kindeft moule, will be both more ready to defend our good meanings, and willing to hinder that hagges proceedings, your wills will be leaft followed, and therefore your wits muft be moft vfed; wherby you, whofe fweete flowing tounges charme more then the Orphean muficke, muft ftraine your melodious notes to that heigh[t], as by your fingularitie you may make Ielofie afhamed, & by folemme vowes, breake the necke of fufpition. You muft difwade with wordes, and perfwade by modeft behauiour, confounding by wit, and confirming with difcretion; Following Robins rules to preuent the diuells practife, and making much of loue, to withftand Ielofies councell. And for that Tell troth tells the truth, which by triall you muft proue, vfe Robins falue to heale your fore, and performe his will to inioy your weale, whereby your confirmation may approue his cunning, and allowe my perfumption in a ² greater matter. Robin hath here but onely touched that generall [² leaf G 2; the back of this leaf is blank.] knowne enimie to a quiet life; but hee meanes, by your further fauourable protection, fhortly to arme you againft many pettie aduerfaries, which worke againft loues welfare. If, in the meane time, your good reportes knocke downe the bufie carppers, it fhall bee a fufficient fpurre to make both Robins wit and my pen to triumph in fpite of them, which fhall, by wading further to anger them, light into that vaine which will better content you. Vntill which time (becaufe I would not be tedious) I will leaue you, fubmitting the wifh of your welfare to the pleafure of your owne wills.

Yours, as he hath euer beene,

Tell troth.

[Mr H. C. Levander has kindly identified the side-notes of *Tell-Troth* by means of his Ovid Index, and copied them out as follows :—

Quo tibi formosam, si non nisi casta placebat?
  Non possunt ullis ista coire modis.—Ovid. III. Am. IV. 41.
Indignere licet ; juvat inconcessa voluptas
  Sola placet, Timeo, dicere si qua potest.—III. Am. IV. 31.
Quicquid servatur, cupimus magis ; ipsaque furem
  Cura vocat : pauci, quod sinit alter, amant.—III. Am. IV. 25.
Ferreus est, nimiumque suo favet ille dolori,
  Cui petitur victa palma cruenta rea.—II. Am. V. 11.
Flectitur iratus voce rogante deus.—Art. Am. I. 442.
Quo semel est imbuta recens servabit odorem
Testa diu.—Horace, Epist. I. ii. 69.
[. . . ex malis eligere minima oportere . . . .   Cic. de Off. III. i. 3.]
* Obsequium tigresque domat *timidos*que leones.
                                Ov. Art. Am. II. 183.
Flectitur obsequio curvatus ab arbore ramus,
  Franges, si vires experiare tuas.—Art. Am. II. 179.
Nec mentem servare potes, licet omnia claudas ;
  Omnibus exclusis intus adulter erit.—III. Am. IV. 7.
Si sapis, indulge dominae ; vultusque severos
  Exue.—III. Am. IV. 43.
Centum fronte oculos, centum cervice gerebat
  Argus : et hos unus saepe fefellit Amor.—III. Am. IV. 19.
Quod licet, ingratum est ; quod non licet, acrius urit :
                            II. Am. XIX. 3.
Nitimur in vetitum semper, cupimusque negata.—III. Am. IV. 17.
Cui peccare licet, peccat minus : ipsa potestas
  Semina nequitiae languidiora facit.—III. Am. IV. 9.
O utinam arguerem sic, ut non vincere possem !
  Me miserum ! quare tam bona causa mea est ?—II. Am. V. 7.
Per Venerem juro, puerique volatilis arcus,
  Me non admissi criminis esse reum.—II. Am. VII. 27.
Haec tibi *sunt* mecum, mihi *sunt* communia tecum :
  In bona cur quisquam tertius ista venit ?—II. Am. V. 31.
Si nec blanda satis, nec erit tibi comis *amica* ;
  Perfer, et obdura ; postmodo mitis erit.—Art. Am. II. 177.
Desine (crede mihi) vitia irritare vetando ;
  Obsequio *vinces* aptius *ipse* tuo.—III. Am. IV. 11.
En ego confiteor ; tua sum nova praeda, Cupido :
  Porrigimus victas ad tua *vincla* manus.—I. Am. II. 19.
Blanditiae comites tibi erunt, *Terror*que, Furorque,
  Assidue partes turba secuta tuas.—I. Am. II. 35.
His tu militibus superas hominesque Deosque.—I. Am. II. 37.
Nil opus est bello : pacem veniamque rogamus.—I. Am. II. 21.
Pinguis amor, nimiumque patens, in taedia nobis
  Vertitur ; et stomacho, dulcis ut esca, nocet.—II. Am. XIX. 25.
O facies oculos nata tenere meos !—II. Am. XVII. 12.
Non mihi mille placent : non sum desultor Amoris :
  Tu mihi (si qua fides) cura perennis eris.
Tecum, quos dederint annos mihi fila Sororum,
  Vivere contingat ; teque dolente mori.—I. Am. III. 15.]

---

* There are several various readings of the words in Italics.

[THE

PASSIONATE MORRICE,

A SEQUEL TO

TELL-TROTHES NEW-YEARES GIFT, 1593.

By A.]

To the Gentlewomen and others
of *England*.

Nce more (moſt beautiful damſels) I am bold to preſume
of your wonted fauour, thereby being lead to a performance of a vowed duetie : where a kinde zeale bindeth to
offer the acceptance of a ſeruiceable good will, there a
carefull feare that forewarneth to incurre the hazard of offence,
maketh the hart to ſtagger betweene hope and deſpaire ; hoping
through the kindenes of your gentle diſpoſitions, to obtaine a defence
againſt iniurious cauillers, and fearing by an ouer-bolde preſumption,
to offer offence to the affable ſweetenes of your foueraigne curteſie.
But ſeeing my deſire to bee poſſeſſed of the better cordiall, makes me
hart-ſtrong to ſuppe of that potion which is likeſt to lengthen my
welfare, the ſame being an aſſured confidence of your continuall
carefulnes, in ſhrowding with your affection the ſlender ſubſtance of
my humorous Morrice.

It is not long ſince, for *Tel-troths* Newyeeres-gift, I preſented
vnto your liking *Robin good-fellow* his newes, with his inuectiue
againſt Loues moſt iniurious enemie, Ielouſie ; which, though it was
a token to gratifie the day, yet, if with indifferent iudgement, the
matter therein contained be conſidered of, I doubt not, though it was
a New-yeeres day toy, it may proue a many yeeres helpe to hinder
that hagges enterpriſes. The worke tooke his title according to the
time of his creation[1]; but ſhall *Robins* preſcript[2]ions be followed ? [1 *orig.* crea-
the patients maladie ſhall continually finde it a gifte to ſignifie the [2 pt. *orig.*
[3]good beginning, and proſperous proceeding of many new yeeres vnto [3 ſig. A 2,
them. But now to ſend *Tell-troth* packing, *Honeſtie* hath thruſt [back]
himſelfe into your ſeruice, who, though at the firſt fight he may
ſeeme a crabbed companion, yet let me beſeech you to ſtay your

SHAKSPERE'S ENGLAND : TELL-TROTH. 4

cenfure til you haue throughly tryed what is in him; and if then he thewes not himfelfe a diligent pleafer of your immortal vertues, memorize in the Cronicles of Difdaine the fame of that runnagate fimplicitie, and let me, for his faulte, be banifhed from your good thoughts to euerlafting ignominie.

I was rather defirous to trauel altogether inuifible, then to haue had a title which might giue light to the vnderftanding of me your vnworthie profeffed Author; but fince the higher powers denie me that priuiledge, I am content to fubiect my felf to the opinions of courteous difpofitions; befeeching you to beare with my vaine, for that the vanitie of this age regardes no other; nor would any be content to heare of faultes, vnleffe they be tolde them in meriment. I proteft there is nothing fcandalous therein, nor which is ment to offer iniury to any; onely my purpofe is, that if you fhould know any like vnto any of thofe in difpofition, that either you forewarne them thofe monftrous iniurious vices, or accompt of them as peftilent foolifh wretches. To fhun tedioufnes, I commit my intention to your mifticall confideration, my woorke to your courteous protection, my felfe to your fauourable opinions, and your facred felues to the heauens tuition.

Yours in *feruice and affection*
moft loyall, A.

THE PASSIONATE[1]
Morrice.

[1 orig.
PASSOIN-
ATE]

N the moneth of *March*, a time as fit for wooing, as *May* is pleafant to fporte in, *Honeſtie* trauelling, as his cuftome is, to fearch fuch corners as good fellowſhip haunteth, it was my hap, comming into *Hogſden*, to light vpon a houfe, wherein were met fuch a troupe of louers, as, had not the hall been wondrous bigge, a multitude ſhould haue been forced to ſtand without dores. Yet, though the roume was fo fpatious, as an armie might haue lodged therein without peſterment, notwithſtand-ing it was fo well filled at this inſtant, as all the place *Honeſtie* could get amongſt them was, to fit on the rafters on the top of the houfe, which fitted beſt my humour, that defires rather to fee then to be feene. There, feated in my Maieſtie (as ready to heare newes, as the pickthanke is forward to tell newes), I might eafely perceaue my louers mated, as if they ment to make Marche birds, euery man hauing his fweete hart, and euery couple their corner. There were of all fortes, and in many manners forted,—fome batchelers fewed to widdowes, others to maides; widdowers likewife wooed fome maides, and otherfome, widdowes; there was age and youth coupled together, equalitie of yeares courting each other, and diuerfity of difpofitions, arguing to make a fympathie.

[2] Amongſt them I lent my eares firſt to a couple that had chofen forth the moſt fecret corner in the houfe, which were not worſt fitted for yeares; for it was a youth of three and twentie, that had matched himfelfe with a maide of eighteene; hee, holding her vpon his knee, with his right hand clafping hers, & his left about her middle, mạde many proffers to win her fauour, and breathed many fighes to ſhew his loue; he vowed conftancie with proteſtations, and confirmed with

[2 sig. B,
back]

othes the pleadge of his loyaltie; he ſhewed her how long he had
loued her before he durſt tel her of his affection, how many iournies
he had made with loſſe of labour, and how many complaintes to the
God of Loue, not finding any remedie. Hee made her priuie to the
many houres he had at ſundrie times ſpent in watching to haue a
ſight of her, ſhewing vnto her how ioyfull he were, had he, perchance, but ſeene any creature belonging to her fathers houſe, yea,
were it but the little dog that turned the ſpit. ‘ Many times (quoth
he) haue I lookt vp to the windowe, imagining I haue ſeene thy
picture engrauen in the glaſſe, when, with long gaſing to viewe the
true portrature thereof, I haue at laſt recalled my ſelfe, by letting my
ſoule ſee how mine eyes were deceiued, in expecting that true forme
from the glaſſe, which was onely pictured in my heart. Then would
I ſorrowe to my ſelfe, and power forth ſuch paſſions into the ayre, as
my heart, being ouer loaded with the extremitie they would force,
would conſtraine me to ſit downe, ending my ſpeeche with ſuch
ſighes, as my breathed ſorrowe would no leſſe darken the ayre, then
a miſtie fogge doth obſcure the ſkie. But at laſt, comming to my
ſelfe, I would returne home, locking vp my ſelfe within my
lodging, a cloſe priſoner by the commandement of loue; where,
to paſſe away the time, I would write paſſionate lines, amorous
ditties, pleaſing fancies, pleaſant ronddelaies, and dolefull drerelayes.
Now would I thinke to winne thee by letters; anon I thought it
better to pen ſpeeches; but ſuddainely, both miſliking mee, I would
throwe ¹ my ſelfe vppon the bed, ſo long thinking which way to
obtaine thee, as in the end I ſhould fall into a ſlumber. Yet, amidſt
my reſt, my thoughtes concerning thee were reſtles; For then ſhould
I dreame ſometimes thou ſpakeſt me faire, repaying my kindenes with
ſweete kiſſes, granting my requeſts, and forward to doe my will; but
awaking from forth that ſoueraigne eluſion, looking to finde thee, I
ſhould feele the bed-poaſtes, that hard hap, turning my glad heart to
a new bread ſorrow, which was the more painefull, by how much
my dreame was pleaſing; at another time, I ſhould thinke,.that ſuing
to thee for fauour, thou wouldeſt beſtowe frownes, & profering my
ſeruice, thou wouldſt offer ſkornes. If I ſighed, thou wouldſt ſmile,
laughing at my teares, and ioying at my griefe, requiting euery kinde
demande with ſo cruell anſwers, as if thy bitter words could not force

[' ſig. B ₃]

me to leaue my fuite, thy fkornefull farewels fhould fruftrate my wil ; offering to touch thine hand, mee thought thou profereds[t] thy foote, and ftouping to catch that, being glad of any thing, thou wouldft in a rage fling from me, and leaue the doore barred againft me. There fhould I fit till my teeth chattered in my head, and my heart aked in my bellie ; then fhould I fhake for colde, and figh for forrowe ; when, thinking to knock my legges againft the ground to get heate, I fhould kick al the cloathes off me, being in the end conftrained to awake through colde. At what time that colde fare would better content me, then the former flattering cheare did pleafe me, being as glad it was falfe, as I would haue been glad if the other had been true. Many like to thefe did I endure before my acquaintance with thee, not knowing any meanes how to obtaine the fame of thee, vntill happely finding thee in a fommers euening at the dore, I pre-fumed to enter parlie with thee, offering my felfe your feruant, which had been a tweluemoneth your fworne fubieét, doubting of your patience, though you feeme to be a patterne of pittie. How, and after what order I haue fince that time befought your fauour, your felfe fhall [1] be my iudge, for I lift not to rehearfe my dayly fhiftes to fhewe my zeale, my manyfolde conclufions to obtaine your companie, my giftes to wooe the feruants, and my prefents to gaine your good will. But to be briefe, thereby to come to that I like beft, one whole yeare I loued thee before thou kneweft me, & three more are paffed fince firft I fpake to thee ; yet then was I as neare as now I am, and now as farre off as I was then. Say, therefore, fweete, fince to ftay longer yeelds but little comfort, fhall my fuite now end with the verdit, You loue me ? '

[¹ fig. B ², back]

To which long preamble, fhut vp with fo whot a conclufion, fhe no leffe prepared herfelfe to anfwere him, then Frier *Tuck* vfed cere-monies before he fong mattens. She caft her eyes vp to Heauen, as if fhe had been making her praiers to loue, fighing fo bitterly, as I thought hir placket lace would haue broken ; then to the matter thus fhe anfwered : ' Alas, gentle fir, I muft confeffe I haue found you kinde, and you haue been at a great deale more coft then I could wifh you had ; your fuite hath been long, and my kindenes not much, nor doe I hope you expeét more at my hands then you haue had, before my friends haue granted their good will. Maidens are modeft, and

muſt not bee prodigall of their courteſie; children are bound, and
cannot conſent without their parents counſell; pardon mee, therefore, I pray you, if I ſay I loue you not, ſince my father knowes you
not; and thinke not much if I deſire you to leaue to loue mee, vntill
my mother giue me leaue to like of you. At which time, aſſure
your ſelfe I will bee as ready to performe your will, as they ſhall
be forward to wilh me that good; and thus, in the meane
time, I hope you will reſt ſatiſ̈ied.' This was a ſhroade bone
for my paſſionate youth to gnawe on, that being ſo ſtrucken on the
head as his heart aked therewith, thought to eaſe his ſorrowe with
this replie: ' Ah, my ſweeteſt ſweete (quoth hee), Thinke not on thy
fathers counſel, ſeeing a greater friend craueth his deſerte, nor let me
reſt their leaſure without pitie, that hath thus long remained
conſtant vnto ¹thee. I loue thee not ² for thy freendes ſake, though I
loue them for thy ſake; nor doe thou lothe me for their pleaſure
that liues but at thy pleaſure. But, ſweete and ſoueraigne of my hart,
as thy thoughts be not tied to their wils, ſo let not thy loue be linked
ſo faſt to their liking, as their miſlike ſhould end my life by remouing
thy loue. Say, my goddeſſe—' and therewithall, as he was proceeding,
ſhe cut off the reſt with this ſhort anſwere: ' I beſeech you, ſir, to
leaue off your courting, vnleſſe you entend ſome other concluſion then
as yet I can gather; for, of my faith, loue you I wil not, nor conſent;
I dare not, without my freends giue their conſents firſt;' and thereupon ſhe thruſted through the throng, and poaſted out of doores,
leauing my paſſionate louer to ſay his pater noſter alone; where we
will leaue them.

[¹ ſig. B 3]
[² orig. nor]

What I thought I will tell you, and I hope you will not doubt of
the matter, for that *Honeſtie* ſpeakes it. One yeeres loue without
acquaintance, and three yeeres ſuite to be neuer the neerer; either he
was a bad lawyer, or ſhe a monſtrous vniuſt iudge; but be it, both a
paſſionate Aſſe, and a peeuiſh wench were well met. But marke his
folly and her cunning; he, building Caſtles in the aire, and ſetting
trappes in the Sunne to catch the ſhadowe of a coye queane, was
pleaſed by her, with wagging his bawble and ringing his bell, while
ſhe pickt his pocket and cut his purſe. A proper peece of ſeruice of
a paſſionate Souldier, and a prettie ſleight of a flattering Slut; I
would we had more of them, nay, why wilh I that, ſince the worlde

is too full of fuch alreadie? Yet, of my honefty, fhe was as fitte a
match for fuch a foole as might be found in the worlde. A great
deale of fond fancie repaied with a fharpe fhorte deniall, and
three yeeres affeftion rewarded with an ounce of flatterie, mingled
with a pound of difcurtefie, a good cordiall to comfort fo kinde a
hart. Oh, the fubtilty of the diuell, that vnder the fhadow of obedience
couers *the* craft of cofonage. It is hotte loue that buildes on freendes
liking, and peftilent affeftion that relies rather on the mothers [1] loue, [1 sig. B 3,
then on the Louers loyaltie. Such as ftands fo curioufly on their back]
Parents good will, hauing dealt fo craftily without their confent, are
worthie, by *Honefties* doome, to ftand in a Cage, vntill either their
freends good will be got, or her fweet harts licence obtained for her
deliuerie. And this is too good, for that the kinde Affe wil too too
foone releafe her ; I thinke this punifhment would be worfe welcome
vnto her, namely, that fhe be bound from mariage, fo long as fhe
hath kept him without his anfwere, which will fo pinche her prodigall defire, as either fhe will forfweare honeftie, or neuer commit the
like knauerie. Oh, there is a companie of minions which delight to
haue many futors, that they may bragge amongft their mates of their
diuerfitie of louers; they thinke it commendable to haue ftore of
cuftomers. But knewe they fo much as I know, they were better to
goe once in a fortnight to *Greenes* Cunnyberries, then to haue fuch
reforte to haunt their companies.

Honeftie honours the confent of Parents, but abhorres fuch loue
as is built on their liking ; if there be no remedie but that either they
fhall like, or thou wilt not loue, let him haue thy Fathers good will
before he obtaines thy countenance; for doubtles fhe that will entertaine louers, and repay their courting with kindenes, will care as little
for her freends counfell, hapning on a mate fhe can fancie, as the
horfe wil for haye, that hath his manger full of prouender. And,
what is the caufe why fo many ftande fo curioufly on their freends
confent? nought, forfooth, but the prefumption of a double baite,
that being fure of their countenance, they may be affured of an
other dinner if their owne likes them not ; or otherwife to haue a
hole to hide a Fox in, for that her owne denne is not fecret enough.
If her Hufband controlle her for any mifdemeanour, or reproue her
of any difhoneft behauiour, then on goes her pantoples, building the

reckoning of her honefty on her fathers countenance, fo far prefuming
of his bounden duetie for the match making, as if he kept the keye
[¹ leaf B 4] of ¹ her hufwiferie. Her long toung vtters large fpeeches, ftanding at
defiance vnder the banner of her Fathers defence, and his houfe muft
be her Caftell to keepe her from her Hufband. This is the commoditie
a man fhall reap by fuch a match; and this is their meaning that
would couer their rebellion with the cloak of obedience. Is not he
wel preferred that is fo well married? and how can he mend it?
Marry, no way but this, that he which is mated with the like inconuenience, to learne more wit againft the next time, ftriuing, in the
meane time, to pleafe both her and her freends, fince he had fo
much reafon to woo both her freends and her, to be bound to fo bad
a bargaine.

It is follie (quoth a wife man) to be forrowful for things irre-
couerable, and *Honeftie* thinkes it madnes to repent for deedes done,
whereof her felfe is culpable; can any man be fo witles (efpecially in
matter wherein wifedome is fo much required) as to doe, and with
vndoone in a moment? yea, doubtles, *Honeftie* knowes fuch, they
being the hotte fpurres of our age, that thinke euery day a twelue
moneth vntill they be married; and after they are matched, euery
houre feauen yeeres vntill they are parted. It was hotte loue that
will be fo foone colde, fome of you will fay; but I fay, if it had been
hot loue (as it was burning luft), it would not haue been fo foone
colde. For whereas *the* prouerb goes, that *hot loue wil be foone colde*,
it is ment by fuch affection as wants matter therby to continue longer.
For as that is the pureft wood which yeelds the perfecteft heat, and
the purer it is, the fooner it wilbe it own deftruction, leauing the
fitters by without fire, vnles a frefh fupply be as neede requires
added,—fo wil our hotte loue (whofe kindled affection is come vnto
it perfection, the hart being on fuch a blaze, as euery part of it is on
a light flame,) decay (as reafon and nature requireth), vnles new
faggots of kindenes adde frefh matter for fiering, the fupply thereof
remouing all fufpition of want of affection. How pure *the* loue is
where there is fo light a regarde of proffered kindenes, as 'my Fathers
[² leaf B 4, will,' or 'my Mothers leaue' muft be a Spurre ²to my liking, let euery
back] one iudge that knowes loue.

But, in my opinion, as I confeffe that the duetie we owe to our

Parents may doo muche where the knowledge thereof bindes to obeye; fo muft I confirme that loue is a duetie, himfelfe binding to fo great obedience, and tying with fuch ftrong conuaiances, as he remoues all thoughts of lower dueties; I, tearming al dueties lower, for that by commaundement thofe dueties muft be reiected in refpect of the louing duetie that a Hufband fhall require. Now, how far my nice Minion was from knowing this duetie, her coye demeanour and cunning behauiour hath manifefted. Yet how happie was my youth at laft to be rid of fuch a monfter! And monfter may I tearme her, in refpect of her lewde behauiour; for was it not much better that her inconftancie fhould haue beene knowen before he was faft linked vnto her, then it fhould haue beene found when it had been incurable? Doubtles it was a good caufe he had to double his orifons vnto loue, for fo louingly preferuing him from fo peftilent a prittie-bird,—I fhould haue faid pricking-burre, or paultry bauble.

BUt to come to my fecond couple, which were feated oppofite to thefe in an other corner, being a luftie widdower that was courting a gallant wench, both of them being highly beholding to nature for her liberall fkill in their making, which were thus placed: She was fet down, ouerlooked by him ftanding before her, hauing one of his hands leaning on her lap, and the other refting on the wal, hauing therby (as I geffe) the more libertie to vfe his pleafure, in beftowing kinde kiffes and louing fauours; fo he was feated, and thus he began to fue: 'Faire Maide (quoth he), I know my experience to be greater then your practife, for that I haue tried, rules me by reafon; hauing loued and liued with my loue, vntill by the fates I was bereaued of that fruit. fo well liked I of my laft loffe, as my former good hap breeds an affured hope of the like good fortune, that being a helpe to further my will, and a meane to make a new choife; which change, what good it fhal yeeld, ¹your felfe fhall chal- [¹ sig. C] lenge, whofe good reporte hath bound me to commence my deferts, to receiue their cenfure by your doome. To boaft what I am, were friuolous, for that your freends are alreadie priuie to my eftate; and to fay how well I loue you, were booteles, for that women loue to trie ere they truft; yet, vnles I fhould fay more then I haue faide, I fhould feeme to fay nothing; though to fay more then is fpoken

already, were meerely foolifh. For thus ftands the cafe : I haue made
choife of you for my fecond wife, and haue already your freends good
will ; there reftes therefore nothing but a confirmation of your duetie,
in agreeing to that they haue confirmed : ' thus comming to a full
point, he clofed vp his period with a brace of fmirking kiffes, which
wrought with his Louer, as a ftrong pyll dooth with a fore ficke
patient ; namely, they forced her to anfwere him thus fhrewdely :
' The affurance of your good fortune, Sir, hath made you highly
beholden to her deitie, that dauncing in the morrice of good matches,
you fhould be led by her to fo good hap ; but, belike, it was ouer good
to continue long, either her kindenes being ouermatched with your
vnconftancie, or your good happe ouer ruled by fortunes cruelty ;
They euer change, and lightly, neuer but for the worfe ; which the
rather feemes fo vnto me, by the fure knowledge I haue of your
fecond choice, that is fo far vnequall to your reported firft match, as
I know your liking would not remain long, or my mifliking would
come too too foone ; becaufe I am not able to follow what your firft
wife hath performed, and you will be vnwilling to beare with the
wants your fecond choice muft be enriched with. But, peraduenture,
I miftake your meaning ; for whereas I thinke you fue to haue me
to your fecond wife, you feeke but to haue my good wil to liue with
my freends ; alas, good fir, my duetie (as you fay) muft not gainfay
their pleafure, nor will I, for that matter ; but with all my hart, if you
haue their licence for your boord, haue my good will to obtaine your
bed there alfo, for their houfe is at their owne commaundement.'

[' sig. C,
back]

'Then doubt I not (replyed he) to ' haue you for my bedfellow.'
' But that doubt I (anfwered fhe), for that I know the contrary.'
' Why dare you (quoth he) to difobay your Fathers commaundement ? '   ' No (fayd fhe), fo it be for my commoditie.'   ' It fhall be
both for your profite and preferment.'   ' Make me to beleeue that
(quoth fhe), and then, peraduenture, it may be a bargaine.'   ' Why,
woman (faide he), I deferue your better.'   ' Take her (anfwered fhe),
and I will not be matched to your inferiour.'   ' Why, then, I fee you
do fcant loue me ? '   ' I vfe it not (quoth fhe), and yet I fweare I
will mocke you, rather then marrie with you.'   With which, being
highly difpleafed, he beftowed three or foure crabbed tearmes, being
liueries of his cholerick long toung, and fo departed.

A fhame goe with him, thought *Honeſtie*, whatſoeuer ſhe thought,
and with all ſuch Louers! louers, with a halter,—lubbers, I may
better tearme them. What monſtrous matches are ſuch as are
ſhuffled vp after the ſelfe ſame order! Suppoſe ſhe had beene fearefull, and durſt not to haue refiſted the receipt of what ſhe lothed;
imagine ſhe had beene fooliſh, and could not haue iudged of affection? thinke ſhe had beene forward, and would haue beene glad of
any one? alas! poore wretch, I pittie the ſuppoſition; what ſhould
I haue ſaid to the confirmation? I know aſſuredly the ſhould haue
ſighed, whatſoeuer I had ſaide; and mourning ſhould haue been her
companion, what ere had been my communication: he would haue
daunſt with her portion, while ſhe had drooped through want
of affeƈtion; he would haue loathed her company, for that ſhe was
not a dayly commoditie; her life ſhould haue been like the hacknies
that are at euery mans commaundement for the hire, and her ioy as
momentary as the floriſhing greene graſſe in Iuly. Pitifully ſhould
ſhe haue liued, puniſhed by him without pitie: and this is my reaſon
of the poſſibilitie; for that it is moſt likely he loued her not, & how
well any body vſe them they loue not, let them ſpeake that ſuſpeƈt
not. Now, that he loued her not, may be proued both by his kinde of
wrong, careleſlye ſuing vnto her, peremptorily vſurping her Fathers {¹ ſig. C ³}
authoritie, which was a band to tye her to obedience, though a bad
meane to obtaine her curteſie. For affeƈtion is not to be limitted,
nor loue to be compelled; but, contrarily, hatred followes feare, and
feare forerunnes miſlike; and how we loue thoſe we regarde not,
iudge they that woo and obtaine not. But this cuſtome is too common and ouer cruell, namely, a wooing of freends, and a conſtraint
of loue, I would not ſay compelling, but for feare it ſhould haue
been taken for compelling. Were *Honeſtie* a Iuſtice, they ſhould
either lye in the ſtockes a fortnight, or marry her I would match
him with, which ſhould ſeeke a wife after this order. I thinke,
verily, he would rather ſtay his ſtint by the heeles, then be bound to
the other inconuenience; and yet he could finde in his hart to binde
another to *the* bad bargaine. This is charitie, yea, & neuer a whit of
honeſtie, being ſo farre from ciuilitie, as the Millers craft is from true
dealing. Now, truely truly, to deale as we would be dealt with, is
ſent to the hedge a begging, and neighbourly loue is made a hacknie,

being fo worne to the bones with feeking a good Maifter, as his fkinne will hang on the bufh fhortely.

I haue heard a reporte of a paffing kinde man that complained of his wife at a Seffions for piffing a pot full, iudging thereby fhe was difhoneft; and that fame man fhortly after burying his wife, fued to a maide, after the manner aforefaid; he had obtained her freends good will, and were at a point for the Maidens loue; yet on a time fhe was troubled with the head-ake at his being with her, whereof he fo mifliked, as in the morning he went to the Phifitions to haue their opinions to what difeafe it coulde turne, and vpon their reporte left her. I am affured I haue erred in no point, vnleffe I haue miftooke the laft, putting the Phifitions opinion in the roome of his owne bad meaning : it was no difeafe, indeede, that mifliked or mifled him, but it was of the Fathers purffe, not of the Daughters head; well, fhe was well prouided for in miffing of him, and if he fped any thing the better, let him boaft of it; but [1]Honeftie can iudge no better of the remnant of his companions, then his action giues the verdict of him, which is as bad as may be.

[1 sig. C 2, back]

But to another that hapned on one that had the toothake, with whom he would not marry for feare the hollowneffe of her tooth fhould corrupt her breath, and fo annoye his colde ftomack. It was colde indeede, and I would fuch ftomacks might be heated with redde hotte gold, as cheerfull as fcalding leade. Well, to a third : he liked her parents wel, for that they were honeft & godly, and as well of the maiden, becaufe fhe feemed modeft; to be breef, he could find no faulte in either of them, onely his feare was that the Daughter would be fomewhat fhrewifh, for that fhe had a long nofe, and thereupon gaue her ouer. If her nofe had beene long enough, I think fhe might haue fmelt a knaue, but I am affured fhe knewe a churle, and fo let her claime him wherefoeuer fhe fees him. Yet one more of the fame ftampe, and fo we will leaue them. This was a wooer in graine, who had gone fo far, as they were at next doore to be afkt in the Church. The wedding apparel was bought, the day appointed, yea, and I may tel you, many of the geffe bid, only there was no affurance, for that he abhorred; but it fortuned that before the day there dyed a rich man that left a welthie widdow, to whom he made fo fecret loue, as he wonne her good will within a fortnight after the death of his predeceſſour; well, notwithſtanding, to ſaue his counterfeit credit and preſerue his hypocriticall honeſtie, he reſorted dayly to his olde ſweete hart, with whom vpon ſome final reaſon he fel at ods, vſing her ſo vnkindly in ſpeeches, as he drew teares for ſorrow. Glad of this, though turning his earneſt into ieſt, he called her vnto him, in the preſence of many of her Fathers ſeruants; then ſwearing that if ſhe tooke him not about the necke & kiſſed him, he would neuer marry with her as long as he liued. Which *the* yong Gentlewoman refuſed to doe, partely for that he had iniured her highly, but *the* rather leaſt ſuch fondnes ſhould ſeeme immodeſtie to the ſeruants; vpon whoſe denial, in a great [1] fume he [¹ ſiz. C 3] flung forth of the doores, and in a rage as if of ſpight, within one fortnight after he matcht with the widdowe aforeſaid. But to tell you what a life ſhe lead with him, were to hunt from the purpoſe; yet aſſure yourſelfe it was ſo bad, as *the* world iudged this maid neuer better bleſt then in not being beſtowed ne caſt away vpon him.

Such, and of the ſame ſorte, are theſe money-woers, that ſue firſt to the Father, to ſaue labour; for, ſpeede they will; and if they miſſe in one place, they knowe another where they will practiſe. And how can it be iudged otherwiſe, ſeeing their meaning in vſing that meane importes no leſſe? for, thinke they, 'if I haue the Fathers good will, the daughter will be eaſilie wonne; and if I miſſe of his, I ſaue that time and labour, in ſuing to the maide, beſides the giftes I ſhould beſtowe.' Ha, ha! I haue him by ſent: and what thinke you of him? in faith, no otherwiſe then *Honeſtie* beleeues. You ſmell a Foxe? I, and a ranke one too, whoſe breach is ſo ſtainde with this gilding matter, as it may eaſely bee iudged what muck hee loues. Alas! good hearts, that are coupled with ſuch bad mindes, this is loue; true; but what loue? couetous loue, hatefull diſſimulation, hipocriticall affection, and what not that is contrarie to the ſweete ſoueraigne loue, which ſues for kiſſes and not for coyne, which craues the heart & nothing elſe; for with it, al ſhe hath is his; and he that wil looke for more, I would he had a halter; and he ſhall not want it in hell, howſoeuer he ſpeedes here. Fie, fie! mariages, for the moſt part, are at this day ſo made, as looke how the butcher bies his cattel, ſo wil men ſel their children. He that bids moſt ſhal ſpeed ſooneſt; & ſo he

hath money, we care not a fart for his honeſtie. Well, it hath not
been ſo, and I hope it wil not be long ſo; & I wil aſſure you, loues
common-wealth wil neuer floriſh vntil it be otherwiſe. Why, it is a
common practize to aſke the father what hee will giue with his
childe; and what is that differing from cheapening an Oxe? And it
is as common, that if ſhe be fat, it is a bargaine, but if leane, ſhe
muſt ſtay another cuſtomer. Out, alas! what loue is this? in faith, if

[¹ ſig. C 3,
back]

I ¹ might haue ſped better in another place, come to notice after I
haue bought your daughter, ſhe ſhall pay for it, or I will make dice
on her bones. A pittifull partnerſhip, where there is no greater loue;
and how can but one of them be vndone? He will vſe her ill,
becauſe he loues her not; and ſhee cannot loue him for not vſing her
well; for whome we feare we hate, and what then? Hee will
practiſe her ende; ſhe will wiſh his death; and while they liue together,
it will be ſo full of heartbreakings through quarrels and contentions,
as woe to them both, I, and to the third too, that was ſo forward to
make ſo bad a matche. But, howſoeuer they two ſpeede, I am
aſſured ſhee will ſpeede worſe: as for hir huſband, he will not want
excuſes to defend his knauerie; and hir Father muſt beleeue him,
becauſe of hir former credit giuen vnto him; ſo that contented ſhe
muſt be, how diſcontented ſo euer ſhe liues; and beare it ſhe
muſt, vntill her hart breake; which happie day muſt ende her miſerie,
and ſet my craftie wooer at libertie.

Thus much for my ſecond corner: and now to my third couple,
which were ciuilly ſeated on a benche together, they being, the one a
batcheler, and the other a widdowe, which was wooed by him after
this like order: 'It were follie, forſeeth (quoth he), to vſe circum-
ſtances, ſince you are ſo well acquainted with the like practize; but
to leaue them and come to the matter, which is (as I thinke) the beſt
meane to pleaſe vs both, you ſhall vnderſtand that vpon the good
reporte your honeſt life hath deſerued, I haue conceiued ſo good
liking of you, as I ſhould thinke my ſelfe happie if I ſhould ſpeede
no worſe.' 'I thanke you (anſwered ſhe) for your good will; but
ſurely, Sir, I thinke you haue deceiued your ſelfe. For, peraduenture,
you imagine, or it hath been vntruely reported, that I am the woman,
which indeede I am not; namely, ritche, for that my deceaſed huſband made ſome ſhowe to the world; but if that bee your thought, I

aſſure you you are deceiued.' 'You miſtake my meaning (replied hee), for it is no ſuch matter; I re¹ſpect not ſo much your wealth, as [¹ leaf C 4] I doo your matronlike modeſtie; my ſelfe is young, and I haue a trade, and am, I thanke God, of my ſelfe able to maintaine a woman. But I doo rather deſire to match with your like, then with a younger, for that you knowe better both what belongs to a man, as alſo to vſe thriftely what I get. And, moreouer, my ſelfe is not ſo young, but that I am meeter to match with a widdowe then to marrie with a maide, and would be moſt glad if it might be my good happe to ſpeede with you.' 'I cannot tell (quoth ſhe) what your good ſpeede may be; I knowe you not, and therefore I hope you will giue me leaue to enquire of you; which done, I will ſend you your anſwere by ſuch a day; in the meane time, I wiſh you well.'

I, mary, *Honeſtie*, & what then? no marry theſe: forth ſhe went to her broker, to will him to ſearch after his ſubſtance, vſing that manner which vſurers can beſt diſcloſe, which is their practiſe in putting forth their money. This was a paſſing commoditie; for what better then a ritche widdowe? but that fooliſh enquirie ſpoyled all; had ſhee thankt him heartily, deſired farther libertie, and had made ſearch into his eſtate ſecretly, ſhee had ſhewed her ſelfe the wiſer; but ſo bluntly to ſaie, 'giue mee leaue to enquire of you,' ſhewed as bad bringing vp as might bee poſſible. But, tut! I like her the better, becauſe ſhe could not diſſemble; for ſhe, alas! did but followe the common trade, dooing with the ape but what ſhe had ſeene done before her. She had heard her huſband inſtruct his prentices to make a profit, and ſhe thought ſhe might trie the ſame for her own good. I would ſhee and others knewe what was good for them; they would then rather reſpect the man then money. But this couetouſnes ſpoyles all, though 'I would I had more,' is too much in our mouthes; for, followed ſhe not the gréedie deſire of adding muck to muck, might ſhee not as well haue liued with this man, that had a trade as good, yea, much better then her huſbands was, as ſhee did before with him? Shee had no children; ſuppoſe ſhe had, they ² were [² leaf C 4, back] prouided for well; and what greater charge woulde this haue brought? he had a care to liue, or elſe hee would haue ſought to loue without reſpect; for who knowes not that ſhe is as able to ſatiſſie a mans deſire that hath little, as ſhe that hath much,

if we onely regarde pleafure? Take this on *Honeflies* credit, that
hee that buildes his loue on fuch reafon, as hauing little, hee will
chofe one that hath fomewhat, wil proue a better match vnto thee,
then him that brings mountaines. Beware when loue is vpholden
with maintenance; if the heart remembers, ' I am thus much beholden
vnto her, fhee loued mee or elfe fhee would neuer haue matcht with
me; fhe made me a man, being before worfe then nothing; how
much better might fhe haue done, if fhe had not been led with
affeftion,' and fuch like; It will alfo remember the duetie this
kindenes requireth, euen like for like, leaft the worfe crie fhame of
him. How happie fhould parents be, were this in their remembrance
at their mariges making! how bleffed fhould their children be, if
the like praftifes were vfed! and what a florifhing commonwealth
would that be, where equalitie of birth (which alwaies fhould bee
regarded, fpecially on the mans fide) fhould bee linked to abundance,
whereby the number of gentle beggers fhould be decreafed, and the
mifgouernement of wealth will be auoided. One man fhould not
haue his cofers ful, and twentie want it that better deferue it. How
many able men fhould we haue (if this were vfed) to ferue and fet
forth men for the princes feruice, where now I am but one man,
and I am bound but to my ftint, to finde one mans charge, though I
haue fiue mens liuings. But no more! this is too ferious for *Honeflie*,
& I meruaile how I fell into this vaine, fince I ftudied to bee pleafant. What, thinke you, did my widdowe after her fearch of
enquirie, for you muft thinke that the batcheler longed for his
anfwere? Marry, though fhe was not a foxe in her fpeeches, yet
fhee proued no leffe in her dooing, for now fhee kept her houfe as
clofely, as hee dooth his holde craftely. She miflikt of the man : for
[¹ sig. D] what caufe, geffe you? ¹ if you knew as much as I knowe, you would
fweare, not for lack of honeftie, or becaufe he was vnthriftie. But
wil you knowe whie? he had not the hundreds lying by him, as the
reporte went fhee had left her, and therefore fhee thought it needeles
any one fhould lofe fo much labour, as to fulfill her promife in carrying his anfwere. Yet, if that were all, it were well; I, and it had
been well for him (for the fauing of fhoo lether) if fhe would haue
fpoken with him at his comming to fetche it : But my widdowe
would not be within, or elfe fhe was bufie ; and thus was his kindenes

requited. Now, fie of the diuell! is this a meete reward for affe&ion?
nay, fuppofe it be no more, the good will, was it well requited? Me
thinkes that if his dog had come, hee deferued better entertainement
then to haue been beaten away; and fhee had dealt better if fhee had
fent himfelfe away with a crabbed anfwere, then fo vnmannerly to
vfe him by fleeueles excufes. And well it were if fhee had no
more fellowes; but out vpon them! there are too many fuch, whofe
coye nicenes exprelle their mifchieuous fondenes; for, fpeake they
will with any man that come, vnles a Herald fore runnes the
fewtor.

In my opinion, and it fhall bee grounded vpon reafon, fuch widdowes are worthie to fit while their breeches growe to their feates, as
refufe to anfwer all commers of what degree foeuer; and becaufe I
promift you reafon, this fhall be it. Who knowes not, that whofoeuer fues for the like match, winneth a thoufand incombrances with
his good fpeede? for he that knowes not that care fhal be mingled
with his beft contentment, fhall fall into a pitte before he be ware of
it. And who, were it not for his foules health, would imbrace fuch
an inconuenience for a little commoditie? I, and the beft mariage
is but a little commoditie, in refpe& of the continuall carking that
comes with it. If, then,—as who faies it is otherwife?—a man makes
fo great fuite for fo fmall hearts eafe (refpe&ing the earthly pleafure),
deferues not he a good countenance, or at leaft a welcome, that longs
for fo bad a bargaine? In my iudgement, [1] and it fhall iumpe with [¹ sig. D,
mine opinion, that woman is much more beholden to the man that   back]
would match with her, then to her parents that haue brought her vp;
for they did what ere they did, of duety, & this doth what might be
vndone, of mere deuotion. Why, thinke the beft you can, thinke
for your felues: fuppofe one that hath nothing, comes to craue your
loue: did he only refpe& your wealth, without his owne welfare (and
hee that thinkes to haue welfare without dealing wel with you, he
reckens without his hofteffe, and fhal finde a new bil of charges), had
he not much better to hazfard the taking of a purfe by the high
way? Yes, doubtles; for were hee by that means brought vnto
miferie, he might haue death at his cal, to rid him from extremitie;
but now being grieued vnceffantly, he may feeke for death, but
meete with the diuell; hope for an ende, but feele the want of it con-

tinually. Yet come we to one further point : imagine fome men
that bee ouer-unruly, defire to haue accefle into your companie : if
you knowe them for fuch companions, I would holde you vnwife to
admit them into your prefence ; but fhall your hart but fay, I fufpeCt
without trial, you cannot out-runne the crime of want of defcretion.
It is beft, therefore, you that feare fuch reforte, to harbour your
felues, during the time of the heate of the market, in fuch places as
the countenances of your proteCtors fhall preuent fufpeCt, and dif-
parage the praCtife of fuch vndecent behauiour ; or otherwife, to
appropriate vnto your houfes fuch helpes as fhall bee likely to foreftall the like mifchiefe. That euery one may bee anfwered, is
Honeſties meaning ; for vnles they bee, they haue not their due, nor
doo you fhewe your felues to be inriched with that curtefie which
widdowes defcretion dooth challenge. For, let me tell you, and
enfure as many as knowe it not, that a man fhall finde more pleafure
in lying in the campe, being dayly threatned with the bullets of his
enemie, then in lodging with a wife, vnles his wifdome be the
greater. And I knowe you looke for my reafon : then for this
caufe, for that their vnconftancie [1] breedes more feare then the fhot
brings hurt ; and their tender heart will craue more gouernement to
content them, then the other will afke forecaft to preuent the danger
they bring with them. For a fteele coate refiftes the harme of a
mufket ; but what garment fhall out ftand her threatning of the
horne ? That man amongft Souldiers is counted accurft that is
ftrucken with a great fhot ; and that hufband thrife bleft among
married men, that is not continually wounded with fome mifde-
meanor or other he fhall efpie in his wife ; well, I fay no more,
becaufe I am a batcheler ; but *Honeſtie* muft fpeake the trueth, or
fhame will follow him.

It is wifdome to looke before lepping, but extreame follie to ftand
vpon nothing ; hee or fhee that makes many doubtes, fhall neuer
want care ; and fhe wil il rule a charge, that cannot charme a knaue.
Speake the diuell faire, and he will be fatiffied ; and what woman
knowes not how to flatter ? It is good to knowe vice, that we may
fhun that euill ; and as good to trie the honeftie of wooers, that you
may not fpeede the worfe. You fhall often finde a kings heart clad
in a thred-bare coate, and a fenators wifdome harbored in a youthfull

[¹ sig. D 2]

head; vertue goes not by birth, nor defcretion by yeares, for there are olde fooles and young councellers, counterfeit knaues & crabbed churles, the one being clad in a lambes fkinne, and the other kept warme with Foxe furre. Nature makes, but fortune clothes; a ritch knaue therefore may march in the habit of a true meaning gentleman, when poore *Honeftie* muft goe as he is able, bee it in a mouldie caffock. I haue heard it credibly reported, that there was a ritch widdowe fell here in England, which had left her liuing enough to maintaine a younger brother; and vnto her did reforte fuch an one, as had not fildome flung out at a bootie, nor would haue cared much if it had been his father, fo he had met him in a conuenient place. This young gentleman (yet not very young, for he was about fortie) came vnto this widdowe, to craue her good wil, vfing as fpeedie tearmes as he [1] defired quicke fpeede. Hee tolde her his name, fo [1 sig. D 2, well knowne throughout the countrie for a fhifting liuer, as he fpake back] no fooner then hee was well knowne vnto hir. Whome fhe vfed courteoufly, anfwering him after this order: 'I hope, gentle fir (quoth fhe), you will giue me leaue to anfwer you as fpeedely as you bluntly afke the queftion.' 'And with all my heart (replied hee), for that is my defire.' 'Then affure you thus much (faid fhe), that if there were no more men in the world befides your felfe, I would not marrie with you.' 'A fhort and fower anfwere (quoth he); yet let mee affure you, that onely fuch an one (naming himfelfe) will haue you,' and fo tooke his leaue, departing in as good order as fhee had in kinde manner vfed him. Shortly after, at a meeting with many of his companions, he craued their aide, finding them as forward to performe any thing hee fhould require, as hee would wifh. Vnto whome hee fhewed his whole intention, the rather defiring their helpes, for that they had been partners with him in as great hazards; well agreed vppon the match, they rode towards the widdowes houfe, comming thither in the euening about fupper-time, when it was very darke, whereby their companie coulde not bee defcried. They knockte at the gate, and was anfwered by the porter, that being afked who was within, certified them according to his knowledge. Him they fo hampered, as gagde hee was and bound, being laide forth of the way; which done, they paffed further, entring the hall with their drawne fwordes, where they found all the feruants at Supper. They

had no weapons neere them but bones, being vnmeete inftruements
to refift armed men; and dogges, they were not to be wonne by fuch
baites. Therefore, eafily one by one they were bound and laide on
a heape; the wooer in the meane time, with two of his mates, being in
the Parlor with the widdowe that was garded with two futors, being
Gentlemen of account in that Country, he vnmafked himfelfe, for
they had al vifards, and tolde the widdow he was [1] come for her; at
what time one of them grewe cholerick, and I thinke it was he that
was likeft to haue fped beft, for he was placed on the benche neereft
to her hart, and drew his poyniard, the beft weapon he had at that
inftant, making as if he meant to darte the fame; but vpon better
confideration had, he put vp his Dagger, and was contented to be
bound with his fellowe. All of them being bound, they got *the*
Widowe foorth, and bound her with a towel behinde one of them,
hauing before their departure hid all the Saddles, and turned forth
the Horfes out from *the* houfe. Ouer a long plaine they rode, & fo
through a wood, where, being out of greateft danger, he himfelfe, the
wooer, got vp before the widdowe, entreating her to confider of their
eftates, not fo much he himfelfe refpecting his own weale, as he
regarded his freends welfare, whome he had drawen into that defperate action. But it was all in vaine, for agree fhe would not; fhe
fware rather to dye then to confent, which feemed little to remedie
his affection. Wel, in fhort time they were come to a place prepared
for *the* nonce, where they found a good fire with a Parfon, and other
good company affembled together about the fame matter. It was a
wonderfull rainie euening, fo that all of them were throughly wet;
but there fhe wanted nothing fhe could defire, nor fpared he kinde
words to winne her good will, which was fo long in graunting, as
before the obtaining of it, Hue and cry was followed into that
Towne. Whereof he, hauing notice, came to her with his laft hope,
willing her, that as fhe was a woman, either then or neuer to confent
to the fauing of all their liues. When fhe, feeing no remedy, but
either fhe muft relent, or they repent it : ' will you (quoth fhe) be
good to my boy Tom ? ' for fhe had one onely childe called *Thomas*.
' To fay I would (replyed he), in this extremitie, might be faide to be
but flatterie, but affure thy felfe I will, and much better then I will
boaft on; ' vpon which agreement, they were foorthwith maried.

[* fig. D 3]

Soone after he called her afide, and tolde her fhe was now his wife, whofe credit was her good regarde : 'we ¹ fhal, I know (quoth he), be [¹ sig. D 3. back] brought for this before *the* counfel, at which time, vnleffe you vfe *the* matter thus cunninglye, as to affirme this was your owne practife, to fhewe your loue, and fhun a bad reporte, we fhall, notwithftanding, fmart for it.' Which fhe promifed to doo, and did indeede no leffe, all them being fhortly after apprehended, and brought vp to anfwere it at the counfell Table, where fhe tolde fo good a tale for him and his fellowes to the effect aforefaide, as the faulte was remitted, and they difcharged. Now, that you may vnderftand how well he re- quited this her kindnes, fhe liued with him a long time, and yet leffe then a dofen yeeres; and dying, left this good reporte of his vfage towards her : namely, that neuer woman liued with a more kinde -man then fhe had found him, with other fuch probable tokens or the certainty thereof, as a Countrie can witnes the fame. Him felfe liued not long after her, at his death leauing her fonne *Thomas* fiue hundred pounds by the yeere, ouer and aboue his own Fathers liuing, which he himfelfe had purchafed by his good hufbandrie.

What fay you to this vnthrifte ? was not fhe put to a fhrewde triall ? fhe was, and it proued paffing wel. Wherfore, then, fhould yonger brothers be reiected, or why they that haue little, be vnre- garded ? furely, becaufe the hart is couetous and miftruftfull, and womens mindes are afpiring, being neuer contented. They fo much thirfte after preferment, as often they ouer-leape amendement, and iumpe iuft into a worfer predicament.

Many looke fo long for aboundance of mucke, as ² they fall into [²*orig.* as as] a quagmire of miferies, hauing filuer to looke on, though wanting mony to fupply many wants; hauing a faire fhewe and a fhrewde keeper, one that hath more then enough, & yet will not part with any thing : *Honeflie* knowes many of thefe, and they feele more then I can tell you. Who goes, for the moft parte, worfe fhod then the Shoomakers childe ? and who hath leffe money in her purffe, then fhe whofe Hufband hath moft in his cheft ? ³ But, for that I am fome- [³ leaf D 4] what ftraied out of my way, I will return to my firft widdowe before my fhooes be quite worne : My forenamed Bacheler, that neither by himfelfe or his freends could fpeake with her to know her anfwer, deuifed this conclufion, to fend her a Letter by a freend, not fo much

for the matter there in fet downe, as that *that* might be a meane to
entice her to be fpoken with, which, indeede, proued to fome purpofe. For to the Meffenger fhe came, and after notice giuen from
whome the Letter was fent : ' gods Lord (quoth fhe), did not my
freend giue him his anfwere ? ' ' No,' replyed the Meffenger ; ' for he
craues no more by this Letter.' ' Surely (quoth fhe), I thanke him
for his good will, but I am not minded that way.' ' What way ?
(replyed he), not to marry ? ' ' Yes,' faide fhe, ' but not with one fo
yong.' Now you fhall vnderftand her fimple excufe, cleanly made ;
for in a mans iudgement it would not be thought there was much
difference betweene their ages. And, as it was gathered after, fhe
meant one way, and the Meffenger tooke it an other ; for fhe meant
yong in fubftance, though he vnderftood it for yeers ; as, after further
talk, fhe plainely expreffed. What fhall *Honeftie* fay more of her ?
in footh, nothing, but to pray, either for the amendement of her and
her companions, or elfe that this punifhment may be inflicted vpon
them ; that is to fay, that they may be fo haunted, vntill they deale
better, as they may not peepe foorth of their houfes, without as much
wondermen[t] as the Owle hath that flieth in the day time. And doo
they deferue leffe that make fooles ? it hath beene a fuftie faying,
Qui moccat moccabitur, and, vntill that proue true by practice, as it
falles out true often vnlookte for, we that are to fpeed fhall neuer
finde better. If all men will agree to *Honeftie*, we wil keepe a
Cronicle of fuch wenches ; my felfe will be fpeak the regiftrefhip, and
though it be no great office, yet it may doo much good. But now
to a fourth kinde.

    Which were a thrife-made, not a threed-bare Widdower, and a fiue
times left Widdowe, both of them being fo much in Fortunes bookes,
as they were endowed with the [1] thoufands. They foone agreed vpon
the matter, and within a fhorte time were married ; vnto whofe houfe,
hauing heard them boaft of their fubftance, I often reforted to fee
what good cheere they kept ; I was twife there together in Chriftmas
time, but neuer could fee hotte meate, yet good ftore of cold, by
reafon they had had foure daies before many guefts. But fince the
holly dayes, hoping for hotter fare, I found him and fhe fet at a
couple of red Herring & a flice of barrel butter : colde fare, as I
thought, for a tuefday fupper. Alas ! how were the feruants dieted,

[¹ leaf D 4,
back]

when they had no better? I would haue thought *the* faulte to haue beene in her, vntill ſhe ſaide vnto me, that ſhe was ſorrye ſhe had no better fare for *Honeſtie*; when the olde Churle replied, ' holde thee content, wife; he is welcome, I thanke God I haue this for him!' 'I thanke your worſhip,' ſaide I; though I thought, ' I beſhrewe the Churles hart!' But there of force muſt I lodge too, for that I had ouer farre home, and he that had fedde me ſo hungerly, had found talke enough to keepe me with him till midnight. I muſt confeſſe I lay better then I had ſupped; lodgde in the next Chamber to themſelues, there being nothing but a thinne wall betweene vs. After my firſt ſleepe, I heard them two very lowde, and though I did not greatly deſire to be a partaker of their ſecret, yet I could not chooſe, vnles I had beene either naturally or artificially deafe. They were at ſo hotte words, as he cryed, ' out vpon thee, old beggarly whore!' with other moſt ſhamefull tearmes; ſhe therby being forced thus to complaine: ' Alas, that euer I was borne to ſee your face; I was no begger when I met with you, for I brought with me as good . as twentie thouſand pounds, which now being at your diſpoſition, you deale thus crabbedly with me; meeting together in reſpeⱷ but yeſterday, what hope reſteth to me of the end, ſeeing the beginning is ſo bad? you diet me with hardmeat, and cheer me with crabbed vſage; I can neither haue a penny in my purſſe, nor a good ſhooe to my foote. I greeue to heare my ſeruants repine thereat, though I cannot amend it, and [1] for that I tell you of it which may redreſſe it, [1 ſig. E] thus you reuile me.' ' Holde thy peace, olde whore (quoth he), or I will make thee; if they like it not, let them mend theirſelues, and either charme your toung, or I will clapperclaw your bones;' with which cooling carde, ſhe was glad to be quiet, as I geſſe, for I could heare no more of her at that time.

Now, *Honeſtie*, hauing leaſure to thinke of what he had heard, ſtill harpt of *the* twentie thouſand pounds, which, as I thought, was meeter to haue made a King, then to haue pleaſed a churle; with *that* I condemned his cruelty, and pitied her chaunce, ſo long thinking on her hard fortune, as I fell a ſleepe, taking vp the remnant of my mornings nap. Well, before I roſe, my olde carle was vp, and before 1 was ready, gone abroad; when ſuddenly comming foorth of my lodging, forced to paſſe through his Chamber, I found the good olde

woman fhedding teares fo aboundantly, as I could not but greeue for
company. But, feeing me, fhe rowzed vp her felfe, and would haue
fhadowed her difcontent; yet, at laft, affured I had heard the iarre, fhe
faide fhe was forrie I had beene difquieted; the which I excufed,
faying, 'I was more greeued for her then for my difquieting, for had
that beene the worft, *Honeftie* hath beene farre woorfe troubled.' ' Ah,
good fir (quoth fhe), this is their fortune that are couetous; for I had
enough left me to haue liued like a woman, if I could haue been fo
contented; but aiming at dignitie, hath been my deftruction, and
longing after promotion hath brought me to this miferie; my laft
Hufband was accounted a good houfholder, and companion to the
beft in the parifh; but he being gone, and my hope to become a
Lady, hath ledde me to this ill bargaine. Ah, gentle *Honeftie*, I was
no meane woman when I met with him, but he thinkes, for that I
haue turned my Cloth to filke, he hath made me happie. How
happie had I beene, if I had neuer feene him; but too late it is to
wifh, and folly to complaine, for that it was my owne choice that
hath matcht my felfe with fuch a churle. He clothes me in gay
[¹ sig. E,
back] ¹coates for his owne credit, but with them cloyes me with multitudes
of difcontentments; abroad he is gone, and perchaunce I fhall not fee
him till bed time; nor are fuch trickes plaide feldome, when he
leaues nothing, what need foeuer we fhould haue of any thing, but
what the houfhold prouifion is, the beft being no better then your
yefternights fare. If he brings any bodie home with him, we muft
run to the Cookes to faue fiering; nor can a bit of bread be eaten
without an account giuen to him; he fearcheth euery corner, & chides
for euery candles end he findes mifplaced; and if, perchaunce, he
happe on a cruft, he will make as much ftirre as if it were the loffe of
a Cow; he will prie into the greace pot, and hunt after the Tappe
droppings: to be breefe, the creame pot fhould be ouerlooked by him
euery day, once at the leaft, and his fiering furucied as often; a
Cheefe cannot be cut without his leaue, nor a fticke be burned without grutching. Nor doo I fo much greeue at this in refpect of my
felfe, as for that my feruants want their due, their want being more
irkefome vnto me, then this fcant; for what will they let to reporte?
and who can blame them? or who will ftaye in fuch an houfe, and
not without reafon? fo that dayly difcredit is heaped on vs, and con-

tinuall care for looking after new feruants, neuer from vs. This is my greateſt hart breake; and my fute to haue this redreſſed, is our only breake-peace. He fumes when I informe him of what I haue heard, and ſtampes when I tell him it is not well; nor wil I tel thee all, for that this is too much, nor ſhouldſt thou haue knowne of thus much for me, except his crabbednes had made the path. But, hark ! he is come in; for the paſſion of God, hide thy ſelfe ! for if he ſhould know thou wert not gon, he will miſtruſt vs, and ſmart I ſhall for vs both.'

Now, the Diuell breake his necke, or God amend him, thoght I; yet, for feare of her harm, I was content to be lockt vp by her into a cloſet, where I was conſtraind to ſtay, while the teeth chattered in my head, before we could be rid of him. Well, at laſt, by good fortune, a companion of his fetcht him [¹ forth to dinner, who, being [¹ ſig. E 3] gone, I was let forth, an extraordinary fier being made for my wel-come down ; & to make me a mends, ſhe had ſent a bracelet ſhe had, of which he knew not, to paune, prouiding ſo good fare for my Dinner, as I was not at better all the Chriſtmas. But while we were eating of it, our mirth could not be much, her feare was ſo great of his comming home ; but we, making as quick ſpeede as our teeth would let vs, after we had doone, I thanked her, taking my leaue and departing. Wel, my backe was ſcarce turnde, when ſhe bid her men and maids to beſtirre them, that the kitchen might be dreſt vp, and the remnant of our Chriſtmas fire to be quencht and caſt into the priuie, leaſt his ſearch ſhould finde out the brandes, and that breede no little diſquietnes to them all. Alas ! poore wretch, thought I, how much feruants are there which liue at more eaſe, and ſtand in leſſe awe, then thou dooſt ! Is this a wiues portion? doubtles, no; but a iuſt plague for couetouſnes ; for they which cannot vſe a benefite when they haue it to a good purpoſe, ſhall want it when they would, and feeke it when they cannot finde it. Couetouſnes ſhall not eſcape hell ; for how farre, I pray you, was ſhe from it ? her good daies died with her matching with him ; and if there be any purgatory betweene vs and hell, ſhe was in it, and thereby at the next doore to that dungeon. I would but all couetous mindes were plagued but with a dramme of the like diſcontent; I would haue theirs but a ſeauen-nights puniſhment, whereas ſhe muſt endure, peraduenture, ſeauen yeeres torment. *Honeſtie* thinkes ſuch a meſſe of miſerie would bring them to a banquet of happines at their deliuerie from that wretched-nes. If many of our coye dames, that cannot be content with any thing, and are ſo curious, as daily dainties ſeeme nothing vnto them, were but pincht a while with her morſelles, I am perſwaded it would ſaue their huſbands a great deale of charges in their diet thence after, and would make their ſeruants much happier, by being freed from much needeles labour. Their houſes would be pulled downe, and the ¹delight of their curious poked ruffes would be ſet aſide; they would not reſpect *the* ſuperfluous diſhes they vſe, nor regarde their ſuperſtitious curioſitie in rubbing *the* flowres of their houſes: what ſhould I ſay more? they would vſe obedience towards their Huſbands more, and brawling with their ſeruants leſſe, they would thinke of their owne happie liues, & pittie others: they would ſeeke to pleaſe, and be more eaſily pleaſed; they would liue contentedly, and be thankfull for ſo great proſperitie.

[¹ sig. E 2, back]

The fiſhe that hath beene ſtricken with the hook, feares the baite; the childe that hath burnte his fingers, dreades the candle; the horſe that hath beene puniſhed with the ſpurre, ſuſpects the wagging of the heele; and the apprehended theeſe begins to thinke on the halter. What delight brings ſweete things vnto them that neuer taſted of ſharp ſauce? or, what an indifferent opinion carrie they of proſperitie, that haue neuer beene in miſerie? The vnridden Colte bites the ſnaffle, while the olde horſe is glad to play with the bit; and they that are vſed to ſhackles, weare the*m* without much annoiance; for that it is vſe that gets experience, and experience that brings profit. When a curſt Cow hath ſhort hornes, harme is leſſe ſuſpected; and if a crabbed cur be mufled, there can be no danger. There are bo:h baites to entice, and bobbes to make to forbeare; allurements to winne, and corrections to driue away; and he that thought this to be needefull, knowes beſt to vſe it, which happens alwaies to vnbrideled nouices, once good ſpeede egges vs to a ſecond aduenture; and, it twiſe a theeſe hath eſcaped the halter, he will neuer leaue vntill he purchaſe tiborne. ‘My laſt Huſband was ſo good,’ makes ſome ſo deſirous of a ſecond, as their haſtie bargaine bringes ouerlate repentance. ‘Like will to like,’ quoth the Diuell to the Collier, and ſome will neuer be ſatiſſied vntill their mouthes be filled with Clay. He that hath enough, feekes for more, and fo I carrie a great countenance, I care not how I am beloued. Indeede, what cannot money doo, that will buye any thing? and yet honeftie will purchafe that [1] which all the muck in the world cannot compaffe, [1 sig. E 3] namely, a good report for euer. Who knowes not that the couetous man cannot liue quietly? and why wil we not knowe that the afpiring minde fhall be brought lowe? The loue of your wealth is in your owne hands, but the key of your wittes kept by a higher guide. You may chofe a ritch man, and hunt after an honeft (yet ritches and honeftie goe fildome together), but to fay it fhall be for your weale, muft craue anothers leaue. Hee that giues all things, can giue thee both; and if thou wilt tafte of his liberalitie, built on his charitie, fufpect not, and fpeede well, feare, and fpeede ill; let therefore all thy care be built on his kindenes, and thou wilt be better contented with a kinde begger then a crabbed churle. To take heede by another mans harme, is a louing warning; but if thou wilt needes try, take the hazard. When our neighbours houfe is on fier, we haue neede to beftirre vs; and he that fits ftill at fuch an extremetie, is worthie to tafte of the like miferie. To looke ere we lep is good counfell, yet, to looke hartely, and lep faintly, makes many to fall into a ditch dangeroufly; well, a word to a wife man is enough, and there are few women but haue ftore of wit, if they adde difcretion vnto it. *Honeftie*, therfore, wifhes them to vfe it fo well, as they neuer fpeede ill.

A fift forte now followeth, which was a couple ftanding in the midft of the company, both of them being of equall yeares. He was a young ciuill gentleman, no leffe proper then hee feemed wife, his difcreet gouernement beautifying both; but fhe, though fhee had wit at will, and was very proper, yet lacked fhee the other ftep to wif-dome, namely, difcreetenes in her behauior. Her immodeft fondnes gaue fufpect of vnciuill lightnes, fo that her ouerforwardnes feemed to ouerlay her louers affection. Shee would hang about his neck before all that company, as a iacke of Napes doth fitting on the bear-heards fhoulder, and kiffe as openly, as a dog fcombers careleffy. She followed him at heeles like a tantinie pigge, and hong about him as if pinned to his flieue. He could not ftirre without [2] her company, [2 sig. E 3, back] nor fcarce goe to make water, but fhe would awaite on him. Thus

much did fhe not let to doe openly, and therefore I had the more
defire to fee how fhe fpent her time fecretly, which was as contrarie
as might bee; for whereas fhe would bee mad merrie in his company,
in his abfence fhe would be as mad melancholie. Shee then would
fit in a corner, as a dogge doth that is crept into a hole, hauing done
a fhroude turne, wetting her couch with teares for the lack of her
fweet heart, as a childe doth the bed for want of a chamber-pot. But,
being in a good vaine, fhee would pen paffionate fonnets, and, in that
humor did I once take her, when fhe had newly finifhed this
amorous dittie :

  S Ad is the time while my deare loue is abfent ;
    Eife waile my miffe, and tongue bewailes him wanting ;
  Heart bleedeth teares that doo encreafe my torment,
  And yeelds forth fighes which fet it felfe a panting ;
  While he is abfent, fuch is my delight,
  As is the faylers in a ftormie night.

  If I chaunce fing, with fighes my fongs be graced,
  And in my tunes, my grones my baces be ;
  Grieuous complaints are for the trebles placed ;
  The meanes be teares, the tennor miferie.
  Foure partes I beare, and want the fifte alone,
  Which is my ioye that with my loue is gone.

  When I fhould fpeake, my tongue forgets it talking ;
  When I fhould write, my fingers are benommed ;
  When I fhould goe, my feete haue loft their walking,
  And euery part is dead, of fence bereaued :
  Nor can I tell what is the caufe of this,
  Except becaufe my heart with him gon is.

  Thus dayes are nights to me, while he is wanting,
  And merieft fongs are plaintes for ioy departed ;
  ¹ My mirth is mone, my forrowe fuccor wanting,
  And fences gon, my bodie haue vnharted :
  So that I liue aliue, as being dead,
  And by his abfence fole, this death is bread.

[¹ leaf E 4]

After the felfefame order fpends fhee her well fpent time, yeelding

fuch bitter fighes, while fhe is fetting down the like paffions, as a
horfe doth hartie neefes, that is troubled with an extreame colde.
Then, paufing a while on that fhe hath done, weighing the eftate of
her lamentable cafe, fhee caftes her felfe vpon hir bed, breathing
againft the fates the rancor of her heart, after this manner : ' Vniuft
and cruell fifters, that haue prolonged my dayes to endure this
miferie; is this the force of your decree, to decreafe my ioy by
increafing my dayes ?   Haue you drawne to this length the thread of
my life, now to cut the fame with fo fharpe an edge-toole ?   Cruell
and vnkinde are ye, fo crabbedly to deale with a poore virgin, fuffer-
ing me to liue to endure this crueltie.'   There, making a full point,
would fhe lie gafping as if fhe were giuing vp the Ghoft; till at length,
hauing gathered winde, fhee would thus begin to murmur againft
Fortune : ' Vnconftant dame, fo much delighting in mutabilitie, as all
thy ioye is to alter chances !   How wauering is thy wheele, and how
vncertaine thy fauours ! the one ftill turning, and the other neuer
remaining long, where fo ere they are beftowed.   Was this the pittie
of your heart, to fet downe fo vnmercifull a doome, as I fhould
alwaies reft vnhappie ?   You whirle your wheele about to pleafe your
felfe with the turning, toffing thereby vnto me oue miferie vpon
another; then eafing me of that burthen, to make the next feeme
more difpleafing vnto me; thou fhewes me my harts ioye, and fets
me on the top of delight, to beholde the difference betweene weale
and woe.   But, from thence thou throweft me as quickly downe, as
I was ioyfully feated, letting thy wheele reft as ouerlong, while I lie
in the dungeon of vnceafing paine, as it did too too little ftay at the
[superscript 1] height of my pleafure.   Thou giues me kinde words and cruell fare, [right margin: [¹ leaf E 4. back]]
happie fightes and horrible heart-akes ; thou fhewes me reft, and fees
me with trouble, fetting me at the table of dainties, yet binding my
hands leaft I fhould touch them, fo far am I from tafting of their
fweetnes.   Vnkinde and vnconftant fortune, what chance had man-
kinde to be charmed to thy beck ? and, wherein are we more vnfor-
tunate, then in being forced to obay fortune ? '   To which interrogation, her felfe would anfwere with a flat mad fit; curfing her
parents that begot her; her birth day wherein fhee was brought forth;
the nurfe that gaue her fucke; the cradle that lulled her afleepe;
death, for that hee ended not her dayes ; and her felfe, for that fhe

was. Now tearde fhe her haire from her head ; anon fhe vnapparel-
led her felfe to hir fmooke ; then, like a fpirit would fhee daunce the
Morrice about the chamber, and foone fofling her felfe downe by the
fiers fide, fit no les fenceles then her actions had been witleffe, a long
time refting as in a traunce. But, at laft, as ouerlate comming to
her felfe, fhee would, looking on her felfe, feeme to bee afraide of
her felfe ; forrowfull to fee the fruite of her forfaken reafon ; and
rifing, would foone make her readie. Being readie, fhee fell vpon
her knees, crying the Gods mercie, and powring forth aboundance of
teares, in token of her penitencie. And after that, being indeede in
her righteft minde, fhee tooke her lute, finging to her fingering this
fonnet :

> WHat booteth loue, that liking wants his ioye ?
>   Grieuous that ioy which lackes his hearts-content ;
> The fight of fweete in tafling of anoy,
> Ads but more griefe to former hearts-torment.
>
> What fweet in loue to liue debarr'd of loue ?
> Soure is that fweete as honny mixt with gall ;
> Loue with vnreft the heart to paffions moue,
> That fighing fing, and finging figh withall.
>
> 1 While eyes beholde the pleafure of my heart,
> Heart ioyes through eyes in gayning of that fight ;
> But when that pleafure from mine eyes doth part,
> Heart partes with ioy, and refts in heauie plight.
>
> And tongue may fing a hei ho for my heart,
> That through mine eyes doth finde both ioy and fmart

[¹ sig. F]

Which mufick would bee fo metamorphofed, as, in truth, her
finging would turne to fighing, and her playing to complaining, when,
in a rage, fhe would throwe her lute downe, beginning to dilate on her
loues vnkindnes, that could be fo cruell to ftay foure and twentie
houres from her. Now, found fhe fault with her felfe for being fo
fond on him, that forbeared fo careleffy her companie ; and, by and
by, in a great rage fwearing to forfake him, fhe fetled her felfe to
frame a rayling letter for a laft farewell. But, before fhee had fcarce
written an vnkinde worde, fhe paufed on the matter, cafting both pen,

inke, and paper from her; yet, vpon her fecond aduice, about fhe goes with a frefh charge to pen a crabbed charme, and had gone fo farre as fhe had fet downe, *Fie, vnkinde wretch!* And there, againe, in a doubt of going forward, or leauing the reft vndone, fhee gnawed fo long vpon her pen in ftudying what to doe, as fhe had eaten it almoft quite vp. But, at laft, with a refolution, fhe played the woman, falling into fo kinde a vaine of fcoulding, as fhe had charged him with a thoufand difcourtefies for miffing one nights reforte vnto her. And, as fhe was concluding her colour, with a proteftation neuer to defire to fee his face againe, in came one of her fifters with newes that Mafter *Anthony* was belowe. Which fo quite purged her of her melancholie, as in a rage fhe rent the paper, and caft all her anger with it into the fier, pofting with fuch hafte to her fweete-heart, as in ftead of running downe, fhe tumbled downe a whole paire of ftayres. Which bad beginning was carelefly put ouer with the conceiued ioy of his prefence; fhee entertaining ¹ him with a kiffe, for that he was ¹ ⁱⁿ ᵗʰᵉ margin: [¹ sig. F back] not forward enough to beftowe on her the like fauour. But ere long, fhee began to perceaue that Mafter *Anthonie* was changed, being nothing fo frolick of his kindnes as bee had been, and it was no maruel. For fome reporte of her fore-ufed fondnes was come to his eares, that being no fmall froft to nip his former affection; fo that his onely comming was to make that conclufion fhe was of late imagining, foone finifhing in wife and difcreet tearmes that her fuf-pect was penning. Vpon whofe departure, with the paine left of his refolution, my minion fel into a found, there being fuch a ftirre for her recouerie, as what for running for *aqua vitæ*, pofting for ale, plying warme cloathes, and fuch like, there was no leffe rule then is in a tauerne of great reforte. ‘ Here, forfooth,’ faith fhe that had the *aqua,* ‘ *come quickly;* ’ ‘ By and by,’ anfwered fhee, being called that went for the ale; the reft no other wife replying to euery queftion and commaunde. Well, at length life was got in her; though no words could bee drawne from her; but, being got to bed, fhe fong ere long like a bird of Bedlam.

In which fit I left her, more pittying her peeuifhnes then her paffions; the rather leffe regarding either, for that I knew that violent fit would not ftay long. But, to tell you what *Honeftie* thought all this while, for I knowe that is your longing; and, if you

beſhrowe any body, blame her for not letting you haue your will
ſooner, by keeping me ſo long there againſt my will.   For vnwilling
I was to ſtay there ſo long, and as loath to leaue her before ſhee had
left at a full point.   That you might know all, was my wiſh; and
ſince I haue mine now, you ſhall not bee long without your wil.
She neuer ſighed hartely, but I laught as merely, being as often
readie to piſſe my breeche for ioye, as ſhe was to ſhed teares, which
came from her as had at commandement.   And, wherefore was
Honeſtie thus vncharitable, thinke you, reioycing at his neighbours
miſerie?   Surely, becauſe her ſelfe was ſo fooliſh to bee ſo diſquietly

[¹ ſig. F ₂] moued with nut-ſhels: would it not haue made a ¹ horſe breake his
halter, to ſee her mumble to her ſelfe as an ape mowes at his own
ſhaddow?   Doubtles,—may I ſpeake it without the ſuſpeᴄt of arro-
gancy?—*Honeſtie* hath as much holde of his ciuilitie, as a mare hath
of her honeſtie; and yet, I might as well be hanged as be kept from
being merry when ſhe mourned.   A Camelion cannot change her
ſelfe into more kinde of colours then ſhee would vſe change of
motions.   Sometimes ſhee would walke with her hands claſped, and
her eyes caſt vp to heauen, as if ſhee were ſent for, with all ſpeede to
render an account of her paſſions.   Anon, ſhe would runne about the
chamber like a hare that had loſt her way; then, by and by, would
ſhe houle like a kinde dogge that had loſt her maſter.   After that,
girne like a Monkie that ſees her dinner; and ere long be as dead as a
dore naile, lying by the fier ſide as a block doth at the backe of a
chimney.   And this laſt *ſimile* proues not worſt, for ſhe burned no
leſſe through the cinders of too kinde affeᴄtion, then the logge dooth
with the helpe of charke-coles.

Was not this a monſtrous fit, that had ſo many motions?   Why,
if *Honeſtie* ſhould tell you how ſhee would ſometimes bite of her
owne nailes, knocking the wall with her feete, praunſing on the
ground, and lepping of and on the bed, you would thinke hee had
to doe with an vnruly iade.   Fie, no, ſhe was a mankinde creature!
and I would not offend them for a kingdome; but this *Honeſtie* is
ſuch a peſtilent ſpie-fault, as he cannot ſee a wench out-ſtart the
bounds of modeſtie, but ſtraight he hollowes the ſight of a ſtriker,
thinking it vnpoſſible that if ſhee want maidenly behauiour, ſhee can
haue womanly honeſtie.   Well, I knowe ſome will ſay hee is a pick-

thanke; but were not they fhonne-thankes, they would fpeake better of *Honeflies* fonne. But thus much for *Honeflies* credit; and now, againe to my craft-loue, that had crauled fo farre into affeftions extremitie, as fhe had loft the habit of her cuftomers curtefie. I went once more of deuotion to fee her, becaufe I left her in fo extreame an agonie, and it was ¹within two dayes after; Whome then I [¹ ſig. F 2, found clafped within a new louers pawes, as iocunde with him of ᵇᵃᶜᵏ] mine honeftie, as euer I fawe her pleafant with Mafter *Anthonie.* And what thought *Honeflie*, then, thinke you? in faith, no otherwife then I am affured you doe now. I thought vpon fuch fondnes the prouerbe was builded, 'hot loue wil be foone colde;' but enough of that in another place, and thus much more of her at this time.

She was as glad, I warrant you, of a louer, as a weried iade is of a faire way; and he, being tyred, is not more glad of a ftable, then fhe was defirous of a babell; it is onely for rime at this inftant, and therefore let it paffe (I pray you) with your fauour; but, whether it doth or no, I befhrewe, my name if I get any blame. For my tongue will not amble out of the trueth, though I fhould digge out my guttes with the Spurre, 'Beware leaft you offend.' There is one ftill at mine elbowe, and fayes I muft take heede how I diffemble, fince *Honeflie* is become a deitie. I would I were not, or went not fo vnuifible: for then I fhould not craule fo eafily into maydens chambers, and heare them boafte of fo many fauours beftowed by them on this day; fo many kiffes giuen to one; another vnloofing her garter, yea, and fhe thought hee went not high enough. Well, but that I am mercifull, and will not name you that are fo immodeft as to boaft of fuch lightnes, for if I fhould, I fhould quite fray away many of M. *Anthonies* companions from beftowing their affeftions on fo liberall whipfters. But I faye no more, for fhame, hoping I fhall haue no caufe to fpeake of the like againe, you will become fo ciuill; then, thus much for you, and now to another.

This way a coy dame, whofe nice ftrangenes moued me not to the leaft admiration; fhe ftoode iuft at the doore, to whom not fo few as twenty had in my veine made fuite. They were of fundrie fciences, and of all degrees, that had tooke the deniall of her, which made mee the rather to admire the caufe; and, to obtaine my longing, I lodged my ²felfe that night vnder her bed. When fhe was layed, and one of [² ſig. F 3]

her mothers maides with her, fhee began thus to parly : ' Wot you
what, *Nan* (quoth fhe), how many futors thinkes thou haue I fent
packing to daye ? ' ' Not fo many (anfwered the maide) as you did
the laft time you were there.' ' Yes, faith, girle, double ' (replied fhe).
' And found you fo many faultes in thefe (quoth *Nan*) as you did in
the other ? ' ' Nay, I trow, wench (anfwered fhe), I let not them
paffe in whom I difcouer not many ouer-flippes.' ' And what were
their faults, I pray you ? ' quoth the girle. ' Some of them had ftore
of wealth (anfwered fhe), but little honeftie; other were honeft
enough, but too too hard fauoured; fome had good faces and bad bodies;
other being proper, had crabbed countenances ; fome were amiable for
fauour, perfeét of bodie, yet ill legged ; other, which were well legde,
fhaled with their feete, or were fplafooted; and, to be briefe, they
that trode right, were either clouterly caulfed, tree like fet, fpindle
fhankte, or bakerly kneed; onely there were two exquifitely fhapte,
whereof one was too tall, and the other too too lowe. Thus much
for their parts, and now to their properties.

' They that were wealthy were meanely qualited, and they that
had many good properties were moniles; fome had good toungs, and
fpake well, hauing as ill geftures; others were rich and feemed wife;
thofe I fufpeéted to be wenchers. And, to make as fhorte woorke in
telling thee of them, as I made fpeedie hafte in fending them packing, either I miflikte their eftates, fcorned their perfonages, lothed
their want of qualities, or could not away with their kinde of wooing.'
' But fhal I be fo bolde (quoth *Nan*) to afke you one more queftion ? '
' I, twentie, and thou wilt ; for, in faith, I haue no lift to fleepe.' ' In
footh forfooth, then (quoth the girle), what manner of man fhall he
be with whom you will match ? ' ' Mary, fuch a one (anfwered fhe)
as fhalbe the onely matchles creature in the worlde.' ' But how will
you meete with him ? ' replyed *Nan*. ' As he fhall light vpon me by
Fortune.' ' But Fortune is blinde (quoth [1] the wench), and may lead
him to another in fteade of you.' ' Yet, as fhe is blinde (replyed the
other), fo is fhe a Goddeffe, a good fupporter of my chaunces; and I
know my reporte is fet fo neere her elbowe, as fhe cannot forget me
if fhe would.'

I, marry, firs, you talk of a wench, and what w[o]ts this of a proud
one ? is it not great pittie but nature fhould haue compaffion on this

neate creature, and ſhape for her a mirrour of meane worth ? Now,
of my troth, *Honeſtie* likes ſuch an one; and why, thinke you ? I will
tell you my reaſon, and if it iumpes with your conceite, ſay you mette
with a kill Crowe. I am aſſured that they that are of my minde
ſhall eſcape a great deale of trouble; for, of mine honeſtie, if I ſhould
light on ſuch an one, I know certainely I ſhould be quickly rid of a
neere miſhap, in being preuented of matching with a nice ninnie by
a nice body ; for not being the paragon of the worlde, would keepe
me from marrying with the onely paltrie one of *the* worlde ; whether,
then, thinke you ſuch to be profitable members of a common wealth ?
Howſoeuer you think, *Honeſtie* hath ſaid, he thinks them hurtfull to
none that eſcape the*m*, for *that* their folly onely hurtes themſelues,
dooing good to others, in the like manner as he hath tolde you. Trot
you, and you will, to trye your Fortune, and runne to wooe ſuch
curious cuſtomers ; but ſay I bid you take heede, leaſt you refiſt good
lucke, by being importunate to wooe them, with whome you ſhall
winne a maſſe of manner-les Monkiſh trickes. And I ſpeak eſpecially
to you, that hunt after monſters of modeſtie, defiring to haue the
maidens you would matche with, as very matrones as your mothers.
Beware you light not vpon an ouerwearied, conceipted follom-bird,
being one that hath beene ſo curious to be talkte with of any, as, hauing
liued ouer long without one, is become glad of any. *Honeſtie* knowes
ſuch, and you may be troubled with ſuch, and how can you thinke
your ſelues vnworthie ? In faith, ill conceited birds, if you thinke
your ſelues ſo vnwiſe, as you are vnable to gouern a wilde wench, you
will [1] ſhewe your ſelues more fooliſh if you match with a nice no- [1 leaf F 4]
maide. But what ſaide *Honeſtie* ? be there any ſuch ? I, that there
are, ordained, for the nonce, to nurture ſuch noddies. It is as eaſie to
be miſlead by hypocriſie, as it is follie to truſt to an vncertaintie ; and
it is more vncertaine to know now a daies whether a woman bee
honeſtly modeſt, or knauiſhly coye, then whether a Smithfeelde horſe
will proue good or iadiſh.

See how I haue a tale by the end, of a ninnie of my now handled
maidens qualitie, which was a Miſers Daughter in the low Countries.
Who was ſo proper a peece of fleſh, as I can tell you we haue not
many Oyſter women that out goes her in hooke ſhoulders. By
reporte ſhe was a louely one ; but that ſhe was monſtrous blobber

lipt, and ftoopt fomewhat vnreafonably in the vpper parte of her
backfide ; but that is no matter, her father was richer then moft in
that Countrie, and why fhould not fhe thinke her felfe the propereft
of a thoufand? of *Honeflies* word, fo by likelyhoode fhe did; and if
you fay not fo anon, then fay I haue heard a lye.   She thought her
felfe fo proper, as none vnder a Burges his eldeft Sonne might fue
vnto her, and he too to be no faultie gallant; for he with all commers fhould be fo furely fifted by her, to fee whether they trod their
fhooes awry or no, as the Miller doth the grift before he mingles
chalke amongft it.   She would haue a fling at their heades, to fee
whether they were round like a ball, or long like a bottell; and fo
from euery parte, til fhe were paft the vndermoft parte of their
Pantoples.   And, in all of them fhe would be fure to finde fome fault
or other, the leaft being a fufficient caufe to cut off their proceedings.
Thus dealt fhe fo long, as at laft her doultifh age was vnawares come
vpon her, making her fuftie curiofitie a fhamefull mockerie throughout the Countrie; fo that the generall reporte of her bruted ignomynie
made her growe glad of any companie; and now faine would fhe be married, though loth to encreafe her fhame by matching with farre worfe

[¹ leaf F 4,
back] then fhe had refufed being offered, and ¹ therefore, thinking to hinder
the make-fpeede of murmured ignominie, with a craftie colour of a
continuing care to couple her felfe to one of Fortunes darlings, fhe
concluded there fhould be a Lotterie, and whofe chaunce it was to be
drawen by her fhould onely poffeffe her withered felf.   You muft
thinke that many were glad to win her ; for whom almoft will not
wealth wooe to a bad bargaine ?   My ftorie reportes that of all fortes,
fome for paftime, and others for profite, put their fcrolles into
fortunes budget, and on the day when my minions draft fhould be
manifefted, who fhould baue her by lot, but fuch an one as *Tom-
witles* is, that will cry if one offer to take away his bable !

A futable mate for fo long a fearch ; there was but one grand
foole in a Country, and fee how Fortune had kept her for him.
Now, fuch chaunce follow like curious coye wenches ; and may
neuer wifer perfons match with them.   And are they not, thinke you,
the meeteft for them ?   For they defire to haue them that haue the
fmalleft faults, and *Honeflie* thinks it *the* leaft fault in a man to be a
foole.   Who is more proude then a foole? and what woman more

coy, for the moſt parte, then ſhe that hath leaſt reaſon for it ? The
Crow likes her own birde beſt, though it be the blackeſt ; and would
not we haue women thinke well of themſelues ? I pray you let them
haue their willes ; or they will, whether you will or no ; and if you
like them not, you may leaue them ; and with as good reaſon as they
will be ſure to deale ſo with you, vnleſſe you highly pleaſe them.
The Aſſe hath a curious eye, and _that_ makes his pace ſo ſlowe ; for
ſhort legges will trippe at euery ſtone, and what, ſhe is not afraide to
fall on a ſtone ! And reaſon too, but they will neuer be happie,
vntill Tom foole and his fellowes be baniſht for throwing ſtones at
them, which often hurt their bellies, whereas their falling breakes but
their knees. Alas ! poore aſſes, that your eyes cannot keepe you
from burthens, as they make you ouer-leape often vnknowne dia-
mondes. But what are more pretious then pleaſing thoughts ? and
what fancies are more full of pleaſure then ¹ thoſe that moſt extoll [¹ ſig. G]
our ſelues ? This arrogancie is an infectious peſtilence ; for we get
pride one from an other, as we purchaſe the ✦plague in a mortalitie.
But once more returne we to the merry talke of our coye Maiden.

After a long progreſſe paſſed in deſcription of the ſweet hart ſhe
would haue, being ſuch an exquiſite proper qualited Squire, as is
ſcarſe one in a whole Countrey, _the_ maid fell with her to this point :
' Now, of my troth (quoth ſhe), by your leaue, I am not of your
minde ; for ſuch a matchles fellowe is as meete a baite to entice many
women to doo his wife wrong, as a faire woman ſhall haue ſutors to
doo her Huſband a ſhrewde turne. And, therefore, as I would not
wiſh to be matcht with ſuch a crabbed peece of fleſh as none can
fancie, ſo deſire not I to holde a mark for euery one to ſhoote at, the
rather for that there are fewe men which will refuſe a kinde offer.
Beware when the woman wooes ! if ſhe be perceiued to be forward
to ſome diſpoſitions, ſhe ſhall not want the offering of a bob ; ſo
that the bobbing bable ſhall bob the foole with her own curious
choice.' Which knauiſh quip did ſo nip my Miſtres Daughter on the
head, as in troth ſhe left arguing, and fell harde to ſcolding.

This is bobbing with a witnes, thought _Honeſlie_ ; but ſurely it
were pittie it ſhould not be true in ſome caſes ; and in thoſe onely
would I wiſh it true, that ſtriue ſo far to out-goe their fellowes in
ſuperexcellent obiectes.

Beware the Foxe that hath the fmootheft fkinne! it is figne his coate is olde, and his wit not young; he will be fure of a goofe in ftore, when many of his neighbours fhall want one. I know fome, about whome Nature hath beftowed fo long time in fhaping faire faces with proper bodies, as fhe hath at laft for hafte beene conftrained to let them paffe with vnperfect hartes. She muft performe her ftinte, and a time is limited her to fafhion euery childe; by reafon, then, they muft haue the pureft harts, *that* haue the vnlikeft fhapes. I know what you will fay, and therby, wil onely feeme to gainfay *Honeftie*, for that it is a Prouerbe, *'Crooked without, and crabbed within.* Of troth, I muft confeffe, that it is very likely, though not alwaies true (for, no work-man but hath fometimes a mifchaunce happen to his moft curious worke, after the finifhing therof, either by a fall or fuch like cafuall chaunce), that a halting bodie hath a diffembling hart, and a mifhapen creature a crabbed difpofition; and we doe finde it commonly, that vnder fouleft afpects are hidden the faireft harts, though I know women accompt blacke thinges to be of leaft worth. But fearch againe, and looke what dye is more perfect, or what will take foile fooner, then the milke-like white? well, the maidens propofition pleafed *Honeftie* ouerwell, as you may geffe by my long ftay vpon it; but I will affure you it difpleafed no les my yong miftres. Alas! it is a little thing that will not difpleafe them whom nothing can pleafe: and fhall we thinke a wench could poffibly pleafe her long, vnto whom fo many men were difliking? Now furely he fhall haue a new accompte, that reckons on leffe then this; namelye, that his matching with fuch a minion, which was fo curious to be pleafed, will craue as great care to be kept pleafed, as a iade will require arte to be kept from tiring. Nor doo I fay fhe wil be tired; I would rather be driuen to affirme he fhalbe iaded, though with fuch an one as will neuer be tired.

But let fuch as my Miftres Many-miflike is, take heede leaft by their coye kindenes they kill their harts whome they would gladly faue after, with all their arte, and cannot. How eafie is it to put that away with our little finger, which we would willingly recouer againe with both our hands. I haue knowen fome Faulkoners that haue beene fo curious in dieting their Hawkes, as a nice curtefan is of her fare; and yet fometimes they haue fearcht a whole day after the kill-

[1 sig. G, back]

ing of a carrion Crowe, and mift of it too. The faire laftes not alwaies; and fuch as lightly regarde a good bargaine when it is proffered, may trie the market a twelue moneth after, and miffe of the like offer. The rolling ftone gathers no moffe, nor the running fan¹cie is worth the catching. They fhalbe fure to meete with a fickle [¹ sig. G ²] hart that match with fuch a wauering loue; and an vnconftant affection is better loft then found. And for that I am entred into the path of vnconftancie, I wil come to a feauenth enemie, which a couple harboured that ftood behinde the doore.

He was a Prentice that had foure yeers to ferue, which I certainely vnderftoode afterwards, though at that inftant I gefte no leffe by his fearefulnes to be feene; wel, thefe had fo wooed and wonne the one the other, as fure they were, hauing remained fo by the fpace of three yeers; yet now there was diflike growen betweene them; firfte, fpringing from the woman, that was difcontented that fhe had alreadie loft fo much time, being yet bound to endure a longer ftay. Who knowes not the certaintie of her prefumption, confirmed by an order of the Cittie of London (which is, that if any man, ftanding bound for the feruing of yeeres, entangle himfelfe and marrie before the tearme of his yeeres ended, he fhall double his prentifhip), and, therfore, muft fhe either out-ftay them, or binde him by the haftie match to feauen yeers more feruice. Vpon this inconuenience, miflike harboured in her bofome, hauing tied that with her toung which fhe could not loofe with her hands; fo that mad melancholly fhe was for the matche made by her felfe, that tooke fo fmall delight therein.

Now, I would all might be ferued with *the* fame fauce, thought *Honeftie*, that fo foone tying themfelues, defire as foone to be loofed; and, it is great maruell when it falles out otherwife, efpecially in thefe daies, wherin conftancie is made a hackney. *Lingring loue breedes miflike*; and how can that loue be faithfull that is faftned with fo flender a thong? There is a thing which maintaines the coherence of two harts, which, if it be long wanting, our loue will proue but watrifh affection; I meane, that certaintie of an euerlafting happines, with an affurance of a continuall earthly pleafure. There comes many faire Horfes into Smithfeelde in a twelue moneth, which make many that ²are fped alreadye, to wifh themfelues vnprouided, to [² sig. G ², back]

deale with them; for all men haue not keeping for two Geldings.
It is time that makes a iade knowen; and our knowledge *that* wifhes
him further from vs. Many thinges muft alter in feauen yeeres, for
that wonders happen in a moment. In one day a begger and a King
are made equal; both the pompe of the one, and the poore eftate of
the other, being buried in duft. Loffes come fooneft vnlooked for,
and the worft bargaines are gotten with the greateft fearch; neede
raifeth the market; and much enquirie after a commoditie engenders
fufpect there is fcarcitie thereof. What cannot golde doo? and may
it not, then, eafily conuert a hart that longes after it? There are many
entifing baites that change many mindes; & who wil not ftriue for the
golden Apple? onely except thofe that know they cannot get it,
though they are deferuing thereof, which impoffibilitie muft needs
hatche miferie. How be cormorants more plagued, then by a difap-
pointment of their purpofe? They that foreftall markets, make often
times but bad bargaines, as well as the fluggard that comes a day after
the Faire.

Is it not folly to ftriue to keepe a wet Eele by the taile? or what
commoditie arifeth of holding the Diuell by the great toe? the one
is ouer-quick, and the other wonderous ftrong; and, in *Honefties*
iudgement, a knowne loffe, the fooner it comes, the leffe it greeues;
and better it is to be without company, then to be matcht with an
enemie. Slipperie ware is not *the* beft Marchandize; and what
requires more care, then Glaffe that is moft brittle? I know you wil
fay a womans hart is as tender, and *that* I think no leffe. Then, fince
we muft hazard our welfare, that are conftrained to deale with fuch
pure metall, being tied to that traffique; let vs not beftowe all our
hope on a peece we know muft ftay fo long by vs, before we can
make profite thereof. *Honeftie* is rather a profeffed folicitor for a
woman, then a counfeller to a man; but, for that both men and
[¹ sig. G 3] women are troubled with the like difeafes, let them ¹ vfe my plafter
that like beft of my knowledge. Where loue ftrikes the bargaine,
their liking cannot ftart backe; but vnles he be bound by his agreement, affection is a fickle fellowe. What furer couenant then fetled
loue? But they which refpect not their worde, will hardly regarde
an oathe. Honeftie is all, for hee is the father of conftancie; and a
fig for that loue which muft be tied by the lawe! If we fofter a

fnake, fhe will fting vs by the bofome; and hee that fues for an enemie, is worthy to haue his pate broken with want of honeftie. A tedious fuite makes ritch lawyers and leefing clients; and a defire to haue all, makes vs often to loofe all.

I haue heard of a Gentleman that tied himfelfe to a poore maide after the manner aforefaide, meaning to marrie with her after the death of his father, for that hee durft not doe it while hee liued. Hee maintained her paffing brauely, running himfelfe greatly into debt, through the large expenfes fhe lafht out. Which curious and ritch fetting forth, made many to looke after her, which otherwife would not haue thought on her. A blazing ftarre prefages alteration, as the Aftronomers holde it; and doubtles, a proper woman gayly ap-parelled, breeds miracles in mens mindes. A prancing horfe moues wondring, when a fure nagge onely pleafeth the rider; fo while fhee liued according to her birth, few or none regarded hir; but now fet foorth as readie for fale, her gallantnes engendred thoughts of fome great portion to be fallen by an vnlooked for accident. Nor will friends let to fpeake, to make a friend fpeede well, and hire of the fame minde gaue forth that it was fo indeede; vpon which reporte many wooers were drawne to trie their fortunes, and amongft them a ritch farmers fonne fet in his foote to hazard his happe. Whome her parents and friends fo well liked, being his fathers onely childe, as they began to perfwade their daughter to take it while it were offered, after this maner: 'Tut, wench (quoth they), while the graffe growes the fteed ftarues; and, as foone goes the young fteare as the ¹olde oxe [¹ sig. G 3, to the market. Young heads are fickle; and fuppofe he fhould play back] falfe, how fhould we remedie it? Golde bies lawe now a dayes; and may not a bribe eate vp a fure title, as wee haue heard a fat hog did a poore mans glaffe of oyle? He that can giue mofte, fhall be fure to fpeed beft; and you knowe, daughter, your father is not able to wage lawe againft fo ritch an enemie. Why, woman, you haue not feene him this fortnight; and how knowe we but he hath a wife in a corner? By our Lady, girle, fuch windefalles happen not often, as is this day put into your mouth. By cock and pie, doo as you will, but if you doo refufe this proffer, we will denie you our bleffing.' Which counfell ftroke fo deepe into her confcience, as it fent packing all the affe&ion her protefted loyaltie had promifed, and turned it fo to the farmers fonne, as in fhort time hee maried with her.

By that time, as my minion had been married three or foure dayes, thither comes pofting my out-ioynted Gentleman : of whofe ftarke ftaring mad difcontentment, vpon the hearing of his willow guift, *Honeflie* lifts not to ftand, fince you can imagine it was great : but what remedie ? What wife man would fue for a falfe-hearted begger ? or what gaine fhould be got by the recouerie of a broken pipkin ? In feeking to haue plagued her, he fhould haue punifhed himfelfe, adding but fhame to the loffe of a greater expence, and in the ende, recouered a flap with a foxe tale. Well, I pittie him, becaufe of his kindnes which was fo croffed ; but if *Honeflie* heares of any fuch kinde affes hereafter, he will make as good fporte thereat as the boyes doo at the foole of a Morrice. Are they not worthie to lie by the heeles, that purchafe the countertenor with fo plaine a prickfong ? I warrant you it prict and pincht him too ; but his father was the more willing to releafe him, for that he hopte that loffe had gaind him more wit. *Honeflie* could tell you of a thoufand that haue been ferued after the fame order, they hauing promifed to ftaye one for another ; fome a yeare, others more or leffe, whereof fome haue had their [1] hope found within a fortnight of their day, and then, thinking themfelues neereft to haue their willes, in come takers, putting their nofes quite befides the fweete fent of their forefpoken bedfellowes. This can be no fmall griefe to a kinde, conftant heart, that hath, peraduenture, refufed many good likely hoods to ftay for fuch a light hufwife. He that will thinke himfelfe fure to a woman, or fhee that will build on a mans conftancie, till the parifh prieft hath faide *God giue yee ioye*, and the brides bed hath borne it firft nights waight, he is not of *Honeflies* minde, though I wifh it were otherwife.

It is as good to bee affured of the horne, as to bee made fure to an vnconftant heart, for they that looke for les fhall be difappointed. God forbid *Honeflie* fhould fay it were vnpoffible, that two may loue conftantly vnmarried feuen yeres ; but he may aboue that two fay, fuch are fcarce found in feauen ages. Walke but to Weftminfter,—a place, in faith, where conftancie is as little vfed as wit in Bedlam,—and yet there (I warrant you) you fhall haue your head filled with tales

[1 leaf G 4]

of vnconftant louers. Goe, likewife, to Poules (a path as well haunted
with hunters of honeftie as *Kemps* head is fometimes peftered with
knauerie), and blame *Honeftie* if there you heare not outcries of
wauering wenches. Long lanes and broade ftreetes, little cottages
and manner places, are at this day, by report, bolftred with naught fo
much as with vnconftant mindes. Whereby, what through the
forrowe Conftancies complainte moues, and the griefe honefties
broken pate procures, it is great pittie wee fhould not haue many
knackes to knowe knaues by, and as many Iigges to gird garifh girles
with. I[n] peticoate lane is a pocket ful of new fafhions, the drift
whereof is, that firft commers fhould be firft ferued; but they meane
no commers which enter not the placket. In Shooelane there is one
that felles running lether, the vertue whereof is maintained with
liquor of a careles heart; fo that hee or fhee that cannot play light of
loue, fhall not be cuftomed there. Withdrawe your felues [1]to Crooked [1 leaf G 4, back]
lane, and, of *Honeflies* credite, you fhall finde more traps to catch
Rats and Mice there, then conftant louers in *Shordich* Church at
midnight.

What fhall I fay, fince the art of Cony-catching hath foreftalled
good inuention? but fie on the diuell that driues fuch wits to fo bad
a bargaine, as to be forft to fpend their time in no better ftudies.
They haue need of good intelligencers that fhall intermeddle with
trickes of Coning-fhifts; for mine own part, I had rather wade to
the middle in Loues whirle-poole, then to the anckles in the brooke
of vnconftancie. And yet, force perforce, by Loues appoyntment, I
muft haue a fling at her followers. Let them flye to the gallowes,
for *Honeftie*, that loues her fo well; and my fling will driue
them to a worfe place, vnleffe they leaue her. Vp hill and downe
hill is a very troublefome labour; but vp the ladder and downe
the rope ends many ones miferie. What fteeper way then to
the height of affection? and how many often poft vp and down
betweene that and the valley Likings-recantation. ' I recant' now a
daies followes Loues heeles like his fhadowe; it is a halting crack-
halter, and a hurtfull hinderloue, and beft he fhall be knowne by his
ftumpe foote. I meane not a mifhapen ledge, but a refting loue,
that either makes fuch a full poynt in the beginning, as he can goe
no further, or els ftands at a ftay two or three quarters, not knowing

whether it were beft to goe forwards or backwards. Extreames are
as daungerous as ftretches : for, as many ioynts are out-fet or crackt by
the one, fo many vncurable hurts are receiued by the other. *Honeftie*
thinkes a feuen nights fpace is too fhort a time to faften a true louers
knot; but he that out ftayes *the* moneth, may learne as much in that
time as is needfull to be knowne. A longer time is pleafing to them
that haue barres to hinder their forwardnes, but he that may goe on
without hinderances, if hee aimes at a longer refpite, take it on
Honeflies word, hee workes but vpon aduantage. They that build
their affection vpon reafon, are like to remaine moft conftant; for
[¹ sig. H]   ¹ where a condition of profite binds the futors, there a long day will
not likely be broken. But this reafon craues wifedome, the experience whereof muft awaite on Loues followers, the practife being
nothing but this, a care in our choyce to maintaine the maine
chaunce. That is, that they which haue little, doe fancie none but
fuch as haue fomewhat, and they that haue nothing, either to match
with fuch as haue enough to ferue themfelues and others, or els to fit
ftill in the chimney corner. Al muft meafure their liking according
to the depth of their defire, to the end they may liue with contentment, which will (I warrant you) nourifh conftancie.

Now followeth another fort, which are not the leaft enemies Loue
hath, being our common courting lads, who take fuch pleafure in
their pregnant wits, and fo great glorie in their readie tongues, as a
wench cannot peepe forth the doores, but they muft haue a fling at
her beautie. Firft comes, 'faire ladie, God faue you'; and then followes,
that the fight of fuch a blazing Commet makes them ftand at the
gaze, for that fuch fights are feldome feene. After, enfues their
application, falling from the celeftiall creatures to their earthly Goddeffes, extolling their beauties to fuch a height, as, when they can goe
no further, hauing forgotten their way backwards, they fall downe
headlong, breaking the necke of Good reafon. Then come they to
the good parts of their bodies, and from thence to a fupernaturall
view of their hidden vertues, building vpon the prouerbe, *A faire
face cannot haue a crabbed heart*, though many of them find by experience, but crabbed entertainment to proceede from thofe their
celeftial obiects; yet the moft, what through their quicke conceipts,
falfe proteftations and vfuall reforting into their companies, bring

many into fuch a fooles paradice, as they harpe on nothing but
mariage. And maruell not, feeing we haue many fo forward
wenches, that if a man looke but earneftly vpon them, they thinke
verely hee is inamoured of their beautie; but fhal he fpeake, and fay
he loues them, "my father, my mother, [1] and all my friends muft be [1 sig. H,
made priuie to his proceedings, for I know he will haue me." back]

Alas! light hearts that are lead away with euery kinde blaft;
know ye not that our age flowes with fine wits, that muft borrow
their practife of fuch like patients? Doe not many men cheapen,
that meane not to buy? & think you to want fuch cuftomers? How
many come into a Faire with neuer a farthing in their purfes, and yet
for fafhion fake will afke the price of a coftly peece of worke! Our
tongues ftand vs in little charges for reparations; and feeing they
weare not, we will not fpare to wagge them. But this is beft knowne
to you women, whom nature bindes to the greateft practice, hauing
giuen you no other weapon; yet, I may tell you, men cannot want
that inftrument, efpecially in their wooing matters. But did many of
both kindes vfe it leffe, both you and they fhould fpeede neuer the
worfe, for you fhould miffe of many fond faithles fpeeches, and they
fhould march without as many kinde hit-home floutes. They fhould
not, playing with the fire, be burnt with the flame, and remaine
helples through your careles pitie; nor fhould you be intrapt in the
fnares of their fmoothe words, decreafing your glorious beauty by
hopeles conceites of obtaining your wifhed happines.

Many honeft mindes taken at their words, are bound to bad bargaines, when, on the contrarie part, a crackt credit regardes neither
his own reputation or anothers welfare. How eafie is a free horfe
tired, a good edge-toole fpoyled, and a kinde heart furfeited? A dull
iade will rather be fpurde to death then breake his pace; and with a
bad knife we may affay to cut any thing, without dooing it much
harme; but woe bee vnto that heart, whofe mildenes makes it felfe
fubiect to a counterfeit kindnes. You fhall fighe forth your forrow,
while they fmile at their good fucceffe; they, building their affurance
of being no lofers on your good difpofitions, that ferue for ftables to
reft their hopes in; your good natures muft bee but roumes for
hacknies that neuer knowe their mafters, and your kinde [2] hearts to [2 sig. II 2]
ferue for mangers to feede their bad conceites. Their trotting fhall

faften to your heads heapes of proclamations, the claufes whereof
fhall breede thoufand of doubted miferies, and ten thoufands of carefull heartbreakings.   Their counterfeit frendfhip fhall hinder faithfull
and louing proceedings, hurting affe&ion by hindring it from it
defarte, with keeping it from receiuing the due of requitall.   That
bootles conftancie fhall banifh faithfull loyaltie by crabbed croffes,
and purchafe to it felf, through a haples conclufion, a cart-loade of
carefull extremities.   True-meaning thereby fhall be deceaued on
both fides, and kind-heartednes plagued with ouer-furefet affe&ion.
Loue fhal be banded away with the racket of diffimulation, and
beaten at laft into the hazard Defpaire by his fporting enemie.   What
a great loffe will followe fuch a chafe, and how great expence of
hearts griefe muft enfue fo fhroude a game, geffe you, that lie
condemned in the like charges.   Onely *Honeftie* pitties fuch a
paftime that ends with fo fmal pleafure, and wil now come to giue
you warning of what he hath feene happen in the like cafes of little
confcience.

   There was one of this focietie that had fo courted vp a wench, as
through a potion of pleafure he had giuen her, her belly rofe like a
blowne bladder.   Belly round fhe was, fo that, through his craft, her
credit ftoode vpon cracking; which fhe perceauing, entreated her
phifition, that as hee had tafted of her curtefie, fo he would faue her
honeftie, declaring that fhe was with childe, as the truth was.   ' Of my
faith (quoth he), what care I ?   You might haue tooke better heede ;
you are beft to make hafte and get a father for it.'   ' I hope (anfwered fhe) you will not ferue me fo; are thefe your faire promifes ?
and can your vowes bee fo flightly paffed ouer ?   Haue you not
made loue to me by the fpace of a quarter, being vfed kindly of mee,
and can you finde in your heart thus cruelly to requite my extraordinarie fauour, putting me to fhiftes in this extremitie ?   Is it poffible
your profeffed whot loue fhould be fo foone cold, or that ' your large
promifes fhould turne to fo little performance ?   I cannot thinke you,
being a man, can be fo cruell as to caft away a poore maiden.'
' Away, beaft (quoth he), thy perfwafions are as bootles as thy
thoughts; and I am affured thou art not fo foolifh as to build of any
thing I haue faide, or of that I haue done, but as of a ieft; if thou

[' fig. H 2,
back]

dooſt, it will be a bad foundation; ' and with that, he flong forth of the dores, leauing my maimed-maide in a bad taking.

Doe you tearme ſuch dooing ieſting? thought *Honeſtie*; if *Chaucers* iapes were ſuch ieſtes, it was but bad ſporte; well, a ſporte it was, though it proued a ſure earneſt; and who knowes not that ſweete meates craue ſowre ſauce? Her laughing lye-downe came to ſad riſing-vp, a ſhrewde ſporte to turne to ſuch ſorrie paſtime; and if ſuch an earneſt penny cannot binde a bargaine, nought wil holde the like chapmen but a halter. Now, Tiborne and Wapping waite on ſuch for Porters, as poſt to markets, ſo to ieſt with lac'ſt-mutton. If ſaying had been all, ſhee had beene fooliſh indeede to haue regarded a fooles ſpeeches; but, ſeeing he crept ſo farre into credit with her, as he crackt her placket lace, how could he of conſcience call that ieſting? Doth *Honeſtie* talke of conſcience to *Buls* bailiffes, that haue no care of any thing but to ſaue their caſſokes from being his purchaſe? Now, fie of all the Beadles of Bridewell, if they ſpare ſuch a ſporter comming vnder their correction, without double the dole they puniſh one of *Baals* common Prieſts with. I would their blewe coates might fall to be *Hindes* fees, vnleſſe they giue ſuch foure luſtie laſhes at euery kennell and ſtreets corner they paſſe by. Why, vnder the cloake of honeſt ſatiſfaction, to allure an honeſt minde to lewde corruption, is no leſſe thefte then robbing of Churches; onely the Clarkes conſent ſeemes in the one to craue ſome tolleration ouer it doth in the other. Then you will ſay they deſerue both to be hanged, and ſo would *Honeſtie* ſay, but that their chriſtianity merites charitie. But, of my troth, if *Honeſtie* were a Iuſtice, ſuch as ſue after the ſelfe-ſame order, ſhould either marrie with them they [1] haue deceiued, or [¹ ſig. H 3] hang without them, my minion going vnpuniſhed, for that time in hope of amendment. Loue is a kinde hart, and mariage is a ſweete baite; what, then, will not ſuch promiſes gaine of a faithfull louer? This ieſting turnes to lingring loue, when the weakeſt hath ſurfeited in affection. Sweet ſpeeches haue vowed euerlaſting conſtancie; and running in the pleaſant meddowe of kindenes, it growes luſtie, ſpending the remnant of his wooing to winne vnto ſuch bad fare; courting endes with ſuch a charge, changing profeſſed loue into burning luſt. Loue lookes to be maintained with kindenes, and when he hath got

what wordes can affoorde, then falles he to iefting, which turns
contrary to *Chaucers* meaning, to *the* fatiffying of a leachers luft in
earneft. But too too much of this, except it were better; and once
more returne we to our melancholly lefte marde maide.

She, poore foule, fet fo lightly by in her fortie weekes reckoning,
fo thought on her prefent hard hap, as fhe quite forgot her accompt,
wherby now fhe was in a worfe taki*n*g then before; for if, being put
to her othe, fhe fhould miffe of that, his counter othe would make
but a fo fo end for her; and, therefore, thus fhe beftirred her felfe in
the matter. She made her cafe knowne to a freend, and, falling
downe vpon her knees, entreated him, for the paffion of our Lady, to
ftand good helpe vnto her, to draw her mate to marry. with her.
Who, being a very honeft man *that* had fome care of her credit,
laboured fo effectually in *the* matter, as, what through promifes and a
peece of money, he made it a match; fo that, what through a little
honeftie my man was endued with, and a peece of money my maiden
was endowed with, we had a choptlodgicke. Now, woe vnto fuch
wooed fpoufes, if their mates want altogether honeftie, and they haue
no money; and this might haue, perchaunce, wonne the ftanding in a
white fheete without fo good a maifter. Take heede, girles, how you
truft to fuch helpes, for *Honeftie* can tell you they are not ordinarie.
It is harder to finde one fuch in euery parifhe through a Countrie,

[¹ sig H 3,
back]

¹ then to finde a honeft woman in a houfe of Weftminfters Hof-
pitalitie. Alas! how many honeft mens children come to decay
through this practife? Talke with any corrupted Virgine; and,
excepting one amongft twentie, if they all not agree that fuch entice-
ments were the procurers of their miferie, neuer beleeue *Honeftie* for
a halfepennie. Beware if a rich mariage be offered for a rewarde of
breache of honeftie; there are fewe that will not confent to leacherie
with fuch briberie.

But the opening of an other wound remaines, with which loue is
hurt by his courting enemies, for they which haue beene once
deceiued by flatterie, will hardly be drawn to beleeue finceritie,
whereby the faithfull futor is hindred from his due. The beaten
dogge fhuns the ftick; the torme*n*ted patient feares the Pothecaries
drugs; the childe that hath beene fore whipt for a fault, will feare,
by offending, to hazard his breeche. Who is more warie of his wel-

fare, then he that hath been in greateſt extremitie? and if loue hath been wounded with a diſſembled affe&ion, he will be afraide to enter into an a&ion from whence the like ſorrowe may flowe. What giues greater hope of conſtancie, then vowed loyalty? or what ſeemes ſweeter then ſugered flatterie? Affe&ion ſpringeth of kinde vſage, and loue ſettles on a continued ſhewe of profeſſed zeale, which, being ſure ſet, ca*n*not be remoued wit*h*out great danger, except wiſe-dome be a helper. What ſorrowe danger brings, and what care diſ-contentment harboureth, he knowes not. But of the vnceaſing harts-greefe, with the tormenting ſoure-ſauce which ſeaſoneth the deſtruc-tion of entire affe&ion, none can iudge, ſaue thoſe that haue taſted thereof; onely it may be imagined by *the* effe&s that haue followed the like cauſes (as by the vntimely death it hath brought to ſome, a depriuation of their wits to others, languiſhing diſeaſes to many; namely, the greene ſicknes, the mother, and ſuch like; and laſtly, to all mad melancholye fits), that they which are fauoured with the leaſt miſhap that comes through want of their longing, are rewarded [1] with [¹ leaf H 4] the loſſe of a preſent wel-fare, hauing that ſupplyed by a gifte of ſighing heauines. Now, after *the* freedome from ſuch a miſcheefe, who will not ſweare to flie from the like danger? And ſince flatterie cannot, without dangerous triall, be knowen from faithfull freendſhip, who will not ſhunne both, fearing to miſtake the one for the other? If a kinde hart hath beene deceiued by a crooked knaue, clad in the robes of a courteous louer, ſhe will euer after miſtruſt the habite, for that it is vnpoſſible to know the hart. Who can forbid the Tailor to vſe his arte? and doo you thinke that any one for an aduantage will let to trie his crafte? The Diuell can change himſelfe into any ſhape; and the onely meanes to knowe him (as is ſaide before), is his ſtumpe foote.

Liking wil not be long a dooing; and loue that followes is but little, whereby he brings no great harme; but al the miſcheefe comes with deſire, which ſwelles the affe&ions, and predominates ouer loue and liking; he makes the miſ-rule, and keeps the open Chriſtmas; he deſires the ſporte, and maintaines the paſtime, ſo that, though he be long in comming, and ſtaies but little in his Lordſhip, yet the re-membrance of his iolitie is not forgotten a long time after. He keepes his cuſtome euery yeere; and a yeere with him is but a ſhort

fpace; fo that after he comes to his full age, he makes many Chrift-
maffes; for Defire is not fhort liued. It is therefore this lingring loue
that dooth all the harme, becaufe by him Defire is onely begotten.
He that, beating the market, is willing to buye, will not ftand long a
bargaining when he hath met with his liking, for feare a francker
cuftomer fteppe betweene him and his longing ; but if he be careles,
he will not deale without a good penniworth. Very eafily, then, is
the mifcheefe of repentance taken from women, feeing a true-meaning futor may be as quickly difcerned, as a careles chapman may be
perceiued. And how fondly doo they entrude themfelues into the
needles hazard of great difcontent, that will let their loue runne fo

[¹ leaf H 4,
back] farre without reafon, as it ¹ cannot be called backe without great
greefe at the leaft. Though a buyer be not able to giue the feller
his afking, yet will he be earneft to haue it at fuch a price as he doth
offer; and, although this louing cuftomer be not of abilitie to anfwere
thy freends expeҫtation, yet fhall he not be forward to be poffeffed of
thee; he is but a watcher for aduantages. So that if either his abilitie
be fuch, as of himfelfe he can maintaine thee, or be thy poffibilitie fo
great, as by his good endeuour he may winne a liuing, thy freends
good will, by the poffeffion of thee, thy affeҫtion is too too colde, it
thou keepes him lingring without his longing ; and his deuotion is
fmall, if he be not an vnceafing futor for it.

And truely, in *Honeflies* minde (and pardon me, I pray you, with
whofe conceipts it iumpes not), thofe matches fhall profper beft,
where loue is rather refpeҫted then wealth ; prouided there be a care
had of the likelyhoode of poffibilitie which muft come with one of
them. But fhall one that hath nothing, ioyne louing iffue with an
other that hath, or is like to haue as little, he hauing no meanes to
make a liuing, he fhewes himfelf to be a foolifh follower of repentance, and an vncharitable procurer of an others wretchednes? There
are many good wits, that, wanting matter to worke on, wade into the
triall of dangerous conclufions, which otherwife being imployed, would
become profitable members of a common wealth. All cannot be
heires, and many yonger brothers children are but barely left, though
they haue had good bringing vp, which nothing hinders their gentrie,
onely, now a daies, it is a barre to their preferment. For men wil
fooner match their daughters with my yong maifter, a rich Coblers

Sonne, though they be their heires, then with a Gentleman of a good houſe, being a yonger Brother. Heerby comes the decay of ancient gentilitie, and this *the* making of vpſtart houſes; heerby, thoſe that haue had good bringing vp, muſt either goe to plough and carte, being drudges to ſuch drones, or their natures, diſdaining that, and more abhorring to begge, leade them to lewde praĉtiſes to maintaine [1] the [1 sig. 1] ſtate of their birth. And did you, Fathers, which are to match your Children, know the hart-breakings many parents (which haue beene of your mindes) haue found by triall, then would the feare of vnciuill behauiour, which ſpringeth by ſucceſſion from their carterly pro- genitors, turne your greedie deſire of golden gaine, to a ioyfull gaining of your poſterities happines.

But fie of couetouſnes, that is the roote of all miſchiefe; for men that haue enough to make their Daughters Gentlewomen, by match- ing them with houſes of no ſmall antiquitie, will, with the deſire they haue therevnto, wooe men of great liuing with large offers, to match their ſons and heires with them; Who, being drawen therunto, will vſe them their wiues meetely well during the life time of their owne and wiues Fathers, for that their eſtates are by their great portions better maintained, and their beſt freends thereby well pleaſed. But let your Daughters beware, after your and their Fathers death (when all hope is taken away of a further gaine, and a ſearch made of their aunceſtors alliance), for then, ſeeing the baſenes of your pettigree, and *the* noble deſcents of their predeceſſors, that corruption of blood which you, with your corruption of money, hath made, and their Fathers couetouſnes hath purchaſed to their ſucceſſion, will (as for the moſt parte it doth in the like caſes) moue ſuch hartbreakinges, as either quarrelles of diuorcement or ſutes of ſeparation will ſurely followe. When, on the contrary parte, if reſpeĉting gentrie, thereby to aduaunce your houſes, you would match the*m* with Gent. yonger brothers (of whom there ought to be leſſe regarde, the chiefe houſe being main- tained), your Daughters portions being the onely maintenance of their eſtates, would be ſo ſtrong a helpe to encreaſe their affeĉtion towards your children, with purchaſed happines to their poſterities, as knowing no houſholde quarrelles can be without charges, they willbe glad to ſtudie to encreaſe the ſweetenes of vnitie, thereby to continue euerlaſting proſperitie to their following ages.

[¹ sig. I, back] ¹ *Honeſlie* knowes what the fairing-monger will faye, when he ſhall heare of one fo flat againſt his opinion touching mariages, not letting to affirme that it is moſt neceſſarie that the confent of parents ſhould be laſt fued for, and little regarded in refpeft of loue, efpeciallye feeing his Pamphlet buildes fo diuinelye on farre-fetcht arguments to proue the contrarie. Therfore, to preuent him, and to prouide againſt the great danger their matches-making procure, *Honeſlie* muſt tell him, and aſſure all thofe that are of his minde, that were the worlde like vnto that wherein *Abraham* liued, or were Fathers of thefe daies of his difpofition, his argument drawen from the gift of *Euah* to *Adam*, by God, and fuch like, might feeme to proue fome thing. But, feeing thefe times in effeft are quite contrary to thofe, and the difpofitions of men in our daies altogether difagreeing to theirs of that age, his time had beene better fpent in a worke to fome other purpofe. For a little to feeme to flie from my matter, and to haue a fling at him : how many Fathers now a daies are there fo carefull of prouiding con-uenient mates for their children at a feafonable time as our great Grand-father *Abraham* was? Againe, how manye haue children that are fo obedient to bend their loue to their Parents liking as was *Iſaac* ? Oh, Sir, you are deceaued, our yong ones are of riper wits, and far for-warder then Children were in thofe daies, and our olde ones are of more couetous mindes, and far forwarder to be drawen to their childrens good; for what greater good then to enioye them they loue ? and what will offend our parents more then to entreat that he fent his feruant to fearch forth one of his next kinne, not to enquire after one that had moſt wealth ; and fhould fome children entertaine no loue in our time vntill their parents procured it, nor fue for a match before their freends made it, it were requifite their honeſtie fhould be great, or I knowe what will follow. Yet, againe, Fathers liue not now adaies ordinarily aboue a hundred yeeres, whereby they [² sig. I 2] haue a long la²ſting gouernement ouer their Children ; but beholde it is far contrary, and therefore it requires contrary proceedings. And laſtly (for that I will not be long at this time in this matter), the holy writ beares not fuch ſway in our confciences, as it workt wonders in theirs of thofe daies ; and therefore, to helpe our weaknes in the want of that warrant, we muſt vfe the meanes—loue—to drawe vs to that euerlaſting happines.

But once more to my courting companions, to make as fpeedie an
end with them, whofe haire-braine fancying and fickle affection is no
fmall hindrance to loues proceedings. *Honeflie*, hauing fet downe the
meanes to finde out their knauerie, hath alfo prouided a batte to beate
downe fuch flatterie, the inftruement to finde out their diffimulation
being a fearch into their lingring, and the clubbe to match their
clubbe feete, a loathing of their company. But to come to the
punifhment I would haue fuch to be plagued with : in my opinion,
and by *Honeflies* doome, they are worthie to be fet for fcarre-crowes
in newe fowen fieldes ; and the rather thus goes my iudgement, for
that feeing they are fo fkilfull to doo harme in townes and cities, if
that bad-ufed wit were forft to be imployed about that commodious
doo-good, they would inuent excellent meanes to preuent the fpoyle
the rauenous birds commit. Their pregnant wits and cunning
deuices to catch womens affections, that farre exceede crowes in
reafon and difcretion, confirme they would be ftrange, and therefore
profitable ; yet, becaufe it is fomewhat too bace, though their practifes
are as beaftly, I will ende with them with this refolution :—That they
are as worthie to ftand in white-fheetes in Churches, for leauing
women in defperate cafes, hauing drawen them into that fooles
paradice of ouer-paffionate affection, as they that poyfon ftrangers
bellies ; This would make faithfull futors happie, conftant louers
ioyfull, and courting diffemblers fearful.

   Honeflie, hauing noted thefe enormities harbored in lewde difpo-
fitions fhuffled into this Morrice, at laft lent [1] his eares, and beftowed [t fig. 1 2, back]
his eyes, ioyning with him his beft vnderftanding, to fearch into the
natures of *the* remnant, to fee whether *the* multitud were mixed with
thefe in bad conceits. But, behold, fo contrarie practizes were performed by them, as thofe proceedings are difagreeing to the further-
ance of perfect vnitie. Amongft thefe did I beholde *Loue* dandled
with fweete mufick, and conftant affection vpholden with modeft
demeanour. The foueraignes of Virginitie difplayed their heauenly
dignitie, by the imperiall colours of matchles beautie, grounde with
the *Ambrofian* oyle of celeftiall courtefie ; and the matronly deities
proued their ethereall difcreetnes, in following the heauens pre-
fcription for Loues true imitation. I faw Kindenes matched *with*
Goodwill, Affection linked vnto Liking, & Loue embraced with

Loyaltie, Vertue leading them to eternall happines. They liked not
for a moment, loued not vpon aduantage, nor wooed but with a good
intention. Thefe fhaked not hands with hatefull hearts, nor vfed
fmoothe tongues with diffembling thoughts. They courted not
kindely, to corrupt fhamefully, ne protefted with vowes, to wound
with wordes, and kill with deeds; but hand and heart went together,
and the tongue vttered their paffionate conceites; their heart louing
them as faithfully as their tongue labored to winne their courtefie.
And you no earthly creatures, though ioyned with men for their
eternall good (you heauenly faints, I meane, mafking in the fhadowes of terreftriall fhapes), you beautifie this crue with your deuine
motions, whofe mindes are onely inritched with the true wifdome
that vpholdes Loues welfare. Your facred actions ayde his fimple
followers, & naught but your carefull kindnes binds mens weake
affections from vnconftancie. You make their praiers effectuall, their
requeft gayning through you the fafetie of their longing. Your pittie
brings them to pietie, and your almes relieues them from the captiuitie
of Defpaire. Deftreffed *Honeftie* is foly harbored within your milke-
white bofomes, and were it not for your bountifull charitie, his end
[¹ fig. I 3] ¹ would be tormenting beggerie. Your allablafter pappes do wholy
minifter moifture to my confuming welfare, and from their fugered
teates doe I onely drawe my liquor of life, fo that by your motherly
kindnes to decaying *Honeftie*, they reape likewife their bliffe, that
would giue mee my baine; recouering contrarie to their wils the
remaynder of their weale. For how marcheth the paffionate fouldier,
without you found the alarome of his good-fpeede? or, how fareth the
amorous gallant, except you play the galliard of acceptance? Vn-
fortunate eyes, your pearcing fightes fhal be cruelly curft, and
vnnaturall vfage fhall be offered to your obedient hearts; for feeing
and adoring celeftiall obiects, vnles their relenting pittie take mercie
on your deftreffed abiects. And blafpheming tongue, thy vnbridled
impudencie fhall heape vpon thy owne back a bundle of vntollerable
miferies, by being forced to vtter execrable flaunders againft them for
their hard hearts, that were purchafed to worke your hard happe
through your owne iniurious follie. Paffions of difcontent muft
pleafe your fancies, and forrowfull poems muft grace your mufick;
deep fighes muft ftraine your heart-ftrings, and direfull forrowe lull

you a fleepe, when vifions of new deftreffes muft difquiet your greateft
happines, and dreames of frefh vexations forbid you the leaft eafe.
You fhall fue in vaine, becaufe you haue delighted in vanitie; and
hope without obtaining, for that your heart haue harbored diffembling,
except thefe goddeffes, whofe goodnes is vnfpeakable, vouchfafe to
minifter a plafter of pitty to your louing pietie. It is their courtefie
that muft make you chereful, and their good conceits muft cherifh
your dying mirth; their liking muft honour your affeétion, and their
gratefull kindnes muft aduance the zeale of your protefted loyaltie.
It is in their choyfe to change your chance, and in their power to
bridle Fortune; for that the Fates, being their fifters, are at their
calles to fet downe your deftinies. If they fay they doe hate you,
beware, for they can hurt you; but if they affirme they loue you,
ftriue to con¹tinue your prefent happines, and feare to lofe the prof- [¹ fig. I ₂
fered bleffednes. Why are women accounted weake, but becaufe ^{back]}
their nature is pure? Or, wherefore are they neceffarie, but that men
cannot liue without their companie? When we are fuccorles, they
comfort vs; being melancholy, they cheere vs; and they are the
meanes to redeeme vs from the gates of hell. Being mad, their
muficall tongues chafe away the euill fpirits; being bewitched, their
loue charmes the tormenting diuels; and being fwallowed vp by the
gulfe licentioufnes, the heauens haue created them the helpe to
redeeme vs from that hellifh furnace

Thus much for their power; & now, a little of their properties.
O, facred mercie (neuer more honored then in the pittifull bofomes
of thefe feminine deities), thou holds thy chief harborow within their
paffionate bofomes, & only art nourifhed in their relenting harts.
Thou fingft within the clofets of their pittifull confciences, & reioyceft
within the caftles of their celeftiall foules; thou liueft with them
fecure, and makes through them multitudes of miferable wretches
poffeffors of the higheft happines. Thou heares the fighes of fuing
fweet-hearts, & comforts the pinching griefe of pining louers. Thou
meditates of their vowes, and ftudies to requite their carefull affeétion
with kindeft curtefie. Thou pittieft the foolifh maladies of fond
nouices, & forroweft at the weaknes of many mens wifdome. Thou
ftriueft to do no wrong, that thou maift be free from iniurie; and
labours to fhunne fufpeét, that thou maift bee without mifdoubt.

Thou ftudieft to repay, that thou maift reape thy due; and keepeft thy day, that thou maift bee well dealt with.   Yea, much more, and fo much the better for man ; thou pitties them that would fpoile thee, and forgiues them that would hurt thee ; thou wifheft them well that would bereaue thee of thy weale, & loueft them (which is thy only fault), ouer entirely that efteeme of thy proffered kindnes too too carelefly.   Yet let difcretion haue the fecond place with you, for fhe guides them by reafon, and that gouerns men with wifdome.   She knowes when to charme with [1] fweete melodie, and when to correct with louing perfwafions ; fhe vfeth to dandle vertue, and reproue vice, to embrace good and flie from euill, and willingly to fubiect obedient imitation to holfome counfell, as alfo dutifully to defire libertie from ftooping to iniurious doctrine.   Shee fearcheth into the depth of fubiected feruife, and difcouering whether it be offered of curtefie, or proffered of knauerie, regards it according to it value, and rewardes it with it full worth.   She teacheth to like ere they loue, and louing to encreafe, or deminifh the heate of their fancie, according to the proportion of kinde coales that nourifheth the fire of their affection.   She perfwadeth to launce, courting to the bones to finde out the danger ; and feeing what likelyhoode, either of weale or woe is likeft to enfue ; fhee fheweth them what is good to withdrawe the putrified liking, and what is holfome to preferue the found loue.   And fhe ftudies to make them happie, by wifhing men their welfare to make them conftant, by endeuoring to encreafe a fparke of loyaltie, and to make them honored by inftructing them in the true rules of modeftie.

And now ftep in further, thou beautifying modeftie ; for thou addeft no fmall renoune to their adored natures, nor doth thy bafhfulnes meanely adorne their highly prifed excellencies ; thy rofie blufhes bring no fmall honor to their admired beauty ; nor euer dies that facred ftayning colour, vntil by mans corruption that maidenly marke be extinguifhed.   Yet then (but, ah ! that man fhould do fo much !) thy decent fobrietie aduanceth the dignity of their womanly chaftitie, and thy matronly behauiour difplayeth the foueraintie of their motherly nurture.   Thou giues examples that, imitated, preuent occafions of enticing offers to draw to folly, and efcapes the iniurious flanders of fufpitious fearchers, *that* hunt after fhewes of fenfuality.   Thou main-

[¹ leaf I 4]

tainеft peace at home, efcapeft fufpect abroade, and keepeft thy louers
heart from harboring ieloufie, the chiefe procurer of greateft miferie.
And thou gaineft liking, and encreafeft affection, receiuing loue and
loyaltie with an. aſſu'red pledge of neuer-dying conftancie. Neither [¹ leaf I 4,
back]
art thou, euerlafting goddes, a ftranger to mens-helpers; for thou,
with all the vertues, waite vpon thefe beautiful fpectacles, and they,
with the Graces, extol thofe the earths miracles. Their praifes are
vnfpeakeable, for that their worth is vnualuable and their defartes
vnrequited, becaufe through mans weakenes mifprifed; but fuch and
fo great were the adorned excellencies of thefe humaine deities, as
their practifes layde open their princely courtefie, and their perform-
ances made their louers happie. And men reioyced through their
faithfull affection; ftudying to requite womens euerlafting kindnes
with the reward of neuer-ceafing conftancie. Men vfed heauenly
wifdome to obtaine liking, and carefull behauior to confirme loue
being purchafed; and women were forward to beftowe modeft kindnes,
being faithfully dealt withall, and effectually requited proffered
curtefie; neither being too too coye, or fhewing themfelues ouer forward to be wonne. But briefly, and fo to end: euery one of them
rendred like for like with proofes of neuer-altering affection, they
thereby gaining vnto themfelu[e]s the fugred fweetnes of
celeftiall amitie, & tying vnto their kinde thoughts,
the affections of their well-willers, with
euerlafting conftancie.

F I N I S.

TOM
TEL-TROTHS
MESSAGE, AND
HIS PENS COM-
PLAINT.

A worke not vnpleasant to be read,
nor vnprofitable to be fol-
lowed.

Written by Jo. La. Gent.

Nullam in correcto crimine crimen erit.

LONDON.

Imprinted for *R. Howell,* and are to be sold at his shop,
neere the great North doore of Paules, at the signe of
the white horse. 1600.

TO THE WORSIPFULL

MASTER George Dowse, GENTLE-
MAN, Io. La. WISHETH FRVITI-
on of endlesse felicitie.

 F writings may quittance benefits or goodwill. more then common curtesie, then accept, I beseech you, these first fruites of my barren braine, the token of my loue, the seale of my affection, and the true cognizance of my vnfained affection. And for so-much as the plot of my Pamphlet is rude, though true, the matter meane, the manner meaner, let me humbly desire, though slenderly I deserue, to haue it patronized vnder the wings of your fauour; in requitall whereof I will be,

Yours euer to command,

Io. La.

TO THE GENTLEMEN
READERS.

I Vdiciall Readers, wise Apolloes flocke,   1
  Whose eyes like keyes doe open learnings locke;
Daigne with your eye-lampes to behold this booke,
And in all curtesie thereon to looke :   4
Thus being patronized by your view,
I shall not be ashamed of his hew.
    O graunt my suite, my suite you vnderstand,
    That I may you commend, you me command.   8

                                          Io. La.

TOM TEL-TROTHS

Message, and his pens complaint.

. [1]

hou that didst earst Romes Capitall defend,   [p. 7]   1
Defend this sacred relique of thy wing,
And by thy power Diuine some succor send,
To saue the same from carping *Momus* sting :   4
    That, like a tell-troth, it may boldly blaze,
And pensill-like paint forth a iust dispraise.   6

[2]

Goe, naked pen, the hearts true secretarie,   7
Imbath'd in sable liquor mixt with gall,
And from thy master these rude verses carrie,
Sent to the world, and in the world, to all :   10
    In mournfull verse lament the faults of men,
    Doe this, and then returne heart-easing pen.   12

[3]

Time sits him downe to weepe in sorrowes fell,   [p. 8]   13
And *Truth* bewailes mans present wickednes;
Both *Time* and *Truth* a dolefull tale doe tell,
Deploring for mans future wretchednes.   16
    With teare-bedewed cheeks, help, help therfore,
    Sad tragicke muse, to weepe, bewaile, deplore.   18

[]

Mee thinks I see the ghost of *Conscience*,   19
Raisde from the darke graue of securitie,
Viewing the world, who once was banisht thence,
Her cheeks with teares made wet, with sighs made dry :   22
    And this did aggrauate her griefe the more,
    To see the world much worse than twas before.   24

[5]

She wept; I saw her weepe, and wept to see   25
The salt teares trickling from her aged eyes;
Yea, and my pen, copartner needs would be,
With black-inke teares, our teares to simpathize :   28
   So long wee wept, that all our eyes were drie,
   And then our tongues began aloud to crie.   30

[6]

Come, sad *Melpomene*, thou tragicke Muse,   [p. 9]   31
To beare a part in these our dolefull cries!
Spare not with taunting verses to accuse
The wicked world of his iniquities!   34
   Tell him his owne! be bold, and not ashamed,
   Nor cease to speake till thou his faults hast blamed!   36

[7]

I seeme to heare resounding Ecchoes tatling,   37
Of misdemeanors raigning heere and there,
And party-coloured Pyes on greene bowes pratling,
Of foolish fashions raging euerie where :   40
   Then blame not my muse, what so ere she say,
   Sith birds and Ecchoes, mens fond faults bewray.   42

[8]

O world, no world, but rather sinke of sinne,   43
Where blind and fickle Fortune Empresse raigneth;
O men, no men, but swine that lie therein,
Among whom, vertue wrong'd by vice complaineth :   46
   Thus world bad, men worse, men in world, worldly men,
   Doe giue occasion to my plaintife pen.   48

[9]

Sinne, like the monstra *Hydra*, hath more heads,   [p. 10]   49
Then heauens hie roofe hath siluer-spangled starres,
And in his lawes,[1] mens soules to hell he leads,   [1 *orig.* lawes]
Where fierie fiends meete them in flaming Charres :   52
   This Pirate, like a Pilate, keepes each coast,
   Bringing his guests vnto their hellish hoast.   54

[10]

If all the earth were writing paper made,   55
All plowshares pens, all furrowes lines in writing,
The Ocean inke, wherein the sea-nimphes wade,
And all mens consciences were scribes inditing :   58
  Too much could not be written of mans sinne,
  Since sinne did in the first man first begin.   60

[11]

But as the Ægyptian dog runs on the brinke   61
Of Nilus seuen-fold ouer-flowing floud,
And staying not, nowhere, nowhere doth drinke,
For feare of Crocodiles which lurke in mudde :   64
  So shall my pẹn runne briefly ouer all,
  Reciting these misdeeds which worke mans thral.   66

[12]

Nature, that whilome bore the chiefest sway,   [p. 11] 67
Bridling mans bodie with the raignes of Reason,
Is now inforc'd in vncoth walkes to stray,
Exilde by custome, which encrocht through treason :   70
  Instead of Art, Natures companion,
  Fancie with custome holdes dominion.   72

[13]

Ouid could testifie that, in his time,   73
Astraea fled from earth to heauen aboue,
Loathing iniustice as a damned crime,
Which she with equall poised schoales did proue :   76
  And this pen in my time shall iustifie,
  That true religion is constrainde to flie.   78

[14]

The two leafe-dores of *quondam* honestie,   79
Which on foure vertues Cardinall were turned,
By Cardinals degree and poperie,
Are now as heretike-like reliques burned :   82
  Now carnall vice, not vertue Cardinall,
  Plaies Christmas gambals in the Popes great hall.   84

[15]

Well, sith the Popes name pops so fitly in,   [p. 12]   85
From Pope ile take the Latin P. away,
And Pope shall with the Greeke π. then begin,
Whose type and tippe that he may climbe ile pray :   88
    Pray all with mee that he may climbe this letter ;
    For in this praier each man is his detter.   90

[16]

I passe not although with bell, booke, and candle,   91
His bald-pate Priests and shoren Friers curse ;
My plaintife pen, his rayling text shall handle :
Nor doe I thinke my selfe one iot the worse :   94
    Yea, though my pen were in their Purgatorie,
    Yet should my pen hold on his plaintife storie.   96

[17]

Oh, what a world is it for one to see,   97
How Monkes and Friers would religious seeme?
Whose heads make humble congies to the knee,
That of their humble minds all men might deeme :   100
    These be the sycophants, whose fained zeale
    Hath brought-in woe to euerie commonweale.   102

[18]

The Monkes, like monkies, hauing long blacke tailes,   [p. 13]   103
Tell olde wiues tales to busie simple braines ;
The baudie Friers do hunt to catch females,
To shriue and free them from infernall paines.   106
    Thus Monkes and Friers, fire-brands of hell,
    Like to incarnate diuels with vs dwell.   108

[19]

But I as loath, so will I leaue to write,   109
Against this popish ribble rabble route,
Hoping ere long some other will indite
Whole volumes gainst their slander-bearers stout :   112
    Poets and Painters meane while shall descry,
    With pens and pensils, their hypocrisie.   114

[20]

As thus my pen doth glance at euerie vice,   115
Needs must I heare poore Learnings lamentation,
Which whilome was esteem'd at highest price,
But now reiected is of euerie nation :   118
 She loueth men, yet is shee wrong'd by men;
 Her wronged loue giues matter to my pen.   120

[21]

Pallas, the nurse of Nature-helping Art,   [p. 14] 121
Whose babes are Schollers, and whose cradels, schooles,
From whose milch teates no pupils would depart,
Till they by cunning shund the names of fooles :   124
 She, euen she, wanders in open streetes,
 Seeking for schollers, but no schollers meetes.   126

[22]

Englands two eyes, Englands two Nurceries,   127
Englands two nests, Englands two holy mounts,
I meane, Englands two Vniuersities,
Englands two Lamps, Englands two sacred founts,   130
 Are so puld at, puld out, and eke puld downe,
 That they can scarce maintaine a wide sleeu'd gowne.   132

[23]

Lately as one CAME ore a BRIDGE, he saw   133
An OXE stand ore a FORDE to quench his drouth :
But lo, the Oxe his dry lips did withdraw,
And from the water lifted vp his mouth.   136
 Like *Tantalus*, this drie Oxe there did stand :
 God grant this darke *Ænigma* may be scand !   138

[24]

The Liberall Sciences, in number seauen,   [p. 15] 139
Which, in seauen ages, like seauen Monarchs raigned,
And shin'd on earth as Planets seauen in heauen,
Are now like Almesfolkes beggerly maintained,   142
 Whilst in their roome, seauen deadly sins beare sway,
 Which makes these seauen Arts, like seauen slaues ohey.   144

[25]

Grammer, the ground and strong foundation   145
Vpon which Lady Learning builds her tower;
Grammer, the path-way and direction
That leadeth vnto *Pallas* sacred bower,   148
    Stands bondslaue-like, of Stationers to be sold,
    Whom all in free Schooles erst might free behold.   150

[26]

Add *Rhetoricke*, adornde with figures fine,   151
Trickt vp with tropes, and clad in comely speech,
Is gone a Pilgrime to the Muses nine,
For her late wrong assistance to beseech.   154
    Now rich Curmudgions, best orations make,
    Whilst in their pouches gingling coyne they shake.   156

[27]

Logicke, which like a whetstone sharpes the braine,   [p. 16]   157
Logicke, which like a touch-stone tries the minde,
Logicke, which like a load-stone erst drew gaine,
Is now for want of maintenance halfe pinde;   160
    And sith in Colledges no maides may dwell,
    Many from Colledges doe her expell.   162

[28]

Musicke, I much bemourne thy miserie,   163
Whose well-tunde notes delight the Gods aboue,
Who, with thine eare-bewitching melodie,
Doest vnto men and beasts such pleasure moue: 166
    Though wayling cannot helpe, I wayle thy wrong,
    Bearing a part with thee in thy sad song.   168

[29]

Arithmeticke, she next in number stands,   169
Numbring her cares in teaching how to number;
Which cares, in number passing salt-sea sands,
Disturbe her minde, and still her corps incumber: 172
    Care addeth griefe, griefe multiplies her woe,
    Whose ebbe substracting, brings reducing floe.   174

[30]

Geometrie, as seruile prentise bound   [p. 17] 175
Vnto the Mother earth for many yeares,
Hath long since meated out the massie ground,
Which ground the impression of her foot-steps beares.   178
  Great was her labour, great should be her gaine
  But her great labour was repaid with paine.   180

[31]

Astronomie, not least though last, hath lost   181
By cruell fate her starre-embroidred coate;
Her spherie globe in dangers seas is tost,
And in mishap her instruments doe floate: 184
  All Almanacks hereof can witnesse beare,
  Else would my selfe hereof as witnesse sweare.   186

[32]

But how should I with stile poeticall   187
Proceede to rime in meeter or in verse?
If Poetrie, the Queene of verses all,
Should not be heard, whose plaint mine eare doth pierce?   190
  Oh helpe, *Apollo*, with apologie,
  To blaze her vndeserued iniurie.   192

[33]

Horace did write the Art of Poetrie,   [p 18] 193
The Art of Poetrie *Virgill* commended;
Ouid thereto his studies did applie,
Whose life and death, still Poetrie defended.   196
  Thrice happie they, but thrice vnhappie I,
  They sang her praise, but I her iniurie.   198

[34]

O princely Poetrie, true Prophetesse,   199
Perfections patterne, Matrone of the Muses,
I weepe to thinke how rude men doe oppresse
And wrong thine Art with their absurd abuses.   202
  They are but drosse, thine Art it is diuine,
  Cast not therefore thy pearles to such swine.   204

[35]
The sugred songs that sweete Swannes vse to sing,   205
Floting adowne *Meanders* siluer shore,
To countrie swaines no kinde of solace bring;
The winding of an horne they fancie more.   208
   No ma:ueile then though Ladie Poetrie
   Doe suffer vndeserued iniurie.   210

[36]
Like to *Batillus*, euery ballet-maker,   [p. 19] 211
That neuer climbd vnto *Pernassus* Mount,
Will so incroach, that he will be partaker
To drinke with *Maro* at the *Castale* fount.   214
   Yea, more then this, to weare a lawrell Crowne
   By penning new gigges for a countrie clowne.   216

[37]
When *Marsias* with his bagpipes did contend   217
To make farre better Musicke then *Apollo:*
When *Thameras* in selfe conceit would mend
The Muses sweete songs note, what then did follow?   220
   Conuicted both, to both this was assignde:
   The first was hangd, the last was stroken blinde.   222

[38]
And may it happen to those bastard braines,   223
Whose base rimes striue to better Poetrie,
That they may suffer like deserued paines,
For these be they that worke her infamie.   226
   Thus hauing blazed false Poets in their hew,
   Deare Poetrie (though loth) I bid adiew.   228

[39]
As Poetrie in poesie I leaue,   [p. 20] 229
I see seauen sinnes which crost seauen Liberall Arts,
Which with their fained shew doe men deceaue,
And on the wide worlds stage doe play their parts: 232
   As thus men follow them, they follow men,
   They moue more matter to my plaintife pen.   234

[40]

These mincing maides and fine-trict truls, ride post   235
To *Plutoes* pallace, like purueyers proude;
Thither they leade many a damned ghost,
With howling consorts carroling aloude: 238
And as one after one they post to hell,
    My plaintife pen shall their abuses tell.   240

[41]

First praunceth Pride with principalitie,   241
Guarded with troupes of new-found fashions:
Her hand-maides are Fancie and Vanitie:
These three a progresse goe throughout all nations;   244
    And as by any towne they passe along,
    People to see them gather in a throng.   246

[42]

Now fine-ruft Ruffines in their brauerie   [p 21]   247
Make cringing cuts with new inuention:
New-cut at Cardes brings some to beggarie,
But this new-cut brings most vnto destruction: 250
    So long they cut, that in their purse no groate
    They leaue, but cut some others purse or throate.   252

[43]

Bedawbd with gold like *Apuleius* Asse,   253
Some princk and pranck it: others, more precise,
Full trick and trim tir'd in the looking-glasse,
With strange apparell doe themselues disguise.   256
    But could they see what others in them see,
    Follie might flie, and they might wiser bee.   258

[44]

Some gogle with the eyes, some squint-eyd looke,   259
Some at their fellowes, squemish sheepes-eyes cast,   .
Some turne the whites vp, some looke to the foote,
Some winke, some twinke, some blinke, some stare as fast.   262
    The summe is infinite; eye were a detter,
    If all should answere I, with I the letter.   264

[45]

Many desire to foote it with a grace,   [p. 22]   265
Or Lion-like to walke maiesticall :
But whilst they striue to keepe an equipace,
Their gate is foolish and phantasticall.   268
  As Hobby-horses, or as Anticks daunce,
  So doe these fooles vnseemely seeme to praunce.   270

[46]

I will not write of sweatie, long, shag haire,   271
Or curled lockes with frisled periwigs :
The first, the badge that Ruffins vse to weare,
The last, the cognisance of wanton rigs.   274
  But sure I thinke, as in *Medusaes* head,
  So in their haires, are craulling Adders bred.   276

[47]

Men, *Proteus*-like, resemble euery shape,   277
And like Camelions euery colour faine ;
How deare so ere, no fashion may escape
The hands of those whose gold may it attaine :   280
  Like ebbe and flow, these fashions goe and come,
  Whose price amounteth to a massie summe.   282

[48]

The sharp-set iawes of greedie sheeres deuoure,   [p. 23] 283
And seaze on euery cloath as on a pray,   .
Like *Atropose* cutting that in an houre,
Which weauers *Lachese*-like wrought in a day.   286
  These snip-snap sheeres, in al shieres get great shares,
  And are partakers of the dearest wares.   288

[49]

When fig-tree leaues did shroude mans nakednesse,   289
And home-spun cloath was counted clothing gay,
Then was mans bodie clad with comelinesse,
And honour shrouded was in rude array :   292
  But since those times by future times were changed,
  Thousands of fashions through the world haue ranged.   294

[50]

Ambitious thoughts, hearts haughtie, mindes aspiring,   295
Proud lookes, fond gates, and what not vndescreete,
As seruants waite, mens bodie still atyring
With far-fetcht gewgawes for yong children meete :   298
  Wherewith whilst they themselues doe daily decke,
  Brauado-wise they scorne to brooke the checke.   300

[51]

Some couet winged sleeues like *Mercurie*,   [p. 24] 301
Others, round hose much like to Fortunes wheele
(Noting thereby their owne vnconstancie),
Some weare short cloakes, some cloakes that reach their heele.   304
  These Apish trickes vsde in their daily weedes,
  Bewray phantasticke thoughts, fond words, foule deedes.   306

[52]

Bold Bettresse braues and brags it in her wiers,   307
And buskt she must be, or not bust at all :
Their riggish heads must be adornd with tires,
With Periwigs, or with a golden Call.   310
  Tut, tut, tis nothing in th'Exchange to change
  Monthly, as doth the Moone, their fashions strange.   312

[53]

It seemes, strange birds in England now are bred,   313
And that rare fowles in England build their nest,
When Englishmen with plumes adorne their head,
As with a Cocks-combe or a Peacocks crest.   316
  These painted plumes, men in their caps doe weare,
  And women in their hands doe trickly beare.   318

[54]

Perhaps some women being foule, doe vse   [p. 25] 319
Fowles feathers to shroude their deformitie :
Others perchance these plumes doe rather chuse,
From weather and winde to shield their phisnomie.   322
  But whilst both men and women vse these feathers,
  They are deem'd light as feathers, winde and weathers.   324

[55]

Some dames are pumpt, because they liue in pompe,   325
That with *Herodias* they might nimbly daunce,
Some in their pantophels too stately stompe,
And most in corked shooes doe nicely praunce.   328
   But here I doubtfull stand, whether to blame
   The shoomakers, or them that weare the same.   330

[56]

In countrie townes, men vse fannes for their corne,   331
And such like fannes I cannot discommend :
But in great cities, fannes by truls are borne,
The sight of which doth greatly God offend.   334
   And were it not I should be deem'd precise,
   I could approue these fond fann'd fooles vnwise.   336

[57]

A Painter lately with his pensill drew   [p. 26]   337
The picture of a Frenchman and Italian,
With whom he plac'd the Spaniard, Turk, and Iew ;
But by himselfe he sat the Englishman.   340
   Before these laughing, went *Democritus*,
   Behinde these weeping, went *Heraclitus*.   342

[58]

All these in comely vestures were atired,   343
According to the custome of their land,
The Englishman excepted, who desired
With others feathers, like a Iay to stand.   346
   Thus whilst he seeketh forraine brauerie,
   He is accused of vnconstancie.   348

[59]

Some call him Ape, because he imitates ;   349
Some foole, because he fancies euery bable ;
Some liken him to fishes caught with baites,
Some to the winde, because he is vnstable.   352
   Then blame him not, although gainst Englishmen,
   This Englishman writ with his plaintife pen.   354

[60]

But hush! no more; enough's enough; fie, fie,   [p. 27] 355
Wilt thou thy countries faults in verse compile?
Desist betimes, least thou *peccaui* crie,
For no bird, sure, his owne nest will defile.   358
   Well, sith thou brak'st his head, and mad'st a sore,
   With silence giue a salue, and write no more.   360

[61]

The world began, and so will end, with Pride;   361
With Pride this poynt began, with Pride it ends:
And whilst in pleasures Chariot she doth ride,
My plaintife pen, page-like still by her wends.   364
   Thus hauing painted out Prides roysting race,
   At this poynts end, a periods poynt I place.   366

[62]

Now pyning Enuie whining doth appeare,   367
With bodie leane, with visage pale and wan,
With withered face, and with vnkeamed haire;
She doth both fret and fume, sweare, curse, and ban: 370
   She fareth ill, when other men fare well,
   Others prosperitie is made her hell.   372

[63]

She peepes and pries into all actions,   [p. 28] 373
And she is neuer well but when she iarres:
She is the mother of all factions,
She broacheth quarrels, and increaseth warres: 376
   Anger is hot, and wrath doth roughly rage,
   But nothing, Enuies heating hate can swage.   378

[64]

This Trull inticed *Pompey* to contend,   379
And with great *Caesar* ciuill warres to moue:
This dame allured kings their liues to spend
In bloodie broyles, and braules deuoyd of loue: 382
   Incensing subiects gainst their gouernours,
   Sonnes against Sires, Captiues against Conquerors.   384

[65]

As Iron doth consume it selfe with rust,   385
By eating which, it selfe it still doth eate,
So doth the enuious man soone come to dust,
And doth consume himselfe whilst he doth fret.   388
    Thus Ennie still conspires to end his life,
    That liuing with another, liues at strife.   390

[66]

We reade that Enuie twixt two men did grow,   [p. 29] 391
And that the one of them one eye would lose,
So that he might pluck both eyes from his foe,
And plucking both eyes out, his eyes might close.   394
    O who would thinke, a man should beare the minde
    To lose one eye, to make another blinde!   396

[67]

What trade so base but there is Enuie in it,   397
When Minstrels with blinde Fidlers daily striue?
What strife is there, but Enuie doth begin it,
When iusling Iacks, to walls their betters driue?   400
    The truth hereof I shall not neede to sweare,
    Sith *Hesiode* old hereof doth witnesse beare.   402

[68]

What is the cause that many mop and moe,   403
That many scoffe, and scorne, and gibe, and iest,
With rimes and riddles rating at their foe,
Flouting the base, and powting at the best?   406
    What is the cause? the cause one line shall show:
    Enuie is cause, which in mens hearts doth grow.   408

[69]

Knowledge, within the hart of man doth dwell;   [p. 30] 409
And loue, within the liuer builds his nest:
But Enuie, in the gall of man doth swell,
And playes the rebell in his boyling brest.   412
    O would to God men had no gall at all,
    That Enuie might not harbour in the gall!   414

[70]
Enuie and Charitie together stroue
Which of them two a man should entertaine :   415
The one with spight, the other sought with loue;
The first in gall, the last in hart would raigne :   418
   So long they stroue, that Enuie lost the field,
   And Charitie made Enuie captiue yeeld.   420

[71]
Enuie, adiew, and welcome Charitie,   421
The bond of peace and all perfection,
The way that leades to true felicitie,
Filling the soule with most diuine refection.   424
   Enuie shall goe, Ile cleaue vnto thy lore,
   Thee will I serue, and thee will I adore.   426

[72]
Next followes Wrath, Enuies fierce fellow-mate,   [p. 31] 427
Attired in a roring Lions skin,
Ietting along with a giant-like gate,
Which aye a tyrant terrible hath bin.   430
   A butcher like, within his hands doth beare
   Their harts, which he with woluish teeth doth teare.   432

[73]
Wrath moued *Herod* with blood-thirstie hart   433
To slaughter infants from their mothers brest
Like lambes scarce ean'd, or doues new-hatcht to part,
And with liues losse to leaue both damme and nest.   436
   O, had King *Herod* knowne what would ensue,
   He had not done what he did after rue.   438

[74]
He shed their blood; their blood did vengeance craue;   439
They first too soone, he last too late did dye;
They led the way, he followed to the graue;
Both they and he a pray for wormes did lye.   442
   Yet thus they differ, wormes them dead did eate,
   But him aliue, the wormes did make their meate.   444

[75]

Wrath in *Caligulaes* mad head did grow,   [p. 3²]   445
Making him wish that Rome had but one head,
That he might smite off that head at a blow,
Whose pompe he saw, like many heads to spread :   448
  But whilst he thought Romes heads in one to lop,
  Romes heads in one, his flower of life did crop.   450

[76]

Wrath is the cause that men in Smith-field meete   451
(Which may be called smite-field properly) ;
Wrath is the cause that maketh euery streete
A shambles, and a bloodie butcherie,   454
  Where roysting ruffins quarrell for their drabs,
  And for sleight causes, one the other stabs.   456

[77]

Wrath puffes men vp with mindes Thrasonicall,   457
And makes them braue it braggadochio-like :
Wrath maketh men triumph Tyrannicall,
With sword, with shield, with gunne, with bill and pike : 460
  Yea, now adaies Wrath causeth him to dye
  That to his fellow dares to giue the lye.   462

[78]

Mars is the Chieftaine of this wrathfull host,   [p. 33]   463
Whose embrewd standard is with blood dyed red ;
Of many he spares few, and kils the most,
And with their corps his bloodie panch is fed.   466
  Tara tantara, sa, sa, kill, kill, he cries,
  Filling with blood the earth, with scrikes the skies. 468

[79]

Wraths fierce fore-runner is Timeritie,   469
And after Wrath Repentance shortly followes :
The first rides gallop into miserie,
The last procures sadnes, despayre, and sorrow.   472
  Who therefore doe desire to liue at rest,
  Let them not harbour wrath within their brest.   474

[80]

Wraths contrarie is Lady Patience,   475
Who conquers most when she is conquered,
She teacheth beasts that they by common sence
Might teach to vanquish, being vanquished.   478
    Rammes running back with greater force returne,
    And Lime most hot, in most cold springs doth burne.   480

[81]

Patience, a cosin hath calde Sufferance,   [p. 34] 481
Neerely akind, because she is so kinde;
She is most like a Doue in countenance,
And like an Angell in her humble minde;   484
    All Phænix-like she is but rarely found,—
    Would God she might be seene on English ground,—   486

[82]

Then naked swords themselues would neuer cloath   487
With wounded skinnes of men whom men did maime;
Then quarrellers would, after quaffing, loath
With stabs and strokes to kill or make men lame.   490
    Then, then I say, swords might in scabberts sleepe,
    And some might laugh which are constrainde to weepe.   492

[83]

As thus my pen, writing of Vice, spares none,   493
It brings into my sight a lazie Gill,
A sleeping sluggard and a drowsie drone,
Which snorts and snores, and euer sitteth still :   496
    Some call her Sloth, some call her Idlenesse,
    A friend to neede, a foe to wealthinesse.   498

[84]

They tearme her Mother of all other vices,   [p. 35] 499
Bearing a spawne of many new-bred sinnes :
Many she lures, and many she entices,
Whereof most part is trapped in her ginnes :   502
    She is the But at which foule Lust doth shoote,
    And where she toucheth, there she taketh roote.   504

[85]

I once did heare of one *Lipotopo*   505
(Whose pace was equall with the shell-housde snaile)
That to a fig-tree lasily did go,
Whose broad-leau'd branches made a shady vaile :   508
　Thither this lusking lubber softly creeped,
　And there this lazie lizard soundly sleeped.   510

[86]

But as one *Goffo* by the fig-tree went,   511
He wakened him from out his drowsie sleepe,
And earnestly did aske him what he ment,
Vnder that fig-tree all alone to keepe.   514
　As thus he did *Lipotopo* awake,
　Yawning and gaping, thus he idly spake :   516

[87]

Good friend, it is a paine for me to speake,   [p. 36]   517
Because I vse nothing but only sleeping :
Yet vnto thee my minde Ile shortly breake,
And shew the cause of my here daily keeping :   520
　The cause is this, that when these ripe figges fall,
　My gaping mouth might then receiue them all.   522

[88]

As thus he spake, *Goffo* from off the tree   523
Pluckt a ripe fig, and in his mouth did put it ;
Which when he gan to feele, my friend (quoth he),
I pray thee stirre my iawes that I may glut it.   526
　Goffo, admiring this his lazinesse,
　Left him as he him found, in idlenesse.   528

[89]

O would my pen were now a pensill made,   529
And I, a Poet, might a Painter bee,
That picture-like this patterne might be laide
Before mens eyes, that it their eyes might see ;   532
　By which they, seeing Sloths deformitie,
　Might flie from sloth, and follow industrie.   534

[90]

Now doth appeare dame niggard Auarice,   [p. 37] 535
Who, being loden with gold, gapes for gold :
She raiseth cheape things to the highest price,
And in Cheapside makes nothing chaepe be sold,   538
   Which coyne, her chests fild full, fulfill her eye,
   Whilst poore folkes perish in great miserie.   540

[91]

She hath been troubled long with one disease,   541
Which some a Dropsie call, or drouth of gaine ;
She drinkes and drinkes againe, yet cannot ease
Her thirstie sicknesse and her greedie paine :   544
   Still is she sicke, yet is she neuer dead,
   Because her sicknesse still is nourished.   546

[92]

Her bodie grosse, engrosseth all the corne,   547
And of the grossest wares makes greatest gaine :
Yea, Grocers now adaies, as men forlorne,
Auerre that they gainst her haue cause to plaine :   550
   Yet doth she liue, yet doth she tyrannize,
   Because her coyne her works doth wantantize.   552

[93]

This Auarice a cosin-germane hath,   [p. 38] 553
Which many Londoners call Vsurie,
Which like a braue comptroller boldly saith,
She will bring England into miserie,   556
   Who, vnder colour of a friendly lending,
   Seemes of her bad trade to make iust defending.   558

[94]

They hand in hand doe walke in euery streete,   559
Making the proudest Caualiers to stoope :
If with their debtors they doe chaunce to meete,
They pen them vp within the *Poultries* coope.   562
   And if for gold lent, men would counters pay,
   In Woodstreets Counter there them fast they lay.   564

SHAKSPERE'S ENGLAND : TELL-TROTH.   9

[95]

Now Charitie, which is the band of peace,   565
Is turned to a Scriueners scribling-band,
To *Indentura facta*, or a lease,
To racking houses, tenements and land :   568
   All this can gold, all this can siluer do,
   And more then this, if neede require thereto   570

[96]

From whence comes gold, but from the earth below ?   [p. 39] 571
Whereof, if not of earth, are all men made ?
Like will to like, and like with like will grow ;
Growing they florish, florishing they fade.   574
   But where are gold and men? in hell; wher's hell?
   On earth, where gold and men with gold do dwell.   576

[97]

The prouerbe old I doe approue most true,   577
Better to fill the bellie then the eye :
For whilst rich misers feedes on monies view,
Sparing they liue in wilfull penurie :   580
   Yea, more then this, they liue vpon a crust,
   Whilst in their heaped bags their gold doth rust.   582

[98]

Come, plaintife pen, and whip them with thy rod,   583
And plainly tell them their Idolatrie,
Which make their gold their loue, their life, their god,
Which with their gold desire to liue and die.   586
   Tell them, if to no better vse they turne
   Their gold, they with their gold in hell shall burne.   588

[99]

Thus leauing Vsurie and Auarice,   [p. 40] 589
As Sathans limmes, or fire-brands of hell,
As rauening wolues that liue by preiudice,
Or greedie hogs that on mens grounds do dwell :   592
   I post to that which I had almost past,
   But nowe haue ouertaken at the last.   594

[100]

The name of her whom heere I meete withall 595
Is Gluttonie, the mother of excesse,
Which, making daintie feasts, doth many call
To eate with her the meate that she did dresse : 598
  Who being set to eate her toothsome meat,
  Eating doth eate and neuer cease to eate. 600

[101]

This trull makes youngsters spend their patrimonie 601
In sauced meates and sugred delicates,
And makes men stray from state of Matrimonie
To spend their substance vpon whorish mates : 604
  That by their lauish prodigalitie
  She may maintaine her fleshly vanitie. 606

[102]

With gobs she fils and stuffes her greedie gorge, [p. 41] 607
And neuer is her gaping stomacke fed,
Bits vnchaw'de in her bulke, as in a forge,
Kindle the coales whereof foule lust is bred : 610
  Thus doe we see how lazie gluttonie
  Comforts her selfe with Ladie Lecherie. 612

[103]

One other mate she hath, call'd Dronkennesse, 613
A bibbing swilbowle and a bowzing gull,
Which neuer drinks but with excessiuenesse,
And drinkes so long vntill her paunch is full ; 616
  She drinkes as much as she can well containe,
  Which being voyded, then she drinkes againe. 618

[104]

But when the drinke doth worke within her head, 619
She rowles and reekes, and pimpers with the eyes ;
She stamps, she stares, she thinks white black, black red,
She teares and sweares, she geeres, she laughes and cries ; 622
  And as her giddie head thinks all turnes round,
  She belching fals, and vomits on the ground. 624

[105]

Some men are drunke, and being drunke will fight;   [p. 42]   625
Some men are drunke, and being drunke are merrie;
Some men are drunke, and secrets bring to light;
Some men are drunke, and being drunke are sorie: 628
    Thus may we see that druuken men haue passions,
    And drunkennesse hath many foolish fashions.   630

[106]

Fishes that in the seas doe drinke their fill,   631
Teach men by nature to shun drunkennesse.
What bird is there, that with his chirping bill
Of any liquour euer tooke excesse?   634
    Thus beastes on earth, fish in seas, birds in skie,
    Teach men to shun all superfluitie.   636

[107]

Would any heare the discommodities   637
That doe arise from our excesse of drinke?
It duls the braine, it hurts the memorie,
It blinds the sight, it makes men bleare-eyd blinke;   640
    It kils the bodie, and it wounds the soule;
    Leaue, therefore, leaue, O leaue this vice so foule!   642

[108]

Now, last of all, though perhaps chiefe of all,   [p. 43]   643
My pen hath hunted out lewde Lecherie,
Which many sinnes and many faults doth call
To bee pertakers to her trecherie: 646
    Her loue is lust, her lust is sugred sower,
    Her paine is long, her pleasure but a flower.   648

[109]

When chast *Adonis* came to mans estate,   649
Venus straight courted him with many a wile;
Lucrece once seene, straight *Tarquine* laid a baite,
With foule incest her bodie to defile: •   652
    Thus men by women, women wrongde by men,
    Giue matter still vnto my plaintife pen.   654

[110]

Thousands of whores maintained by their wooers,   655
Entice by land, as Syrens doe by Seas,
Which, being like path-waies or open doores,
Infect mens bodies with the French disease :   658
  Thus women, woe of men, though wooed by men,
  Still adde new matter to my plaintife pen.   660

[111]

Whilome by nature men and women loued,   [p. 44] 661
And prone enough they were to loue thereby;
But when they *Ouids ars amandi* proued,
Both men and women fell to lecherie :   664
  By nature sinning, art of sinne was found
  To make mans sinne still more and more abound.   666

[112]

If that I could paint out foule lecherie   667
In her deformed shape and loathsome plight,
Or if I could paint spotlesse Chastitie
In her true portraiture and colours bright,   670
  I thinke no maid would euer proue an whore,
  But euerie maid would chastitie adore.   672

[113]

Then maried men might vild reproaches scorne,   673
And shunne the Harts crest to their hearts content,
With *cornucopia*, Cornewall, and the horne,
Which their bad wiues bid from their bed be sent :   676
  Then should no olde-Cocks, nor no cocke-olds crow,
  But euerie man might in his owne ground sow.   678

[114]

Then light-taylde hufwiues, which like *Syrens* sing,   [p. 45] 679
And like to *Circes* with their drugs enchant,
Would not vnto the Banke-sides round-house fling,
In open sight, themselues to show and vaunt :   682
  Then, then, I say, they would not masked goe,
  Though vnseene, to see those they faine would know.   684

[115]

But in this Labyrinth I list not tread,   685
Nor combate with the minotaure-like lust;
Hence therefore will I wend by methods thread,
And wend I will, because needs wend I must: 688
  Farewell, nay fare-ill, filthie lecherie,
  And welcome vndefiled chastitie.   690

[116]

Vesta, I do adore thy puritie,   691
And in thy Temples will I tapers beare;
Thou, O Diana, for virginitie,
Shalt be the matrone of my modest feare,   694
  That both in one, both beeing Goddesses,
  May of my maden-head be witnesses.   696

[117]

O may my flesh, like to the Ermiline,   [p. 46] 697
Vnspotted liue, and so vnspotted die,
That when I come before the sacred shrine,
My vntoucht corps themselues may guiltlesse trie;   700
  Then shall I glorie that I haue bin taught
  To shun the snare wherein most folkes are caught.   702

[118]

Thus hath my pen described, and descry'd,   703
Sinne with his seuen heads of seauen deadly vices,
And now my plaintife pen hath verified
That sinne, from vertue, mortall men entices: 706
  If any wicked Momus carpe the same,
  In blaming this, I passe not for his blame.   708

[119]

Dictator-like I must confesse I write,   709
And like a Nomothetes criticall,
Pernaps my pen doth crabedly endite
In plaintife humors meerely Cinicall: 712
  But sooth to say, Tom-teltroth will not lie,
  We heere haue blaz'd Englands iniquitie.   714

[120]

And for because my pen doth liquour want,   [p. 47]   715
Heere (being drie) he willing is to rest,
Not for that he doth further matter want,
For so to thinke, were but a simple iest :   718
  And if (as he hath not) he haue offended,
  He hopes (as you) so he wilbe amended.   720

Finis.

TOM of All Trades.

OR

THE PLAINE

. PATH-VVAY TO

PREFERMENT.

BEING

A Discovery of a passage to Promotion
in all Professions, Trades, Arts, and
Mysteries.

Found out by an old Travailer in the sea of
Experience, amongst the inchanted Islands
of ill Fortune.

Now published for Common good.

By

THOMAS POVVELL.

Summum hominis bonum bonus ex hac vita exitus.

LONDON.

Printed by *B. Alsop* and *T. Fawcet,* for *Benjamen Fisher,*
and are to bee sold at his shop at the signe of the
Talbot in *Aldersgate*-street. 1631.

The Epistle Dedicatorie.

P *Oore* TOM *was set on shore in* Kent,
And to the next good Towne hee went;
At whose approach the Bosseldir
Kept a most lamentable stirre,   4.
That TOM *would offer to returne*
Through the good Towne of Syttingborne.
Hee askt him, If hee had a Passe?
And told him what the Statute was;   8
And like a Reverend Vestry wit
Swore hee would not allow of it,
But did advise him to resort
To fetch his Passe at Tonstall *Court.*   12
Our TOM *of all Trades hereupon*
Askt what was his condition
Who was the Owner of that place,
So farre in all the Countries grace?   16
For whom (as hee walkt on the way)
He heard the poore so much to pray,
The Rich to praise; And both contend,
To whom hee was the greater friend.   20
Didst never meete his name there spread
Where thou thy selfe didst vse to tread?
² *No? not Sir* EDVVARD HALES? *Quoth he;*
What TOM *of* Odcombe *may'st thou be?*   24
Hee is a man scarce spends a minute
But hath his Countries service in it;

Spends more to make them all accord,
Then other Knights doe at their boord.   28
Hee call'd him Knight and Barronet,
Both wise and Iust; And what more yet ?
He swore that if hee were but mist,
The Countrey could not so subsist.   32
With that our TOM *repaired thither,*
Conferr'd Report and Proofe together ;
And found Report had wrong'd him much
In giving but an out-side touch,—   36
A tincture of a Painters trade,
Where all was substance and in-layd.
Then TOM *resolv'd to walke no farther*
To finde a Father or a Mother ;   40
No other Patron would hee seeke,
But tender all at this Knights feete :
If hee accept what's well intended,
Our TOM *of all Trades travaile's ended.*   44
Signa virtutum tuarum longe lateque ferens.

THO: POVVELL.

[This text, though copied from the *Douce* copy in the Bodleian, has now been
collated with 4 : *T.* 34. *Art.* Variations in the *Douce* copy :—
    p. 137, l. 4, It it true
    p. 143, l. 3 *from the bottom*, gift
      ,, *last line*, incumbent (with small *i*).
    p. 144, l. 2, Dilecct
      ,,   l. 14, Alchermi
      ,,   l. 16, Parsonadge
      ,, *last line but* 2, inmediately
    p. 146, *last line but* 2, Cantioclucrum
      ,, *last line but* 1, Yf
    p. 147, l. 4, Person
      ,,   l. 10, for Induction.
      ,,   l. 12, peculiar.]

TOM *of all Trades:*

OR

THE PLAINE PATH-

WAY TO PREFERMENT.

(· ·)

RINITY Terme was now ended[2]; For by description of the time it could bee no other parcell of the yeare. In that the Scriveners at *Temple-barre* had no imployment, but writing of blanke Bonds and texting of Bills for letting of Chambers in *Chancery-*lane. The Vintners of *Fleetstreet* discharged theyr Iourneymen; A generall humility more then usuall possest the Cookery of *Ram-Alley.* The Ostlers of *Holborne* had more than ordinary care to lay up theyr Ghuests bootes, rather for feare of theyr slipping out of Towne than for any good observance towards them. And your Countrey Attorneys would no longer by any [3]meanes endure the vnwholsome ayre of an Eightpenny Ordinarie. Every one that had wherewith to discharge his Horse out of the stable, strove who should first be gone. And amongst the rest, my selfe made shift for so much money as wherewith to abate the fury of Mistrisse *Overcount* mine hostesse, and so I departed likewise.

At the top of *Highgate* hill I overtooke a Gentleman of *North-amptonshire*, riding homeward, whom I well knew; Him I saluted cheerefully, and he received me lovingly. But in travayling together (Me thought) he was not Master of that mirthfull disposition which he was wont to carry along with him to shorten the way betwixt his

[1] page 1. [2] In June. [3] page 2.

house and *London*. I gave him to vnderstand how strange and notable this alteration appeared in him; And withall desired to know so
much of the occasion thereof as might be impartible to a freind of so
small growth. To which he answered thus: Sir, I come from
London (It is true), from the Terme (It is certaine true), from *London*
and Terme. True and certaine in nothing but expences in all things;
yet I would have you know that it is neither the Thunderclap of
dissolving an *Iniunction*, nor the Doomesday of a *Decree*, nor Coun-
saylors *Fees*, nor Attornies *Bylls*, in a language able to fright a man
out of his wits, can proscribe me my wonted mirth. It is something
nearer and dearer (my deare friend) that robs me of that cheere which
used to lift me vp into the very Spheare, where *Ioue* himselfe sits to
bid all his guests welcome right heartily.

I remember mee of Children, sixe Soones and [1] three daughters,
of whom I am the vnhappy Father. In that, besides the scars which
my vnthriftines hath dinted vpon their fortunes, the wounds of vnequall times, and a tempestuous age approaching, are like to take
away from them all hope of outliuing the low water ebbe of the evill
day; all meanes of thriving by honest paynes, study, or industry are
bereft them. The common vpon which industry should depasture
is overlayd; Numerousnes spoiles all, And poverty sells all at an
vnder value.

In this case (Sir) what can be aduisd? Wherevnto I thus replyed.

Sir, I haue heedfully attended you in the delivery of your per-
plexed thoughts concerning the care which you have of your children,
taking the true and even levell of the declention of arts, the distent
of trades & trading, the poverty of all professions, and the des-
temper, not of ours only, but of all Christian clymates at this present,
tending rather to a more contagion in the generall ayre then a calmer
temparament (for ought that yet appeareth) : as for the stormynesse
of the sea of state, forraigne or domestick, let vs leave the greater and
lesser vessels that be exposed to it vnto the proper Pylates, Masters,
and Marryners, who have the charge to attend the line or plye at the
tackle; we are but poore passengers, and may assure our selues to
partake in their boone voyage, if they suc[c]eed well,—as they may be
certaine to suffer in the same Shipwracke with vs, if wee miscarry.

[1] page 3.

I addresse me to give you the best advise I can, touching the preferment of every of your [1]six sonnes and three daughters, in manner following.

It is true in most Gentlemen, and very likely in you, as in others, living onely vpon the revenew of lands, That the height of their Husbandry amounts to no more than to cleere the last halfe yeeres booking, and borrowing at the rent day, That their credit may hold vp and keepe reputation till the next ensuing that againe.

When you dye, the eldest Sonne claimes the inheritance of what you leave, thanke God and nature for it, your selfe least of all, and your fatherly providence never a whit.

If you take some course in your life time to make the rest of your Children some small portions or estates out of the whole of your lands, It is tenne to one but you destroy both him and them by that meanes.

For the heire, commonly striving to vphold the reputation of his Ancestors, He abates nothing of his fathers accustomed expences towards the raising of those portions or estates so deducted. And they, on the other side, presume so much vpon the hope thereof, that no profession will fit them. To bee a *Minister* (with them) is to be but a *Pedant;* A *Lawyer,* a *mercenarie* fellow; A Shop-keeper, a man most subject to the most wonderfull Cracke, and a creature whose welfare depends much vpon his Wives well bearing and faire carriage. What is, then, to be done?

Surely it would be wished, seeing God and nature hath provided for the eldest, your younger sonnes, and your daughters especially, being worst [2]able to shift, should bee by you provided for in the first place, while your Land is of virgin reputation, while it is chast, and vndishonested by committing of single fornication with Countrie Creditors, that trade without sheets (that is) by *Pole deed,* only for saving of costs; or, at least, before it have defiled the bed of its reputation by prostituting to the adulterous imbracings of a Citie Scrivener. But especially, before it grow so impudent as to lie downe in the Market place, and to suffer everie pettie Clarke to bring its good name vpon Record, and charge it that it was taken in the very fact betweene other mens sheets,—As in this Statute, or in that

[1] page 4. [2] page 5.

Iudgment : Take heed of that by any meanes. And bee sure to match your eldest sonne when your credit is cryed vp to the highest, while your heire is yet in your power to dispose, and will bend to your will, before his blood begin to feele the heate of any affections kindling about him, or before he can tell what difference is betwixt a blacke wrought Wastcoate with a white apron, & a loose bodied gowne without an apron. Put him of in his best clothes, (I meane) in the assurance of your lands; sell him at *the* highest rate. Then dicotomize the whole portion of his wife into severall shares betwixt your other children. Not share and share like, but to every each one, the more, according to their defects : Let impotencie, decreptnes, ilfavourdnes, and incapacitie, rob the other of so much money as they have done them of comlinesse, activitie, beautie, and wit.

Put them not into any course of living according to any prescript order or method of your [1] owne election, But according to their inclination and addition, seeing that everyone, by instinct of nature, delighteth in that wherein he is like to bee most excellent. And delight and pride in any thing undertaken, makes all obstacles in the way of attaining to perfection of no difficulty.

Now, in the next place, take heed that you put off those your sonnes whom you finde fit and addicted to be bred in the *Ministerie*, or made up to the law, or to be apprentized, betimes, and before they take the taynt of too much liberty at home.

And when they be put forth, call them not home speedily to revisit their fathers house, no, not so much as Hospitably by any meanes.

In the first place, take your direction for the SCHOLLER.

His Education.
His Maintenance.
His Advancement.

FOr his Education. The Free-Schooles generally afford the best breeding in good letters.

[1] page 6.

So many of them also afford some reasonable meanes in ayde of young Schollers, for their diet, lodging, and teaching, given to them by the Founders or Benefactors of such Schooles.

[1] Some of them be of the foundation of some Kings and Queenes of this Land; and they are commonly in the gift of the King, or his Provost, or Substitute in that behalfe. Others be of the foundation of some Bodies or Societies incorporate; And they are commonly in the gift of such Masters, Wardens, Presidents, and their Senior fellowes; such chiefe officers of any other title, or such Master, Wardens, and Assistants, or such Opposers, Visitants, or Committees of such bodies respectively as be appointed thereunto. Others be of the foundation of some private persons: And they are, for the most part, in the gift of the Executor, Heire, or Feoffees of such Donor, according to the purport of his Will, or Grant, or both.

Of every of which severall kindes respectively are:

> *Eaton.*
> *Westminster.*
> *Winchester.*
> *The Merchantaylors Schoole, London.*
> *The Skynners at Tunbridge.*
> Sutton's *Hospitall.*
> *St.* Bartholomews.
> And very many other the like.

Briefly, few or no Counties of this Kingdome are unfurnisht of such Scholes. And some have so many, that it is disputable whether the Vniversities, with the Innes of Court and Chancerie, have where to receive them or no.

Some of such free-Schooles, againe, have *Scholerships* appendant unto them, in the one of the Vniversities, or both.

To which, upon Election yearely, they are removeable, As

> *From Eaton to Kings Colledge, Cambridge.*
> *From Westminster to Trinity Colledge, Cambridge, or Christchurch, Oxon.*
> *From Winchester to New Colledge, Oxon.*

[1] page 7.   [2] page 8.

From the Merchantaylors to St. Iohn's, *Oxon.*
And the like, from many the like.

Some other Free-Schooles have pensions for preferment of their Schollers, and for their maintenance in the Vniversitie.

Some Companies Incorporate (especially of *London*, having no such pensions in certaine) doe usually out of the Stocke of their Hall allow maintenance in this kinde.

Besides that, there be many other private persons (upon my knowledge) who doe voluntarily allow yearely exhibition of this nature.

Now if you would know how to finde what is given to any such Free-Schooles, and in whose disposing they now be,

Search

In the Tower of London, *till* } { For Grants *and for License*
the end of Rich. the 3. { *of Mortmaine,* inde.

And in the Chappell of the
Rolles. } { And *for the like.*
From thence till the present.

[1]*In the Register of the Prerogative Court, for* } { For such Grants
such things devised by Will, by King, Queene, { *given by Will.*
or Subiect.

And sometimes you shall finde such things both in the *Tower* and the *Prerogative*, and in the *Rolls* and *Prerogative* respectively.

For the time since our reformed Church of *England* began here,

Search { Doctor Willets Synopsis. } { For all from the King, or from any other.

Search

In divers of our Chroni-
cles. } { For the like.

Next, adde certaine helpes for discovery and attayning thereof.

First (if it may be) procure a sight of the Liedger Bookes, of such as in whom the disposition of such things resteth, which they keepe for their owne use.

[1] page 9.

Next, be acquainted with some of the Disposers themselves.

Next, take the directions of the Master or Teacher of such Free-Schooles.

Especially to be interessed in the *Clarkes* or *Registers* of such *Societies* as have the disposing of any such things.

Also to use means by Letters of persons powerfull and usefull to such disposers.

[1]For (indeed) it is not the sound of a great mans name to a Letter in these dayes, wherein they are growne so common and familiar to our Societies (of *London* especially), can prevaile so soone as the Letter subscribed by the *Lord Maior*, or other eminent Officer of the Citie, to whose commandement they be immediately sub-jugate.

Lastly, if you use the meanes least seene, most used, and best allowed, together with these, For discoverie and attaining of any such thing, it will not be besides the purpose, as I take it.

Now suppose your sonne is brought to the Vniversitie by Election or as Pensioner.

THe first thing you must take to your care is: In case he come not by election, but as a Pensioner to live for the present upon your owne charge, how to procure him a Schollership in the Colledge where you bestow him.

Or in case he come elected into one, how to procure a farther addition of maintenance to him.

To bring him into a Schollership, place him with a Senior fellow of the house (as Tutor), though you allow to some Iunior fellow somewhat yearely for reading unto him.

This Senior fellow, if the number of places voide will beare it, may nominate your sonne for one in his owne right; if it will not beare it, he may call to his ayd some and so many suffrages of the rest, as, with the speaking merit of your sonne, may worke your desire.

[2] Then how to procure a pension for addytament of meanes.

The chiefe skill is to finde it out, being eyther in the gift of some

[1] page 10.   [2] page 11.

body Incorporate, Or of some private person, Wherein the discovery is to bee made (as aforesaid).

If you sue to a Company consisting of many persons Tradesmen, you must enquire who bee the most potent Patritians, and best reputed Vestrie wits amongst them, such as carry their gloves in their hands, not on their hands.

Amongst an *Assistance* of many, onely two or three strike the stroke, and hold the rest in a wonderfull admiration of their extraordinary endowments. And how to speake sensibly to these two or three is no Mysterie; You know they are faithfull fiduciaries in the election; And, therefore, you must not presume to offer any thing by any meanes. Onely you may desire them to accept this poore peece of plate, with your name and Armes upon it, and binde you unto their love, in keeping the memory of you hereafter. Doe but try them in this kinde, and attend the successe. I tell you, this, with a Bucke at the Renter Wardens feast, may come somewhat neere to the matter.

But for the pension to be obtained of a private person, the way is not the same. It proceedeth of the givers meere charity, and must be taken by the hand of a desertfull receiver. Though withall it may sometimes fall out, that merit is made by mediation, especially of some such reverend Divine, as he doth most respect and frequent. For other, let[1]ters can little prevaile with such persons.

The best note to discover a man inclinable to allow such a pension, is to examine how wealth and charitie are equally and temporately mingled in him; And be sure, withall, that he be a man of some reasonable understanding in what he doth in this kinde. For a Fooles pension is like a new fashion, eagerly pursued at the beginning, but as scurvily left off in the proceeding.

Your next care is, in his due time to put on a fellowship, when he shall put off his Schollership, seeing the Schollership keepes him company no farther than to the degree of Master of Arts, and a quarter of a yeare after, in those Colledges, where Schollerships are longest lived, And in some not so long.

In some Colledges The Fellowship followes the Schollership of course; and as the one leaveth him, the other entertaines him. But

[1] page 12.

in the most it is not so, but comes by Election. Which Election passeth by the Master and Senior Fellowes, whereof every one doth name one, if the number to be Elected will beare it; or if not, then they passe by most voyces.

Where note, that the Master hath a double voyce, and in some places hee hath the nomination of one, if there be two places voyd, yea, if there be but one at sometimes.

In Colledges, the letters of great persons, especi[ally] of the Lords grace of *Canterburie*, and the Vniversitie Chancellor, have beene of great prevailance ; But it is not so now in these dayes.

[1] There bee beneficiall gradations of preferment likewise, for Fellowes in their Colledges; as *Lecturer*, *Deane*, *Bowser*, *Vice-master*, and *Master*. But, for my part, I better like and commend those who, when they find themselves fit to put forth into the world, take the first preferment that is offered unto them, rather than such who live cloystered like Votaries; who have Sacraments to fill up their places, be it but to keepe out others, such as use no exercise but wiping the dust off their bookes, and have an excellent activity in handling the fox tayle, such as hold no honour like to *Supplicat reverentijs vestris;* And to be head *Bowsier* of the Colledge, as good as to be Chiefe Butler of *England.*

These preferments of the Colledge, all but that of the Master, comes of course by order and antiquity. Therefore, no meanes but patient abiding, needs for the acquiring of them in their due time.

I hasten to send your sonne out of the Cloyster into the Common-wealth, and to shew you how many wayes of Advancement are open unto him abroad, with the meanes to discover and attaine.

And first for the Ministrie.

First, for his ease, let him looke no farther then next to hand, and enquire what benefices belong [2] to their owne Colledge, and are in the guift of their Master and Senior fellowes (as most Colledges have divers such); and amongst them, which are void at the present, or whose Incumbent is not like to live long. And if he

[1] page 13.   [2] page 14.

find out any such, than, if he know not, after so long continuance among them, to speake in his Seniors owne *Dilect*, let him never travaile beyond *Trumpington* [1] for me.

More indigitly, For attaining of such a Benefice, let him enquire where the Mattens are read with Spectacles, or where the good old man is lifted vp into the pulpit, or the like, and make a way for Succession accordingly.

Where note, that many times a fellow of the house may hold such a Benefice together with his fellowship, or a Pension, for increment of livelyhood. And such tyes as these are commonly the bond of matrimony, whereby they are so wedded to the Colledge.

Next, he must clime vp to the maine top of *Speculation*, and there looke about him to discover what Benefices are emptie abroad, where the Incumbent lives only vpon the Almes of *Confectio Alchermis;* Or where one is ready to take his rise out of Sierge into Sattin, out of Parsonage and a Prebendarie into a *Deanarie* and a *Donative*, let him not be slow of footmanship in that case, by any meanes.

[2] *For Benefices abroad.*

Benefices a broad are in the gift of

> *The King* imediately,
> *Or the Lord Keeper for the King :*
> *Some Lord Bishop :*
> *Some Deane and Chapter :*
> *Some Bodie incorporate* :
> *Some Parish :*
> *Some Private Patron.*

You shall find in the Tower a collection of the Patent Rolls gathered of all Presentations made by the King in those dayes to any Church Prebendarie or Chappell, In right of the Crowne, or otherwayes, from i. of *Edward* the first, till the midst of *Edward* the third.

The King himselfe, only and immediately presenteth in his owne right to such Benefices as belong to him, and are aboue twenty pounds value in the *first Fruits* Bookes.

---

[1] Near Cambridge.   [2] page 15.

For attayning of any which, I can advice you of no better course, than to learne the way to the backe stayres.

The Lord Keeper presents for the King to all such benefices as belong to his Majestie, and are under twenty pounds value in the bookes.

Now to know which of these are full, and who are Incumbents in any of these,

Search

The first Fruits Office.

The Clarke, who hath the writing of the Presentations.

[1] *The Lord Keepers Secretarie being.*

Where note, that the King hath used very seldome to grant any such living in Reversion.

And the Lord Keeper now being, His care is so great in this, as in all cases of common good to provide for mans merit, and cherish industrie in the growing plants, that no one can offer unto him a request[2] of this kinde without trespasse to his good disposition.

In the next place, concerning Benefices in the Presentation of any of the Lords Bishops.

Note, that most Bishopricks in *England* have presentation to divers Benefices belonging to their Seas.

For the number and present estate of these

Search

Their owne Leidgers.

Their Registers.

Enquire of

Their Auditors.

Their Stewards of their Courts. .

And sometimes you shall light upon some of theyr bookes of this kind, in the hands of the heyres or Executors of such as have borne such offices under them. .

He that is Chaplaine to such a Lord Bishop hath, for the most part, the best meanes, accesse, and opportunity, to ataine to such a Benefice.

The commendations of such a great personage, as to whom this

[1] page 16.   [2] *orig.* repuest

Patron oweth greatest respect, especially for his affairing in Court, may doe some good in the matter.

The like wayes of discovery, and the like meanes [1] of attaining any Benefice in the Presentation of any *Deane* and *Chapter*, are to be used with them respectively, as with the Bishops.

With every *Deane* and *Chapter* are likewise divers *Prebendaries*, to be obtained of their gift after the same manner, and by the same meanes also.

The other bodies Incorporate, besides those of *Colledges* and *Deanes* and *Chapters*, have many of them (especially of London and some subordinate Societies thereof) right of the presentation to divers Benefices.

Also some Parishes, by prescription, doe present to their owne perochiall Benefices. And many Patrons are content to present, according to the approbation of the Parishioners, upon their hearing, and allowing, and due exclamation of the integrity of the life of such suitors, and no otherwise; divers governors, and gradations of the lands of divers Hospitals, and *Mesons de dieu*, have like right of presentation to Benefices, as have other bodies Incorporate. And the meanes of discovery and attaining are likewise the like.

In Parishes and Companies of Tradesmen Incorporate, some very few rule the roast.

Your Alderman of the Ward, his Deputie, your Common Councell-man, Yea, sometime that petty Epitomie of Wardemote Enquerst, that little busie morsell of Iustice (the *Beadle* of the Ward), will make a strong partie in the election, if he be put to it. The Probotory Sermon, that must be made upon such tryall before such an *Auditorie*, would be according to the capacitie in generall, But more [2] especially according to the humor and addiction of those whose wits the rest have in singular reverence, As Mr. *Francis Fiat*, a good vnderstanding Fishmonger (I assure you); you may give the stile of right worshipfull to them, though the best man of the company be but a Wine Cooper, and his iudgement better in *Claret* then in *Contioclerum* a great deale.

If your sonne vpon his tryall can but fit their pallats smoothly, which is hard to doe, In regard that they are so hallow mouthed,

let him be sure, though he misse the Benefice for want of prepera-
tion, yet tenne to one but they will straine themselues to bring him
in as a *Lecturer*, which is a thing they reverence farre beyond the
Parson of the Parish, by many degrees.

Lastly, for private *Patrons* and the Benefices in their guifts,

Search,

The Bishops *Register :*

for Institution and Presentation.
The Archdeacons *Register :*

for the Induction.
The Archbishops *Register :*
if it be a Peculiar.

It was my chaunce lately to see a booke of all the Benefices
within the Diocesse of *Canterbury*, with the manner of their tything
in every each one respectiuely. In which I find that there are, or
should be, with the *Register* of every Lord Bishop, seaven Bookes
kept for Entrie of the matters and busines of their Diocesse, of which
this of Benefices is [1] the cheife.

[2] The like I saw formerly of the Diocesse of St. *Davids*, which
confirmes mee in the institution and custome of keeping the said
bookes also in other Diocesse.

And seing that severall private[3] patrons are of severall dispositions; some more Lucrative and Covetous, Others more charitable
and religious; I can give you no other rule of attaining the Benefice
than this, *viz.*

That your sonne bring with him abilitie of learning, Integritie of
life, and conformitie of behaviour, according to the order of the
Church establisht amongst vs; and these shall make his way with[4] the
good and generous Patron. But for the other patron, it makes no
matter at all for learning, and a very litle for manners, or whether
he be a man conformable or no. Truely he is indifferent; for his
part, very indifferent.

To such a patron your sonne must present himselfe thus (if he
meane to be presented), according to present necessitie : He must

[1] in *in orig.*   [2] page 19.   [3] privare *in orig.*   [4] whith *in orig.*

both speake and prove himselfe a man indued with good gifts, For
he shall have to deale with a Patron of a quick Capacitie, more
dexterous in apprehension than your sonne or you can be in deliverie.

Be this Patron what he will, your comfort is, the Benefice must
be fild, and that within a limited time; howsoever, it is dangerous to
attend the ending of the day in this case, (For seldome doth the
Clarke of the market get any thing by their standing too long and
above their accostomed houre.)

[1] Lapse by reason of *Simony*, and Lapse for not presenting in due
time; Both offer advancement to learning; But the first is as hard to
discover as a witch, And the second as rare to find out as a faithfull
fiduciarie or a fast Freind.

The degrees of rising in the Ministrie are not easier knowne then
practized by the industrious man.

Breifly, if all Church livings in *England* were equally [2] distributed,
There is noe one of the Ministry, if he want not learning or good
manners, needs want maintenance or good Livelyhood.

Here I could wish to God, That it might please the right reuerend
Fathers of the Church the Lord Bishops, That they would once in
every of their times cause a true Catalogue of all the Benefices within
their severall Diocesse, with the names of the Patrons thereof, according to the last presentation, to be sent into the office of the *first
fruits*, for the better information of all such as deserue, and would
gladly attaine to, some meanes of maintenance, which they may the
better doe by hauing recourse thither, there to take notice of all
things of this nature. For I know that many sit downe in their
wants, having good meanes to many private Patrons, onely for lacke of
knowledge of the same.

Note that it is an vsuall thing in private Patrons [3] to graunt
reversion and Advowson of such livings.

My selfe intended heretofore to collect all such Benefices, with
their Patrons, into a certaine Cal[4]lender, for such direction (as afore-
sayd), and made some passage into it. But the farther I went, the
more impossible I found it. And I am now resolved, that without
the Bishops assistance it cannot be done.

And so much for the Ministerie.

[1] page 20.   [2] epually *in orig.*   [3] Parons *in orig.*   [4] page 21.

The Lawes promotions follow.

By
Civill Law
and
Common Law.

FOr breeding of your youth in the Civill Law, there are two Colledges of especiall note in our Vniversities : the one is *Trinitie-hall* in *Cambridge ;* the other is *New-Colledge* in *Oxford.*[1]

I remember me not of any Free-Schoole in *England* that have any place appendant in *Trinitie-hall* in *Cambridge.* But in new Colledge of *Oxford,* the Free-Schoole of *Winchester* hath claime both of Schollerships and Fellowships, the whole Colledge consisting of none other, as I take it.

It is to be confest, the charge of breeding a man to the Civill Law is more expensive, and the way more painefull, and the bookes of greater number and price, than the Common Law requireth. But [2] after the Civill Lawyer is once growne to Maturity, His way of Advancement is more beneficiall, more certaine, and more easie to attaine, than is the Common Lawyers; and all because their number is lesse, their learning more intricate. And they admit few or no Sollicitors to trample betweene them and the Clyent. So that the Fee comes to them immediately and with the more advantage.

The Preferments at which they may
arrive are these :

Chancellor to the Byshop.
Archdeacon.
Commissarie, where they have Commissarie Officiall.
Iudge, and Surrogate.
Advocate for the King.
Mr. of the Chancerie.
The Kings Proctor.
Advocate, and Proctor at large.

[1] *MS. note in the Art copy,* rather Alsoules by farre.   [2] page 22.

In these Courts, *viz.*

The High Commission.
The Delegates.
The Prerogative.
The Consistorie.
The Arches.
The Bishops Courts.
The Archdeacons Courts.
Chancellors, Commissaries, and Officials Court.
The Admiraltie Courts.
The Court of the Kings Requests.

In times past
The countenance of some Byshop, especially of the [1] Lord *Archbyshop*, upon a *Civilian*, will much advance his practice as an Advocate, and give him promotion[2] as a Iudge.

There are under the greater officers aforenamed divers other
inferiour Officers : as
Register.
Arctuarie.
Examiner.

The number of the Doctors, (though I finde them never to have beene limited,) Yet it is certaine that the time was within memory of man when the house of their *Commons* did commonly give them all sufficient lodging and dyet. And as for the number of *Proctors*, they were of late times limited. How it is now, I know not.

For the Common Law.

FOr breeding of *Students* at the *Common Law*, take directions for their *method* of studie out of that *Tractate* which Mr. *Iustice Dodridge* did in his time pen for the purpose. Onely (for my part) I doe much commend the ancient custome of breeding of the younger Students. First, in the Innes of *Chancery ;* there to be the better prepared [3] for the Innes of Court. And this must needs be the

---

[1] page 23.   [2] promorion *in orig.*   [3] preparded *in orig.*

better way, seeing too much liberty at the first prooves very fatall to many of the younger sort. I have observed, and much commend also the breeding of some Com[1]mon Lawyers in this kinde, *viz.*

That when they have beene admitted first into an Inne of the *Chancerie*, they have beene withall entred as *Clarkes* in the office of some *Prothonotarie* of the *Common-Pleas*, to adde the skill of the Practicke to their speculation. And if a Student be thus bred, by his foundation in the one, and his experience in the other, he shall with more facilitie than others, who step into the Inne of Court at first, attaine to an abilitie of practise:

Besides other ordinary requisite parts and Arts in a Common Lawyer, Skill in the *Records* of all Courts of *Record*, and in other *antiquities* of President, With some Reading in the Civill Law, also will much inable him.

The Common Lawyer is to be bred onely upon the purse. The charge most at the first. For after he hath spent some few yeares effectually, He may attaine to the imployment of some private friends, for advising with and instructing of greater Counsalle, whereby he shall adde both to his meanes and knowledge.

It is true, that I have knowne some Attorneyes and Sollicitors put on a Counsailors gowne without treading the same usuall path to the barre (as aforesaid). But indeed, I never looke upon them but I thinke of the Taylor, who in one of his Customers cast suites had thrust himselfe in amongst the *Nobilitie* at a Court Maske, where, pulling out his Handkercher, hee let fall his Thimble, and was so discovered, and handled and dandled from hand to foote, till the Guard [2]delivered him at the great Chamber doore, and cryed, " farewell, good feeble ! "

If the Common Lawyer be sufficiently able in his profession, he shall want no practice; if no practice, no profit.

The time was that the younger Counsaile had some such helpe, as

> To be a Favourite,
> A Kindred,
> To marry a Neece, Cosin, or a Chamber-maide.

But those dayes be past, and better supply their roomes.

[1] page 24 ; pages 24, 25 *misnumbered in orig.*   [2] page 25.

As fellowes of Colledges in the Vniversities get pensions or Benefices to adde to their livelyhood, So Barresters and Counsailors of the
Innes of Court advance their meanes by keeping of

> *Courts of Mannors,*
> *Leets and Barrons,*
> *Swanimootes of Forrests,*
> *Stannaries,*
> *Cinque Ports, &c.*

> By places of

> *Iudges of Inferiour Courts.* As
> *London, and other like Corporations.*
> *The Virdge.*
> *The Tower of London.*
> *St. Katherines, neare the Tower.*
> *Borough of Southwarke.*
> *The Clinke.*
> *Wentworth, and like Liberties.*

> [1] By office of

> *Recorder of some Co[r]porate Towne.*
> *Feodarie of some Counties.*
> *The Kings Counsayle in the Marches of Wales, or at Yorke,*
> *or Iudge, or Counsayle of some Countie Pallatine.*

The greater places of preferment for Common Lawyers are

> *The Iudges at Westminster and elsewhere.*
> *The next are all the severall Officers of the Courts of West-*
> *minster, and elsewhere.*

All which you shall finde set forth breifly in *Smiths Common-
wealth* of *England,* and part in mine owne Search of Records. And
all these together, afford suffic[i]ent maintenance for thousands of
persons, who may bee here well prouided for.

Here I should, and here I could, for better direction of yonger
brothers, shew what meniall *Clarkeships* of large exhibition are vnder
the great Officers of the Land, the Iudges, the *Kings Counsayle,* and
other Officers which are not elsewhere publisht. And I know it

[1] page 26.

would open a doore to many a proper mans preferment, especially vnder the *Lord Keeper*, as *Secretaries for Chancerie* busynesse, and Spirituall promotions, the *Comm*[i]*ssion* of the *Peace*, *Iniunctions*, the *Dockquetts*. And other the like vnder the *Lord Treasurer*, as *Secretaries* for the businesse of the *Realme* and the *Custome-house*; besides the Inlets to so many preferments about the Customes and Escheators; places vnder the *Lord Treasurer*, vnder the *Chauncellor* of the *Exchequer*, *Duchie* and *Principalitie* of *Wales*, and *Duchie of* [1] *Cornewall*, as *Seale keeper*, *Secretary*, &c.

Vnder the Master of the Court of *Wardes*, as *Secretarie*; vnder the *Iudges*, as *Marshall*; *Clarke of the Bailes*, &c.; Vnder the *Barrons of the Exchequer*, as *Examiner*; *Clarke of the Bailes*, and other *Clarkes*.

Vnder the *Kings Attourney Generall*, as *Clarke of the Pattens*, *Clarke of the Confessions and entries*, *Clarke of the References*, Booke bearer. Vnder the *Sollicitor Generall*: *Clarke of the Patents*, Booke bearer. Besides many other *Clarkes* vnder the white staues of the Court, and in the Counting house, and many seuerall offices.[2] All which, with hundreds more that I could name, with a plainer and more large deduction, were it not for feare that what I well intend for generall good, would be taken in offence for priuate preiudice. But for the *Clarkeships* of the *Kings* houshold, examine farther the *Blacke booke* in the *Exchequer*.

The Phisition followes.

A Nd heere I remember me of an old tale following, *viz.*
At the beginning of the happy raigne of our late good Queene *Elizabeth*, diuers Commissioners of great place, being authorized to enquire of, and to displace, all such of the *Clergie* as would not conforme to the reformed *Church*, one amongst others was Conuented before them, who being asked whether[3] he would subscribe or no, denied it, and so couse[4]quently was adiudged to lose his benefice and to be depriued his function; wherevpon, in his impatience, he said,

[1] page 27.   [2] offices *in orig.*   [3] whehter *in orig.*   [4] page 28.

'That if they (meaning the Commissioners) held this course it
would cost many a mans life.' For which the Commissioners called
him backe againe, and charged him that he had spoke treasonable
and seditious words,[1] tending to the raysing of a rebellion or some
tumult in the Land; for which he should receiue the reward of a
Traytor.   And being asked whether hee spake those words or no, he
acknowledged it, and tooke vpon him the Iustification thereof; 'for,
said he, yee have taken from me my liuing and profession of the
Ministrie; Schollership is all my portion, and I have no other meanes
now left for my maintenance but to turne *Phisition*; and before I
shalbe absolute Master of that Misterie, (God he knowes) how many
mens lives it will cost.   For few *Phisitions* vse to try experiments[2]
vpon their owne bodies.'

With vs, it is a Profession can maintaine but a few.   And diuers
of those more indebted to opinion than learning, and (for the most
part) better qualified in discoursing their travailes than in discerning
their patients malladies   For it is growne to be a very huswiues trade,
where fortune prevailes more then skill.   Their best benefactors,[3] the
Neapolitan, Their *grand Seignieur*.   The *Sorpego*, their *Gonfollincre*;
The *Sciaticke*, Their great *Marshall*, that calls the Muster Rolle of
them all together at every *Spring* and fall,—are all as familier to her
as the *Cuckow* at *Canck-wood* in *May*;   And the cure of[4] them is the
skill of every good old Ladies cast Gentlewoman; when she gives
over painting, shee falls to plastering, and shall have as good practize
as the best of them for those kind of diseases.

Marry, for Womens griefes[5] amongst *Phisitions*, the *Masculine* is
more worthy then the *Feminine*.

Secrecie is the cheife skill, and virilitie the best learning, that
is required in a Womans Phisition.   But I never read of many
of those to be long liued, or honestly wiued hitherto, in all my
reading.

Hitherto I speake nothing in disrepute of the more reverend
and learned sort of *Phisitions*, who are to be had in singular reverence,
and be vsefull to mankind next to the Divine.   Indeed, I rather
pitty them; and pittying, smile to see how pretily these young game-

---

[1] wrods *in the* Douce *copy*.   [2] axperiments *in the* Douce *copy*.
[3] benefactor *in the* Art *copy*.   [4] page 29.   [5] greifes *in the* Douce *copy*.

sters, *Male* and *Female*, lay about them, and engrosse the greater part
of *Patientrie* in all places wheresoeuer.

And here I may more fitly say (God knowes) how many mens
liues this abused *opinion* had of such *Gamesters*, costs; Because they
be not Masters of that Mysterie, and that science which requires the
Greeke tongue exactly, all the learning and skill of *Philosophie*,
Historie of all sorts (especially naturall), knowledge of all vegetatives
and Minerals, and whatsoever dwels within the foure elements; Also
Skill in *Astronomy, Astrologie.* And so much of the *Iudicialls* [1]vpon
all manner of *Calculations* as may be well warranted; with much other
kind of learning, art, and skill, whereof my young travailing Phisition
and trading wayting woman never heard.

Their meanes of Advancement are in these wayes, viz.

> To be *Phisition of some Colledge in one of the Vniuersities,*
> (as diuers *Colledges* have such places).
> *Phisition to the King or Queenes person.*
> *Phisition to either of their housholds,*
> Or *to some Hospitall,* (as most have such).
> Or *to some great persons* who may preferre them hereafter,
> and be somewhat helpefull in the meane time.
> To *a good old Vsurer,* or one that hath got his great estate
> together vnconscionably: For they feare nothing but
> death, and will· buy life at any rate. There is no
> coward to an ill Conscience.

It is not amisse to make way of acquaintance with Gallants given
to deepe drinking and surfeyting; For they are patients at all times
of the yeare.

Or a Gentlewoman that would faine vse the meanes to bee
pregnant.

Or your Lascivious Lady, and your man in the Perriwigge, will
helpe to furnish with a foot-cloth.

[2]A Citizens wife of a weake stomacke will supply the fringe to it.

And if all faile, And the *Bathe* will affoord no roome; Let them
finde out some strange water, some unheard-of Spring. It is an
easie matter to discolour or alter the taste of it in some measure, (it

[1] page 30.   [2] page 31.

makes no matter how little.)' Report strange cures that it hath done. Beget a Superstitious opinion in it, Goodfellowship shall uphold it, And the Neighbouring Townes shall all sweare for it.

The *Apprentice follows.*

THe first question is, to what Trade you will put your Son, and which is most worthy of choice. For the Merchant, it requireth great stocke, great experience in Forraine estates, And great hazard and adventure, at the best.

And this is not all : For it depends upon the Peace of our State with forraine Princes, especially those with whom we hold mutuall traffique; Or, who lye in our way to intercept or impediment our Trade abroad. Besides that, in time of Warre, they can hold no certainty of dealing, or supplying their Factorie in parts beyond the Seas. Shipping is subject ever, at the let goe, to bee stayed, Marriners to be prest, and many other inconveniences attend them in such times; Besides the burthen of Custome and Imposition which all [1]States impose more or lesse; So that unlesse wee have peace with such Neighbours, there is little hope in that profession in the ordinarie and lawfull way of trading.

Happily you will alledge that some Merchants thrive well enough when the warres most rage, and when the streame of State is most troubled. Some then hold it to be the best fishing; they that gaine then (Sir), if they gaine justifiably, gaine not as Merchants, but as men of Warre, which occupation a man may learne without serving seaven yeares Apprentiship unto it.

And if they gaine justifiably as Merchants, it must be in some generall stocke of a Society incorporated, who have purse to passe to and fro with sufficient power in the most dangerous times; And if such Societies are tollerable at any time, it is at such times. How they be otherwise allowable, I leave to consideration.

For the Shopkeeper, his welfare, for the most part, depends upon the prosperity of the Merchant, For if the Merchant sit still, the most of them may shut up their shop windowes; Little Skill, Art, or Mystery, shall a man learne in Shopkeeping. A man shall never

[1] page 32.

in forraigne parts, being put to his shifts out of his owne Meridian, live by the skill of weighing and measuring. The most use of advantage he can make of it, is to benefit betweene the Mart and the Market, than which nothing is more uncertaine, seeing there is no true judiciall of the falling and rising of commodities, And the casualties that they are subject vnto, (especially) [1]in time of Warre.

Take this for a generall rule, that those Trades which aske most with an Apprentice, are incertainest of thriving, and require greatest stockes of setting up. Amongst Trades, give me those that have in them some Art, Craft, or Science, by which a man may live and be a welcome ghuest to all Countries abroad, and have imployment in the most stormy times at home, when Merchants and Shopkeepers are out of use, (as)—

An Apothecarie.

A Druggist.

A Chirurgion.

A Lapidarie.

A Ieweller.

A Printer.

An Ingraver in Stones and Mettall.

One that hath skill in seasoning of Shipwood.

A Carpenter of all sorts, especially of Shipping.

A Smith of all sorts, especially of Clockes, Watches, Guns, &c.

A Planter, and Gardner of all sorts.

An Enginere for making of Patars, and the like Engines of Warre. And

Hot Presses for Cloth, &c. And

Engines to weigh any Ship, or Guns that are drowned, &c. Skrues, &c.

A maker of all sorts of Instruments for Navigation, Compasses, Globes, Astrolabes.

A Drainer of grounds Surmounded.

A Sale-maker, and

[2] *A maker of Cordage, Tackle, &c.*

A Lymner.

A Clothier, a Clothworker, and a Dyer.

[1] page 33.   [2] page 34.

A Taylor, Shooe-maker, Glover, Perfumer, and Trimmer of Gloves.

An Imbroiderer.

A Feltmaker, a Glasier, and one that can paint in Glasse.

Briefly, any Manufacture or trade, wherein is any Science or Craft.

Onely those Trades are of least use and benefit, which are called Huswives Trades (as *Brewer, Baker, Cooke,* and the like), Because they be the skill of Women as well as of men, and common to both.

I would have you know, that the Maker was before the Retaylor; and most Shopkeepers are but of a sublimated Trade, and retayle but as Attorneyes to the maker. But if the Maker (without dispute of Freedome in any Corporation) might set up Shop and sell his commoditie immediately, it would be a great deale better for the Commonwealth than now it is.

Besides, it is no matter of difficultie, burthen, or disgrace, for a Shopkeeper, yea, a Merchant, or a Gentleman, to have the skill, of some one of these Manufactures, besides his Revenew, or profession, to accompany him what fortune soever may carry him into Countries unknowne.

To my knowledge, a great *Earle* lately of this Land, did thinke it no scorne to indeavour the attaining of the Craft and trade of a Farrior, wherein he grew excellent.

[1]And when our acquaintance tooke first life with those of the Low Countries, upon a Treatie wherein our Embassador strove to set forth the worthinesse of our King and Kingdome with the Native commodities thereof, The *Dutch* (ignorantly conceiving that no man could attaine to wealth without some good occupation or manufacture) askt him what handicraft our King was brought up unto, or what trade he had used to get so much wealth withall.

I admit the Merchant Royall that comes to his Profession by travaile and Factory, full fraught, and free adventure, to be a profession worthy the seeking. But not the hedge-creeper, that goes to seeke custome from shop to shop with a Cryll under his arme, That leapes from his Shop-boord to the Exchange, and after he is fame-falne and credit crackt in two or three other professions, shall wrigle

[1] page 35.

into this and that when he comes upon the Exchange, instead of enquiring after such a good ship, spends the whole houre in disputing, whether is the more profitable house-keeping, either with powder Beefe,[1] & brewes, or with fresh Beefe and Porridge; though (God wot) the blacke Pot at home be guilty of neyther : And so he departs when the Bell rings, and his guts rumble, both to one tune and the same purpose.

The Merchant Royall might grow prosperous, were it not for such poore patching interloping Lapwings that have an adventure of two Chaldron of Coles at New-castle; As much oyle in the *Greene-land* fishing as will serve two Coblers for [2] the whole yeare ensuing. And an other at *Rowsie*, for as many Fox-skins as will furre his Long-lane gowne, when he is called to the Livorie.

The Shopkeeper is a cleanly Trade, especially your Linnen-Draper; which company hath the greatest Commonalty, and the largest priviledges of all other, and yet they maintaine nothing by Charter, for (indeed) they have none.

But a manufacture for my money, especially if he sell to the wearer immediately.

Now, for the better incouragement of men of Trade, Know that in most Companies of Tradesmen incorporate (especially in *London*), there is provision made by divers benefactors of their Societies deceased for the enabling and setting up of young beginners, by stockes of money remaining in the hands of some few of the chiefe of their Company (how faithfully disposed I leave to their owne consideration,) But surely the poorer sort complaine much of the mis-imployment of it generally

There is but one little Crevis to peepe in at their dealings, And that is betweene their Masters conscience & the Clarks connivence, which is so narrow, that you may sooner discern the South Pole through the maine Center, than discover their mysterie.

Indeed, in times past, the Clearkship of the Company hath beene bestowed upon some ancient decayed member of the Company for his livelyhood. But the Attorney and Scrivener, and some petty Clarkes of the Citie, by the Letters of, &c. pre-occupy those places.

[3]And here I could wish, for righting of the dead, and releeving

---

[1] Salt beef.   [2] page 36   [3] page 37.

of the poorer members of such Companies who are kept in ignorance,
That some paines were taken in the *Prerogative* Office, for the
collating of all guifts of this nature, to be publisht in print, that the
meanest might thereby be able to call their Grand Masters to
account, if they abuse the trust in them reposited in this behalfe. I
acknowledge the youth of mine age to be determined, And (God
knowes) how poore a remaine of life is left in my Glasse; yet if it
may please those in whom the power resteth to give me leave to
search (*Gratis*) for all Grants and guifts of pious use in all kindes
whatsoever, I could willingly bestow that little of my Lampe in
collection of these things, and publish them to posterity. Provided
alwayes, that I and mine may have the priviledge of imprinting the
same for some fitting number of yeares to come

The Navigator

NExt to the man of Trade, or rather equally with him, I must
give the *Navigator* his due, for that his profession is as full of
science, as usefull to the Common wealth, and as profitable to himselfe, as any trade whatsoever. If he attaine the skill of knowing,
and handling the tackle, the certaine art of his Compasse; the knowledge of languages, and dispositions of forreigne Nations where [1] he
travailes and trades, he may rise from a Squabler to a Master, from a
Master to be a Generall, honestly, and with good reputation, in a
short time.

The Nauigator his way of Advancement
and imployment is, by

The Lords of his Maiesties privie Councell,
The High Admirall,
Commissioners for the Kings Navy,
Chiefe Officers of the Navyes of Societies,
    incorporate,
Private Merchants and the like,
    With the *Trinitie* house.

But if he get to be an Owner, he may trade as free as bird in ayre,

[1] Page 38.

as a man of warre, or a man of trade and Commerce. If he take heed that he intrench not vpon the incorporated Companies, especially the *minotaur.* He cannot do amisse (with Gods assistance [1]). He may liue merrily and contentedly, be it but in trading as a meere Carryer of home commodities, Imported from one port to another within the kingdome.

The Husbandman.

THe Husbandman may likewise for the happie content of the life, and the honest gaine which it brings with it, be worthy to inuite a right good mans sonne to vndergoe the profession.

Your sonne whom you intend for a *Husbandman,* [2] must be of a disposition part gentile and rusticke, equally mixt together. For if the Gentleman be predominant, his running Nagge will out run the *Constable.* His extraordinary strong Beere will be too headstrong in office of *Church-Warden.* And his well mouthed dogges will make him out-mouth all the Vestrie. But if the clowne be predominant, he will smell all browne bread and garlicke. Besides, he must be of a hardier temper than the rest of his brethren, because the vnhealthfullest corners of the Kingdome are the moft profitable for Fermors. He must especially aime at a Tenancie vnder the *Crowne,* or some *Bishops Sea, Deane,* and *Chapter,* some *Colledge,* some *Companie,* some *Hospitall,* or some other bodie incorporate. Wherein the *Auditor* or *Receiver* must be his best Intelligencer and Director. Young vnthrifts acquaintance, when they first arriue at the age of one and twentie, And good old conscionable Landlords, that hold it a deadly sinne to raise the rents of their Grandfathers, or hope to be deliuered out of Purgatorie by their Tenants prayers, will doe well.

> These professions before mentioned, be (as it were) the orbs to receiue all fixed starrs, and such dispositions as may be put into any certaine frame.
>
> But for a more libertine disposition.
> Fit it with the profession of a *Courtier.*
> For an overflowing, and Ranker disposition, make him a *Souldier.*

[1] assistnace *in orig.*   [2] page 39.

But, beyond this, he is a lost man, not worthy a fathers remembrance or prouidence.

---

¹ *The Courtiers wayes of advancement be these:*

BY the generall and most ancient rule of Court, if you would have him to be preferred unto the Kings service in the end, And, in the meane time, to have sufficient meanes of maintenance, Place him with one of the *White Staves* of the Houshold.

By the more particular rule (if you can), put him unto the Lord High Steward his Service (who, amongst the white Staves), hath the chiefest hand in preferring to any office beneath stayres.

If the High Steward be full, seeke to the Lord Chamberlaine, who hath the chiefe power to preferre to the places above stayres, and to the Wardrobe.

And, if there be no entrance there, then seek to the Treasurer of the Houshold, and next to the Controllor. The Master of the Houshold. The Coferer, and the rest of the greene Cloth.

The Master of the Horse preferres to the Avenanarie and other Clarkeships offices, and places about the Stable.

The principall Secretary hath heretofore had a great hand in preferring to the Clarkeships in the office of the *Signet,* and the Lord privie Seale into the privie Seale office.

The Master of the great Wardrobe into the Clarkeships and offices there. The Master of the Robes. The Master of the Jewell-house. The Keeper of the privie Purse. The Master of the Toyles ² and Tents, with some other the like, have whilome beene the meanes of preferring divers their followers into the service of the King, in divers beneficiall places and Clarkeships, in their severall offices respectively.

The Lord *Treasurer* without the house, preferres to his Majesties service, in most places in, or about the Custome-houses, in all the parts of *England.*

And, besides these, I finde no meanes used of old, for preferment into the Kings service, for these kind of places.

¹ page 40.   ² page 41.

The yeomen of the Guard were wont to come in, for their personage, and activitie, by their Captaines allowance.

And the Bed-chamber mens servants, ever were in way to be preferred for Pages of the privie Chamber, or Groomes, or placed at the back staires, not of right, but of custome.

For the Clarkes of the Houshold, they were wont anciently to rise by certaine degrees, according to the prescription of the *Black Booke;* but how it is now, I know not.

For your better satisfaction of Court Offices, their order and Fee, *Search* the *Blacke Booke* in the *Exchequer,* and in the Court; And for all Offices whatsoever under the King throughout the whole Kingdome, Either in *Castle, Parke, Chase, Court,* or *house* of the Kings royalty or place soever, with the then Fees of the same, I referre you to a booke, Whereof many hundred Copies are extant, which was collected by the Lord *Treasurer Burleigh,* and [1]by him delivered to the late Queene *Elizabeth* of famous memorie. And so much for the *Courtier.*

The Souldier followes.

ANd the question is first.

Whether the better way of thriving is to be a Sea Souldier, or a Land Soldier?

Questionlesse, the better way of thriving is to be a Sea Souldier, In this Kingdome of *England,* being an Island, for that he is more vsefull to his Country. More learning is required to be a Sea Soldier than to be a Land Soldier. A Sea Soldier is certaine of victuals and wages, where the Land Soldiers pay will hardly find him sustenance. A Sea Soldier may now and than chaunce to haue a snapp at a bootie or a price, which may in an instant make him a fortune for ever, where the Land Soldier may in an age come to the ransacking of a poore fisher Towne at the most.

More valour is required in a Sea Soldier than in a Land Soldier; because the extremitie of the place requires it. The Sea Captaine is exposed to as much danger during the whole fight as the poorest

[1] page 42.

man in the Ship; where the land Captaine vseth but to offer his men to the face of the enemy, and than retreateth.

The way to rise to preferment at Sea, is by the *Admiralls* Countenance, and the *Vice Admiralls* in the Kings seruice, or in other service by the favour of great traded Merchants, and especially of your [1]bodies incorporate, and their chiefe Officers: and more especially their President and Treasurer for the time being.

His breeding is a matter of more moment than his age regardeth.

If he be true bred, he should be first made a perfect Nauigator, able to direct the Sterage of their course, able to know the tackle, and appoint every Sayler to his charge. He should know what number of Saylors, what Ordinance, and what munition, should be requisite for a Ship of such a burden.

He should be a skilfull *Caneere*, and able to direct the *Gunner*[2], to say what quantity of powder a *Peece* of such bore and[3] depth requireth, and of what weight the bullet should be where such a quantity of powder is vsed, whether the *Peece* be sound or honycombed. He should be able to know and direct what quantity of victuall should be required for so many men for such a voyage, And what quantity of powder and shot.

Also to ouersee and direct the *Purser* and *Steward* in the expence of their victuall without profusenesse, or too much percemonie.

Likewise skilfull in all manner of Fire-workes, and fitting Engines for sea fight.

Briefly, he should be so compleat, as that none should be able to teach him in his place, and he skilfull to controle every other in their places. He should be courteous and louing to his men; Above all things, he should be zealous of the honour of God. See that the divine service be duely read on board Evening and Morning, and that swearing be severely punished. A Sea Captaine is not a place for a young [4]man to leape into instantly, and imediately out of a Ladies Vshership, a Great mans bed chamber, or a *Littletons* discipleship.

It is not your feathered Gallant of the Court, nor your Tauerne Roarer of the Citie, becomes this place, I assure you.

I find not any *Meson de dieu* for relieving of mayned Marriners

[1] page 43.   [2] *Gnnner in orig.*   [3] ond *in orig.*   [4] page 44.

only, but that erected at *Chattam* by Sir *Iohn Hawkins* Knight, Treasurer of the Navie of the late Q. *Elizabeth*, wherein it was provided that there should be a deduction of Sixpence by the Moneth, out of every man and boy their wages in every voyage towards the same, Which I could wish were aswell imployed as collected.

The Land-Souldier followes.

IF the Land-Souldier thinke to thrive and rise by degrees of service, from a Common Souldier to a Captaine, in this age, (alas) hee is much deceived.

That custome is obsolete, and growne out of use. Doe what he can doe in Land-service, hee shall hardly rise by his single merit.

His happinesse shall be but to fill his hungry belly, and Satiate himselfe upon a Pay day.

But if hee be of Kinne, or a favourite to some great Officer, hee may carry the Colours the first day, bee a *Lieutenant* the second, and a Captaine before he knowes how many dayes goe to the weeke in their Regiment.

The Land-service, where a man may learne most experience of Warre discipline, is in the *Low-Countries*, [1]by reason of the long exercise of Warres and variety of Stratagems there.

Beyond that, Northward, the service is both more unprofitable and more dangerous, and lesse experience is to be there learned.

The more your Sonne turnes his face to the South, the more profitable the Land-service is.

Lastly, if hee have no friend or kindred to raise him in the Land-service, I assure you that there is no Law against buying and selling of Offices in the *Low-Countries*, for ought that I have read; Neither is it markable amongst them.

After the Souldier returnes home, it makes no matter what number of wounds hee can reckon about him.

All the wayes of reliefe for him that I can number are these :

A poore Knights place of *Windsor*; If the Herald report him a Gentleman, And the Knights of the Honourable Order of the *Garter* will accept him.

[1] page 45.

A Brother of *Suttons* Hospital; If the Feoffees have not
Servants of their owne to preferre before him.
A Pensioner of the County; If the *Iustices* find him worthy,
And that hee was prest forth of the same County.
Saint *Thomas* in *Southwarke,* and St. *Bartholmews, Smith-
field,* onely till their wounds or diseases be cured, and
no longer; And that if the Masters of the sayd Hospitals
please to receive them.

For the *Savoy,* where Souldiers had a foundation, I know none
now.

[1]And other Houses appropriated for reliefe of Souldiers, now in
use, I remember none.

For the chiefe are long since demolished, The *Templarij* are gone,
The Knights of St. *Iohn* of *Ierusalem* forgotten, That famous
House upon *Lincolne greene* is rac'd to the ground, And many the like,
now better knowne by the *Records* than the remaines of their ruines,
with their Revenue, are all diverted from the uses of their first
foundation to private and peculiar Inheritances, which I pity more
than the dissolution of all the Monasteries that ever were.

Heere, you see, is preferment enough for your sixe Sonnes, though
you bestow every one upon a severall Profession; Onely take this
generall Rule for all, *viz.*

To what course soever your sonnes shall betake them, Bee sure
that they all have *Grammar* learning at the least, So shall they bee
able to receive and reteyne the impression of any the said Professions.
And otherwise, shall scarce possibly become Masters in the same, or
any one of them; Or if they due, It will bee with more than ordinary
paines and difficulty.

Your three Daughters challenge the next place.

FOr theyr Portions I shewed you before, how and when to raise
them; That is, by the Marriage of your eldest Sonne, or out of
that part of your personall estate which you may spare without pre-
judice of your selfe.

[1] page 46.

¹*For their breeding.*

I would have their breeding like to the *Dutch Womans* clothing, tending to profit onely and comelinesse.

Though she never have a dancing Schoole-Master, A French Tutor, nor a Scotch Taylor to make her shoulders of the breadth of *Bristow* Cowsway, It makes no matter, For working in curious *Italian* purles, or *French* borders, it is not worth the while. Let them learne plaine workes of all kind, so they take heed of too open seaming. In stead of Song and Musicke, let them learne Cookery and Laundrie. And in stead of reading Sir *Philip Sidneys Arcadia*, let them read the grounds of good huswifery. I like not a female Poetresse at any hand. Let greater personages glory their skill in musicke, the posture of their bodies, their knowledge in languages, the greatnesse and freedome of their spirits, and their arts in arreigning of mens affections at their flattering faces: This is not the way to breed a private Gentlemans Daughter.

If the mother of them be a good Huswife, and Religiously disposed, let her have the bringing up of one of them. Place the other two forth betimes, and before they can judge of a good manly leg.

The one in the house of some good Merchant, or Citizen of civill and Religious government, The other in the house of some Lawyer, some Iudge, or well reported Iustice or Gentleman of the Country, where the Servingman is not too predominant. In any of these she may learne what belongs to her improvement, for *Sempstrie*, for Confectionary, and all requisits of Huswifery. She shall be sure to be restrained of all ranke company and unfitting libertie, which ²are the overthrow of too many of their Sexe.

There is a pretty way of breeding young Maides in an Exchange shop, or St. *Martins le grand ;* But many of them get such a foolish Crick with carrying the Bandbox under their Apron to Gentlemens Chambers, that in the end it is hard to distinguish whether it be their belly or their bandbox makes such a goodly show.

And in a trade where a woman is sole Chapman, she claimes such a preheminence over her husband, that she will not be held to give him an account of her dealings, eyther in retaile, or whole saile at any rate.

¹ page 47.   ² page 48.

The Merchants Factor and Citizens servant of the better sort, cannot disparage your Daughters with their Societie.

And the *Iudges*, *Lawyers*, and *Iustices* followers, are not ordinary Servingmen, but men of good breed, and their education for the most part *Clarkely*, whose service promiseth their farther and future advancement.

Your Daughter at home will make a good wife for some good Yeomans eldest Sonne, whose father will be glad to crowne his sweating frugality with alliance to such a house of Gentry.

The youngmans fingers will itch to be handling of Taffata; and to be placed at the Table, and to be carved unto by *Mistris Dorothie*, it will make him and the good plaine old *Ione* his Mother to passe over all respect of Portion or Patrimony.

For your Daughter at the Merchants, and her sister, if they can carry it wittily, the City affords them varietie.

[1]The young Factor being fancy-caught in his dayes of Innocency, & before he travaile so farre into experience as into forreigne Countries, may lay such a foundation of first love in her bosome, as no alteration of Climate can alter.

So likewise may *Thomas* the fore-man of the Shop, when beard comes to him, as Apprentiship goes from him, be intangled and belymed with the like springs, For the better is as easily surprized as the worse.

Some of your *Clarkly* men complaine the moysture of their palmes; Others the *Sorpego* in their wrists: both moving meanes.

With a little patience your daughter may light upom some Counsailor at Law, who may be willing to take the young Wench, in hope of favour with the old *Iudge*. An Attorney will be glad to give all his profits of a *Michaelmas Terme*, Fees and all, but to wooe her through a Crevice. And the Parson of the Parish, being her Ladies Chaplaine, will forsweare eating of Tithe Pig for a whole yeare, for such a parcell of *Glebe* Land at all times.

And so much for your Sonnes and Daughters.

I now espy mine Host of the Bull here in *Saint Albans*, standing at his doore upon his left leg, like to the old Drummer of Parish[2]- garden, ready to entertaine us.

---

[1] page 49.   [2] *for* Paris (*MS. note*).

Therefore I will here conclude with that of the Poet,

—————————————*Navibus atque*
Quadragis petimus benevivere, quod petis hic est,
Est Anglis, animus si te, non deficit equus.

F I N I S.

[1] LONDON,
Printed by B. ALSOP and T. FAVVCET for
Ben: Fisher, and are to bee sold at his Shop
at the signe of the *Talbot* in *Alders-*
*gate-*street.   1631.

[1] page 50.

THE GLASSE

of godly Loue.

Wherin all maried couples

may learne their duties, each toward o-
thers, according to the holy Scriptures :

Verye necessary for all maryed
men and women, that feare the Lorde,
& loue his lawes, to haue it in their
Bedchambers, daily to looke in : whereby
they may know, and do their duties each vnto
others, and leade a godly, quiet, and
louing life togeathers, to the glory of
God, and the good example of their
Christian Bretheren.

Iames .1. See that ye be not only hearers of the
worde, but alſo doers, leaſt that therby yee
deceaue your ſelues.
Coloſſians .3. Aboue all thinges put on Loue,
which is the band of perfeċtion.

To all Chriſtian men and wo-
men that are maryed.

Oraſmuch as the Diuel is moſt ready to make
ſtrife, where there ought to bee moſt loue; and hath,
with heddy wilfulneſſe, concupiſcence, and ignorance, ſo
blinded the hartes of thoſe which liue vnder the yoke
of Matrimony, that (as I may iudge by their fruites) there be very
few that leade their lyues therein according to the lawes of Chriſte :—
Therfore, (my deare & welbeloued Chriſtians, which profeſſe the
Goſpell) to the intent that you ſhould liue therin, according to your
profeſſion and knowledge, I haue here breefely and plainely ſet forth
what it is, and how you ought to leade your lyues therin, accordinge
to the Rules of the holy Scriptures, ſo that your pure and godly
lyfe may bee a good example, and alſo make ſuch aſhamed as would
ſclaunder the holy Goſpell, and profeſſours of the ſame ; yea, and
that their wonted worde (which is, ' marke theſe new men by their
lyuinge') may found to Gods glory, to the honour of his moſt holy
worde, and praiſe of al them in Chriſt which do profeſſe the ſame.
Farewell in the Lorde.

¹ page 76.

[*This* Glaſſe of Godly Love *forms pages* 75—87 *of my imperfect
copy of a tract, stated by Mr W. C. Hazlitt to be unique, entitled*
The Schoole of honest and vertuous lyfe : Profitable and necessary
for all estates and degrees, to be trayned in : but (cheefely) for the
pettie Schollers, the yonger sorte, of both kindes, bee they men or
Women. by T. P. [Thomas Pritchard]. *No date. The tract contains*, p. 47—74, Also, a laudable and learned Discourse, of the worthy-
nesse of honorable Wedlocke, written in the behalfe of all (aswell)
Maydes as Wydowes, (generally) for their singuler instruction, to
choose them vertuous and honest Husbandes : But (most specially)
sent written as a Iewell vnto a worthy Gentlewoman, in the time of
her widowhood, to direct & guide her in the new election of her
seconde Husband. By her approoued freend and kinseman, I. R.
[John Rogers]. Imprinted at London by Richard Johnes, and are
to be solde at his shop ouer against S. Sepulchers Church without
Newgate. [1569.] *4to, black Letter, A.—L. in fours.* Hazlitt.]

'What Wedlocke is.

Ou ſhall firſt vnderſtande, that Wedlocke is an hie and bleiſed order, ordained of God in Paradiſe; which hath euer bin had in great honor and reuerence, wher[i]n one man and one woman are coupled and knit togeather in one fleſhe and body, in the feare and loue of God, by the free, louing, hartie, and good conſent of them both, to the intente that they two may dwel togeather, as one fleſh and bodye, of one will and minde, in all godlyneſſe, moſt louingly to helpe and comfort one another, to bring forth children, and to inſtruct them in the lawes of God. Alſo, to anoyde Fornication and all vncleaneneſſe, and ſo in all honeſty, vertue, and godlyneſſe, to ſpend their liues in the equall partakinge of all ſuch thinges as God ſhall ſend them, with thankes gyuinge.

And, becauſe that the Wife is in ſubiection to her Huſband, I will begin with her, & ſhortly declare what dutie and obedience ſhee oweth vnto him, by the commaundementes of the Scriptures.

Ephe. 5. The duetie of the Wife to her Huſband.

Saynct Pawle ſayth: *Yee Wiues, ſubmit your ſelues to your owne Huſbandes, as to the Lorde; for the Husband is the Wiues head, as Chriſt is the head of the Congregation: Therfore, as the Congregation is in ſubiection vnto Chriſte, likewiſe let Wiues be in ſubiection to their Husbandes in al thinges.* So that the wife muſt bee obediente vnto her huſband, as vnto Chriſt himſelfe; whereout it foloweth, that the ſaide obedience extendeth not vnto any wickedneſſe or euill, but vnto that which is good, honeſt, and cumly. In aſmuch as God delighteth onely in goodnes, & forbiddeth the euill euery where, it foloweth alſo, that the diſobedience that a wife ſhoweth to bir Huſband diſ-pleaſeth God no leſſe then when he is diſobeyed himſelf. For the wife ought to obey hir huſband in all pointes, as [2]the Congregation

[1] page 77.   [2] page 78.

to Chriſte, which loueth Chriſt onely; and aboue all thinges, ſhee is glad and willinge to ſuffer for Chriſtes ſake, ſhee doth all for the loue of him; Chriſte only is her comfort, ioy, and all togeathers; vpon Chriſte is hir thought daye and night; ſhee longeth onely after Chriſt, for Chriſtes ſake (if it may ſerue to his glory) ſhee is hartely well contented to die, yee, ſhee giueth ouer her ſelfe wholly therto, for Chriſtes loue, knowing aſſuredly that hir ſoule, hir honour, body, lyfe, and all that ſhe hath, is Chriſtes owne. Thus alſo muſt euery honeſt Wife ſubmit hir ſelf, to pleaſe hir Huſband with all hir power, and giue hir ſelfe freely and willingly, to loue him and obey him, and neuer to forſake him till the houre of death.

And farther (ſayth *S. Peter:*) *Let the Wiues be in ſubiecton to their Husbandes, that euen they which beleeue not the worde, may without the worde be wonne by the conuerſation of the Wiues; while they beholde your pure conuerſation coupled with feare; whoſe apparrell shall not bee outward with brodred haire, and hanging on of Golde, either in putting on of gorgious apparrell; but let the hid man of the harte bee vncorrupt, with a meeke and quiet ſpirit, which ſpirit is before God much ſet by, for after this manner in the olde time did the holy Women which truſted in God tire themſelues, and were obedient to their Husbandes; euen as* Sara *obeyed* Abraham, *and called him hir Lorde; whoſe Daughters ye are as long as ye do well.*

And *Paule,* ſpeaking vnto *Tytus* (ſayth hee) : *Let the elder Women be in ſuch apparrell as becommeth holineſſe, not beeing falſe accuſers ; not giuen to much Wine, but that they teache honeſt thinges to make the young Women ſober minded, to loue their Husbandes, to loue their Children, to be diſcrete, chaſte, huſwifely, good, obedient vnto their Husbandes, that the worde of God be not euill ſpoken of.*

VVhat a Wife ought to bee.

HEre may you learne, that a Wife ought to be diſcret, chaſte, huſwifely, ſhamefaſt, good, meeke, pacient, and [1]ſober; not light in countenance, nor gariſhe in apparrell, with dyed or curled haire, painted nor paſted, but with a cumly grauitie and a ſad behauiour of a conſtant minde, true tongued, and of few wordes, with ſuch obedience in all godlyneſſe to her Huſbande and head, as it beſeemes

[1] page 79.

a Chriſtian to haue vnto Chriſt; and to the intente that the Huſband in like caſe may learne his duetie, let him harken what *Sainęt Pawle* ſayth, and take heede that hee turne not his authoritie to tyranny.

The dutie of the Husband to his Wyfe.

H*Vſbandes, loue your Wiues* (ſayth hee), *as Chriſt loued the Congregation, and gaue him ſelfe to ſanęlifie it.*
Now muſt you vnderſtande, that the Huſbande is the Wiues head, as Chriſte is the head of the congregation; and Chriſt ſhoweth to the congregation the ſame thinge that *the* head ſhoweth to the bodye; for like as the head ſeeth and heareth for the whole body, ſtudieth and deuiſeth for to preſerue it in ſtrength and life, euen ſo doth Chriſte defend, teach, and preſerue his congregation. For hee is the eye, hart, wiſedome, and guide therof; ſo ought Huſbands (then) to loue their wiues, & be their heads in like manner to ſhow them like kindeneſſe, and after the ſame faſhion to guide them and rule them with diſcretion; for their preſeruacion, & not with force or wilfulneſſe to intreat them. And *S. Pawle* ſaith farther: *So ought men to loue their wiues, as their owne bodies; he that loueth his wife loueth himſelf. For no man hath at any time hated his owne fleſh, but doth nouriſh and cheriſh it, euen as the Lorde doth the Congregation.* Therfore ought euery man moſt feruently to loue his wife, equally wi*th* himſelfe in al pointes; for this is the meaſure of mutuall loue Matrimoniall, that either partie haue nothing ſo deare that they can not be contented to beſtow one vpon another; ye, and if neede ſhould be, they ſhould alſo not ſpare their owne liues one for another, no more then chriſt did for his congregation.

. [1]And like as when we repent and beleeue in the promiſe of God in Chriſt, (though we were neuer ſo poore ſinners), are as ritch as Chriſt, & al merites ours; ſo is a Woman (though ſhe were neuer ſo poore afore ſhe was maried) as ritch as hir huſband, for all *that* he hath is hirs, ye, his owne bodye, and [ſhe] hath power ouer it, as ſaith *Sainęt Pawle.*

And if it ſo chaunce *that* you finde not your wife ſo perfeęt in al pointes as you would, or as your ſelfe; yet muſt you not diſpiſe hir, nor bee bitteer nor cruell vnto hir for hir faultes, but gently and

[1] page 80.

louingly ſeeke to amend and win hir. For, like as Chriſte thought no
ſcorne of his church, diſpiſed hir not, neither forſooke hir for hir vn-
cleanenes and ſinnes; ſo ſhould no chriſtian man ſpurne at his wife,
nor ſet light by hir, becauſe that ſometime ſhe falleth, offendeth, or
goeth not right; but euen as Chriſt nouriſheth and teacheth his church,
ſo ought euery honeſt huſbande (alſo) louingly and gently to informe
& inſtruƈt his wife.

For in many things (ſaith *S. Peter*) God hath made the men
ſtronger then the women, not to rage vpon them & to be tirantes vnto
them, but to helpe them & beare their weakeneſſe. Bee curteous
therfore, (ſaith hee,) and win them to Chriſt, and ouercome them
with kindeneſſe, that of loue they may obey the ordinance that God
made beetweene man and Wife.

Oh how aſhamed be thoſe men to loke vpon this texte, which
with violence in their furye will intreate their wiues; no beaſt ſo
beaſtly, for in the moſt crueſt way is not mete, as when the wife is
ſad and diſquieted, then with ſpiteful wordes and wanton faſhions, ſo
prouoking hir to anger. Where it is not the dutie of the huſband,
but rather aſhamed to his owne head; likewiſe it is worſhip for a man
to haue the feare of the Lorde before his eyes, that he prouoke not
the plague of vengeance.

Let vs therfore haue humilitie in our hartes; For, as a wiſe man
loketh well to his owne goinges, euen ſo pleaſant are the wordes ſpoken
in due ſeaſon, which moueth the woman in hir wrath vnto patience,
whereof *Salamon* [1] ſayth : *Faire wordes are an Hony Combe, a refreſh-*
inge of the minde, and a health of the bones. For it is ſeldome ſeene
that any beaſt is found in the crueſt rage, that *the* Male doth euer
hurte his Female; and how vnnatural a thing is it for a man to hurt
his owne fleſh and body! Who will violently reuenge himſelfe, yea,
on his foote, if it chaunce to ſtumble, but wil not rather, if hee haue
an yll bodye, cheriſh it to make it better?

The ſtrong (ſaith *S. Pawle*) *ought to beare the fraileneſſe of the weake;*
let one ſuffer with another ; beare ye one an others burden, and ſo ſhall
ye fulfill the lawes of Chriſt : and aboue all thinge (ſayth *S. Peter*),
Haue feruent loue amongſt you, for loue couereth the multitude of
faultes. So that loue in all things and at all times ought to bee the

[1] page 81.

whole doore and only inftrument to worke and frame all things betweene man and wife.

VVhat the Husband ought to bee.

B Y all this may yee geather and learne that the man is the head,
gouernour, ruler, & inftructer (with gentil wordes and good
example), the prouyder, defender, and whole comforte of the woman,
and oweth vnto hyr moft feruent loue and affection, all gentle behauiour, all faythfulnes and helpe, all comforte and kindeneffe, as to
him felfe, his owne flefh and body; fo that vnder God there is no
loue, no affection, no freendfhip, no nerenes of kin, to be compared
vnto this, nor any one thing vnder the Sun, that pleafeth God more
then man and wife that agree well togeathers, which liue in the feare
of God. And how can that bee more liuely expreffed, then in that,
that Iefus Chrift the Sonne of God, and the holy chriftian Church,
and the holy body of them both, are fet forth for an example or
Mirror of the ftate of Wedlocke, or coniugall loue? a more holy, a
more godly and purer example could not be fhewed. Undoubtedly
this doth plainely fhow, that loue Matrimoniall is moft highly ac-
cepted afore God; and the [1] contrary muft needes folow, *that* vnquiet-
nes, hatred, ftrife, brawling, chiding, and frowardnes in Mariage, doth
exceedingly difpleafe God, & is clearely forbidden by *Sainct Pawle*,
where hee fayth: *Let all bitterneffe, fierceneffe, and wrath, roaringe,
and curfed fpeaking, be put away from you : be ye curteous and louinge
one to another, and merciful, forgeuing one another, euen as God for
Chriftes fake forgaue you.* Surely it is an highe and pure loue, perfecte and conftant, that God requireth to be betweene maryed couples,
and therfore ought they by all wayes, meanes, and labour to get,
maintaine, and increafe this exceding loue, and to efchue, forbeare,
and cut of all things, that might occafion any parte of the contrary.

What maintaineth loue and quietneffe in Mariage.

A Nd vndoubtedly there is nothing that longer maintaineth concorde and quietnes, nor more increafeth perfecte loue in
Maryage, then fweet and faire wordes, gentle and freendly deedes, and
with a louing patience to take all things to the beft. Freely to breake

[1] page 82.

their mindes togeathers, and al things to be kept ſecret, both[1] glad and willing to amend that is amiſſe, and aboue all thinge, not once one to heare yl of another, for *S. Pawle* warneth you that ye giue no place to the backebiters, but take them as yll willers to you both, though that they be neuer ſo nere freendes or kin.   And God ſayth, *A man shall forſake Father and Mother, and cleaue vnto his Wiſe, and they two shalbe one fleſh, which in like caſe is mente to the Woman.* Therfore ought no creature aliue to be in ſuch eſteemation, credit, fauour, and loue, as each of you with others.   Alſo, to bee of a ſober and temperate dyet, doth much farther a good agreement; and where the contrary is, there is much vnquietneſſe.   For *Salomon* aſkinge where is woe? where is ſtrife? where is brawling? euen amongſt thoſe (ſaith hee) that bee euer at the Wine; therfore it is moſt cumly for chriſtians to be temperate in dyet, tempe[2]rate in wordes, temperate in deedes, and temperate in all things, ſo that at all times ye eſchue al exceſſe and ſurfet, rage and fury, which makes no difference betwixt man and beaſt, and all other things which may breed any part of vnquietneſſe. For *Salomon* ſayth : *Better is a dry morſell with quietneſſe, then a full houſe, and many fat cattell with ſtrife.*   Therfore ought yee to exteeme and imbrace this concord and quietneſſe, as the maintainer and onely vpholder of the whole felicitie in Mariage, which is engendred of feruent loue, faithfulneſſe, and kindeneſſe, and maintained by the ſame, wherin ye ought continually to walke in all chaſtenes and purenes of liuing, which (aſſuredly) ſhineth as a moſt precious thinge in the ſight of God, and in the commendacion of the ſame, ſayth :

The commendacion of Chaſtitie.

Salomon in the Booke of *Wiſedome :* O faire is a chaſt generacion with vertue, for it is with good men, where it is preſent, men take example therat, and if it go away, yet they deſire it; it is alwayes crowned and holden in honour, and winneth the reward of the vndefiled Battel; but the multitude of vngodly Children are vnprofitable, and the things that are planted in whoredome ſhall take no deepe roote, nor lay any faſt foundacion; though they be greene in the braunches for a time, yet ſhall they be ſhaken with the winde, for they ſtand not faſt, and through the vehemency of the winde they

---

[1] *orig.* doth   [2] page 83.

fhal bee rooted out, for the vnprofitable braunches fhall bee broken, their fruite fhalbe vnprofitable & fower to eate, yee, meet for nothing; and why? all the children of the wicked muft beare recorde of the wickedneffe of their Fathers and Mothers, when they be afked, but t[h]o the rightuous bee ouer taken with death, yet fhall hee be in reft.

Here may you fee how vile, filthye, and abhominable, Adultery, Fornication, and Bafterdy is, and how high in eftemacion a chafte life is amongft all good and godly [1] folke, and efpecially in the fight of God, to whom no fecreat finne is hid.

*That maryed folke ought to haue chaſte manners
and communication.*

ANd as a chaft louinge life in Mariage is moft commended, fo ought ye to be of chaft manners, to haue chaft talke, and to efchue all wanton fafhions, vnclenly communication, filthy handling, and all vnfeemelyneffe, and to be the fpeakers and very doores of all vertue and godlineffe, for *Sainɛt Pawle* fayth : *Be ye folowers of God as deare Children, and walke in loue, euen as Chriſt loued you, and gaue himfelfe for vs an offering, and a facrifice of fweete fauour to God, fo that fornication and all vncleaneneffe, or couetoufneffe, bee not once named amongeſt you, as becommeth Sainɛts, neither filthy nor foolifh talke, neither ieſting, which are not cumly, but rather giuing of thankes: for this ye know, that whoremongers, eyther vncleane perfons, or couetous perfons, which is the worshippers of Images, shall haue any entrance in the kingdome of God and of Chriſte.*

Of temperance in Maryage.

ALfo, there ought to be a temperance betweene man & wife, for God hath ordained mariage for a remedy or medecine, to af-fwage the heate of the burninge flefh, and for procreation, and not beaftly for to fulfill the whole luftes of the diuelifh minde and wicked flefh; for, though ye haue a promife that the aɛte in mariage is no finne, if the man receaue his Wife as a guifte giuen to him of God, and the Wife her Hufbande in like cafe, as ye haue a promife that yee finne not when yee eate and drinke meafurably with thankes giuinge,

[1] page 84.

yet if yee take exceſſe, or vſe it beaſtly, vilely, or inordinately, your
miſtemperance make[s] that yll which is good, (beeinge rightly vſed,
and that which is cleane, yee defile through your abuſinge [1] of it: *God
hath not called you to vncleaneneſſe, but vnto holyneſſe,* ſayth *S. Pawle*) :
and farther (ſayth hee), *It is the will of God, euen that you should bee
holye, and that euery one of you should know how to keepe his veſſell in
holynes and honour, and not in the luſtes of concupiſcence, as do the
Heathen which know not God.*

Alſo, *Sainct Pawle* willeth you that yee withdraw not your ſelues,
nor departe not one from another, except it bee with the good con-
ſente of bothe, for a time to faſte and to pray ; which faſtinge and
prayer, I would to God were more vſed then it is, not as Hipocrites
were wont, but as Chriſtians ought, and are commaunded (almoſt) in
euery parte of the Scriptures ; for they that in eating and drinkinge
fulfill the whole luſtes of the fleſhe, cannot worke after the ſpirite ;
and as wee daylie and hourely continually ſinne, ſo ought wee continually to praye and call for grace.   And in all the whole Byble,
you ſhal not finde a more godly example of maryage (which I would
to God all maryed folkes would reade), then that of *Tobiach* and
Sara, the Daughter of *Raguell,* which were knit togeather in faſtinge
and prayer, and oft vſed the ſame, lyuinge a godly, pure, and cleane
lyfe ; for the which they obtayned the bleſſinge of God, and ſaw their
Childerns Children to the fifte generacion.

The commendacion of Children.

C Hildren (vndoubtedly) is the higheſt guift, and greateſt treaſure
of this worlde, and maintenaunce of the ſame.   For Children
is the very ſure band and laſt knot of loue Matrimonial ; by the which
the parents can neuer be clearely ſeperated a ſunder ; In aſmuch as
that which is of them both cannot be deuided, ſeeing both haue parte
in euery one.   And children are their Parents cheefe ioy, comfort, and
felicitie next vnto God ; their ſtay and ſtaffe & vpholders of their age ;
and in their children do the Parents liue (in a manner) after their
death.   For they dye not all togethers, *that* leaue collops of their owne
fleſh aliue [2] behinde them ; and by their children (if they be ver-
tuouſly and godly brought vp) then is God honoured, & the common

[1] page 85.   [2] page 86.

wealth aduaunced, fo that the parents and all men fare the better by them. Your children (moft affuredly) is the very bleffing of god, for the which ye ought to giue him moft hartie thankes, and be contented, and with fuch as hee doth fende you, bee they many or few, Sonnes or Daughters. For if they be many, he wil prouide for them if they be faithful. If they be few, he may fend you more, and giue you more ioy of one daughter then of ten fonnes. Therfore, be content with his will, for hee doth all things for the beft, and knoweth what is befte for you; giue him moft hartie thankes for fuch as you haue, and be diligent to fee them vertuoufly and godly brought vp; and in any cafe, fuffer them not to bee ydell.

How children ought to bee brought vp.

For they that wil not worke (faith S. Pawle), let them not eate; therfore put them to learne fome honeft Science or Crafte, wherunto of nature they be moft apt. For in that fhal they moft profite; in the which they may get their owne lyuinge, and ferue the common wealth. And aboue al thing, let them firft learne to know God & his moft holy worde, which is the right pathe and highe way to all vertue and godlineffe, the fure Shielde and ftronge Buckler to defende vs from the Diuell and all his cruell and craftie affaultes; giue them daily godly and louinge exhortacions, fuffer no vice to take roote in them, but rebuke them for their yll, and commend them in their well dooinge.

Prouide honeftly afore hand for all neceffary thinges, both for them and all your houfehold. For, faith S. Pawle to Timothie: If there bee any that prouideth not for his owne, and, namely, for them of his houfeholde, the fame denyeth the fayth, and is worfe then an Infidell.

[1] The order of your houfe.

OF the Sparrowes may yee learne the order of your houfehold: for as the Cocke flyeth too and fro to bring all thinge to the neaft, and as the dam keepeth the neaft, hatcheth and bringeth foorth hir yonge, fo all prouifion, and whatfoeuer is to bee doone without the houfe, belongeth to the man; and the woman to take charge within, to fee all thinges conueniently faued, or fpent as it ought, to bring

[1] page 87.

forth and nourifh hir children, and to haue al the whole dooing of hir
Daughters and women.

Alfo be louing vnto your children, and be not fierce nor cruell
vnto them. For *S. Pawle* faith : *Fathers, rate not your children, leaft
they be of a defperate minde, but with difcrete admonitions, and with
your pure and good example of liuinge (which is the cheefeft perfwafion),
lead them to all vertue and godlyneffe.*

If all Parentes would vertuoufly bringe vp their children in the
knowledge and feare of God, in the praĉtice & exercife of fome honeft
Science or Craft, Then fhould we not fee fo many ydell as bee; fo
many Vacabondes, Theeues, and Murderers, fo many vicious perfons
of all degrees, nor fuch vngodlynes raigne. But then fhould wee fee
euery man honeftly get his lyuing, preferring his Neighbours proffite
as his owne; then fhould wee fee all men rightly do their duties;
then fhould loue and charity fpring, and all godlyneffe raigne; then
fhould the Lawes and Magiftrates be willingly obeyed, the common
wealth flourifh, and God rightly honoured, for in this point only,
through the grace of God, confiftes the amendment of all the whole
worlde.

Therfore, (my deare and welbeloued Chriftians) feeing that in
this bleffed ftate of Matrimony, and godly houfeholde of hufband,
wife, and children, confiftes (next vnder God) the cheefeft and higheft
felicitie of this worlde, and maintenance of the fame, wherein the
common wealth is wholly aduaunced, and God moft highly honoured,
I [1]exhort you in the name of Iefus Chrift, the Sonne of the liuinge
God, that you walke worthely therin, accordinge to the will of Chrift,
which you profeffe without faining, and that you efchue all woorkes
and deedes of the flefhe, which bee thefe, faith *S. Pawle: Adultery,
Fornication, vncleaneneffe, wantonneffe, Idolatry, Witchcrafte, hatred,
varyance, wrath, ftrife, fedition, fectes, enuyinge, murther, drunkenneffe,
gluttony, and fuch like ; of the which I tell you before, as I haue tolde
you*[2] *in times paft, that they which commit fuch thinges shall not inherite
the kingdome of God.* Therfore, follow yee the fpirit and workes of
the fame, which bee, (fayth *S. Pawle*) : *Loue, ioy, peace, longe fuf-
fering, gentilneffe, goodneffe, faithfulneffe, meekeneffe, temperance, and
fuch like.* And yet once agayne I exhort you with the exhorta-

[1] page 88.   [2] *orig.* you you

cion of *S. Pawle : If there be amongſt you any conſolation in Chriſt, if there be any comfortable loue, if there be any felowſhip of the ſpirit, if there be any compaſſion of mercy, fulfill you my ioy, that ye draw one way, hauing one loue, beeing of one accorde, and of one minde, that nothing bee done through ſtrife or vaine glory, but that in meekeneſſe of minde, euery one eſteeme other better then them ſelfe, and ſo ſhal you leade a ioyfull, quiet, and godly life in this world, and after, through Ieſus Chriſt, come to the life euerlaſting, with God the Father, to whom bee all honour and glory. Amen.*

Rom. 10. *If the roote bee whole, the braunches ſhall bee whole alſo.*

FINIS.

QUOTATIONS FROM THE BIBLE

IN THE

GLASSE OF GODLY LOVE.

Title page, p. 177, *Jam.* i. 22 ; *Col.* iii. 14.

p. 179, Yee Wives, &c., *Eph.* v. 22-4.

p. 180, Let the Wives, &c., 1 *Pet.* iii. 1—6 ; Let the elder Women, &c., *Titus* ii. 3—5.

p. 181, Husbandes, love your Wives, &c., *Eph.* v. 25 ; So ought men, &c., *Idem.* 28-9 ; his owne bodye, &c., 1 *Cor.* vii. 4.

p. 182, For in many things, &c., 1 *Pet.* iii. 7, 8 ? Faire wordes, &c., *Prov.* xvi. 24 ; the strong, &c., *Rom.* xv. 1 ; let one suffer, &c., 1 *Cor.* xii. 26 ? beare ye, &c., *Gal.* vi. 2 ; and above all thinge, &c., 1 *Pet.* iv. 8.

p. 183, Let all bitternesse, &c., *Eph.* iv. 31.

p. 184, A man shall forsake, &c., *Gen.* ii. 24 ; For Salomon askinge, &c., *Prov.* xxiii. 29, 30 ; Better is a dry morsell, &c., *Prov.* xvii. 1 ; Salomon in the Booke of Wisdome, *Wisdom* iv. 1—7.

p. 185, Be ye folowers, &c., *Eph.* v. 1—5.

p. 186, God hath not called you, &c., 1 *Thess.* iv. 7 ; It is the will of ˙ God, &c., *Idem.* 3—5 ; Also, Sainct Pawle, &c., 1 *Cor.* vii. 5.

p. 187, For they that wil not worke, &c., 2 *Thess.* iii. 10 ; If there bee any, &c., 1 *Tim.* v. 8.

p. 188, Fathers, rate not your children, &c., *Eph.* vi. 4 ; Adultery, &c., *Gal.* v. 19—21 ; Love, &c., *Idem.* 22.

p. 189, If there be amongst you, &c., *Philipp.* ii. 1—3 ; If the roote, &c., *Rom.* xi. 16.

NOTES.

p. xiii. *John Lane and Milton's father.* "Besides these, there remains, as evidence of Lane's perseverance, a long manuscript poem in the Museum [Royal MS., 17. B. xv.], dated 1621, and entitled *Triton's Trumpet to the Twelve Months, husbanded and moralized.* In it there is a distinct allusion to the scrivener Milton, in his capacity as a musical composer. Here it is—specimen enough of all Lane's poetry !—

> Accenting, airing, curbing, ordering
> Those sweet parts Meltonus did compose,
> As wonder's self amazed was at the close,
> Which in a counter-point maintaining *hielo*
> 'Gan all sum up thus + *Alleluiah Deo.*"

But, more interesting still, another of Lane's manuscripts—that of " Guy of Warwick "—furnishes us with a specimen of the musician's powers in returning the compliment. This manuscript had evidently been prepared for the press ; and on the back of the title-page is a sonnet headed " *Johannes Melton, Londinensis civis, amico suo viatico, in poesis laudem ;* " that is, " John Milton, citizen of London, to his wayfaring friend in praise of his poetry." The sonnet is so bad that Lane might have written it himself ; but, bad or good, as a sonnet by Milton's father, the world has a right to see it. So here it is :—

> " If virtue this be not, what is ? Tell quick !
> For childhood, manhood, old age, thou dost write
> Love, war, and lusts quelled by arm heroic,
> Instanced in Guy of Warwick, knighthood's light :
> Heralds' records, and each sound antiquary,
> For Guy's true being, life, death, eke hast sought,
> To satisfy those which *prævaricari ;*
> Manuscript, chronicle, if might be bought ;
> Coventry's, Winton's, Warwick's monuments,
> Trophies, traditions delivered of Guy,
> With care, cost, pain, as sweetly thou presents,
> To exemplify the flower of chivalry :
> From cradle to the saddle and the bier,
> For Christian imitation all are here." [1]

[1] " Harl. MS. 5243. Mr. Hunter was the first to print this sonnet ; and also, so far as I am aware, to refer, in connexion with Milton, to Lane's MSS. generally." —1859. D. Masson's *Life of Milton,* i. 42-3.

p. xiii. John Lane's *Triton's Trumpet.* "Phillips . . omits ' *Triton's Trumpet,*' undoubtedly by Lane, and dated 1620, in which the death of Spenser in 1599 is mentioned, with all the particulars of his sufferings and poverty, and the vain wish of the Earl of Essex to relieve them. ('Life of Spenser,' edit. 1862, p. cli)."—J. P. Collier, *Bibliographical Catalogue,* i. 448.—F.

p. xvii, note 1. Powell's *Welch Bayte.*

5to Decembris

Valentine Yt is ordered that he shall presently bring into the hall, to be used
Symms according to the ordonance in *that* behalf. Thirtie bookes of *the welshbate.* and all the ballades that he hath printed of *the Traytours lately Arrayned at Winchester.*

Valentine also Yt is ordered that he shall pay xliis iiijd for a fine for
Symms printing the same book and ballad without Licence. And not to meddle with printing or selling any of the same bookes or ballads hereafter.

Arber's *Transcript of the Stationers' Registers,* iii. 249. See also ii. 837.

p. xxiii. T. Powell's *Mysterie of Lending and Borrowing.* Here is

"The Authors Inuocation.

THou spirit of old *Gybbs,* a quondam Cooke,
Thy hungry Poet doth thee now inuoke,
T-infuse in him the iuyce of Rumpe or Kidney,
And he shall sing as sweet as ere did *Sidney :*
I am not so ambitious as to wish
For black spic'keale, or such a pretious dish,
As Dottrels caught by pretty imitation,
Nor any thing so hot in operation,
As may inflame the Liuer of mine Host,
To sweare I chalke too much vpon the post :
My selfe a damn'd Promethian I should thinke,
If with the Gods Scotch-Ale, or Meth, a drinke,
The vulgar to prophane, Metheglin call,
Or drops which from my Ladies Lembick fall,
In seuerall spirits of a fifth transcendence,
No, no, the hungry belly calls my mind thence :
I wish not for Castalian cups, not I,
But with the petty-Canons being dry,
And but inspir'd with one bare Qu : let any
Compare with vs for singing (O *Sydany.*)
Thy Pot-herbs, prithy, *Robbin,* now afford,
Perfume the Altar of thy Dresser-boord,
And couer it with *Hecatombes* of Mutton,
As fat and faire as euer knife did cut on :
Then will I sing the Lender and the Debter,
The martiall Mace, the Serieant and the Setter,
Ruines and reparations of lost wealth,
Still, Where you see me, Trust vnto your selfe."

p. 4, l. 11. *Lelaps.* A dog of surpassing swiftness given by Diana to Procris, and by her presented to her husband Cephalus. See Ovid's *Metamorphoses,* vii, ll. 771-93, for an account of Laelaps.—S.

p. 5, l. 15. *daughters of twentye . . to rich cormorants of threescore.* Compare Chaucer's *Merchant's Tale* of January and May.—F.

p. 6, l. 2. *Durum pati meminisse dulce.* Cf. *Æn.,* I. 203. Daniello in a note to the Inferno, xvi. 84, attributes this quotation to Seneca, but does not give a precise reference. See Lombardi's *Dante*, I. 351, ed. 1830.—S.

p. 6, l. 7. *Thinges farre fetchte and deere boughte.* See Notes to Stafford's *Examination*, p. 103.—F.

p. 7, l. 3, *for:* from, against : 'now will I dam up this thy yawning mouth *for* swallowing the treasure of the realm,' 2 *Hen. VI*, IV. i. 74 ; 'and advise thee to desist *for* going on death's net,' *Pericles*, I. i. 40.— Schmidt.—F.

p. 7, l. 6. *Sic volo, sic jubeo, stet pro ratione voluntas.* Juvenal, S. vi. 223. The usual reading is " Hoc volo, sic jubeo, sit, &c."—S.

p. 8, l. 4. *women with nothing more contented then to haue their willes.* Compare Chaucer's *Wife of Bath's Tale;* Andrew Boorde's *Brevyary*, chap. 242, in my edition of his *Introduction*, &c. (E. E. T. Soc.) p. 68, and note there.—F.

p. 10, l. 9. *had I wist is a slender remedy to remove repentaunce.* " I write not here a tale of had I wist : But you shall heare of travels &c."— J. Taylor (Water Poet), *Pennilesse Pilgrimage*, Spenser Soc. ed., p. 132, ll. 2-3. " A wise man saith not, had I wist."—Uncertain author in Tottel's *Miscellany*, Arber's ed. p. 244.—P. A. D. " When dede is doun, hit ys to lat ; be ware of hady-wyst."—The Good Wyfe Wold A Pylgremage : *Queene Elizabethes Achademy*, E. E. T. S., p. 42, ll. 119-20.—S.

p. 26, l. 8 from foot. '*Knight of the Post.* Properly, a man who gained his living by giving false evidence on trials, or false bail ; in a secondary sense, a sharper in general. " A *knight of the post*, quoth he, for so I am tearmed ; a fellow that will sweare you any thing for twelve pence."—*Nash, Pierce Penilesse*, 1592.

" But is his resolution any way infracted, for that some refractaries are (like *knights of the post*) hired to witnesse against him ?"—*Ford's* Line of Life, 1620.'—(Additions to) Nares.—F.

p. 26, l. 24. " *A supplication from Pierce Pennilesse.*" An allusion to a satire written by Thomas Nash, entitled " Pierce Penilesse, his Supplication to the Divell ; describing the over-spreading of Vice, and the suppression of Vertue. Pleasantly interlaced with variable delights, and pathetically intermixt with conceipted reproofes," Lond. 1592 ; Watts, *Bib. Brit.*—S.

p. 29, l. 12-13. Three instances of the genitive *it* in two lines : *it* delighte, *it* ioy, *it* beginning. See too p. 90, l. 9 from foot.—F.

p. 30, l. 9-10. This proverb of the Pitcher going long to the water, but getting broken at last, is in Dan Michel's *Ayenbite of Inwyt*, A.D. 1340: " Zuo longe geþ þet pot to the wetere, þet hit comþ tobroke hom," p. 165, l. 7 from foot, ed. Stevenson, for Roxburghe Club.—F.

p. 32, l. 13 from foot. *it was the parte of Mad Men,* &c. A free expansion of " Quare in tranquillo tempestatem adversam optare dementis est, subvenire autem tempestati quavis ratione sapientis."—Cic. *Off.*, I. xxiv. 5.—S.

p. 33, l. 17. *a tooting head:* one with horns, through which men toot or blow, the mark of a cuckold.—F.

p. 33, l. 30. *where Christes crosse standes :* that is, at the head of the alphabet. '*La croix de par dieu.* The Christs-crosse-row'; or Horne-booke wherein a child learnes it.'—*Cotgrave.*—F.

p. 36, l. 3. *mistrisse her necke.* This absurd form of the possessive case came in from the mistake in the masculine, ' Robin good-fellow *his* newes,' p. 49, &c., as if the genitive *-s, -es* was contracted from *hi-s.* In the second text of Layamon's *Brut* are many of these genitives in *his,* some of them to feminine nouns. They arose from the scribe of that MS. being very fond of *h*'s, and putting *h* on to the genitives in *-is,* which *-is* was often written apart from the crude form of its noun.—F.

p. 36, l. 11. *nor so many yeeld uppe the possession of their garmentes to the hangman.* "There was a curst page that his master whipt naked, and when he had been whipt, would not put on his cloaths ; and when his master bad him, 'take them you, for they are the hangman's fees.'"—Bacon's *Apophthegms,* No. 69, *Miscellaneous Writings of Francis Bacon,* 1802.—S.

p. 39, l. 3. *Omnia vincit Amor, et nos cedamus amori.*—Virgil, *Ecl.* x. 69.—S.

p. 39, l. 12. *that babie which lodges in womens and mens eies.* The reflected images of himself seen by a lover in the pupils of his mistress's eyes, or *vice versâ.*

Cf. " So when thou [Love] sawst in natures cabinet Stella, thou straight lookst *babies in her eyes.*"—Sidney's *Astrophel and Stella,* sonnet xi. ll. 9-10.

In Massinger's *Renegado,* II. iv, p. 129, col. 1, ed. Gifford, 1840, Donusa says to Vitelli, " When a young lady wrings you by the hand, thus, Or with an amorous touch presses your foot, Looks *babies in your eyes,* plays with your locks, Do not you find without a tutor's help, What 'tis she looks for ? "—S.

p. 43, l. 14. ' Thirteen Pence Halfpenny was considered as the hang-man's wages very early in the 17th century. How much sooner, I have not noticed. " 'Sfoot, what a witty rogue was this to leave this fair *thirteen pence halfpenny,* and this old halter, intimating aptly,

Had the hangman met us there, by these presages, Here had been his work, and here *his wages.*"

Match at Midnight, Old Plays, vii. 357.

" If I shold, he could not hang me for't ; 'tis not worth thirteen pence halfpenny."—J. Day's *Humour out of Breath,* sign. F. 3.'—Nares.—F.

p. 55, l. 22. *Greenes Cunnyberries,* Robert Greene's Coney-burrows, alluding to his four Coneycatching tracts : I. A Notable Discouery of Cosnage, 1591 ; II. The Second Part of Conny-catching, 1591 ; III. The Third and last part of Conny-catching, With the new deuised knavish arte of Foole-taking, 1592. IV. A Disputation Betweene a Hee Conny-catcher and a Shee Conney-catcher, whether a Theafe or a Whorer is most hurtfull in Cousonage, to the Commonwealth. Discouering the Secret Villanies of alluring Strumpets. With the Conuersion of an English Courtizen, reformed this present yeare 1592.—*Haslitt.*—F.

p. 55, last line. *then on goes her pantoples.* "Such is the Nature of these nouises that think to haue learning without labour, ... that for the most parte they *stande so on their pantuffles*, that they be secure of perils, obstinate in their own opinions, impatient of labour, apt to conceive wrong, credulous to believe the worst, ready to shake off their olde acquaintance without cause, and to condemne them without colour."— *Euphues*, p. 47, ed. Arber.

Sander. . . . "Why looke you now, ile scarce put up plain Sander now at any of their hands ; for and any body have any thing to do with my master, straight they come crouching upon me,—'I beseech you good M. Sander speake a good word for me,'—and then I am so stowt and take it upon me, and *stand upon my pantoffles* to them, out of all crie, why I haue a life like a giant now."—*Taming of a Shrew*, p. 174, ed. Nichols, Six old Plays.

"Stande thou on thy pantuffles, and shee will vayle bonnet."— *Euphues*, p. 117.—P. A. DANIEL.

p. 68, l. 7 from foot. *willing her,* . . . *either then or never to consent to the saving of all their lives.* Abduction was punishable with death. By statute 39 Eliz. c. 9, principals, procurers, or accessories before the fact, were deprived of benefit of clergy. See Blackstone's *Commentaries*, ed. Kerr, 1862, iv. 231.—S.

The preamble of the Act of Elizabeth, passt in 1597, illustrates the story in the text, and runs thus :—

"Whereas of late times diuers women, as well maydens as widowes, and wiues hauing substance, some in goods mooueable, and some in lands and tenements, and some being heires apparent to their Ancestours, for the lucre of such substance bene oftentimes taken by misdoers, contrary to their will, and after maried to such misdoers, or to others by their assent, or defiled, to the great displeasure of God, and contrary to your Hig[h]nesses Lawes, and disparagement of the said women, and great heauinesse and discomfort of their friends, and ill example of others ; which offences, albeit the same be made felonie by a certaine act of Parliament made in the third yeere of King Henrie the seuenth : Yet forasmuch as Clergie hath been heretofore allowed to such Offenders, diuers persons haue attempted and committed the said offences in hope of life by the benefit of Clergie[1] :—Be it therefore enacted &c." Christopher Barker's edition of 1597, sign. E. This edition contains two acts more than the Record Office one, namely, "26 An Act for confirmation of the Subsidies granted by the Clergie. 27 An Act for the grant of three entire Subsidies, and sixe Fifteenes and Tenths granted by the Temporalitie." Chap. 7, ' An Act for the more speedie payment of the Queenes Maiesties debts', looks as if Q. Elizabeth was insolvent : but

[1] Education the excuse for crime ! The doctrine sounds odd now.

'the Queen's debts' were debts due to her, like 'the Queen's traitors' were traitors against her.—F.

p. 69, l. 8. *the counsell Table.* The concilium ordinarium, commonly known as the court of star chamber, a branch of the privy council which assumed jurisdiction over many offences cognizable in the ordinary law courts. See Hallam's *History of England,* vol. I. chap. i.—S.

p. 69, l. 8. *she tolde so good a tale for him,* &c. If a woman was married by her abductor, she was allowed to give evidence against him of the abduction, contrary to the then general rule that a wife's evidence could not be received against her husband. See Blackstone's *Comment-aries,* iv. 231.—S.

p. 71, l. 10 from foot. *cooling carde.* So Suffolk in 1 *Hen. VI.,* V. iii. 83 : " There all is marr'd ; there lies a *cooling card."* Not Shakspere's.—F. A letter from Euphues to Philautus is entitled, "A cooling Carde for Philautus and all fond lovers."—*Euphues,* Arber's ed. p. 106. " Card. (2) A chart. Harrison, p. 39."—Halliwell's *Dict.—* S.

p. 75, l. 3 from foot. *a tantinie pigge.* St Anthony's. See Brand's *Antiquities,* ed. Ellis, 1841, i. 200, note *a,* col. 2. And " St. Anthony's church in Threadneedle street, belonging to an hospital of that Saint, and dedicated to St. Anthony of Vienna as early as Henry III. The found-ation was for a master, two priests, a schoolmaster, and twelve poor men. . . The proctors of this house used to collect alms, and take from the market people lean or ill-conditioned pigs, which they turned abroad with bells about their necks to live upon the public,—whence the saying *an Anthony's pig,* and when fat, they killed them for the use of the hospital."—Stowe's Lond. p. 190, in Nichols's ed. of E. Perlin, *Descr. d'Angleterre* 1558, repr. 1775, p. 13. See the Index below, p. 209.—F.

p. 82. To compare small things with great, set this page beside Julia's description of her lovers in the *Two Gentlemen of Verona,* I. ii., and Portia's of hers in the *Merchant of Venice,* I. ii.—F.

p. 83, l. 7. Smithfield (or smooth-field, an etymology sanctioned by Fitz Stephen, who describes it as *campus planus*) was celebrated for many centuries as a market, and the cheating carried on there, more especially in the sale of horses, was long notorious. A 'Smithfield horse' was the cant name for a particularly bad bargain. Falstaff tells us that his horse was bought at Smithfield (2nd part of *Henry IV.,* act I. sc. ii. ll. 56-7), and Pepys speaks "of the craft and cunning that I never dreamed of, concerning the buying and choosing of horses," *Diary,* Dec. 4, 1668. And see under Dec. 11, 1668.—H. B. W.

p. 83, l. 7 from foot. *a Smithfelde horse.* Smithfield was noted for its horse-fairs (p. 87, l. 2 from foot) ; and at them, as at all other fairs, the buyer takes his chance.

" The Londiners pronounce woe to him that buyes a horse in Smyth-field, that takes a servant in Pauls Church, that marries a wife out of Westminster" [noted for its stews].—Fynes Moryson's *Itinerary,* 1617, Pt. 3, p. 53. On the Fair in Smithfield, see *Bartholomew Fair,* 1641.—F.

p. 83, l. 7 from foot. *whether a Smithfeelde horse will proue good or jadish.* "heere [to Smithfield] comes many Horses, (like *Frenchmen*) rotten in the joynts, which by tricks are made to leape, though they can scarce go ; he that light upon a Horse in this place, from an olde Horse-courser, sound both in wind and limbe, may light of an honest Wife in the Stews : here's many an olde Jade, that trots hard for't, that uses his legs sore against his will, for he had rather have a Stable then a Market, or a Race."—London and the Countrey Carbonadoed and Quartred into severall Characters. By D. Lupton, 1632, pp. 36-7.—S.

p. 85, l. 3. *let them have their willes ; or they will, whether you will or no.* Compare Andrew Boorde's *Breuiary*, Fol. lxxxii. back, "therfore, *Vt homo not cantet cum cuculo*, let euery man please his wyfe in all matters, and displease her not, but let her haue her owne wyl, for that she wyll haue, who so euer say nay," p. 68 of my edition, E. E. T. Soc. 1870.—F.

p. 91, l. 2. *Kemps head.* An account of William Kemp will be found in Variorum Shakspere, ed. 1821, vol. III. p. 197.—P. A. D.

p. 91, l. 9. *Knackes to knowe knaves by.* "A knack how to knowe a knave," one of Kempe's works ?—P. A. D.

p. 113, l. 73. *Ovid could testify*, &c. Ultima cœlestum, terras Astræa reliquit.—Ovid's *Metamorphoses*, 1. 150.—S.

p. 113, l. 84. *carnall vice . . in the Popes great hall.* On the lechery and sodomy seen in Rome by Andrew Boorde, see my edition of A. B., p. 77, with the extract from Thomas's *History of Italye* in the note there.—F.

p. 118, l. 216, *gigge*, jig. Cp. in Arber's *Transcript of the Stationers' Registers*, iii. 49, 50, "A pretie newe *Jigge* betwene Francis the gentle-man, Richard the farmer, and theire wyves," Oct. 14, 1595 ; and on Oct. 21, "a ballad called Kemps newe *Jygge* betwixt a souldiour and a Miser, and Sym the clown." "The word '*jig*' is said to be derived from the Anglo-Saxon ; and in old English literature its application extended, beyond the tune itself, to any jigging rhymes that might be sung to such tunes. The songs sung by clowns after plays (which like those of Tarle-ton, were often extempore,) and any other merry ditties, were called *jigs.* 'Nay, sit down by my side, and I will *sing* thee one of my countrey *jigges* to make thee merry,' says Deloney, in his *Thomas of Reading.*"— Chappell's *Popular Music*, ii. 495.—F.

p. 118, l. 230. Seven Deadly Sins. Compare 'The Seuen Deadly Sinnes of London : Drawne in seuen seuerall Coaches, Through seuen seuerall Gates of the Citie, Bringing the Plague with them. Opus septem Dierum. Tho: Dekker. At London Printed by E. A. for Nathaniel Butter, and are to be solde at his shop neere Saint Austens gate. 1606. 4to, black letter, 31 leaves.'—*Hazlitt*. Also Dekker's 'Belman of London,' 1608 ; 'Lanthorne and Candlelight,' 1609 ; 'O per se O,' 1612 ; 'Villanies discovered,' 1616 ; and the successive versions of his 'Eng-lish Villanies,' 1632-48.—F.

p. 121, l. 304. *Some weare short cloakes, some cloakes that reach the heel.* "In the time of Queene *Mary*, and the beginning of the Raigne of Queen *Elizabeth*, and for many yeeres before, it was not lawfull for any man either servant or others, to weare their Gowns lower than to the calves of their legges, except they were above threescore yeares of age, but the length of Cloakes being not limited, they made them Cloakes downe to their Shoes . . . ."—Stow's *Annales*, continued by Edmund Howes, ed. 1631, pp. 1039-40.—S.

p. 121, ll. 307-10. *Bold Bettresse*, &c.; p. 122, l. 333. *fannes by truls are borne.* · "Womens Maskes, Buskes, Muffes, Fanns, Periwigs and Bodkins, were first devised, and used in Italy by Curtezans, and from thence brought into France, and there received of the best sort for gallant ornaments, and from thence they came into England, about the time of the Massacre of Paris" [1572].—*Idem*, p. 1038, col. 2.—S.

p. 126, l. 451. *Wrath is the cause that men in Smith-field meete.*
"This field commonly called West-Smithfield, was for many yeares called *Ruffians hall*, by reason it was the usuall place of Frayes and common fighting, during the time that Sword and Bucklers were in use.

"When every Serving-man from the base to the best, carried a Buckler at his backe, which hung by the hilt or pomell of his Sword which hung before him.

"This manner of Fight was frequent with all men, untill the fight of Rapier and Dagger tooke place, and then suddenly the generall quarrell of fighting abated, which began about the 20 yeare of Queene *Elizabeth* [1577-8], for untill then it was usuall to have Frayes, Fights, and Quarrells, upon the Sundayes and Holidayes, sometimes twenty, thirty, and forty Swords and Bucklers, halfe against halfe, as well by quarrells of appointment as by chance.

"Especially from the midst of Aprill, untill the end of October, by reason, Smithfield was then free from durte and plashes. And in the Winter season, all the high streetes were much annoyed and troubled with hourely frayes of sword and buckler men who tooke pleasure in that bragging fight ; and although they made great shew of much furie and fought often, Yet seldome any man hurt for thrusting was not then in use : neither would one of twentie strike beneath the waste, by reason they held it cowardly and beastly. But the ensuing deadly fight of Rapier and Dagger suddenly suppressed the fighting with Sword and Buckler."—Stow's *Annales*, continued by Edmund Howes, ed. 1631, p. 1024, col. 1 and 2.—S.

p. 127, l. 497. *Idlenesse.* See Andrew Boorde's amusing 151st Chapter of his *Breuiary*, on 'an euyl Feuer, the whiche dothe cumber yonge persons, named the Feuer lurden.' His remedy is : "There is nothyng so good for the Feuer lurden as is *Vnguentum baculinum*, that is to say, Take me a stycke or wand of a yerde of length and more, and let it be as great as a mans fynger, and with it anoynt the bake and the shulders well, mornynge and euenynge, and do this .xxi. dayes," &c. : see my edition, p. 83-4, and the Index to my *Babees Book.*—F.

p. 129, ll. 562, 564. There were two Compters or prisons for debtors in the city of London ; each being under the superintendence of one of the Sheriffs. The Poultry Compter stood a few doors from St Mildred's church until 1817, when it was taken down. Stow wrote of it, " this hath been there kept and continued time out of mind, for I have not read of the original thereof." Wood Street Compter stood on the east side of Wood Street, Cheapside, and was first established there in 1555, when the prisoners were removed from the old Compter in Bread Street to the new one in Wood Street. The latter was burnt down in the Great Fire, but rebuilt afterwards. The prison was removed to Giltspur Street in 1791. T. Middleton introduced a reference to the two Compters in his *Phœnix*—" for as in that notable city called London stand two most famous Universities, Poultry and Wood street, where some are of twenty years' standing and have took all their degrees." Quoted in Cunningham's Handbook of London.—H. B. W. Thomas Nash also praisd the Compter ironically in his ' *Strange Newes*,' 1592, (sign. I.) :—

" Heare what I say : a gentleman is never throughly entred into credit till he hath been there ; and that Poet or novice, be hee what he will, ought to suspect his wit, and remaine halfe in doubt that it is not authenticall, till it hath beene seene and allowed in unthrifts consistory. *Grande doloris ingenium !* Let fooles dwell in no stronger houses than their fathers built them, but I protest I should never have writ passion well, or beene a piece of a poet, if I had not arriv'd in those quarters. Trace the gallantest youthes, and bravest revellers about towne, in all the by-paths of their expence, and you shall infallibly finde, that once in their life-time they have visited that melancholy habitation. Come, come, if you goe to the sound truth of it, there is no place of the earth like it, to make a man wise. Cambridge and Oxford may stand under the elbowe of it. I vow, if I had a sonne, I would sooner send him to one of the Counters to learne lawe, than to the Innes of Court or Chancery." (in Collier's Bibl. Catal. i. 277.)

p. 133, l. 679. *light-taylde huswives*. Compare ' A Dialogue bytwene the commune secretary and Jalowsye, Touchynge the vnstablenesse of Harlottes,' John Kynge [1550-61], Collier's *Bibl. Cat.* i. 400.

" She that is fayre, lusty and yonge,
And can comon in termes with fyled tonge,
And wyll abyde whysperynge in the eare,
Thynke ye her *tayle is not lyght of the seare ?*"

This is Hamlet's ' tickle o' the sere,' the sear being the catch of a gunlock, which when stiff, makes you pull the trigger very hard, but when light, turns it into a ' hair-trigger,' one that'll go at the touch of a hair.—F.

William Goddard's *Neaste of Waspes*, 1615, gives the theatres a bad character too (Collier's *Bibl. Cat.* i. 314) :—

" Goe to your plaie-howse, you shall actors have,
Your baude, your gull, your whore, your pander knave,

Goe to your bawdie house, y'ave actors too,
As bawdes, and whores, and gulls, pandars also,
Besides, in either howse (yf you enquire)
A place there is for men themselves to tire.
Since th' are so like, to choose theres not a pinn,
Whether bawdye-house, or plaie-howse you goe in."

As to the round house, compare *The Cries of London* (ib. p. 163, time of Jas. I.)

" The Players on the Banckeside,
The *round Globe* and the Swan,
Will search you idle tricks of love,
But the Bull will play the man."

The Bull was ' The Red Bull' theatre in Clerkenwell. The Rose theatre on or near Bankside was also round. See Norden's Map, 1593.—F.

p. 139, l. 7. *Hee askt him, If hee had a Passe,* &c. " Any two *Justices* of Peace may licence such as be delivered out of *Gaoles*, to begge for their fees, or to travell to their Countrey, or friends : and. may give licence for fourtie dayes to a *Rogue*, that is marked [branded ?] : and may make testimonial to a Servingman, that is turned away from his master, or whose master is dead : 14 Eliz. cap. 5 ; and 18 Eliz. cap. 3 ; and 27 Eliz. cap. 11.

. . . And they may *Licence* diseased persons (living of almes) to travel to *Bathe*, or to *Buckstone*, for remedies of their griefe, 14 Eliz. cap. 5, and 27 Eliz. cap. 11."—Lambard's *Eirenarcha*, ed. 1592, p. 321-2.

" Two such *Justices* may give licence to *Fencers, Bearewards, Common players* in Enterludes, *Minstrels, Juglers, Pedlers, Tinkers,* and *Petite-chapmen,* to goe abroad, so as they shall not be taken as Rogues. 14 Eliz. cap. 5 ; and 27 Eliz. cap. 11."—*Idem,* pp. 341-2.—S.

p. 140, l. 45. *Signa virtutum tuarum longe lateque ferens.* A reminiscence of Horace, *Od.* IV. i. 16. ?—S.

p. 141, l. 1. *folk leaving town after Term.* Compare Lord Campbell's note on p. 23-4 of his *Shakespeare's Legal Acquirements considered,* 1859 :

" Even so late as Queen Anne's reign there seems to have been a prodigious influx of all ranks from the provinces into the metropolis in term time. During the preceding century, Parliament sometimes did not meet at all for a considerable number of years ; and being summoned rarely and capriciously, the ' London season ' seems to have been regulated, not by the session of Parliament, but by the law terms,—

' . . . . and prints before Term ends.'—*Pope.*

While term lasted, Westminster Hall was crowded all the morning, not only by lawyers, but by idlers and politicians in quest of news. *Term having ended, there seems to have been a general dispersion.* Even the Judges spent their vacations in the country, having when in town resided in their chambers in the Temple or Inns of Court. The Chiefs were obliged to remain in town a day or two after term, for Nisi Prius sittings ; but the Puisnes were entirely liberated when proclamation was made at the rising of the court on the last day of term, in the form still preserved, ·

that "all manner of persons may take their ease, and give their attendance here again on the first day of the ensuing term. . . . ."
See Thomas Dekker's 'The Dead Terme. Or Westminsters Complaint for long Vacations and short Tearmes. Written in manner of a Dialogue betweene the two Cityes of London and Westminster. London, Printed and are to be sold by Iohn Hodgets. 1608. 4to, black letter, 27 leaves.'—F.

p. 156, l. 19. "Actuary, (*Actuarius*) Is the Clerk or Scribe, that registers the Canons and Constitutions of the Convocation : Also an Officer in the Court Christian, who is in Nature of a Register."—Cowel's *Law Dict.*, ed. 1727.

p. 158, l. 6. *Swainmootes of Forrests.* " From the *Sax.* swan, a *swain*, as *Country-swain, Boot-swain*, and gemote, a Court or Convention. The *Swanemote* was a Court held twice a year [Spelman and Cowel say thrice.—S.] by the forest officers, fifteen days before *Midsummer*, and three weeks before *Michaelmass*, for enquiry of the trespasses committed within the bounds of the forest."—Kennett's *Parochial Antiquities*, ed. 1695, Glossary, s.v. Swanemotum.—S.

p. 158, l. 12. *The Virdge.* " Verge, Virgata, may seem to come from the French *Verger, viridarium*, and is used here in *England* for the Compass of the King's Court, which bounds the jurisdiction of the Lord Steward of the King's Houshold, and of the Coroner of the King's House, and that seems to have been Twelve Miles Compass."—Cowel's *Law Dict.* ed. 1727.—S.

p. 158, l. 16. *The Clinke.* " Then next is the *Clinke*, a Goal or Prison for the Trespassers in those Parts, namely, in old time for such as should Brabble, Fray, or break the Peace on the said Bank [the Bankside, Southwark] or in the *Brothel* Houses, they were by the Inhabitants thereabout apprehended and committed to this Goal, when they were straitly Imprisoned."—Strype's *Stow*, ed. 1720, II. book iv. p. 8, col. 1.—S.

p. 159, l. 9 from foot. *And here I remember me of an old tale.* This story will be found in Bacon's *Apophthegms*, No. 34, *Miscellaneous Writings of Francis Bacon*, ed. 1802, p. 12.—S.

p. 163, l. 12 from foot. *An Enginere for making of Patars.* Grose (*Military Antiquities*, I. p. 402) gives an engraving of "Pierriers, vulgarly called Pattereros," and says, " Chamber'd pieces for throwing stones, called cannon perriers . . . were about this time [Edward VI. reign] much used in small forts, and on shipboard."—S.

p. 171, l. 1. *Sir John Hawkins' hospital at Chatham.* An hospital for decayed mariners and shipwrights was founded by Sir John Hawkins, in 1592, in which twelve pensioners have each a separate house, an allowance of eight shillings per week, and an annual supply of coal : the management is vested in 26 governors, of which number five are elective.—Lewis's *Topographical Dictionary.*—S.

p. 175, l. 2. *Navibus atque.* &c. Hor. *Epp.* I. xi. 28—30.—S.

INDEX.

JOHN CHILDS AND SON, PRINTERS.

Series I. *Transactions.* 6. Part 11. for 1877-9, Mr Daniel's Time-Analyses of Shakspere's Plots.
Series IV. *Allusion-Books.* 2. *Shakspere's Centurie of Praise*, the 2nd edition, by C. M. Ingleby, LL.D., and Miss L. Toulmin Smith. (*Presented mainly by Dr Ingleby.*)
Series VI. 6. Stubbes's *Anatomie of Abuses*, Part I., Section 2, with extracts from his Life of his Wife, 1591, and other Works, and illustrative woodcuts: ed. F. J. Furnivall, M.A.

The following Publications will probably be issued for **1880**:

Series I. *Transactions.* 7. Part III. for 1877-9, Papers by Miss Phipson, Mr Ruskin, &c.
Series II. *Plays.* 10. *Henry V: c.* a revisd edition of the Play, by Walter G. Stone, Esq.
Series II. *Plays.* 11. *The Two Noble Kinsmen*, by Shakspere and Fletcher; *c.* An Introduction, and Glossarial Index of all the words, distinguishing Shakspere's from Fletcher's, by Harold Littledale, Esq., B.A., Trinity College, Dublin. (*Presented by Rich. Johnson, Esq.*)
Series IV. *Allusion-Books.* 3. A fresh Century of Additions to *Shakspere's Centurie of Praise*, gatherd by Members of the New Shakspere Society, and edited by F. J. Furnivall.
Series VI. 7. *Shakspere's England.* The Rogues and Vagabonds of Shakspere's Youth, ed. by E. Viles and F. J. Furnivall. (*Presented by Mr. Furnivall.*)

The following Publications of the *New Shakspere Society* are in the Press:

Series I. *Transactions.* 8. Part I. for 1880-2, Papers by Dr. B. Nicholson, W. E. Rose, &c.
Series II. *Plays.* 12. *Cymbeline: a.* A Reprint of the Folio of 1623; *b.* a revisd Edition with Introduction and Notes, by W. J. Craig, M.A.
Series VI. 8. Harrison's *Description of England*, 1577-87, Part III, with engravings of West Cheap, the Preaching at Paul's Cross, Norden's Map of Westminster, &c., ed. F. J. Furnivall, M.A. 9. Stubbes's *Anatomie of Abuses*, Part II., A.D. 1583, ed. F. J. Furnivall, M.A.
Series VII. *Mysteries, &c.* Five *15th-century Mysteries, with a Morality*, from the Digby MS. 133. &c., re-edited from the unique MSS. by F. J. Furnivall, M.A.

The following works are in preparation for the Society :—

Series II. *Plays.* Parallel-Texts of the First Quarto and Folio of *Richard III*, ed. T. A. Spalding, LL.B.; of the *Contention* and *True Tragedy*, and 2 and 3 *Henry VI*, ed. Miss Jane Lee; of the two earliest Quartos of *Midsummer Nights Dream*, ed. Rev. J. W. Ebsworth, M.A.
Series III. *Originals and Analogues.* A Shakspere *Holinshed:* the Chronicle and the Historical Plays compar'd : by Walter G. Stone, Esq.
Series IV. *Allusion Books.* Ballad-allusions to Shakspere, edited by the Rev. J. W. Ebsworth, M.A.
Series V. *Contemporary Drama.* *Edward III, a.* a Reprint of the first Quarto, 1596, with a collation of the 2nd Quarto, 1599; *b.* a revisd edition, with Introduction and Notes; *c.* the Sources of the Play, from Froissart, and Painter's *Palace of Pleasure;* edited by Walter D. Stone, Esq., and F. J. Furnivall, M.A.
Series VI. *Shakspere's England.* Wills of the Actors and Authors of Elizabeth's and James I's times, edited, with Notes, by Colonel J. Lemuel Chester.

The following works have been suggested for publication :—

Series II. *Plays.* 1. Parallel Texts of the imperfect sketches of *b.* Hamlet, and its Quarto 2 (with the Folio and a revisd Text); *c.* Merry Wives of Windsor, and Folio 1.
2. Parallel Texts of the following Quarto Plays and their versions in the First Folio, with collations: 2 Henry IV, Q1; Troilus and Cressida, Q1; Lear, Q1. Of Othello, 4 Texts, Q1, Q2, F1, and a revisd Text. The two earliest Quartos of the Merchant of Venice.
Series V. *The Contemporary Drama.* Works suggested by the late Mr Richard Simpson :—
a. The Works of Robert Greene, Thomas Nash (with a selection from Gabriel Harvey's), Thomas Lodge, and Henry Chettle. *b.* The Martinist and Anti-Martinist Plays of 1589-91; and the Plays relating to the quarrel between Dekker and Jonson in 1600. *c.* Lists of all the Companies of Actors in SHAKSPERE's time, their Directors, Players, Plays and Poets. *d.* Dr Wm. Gager's *Meleager*, a tragedy, printed Oct. 1592, with the correspondence relating to it (Univ. Coll. Oxf. MS. J. 18; and at Corpus), &c.
Richard II, and the other Plays in Egerton MS. 1994 (suggested by Mr Halliwell-Phillipps).
Series VI. Edward Hake's *Touchstone*, 1574; edited by F. J. Furnivall, M.A. Dekker's *Gulls Horn-Book*, with its original, *The Schoole of Slovenrie*, edited by the Rev. J. W. Ebsworth.
Series VII. *Mysteries, &c. The Towneley Mysteries*, re-edited from the unique MS. by the Rev. Richard Morris, LL.D. *The Macro Moralities*, edited by F. J. Furnivall, M.A.
Series VIII. *Miscellaneous.* Thomas Rymer's 'Tragedies of the last Age considerd and examined', 1673, 1692: and his 'A short View of Tragedy of the last Age', 1693.